PORTRAIT
of JULIA

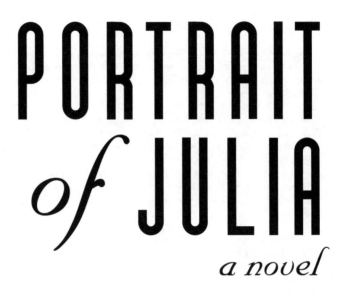

PORTRAIT of JULIA

a novel

ROBERT MACNEIL

Formac Publishing Company Limited

Formac Publishing Company Limited recognizes the support of the Province of Nova Scotia through the Department of Communities, Culture and Heritage. We are pleased to work in partnership with the province to develop and promote our culture resources for all Nova Scotians. We acknowledge the financial support of the Government of Canada through the Canada Book Fund for our publishing activities. We acknowledge the support of the Canada Council for the Arts which last year invested $157 million to bring the arts to Canadians throughout the country.

  Canada

Book Cover: Detail of *Dieppe*, c. 1906 by James Wilson Morrice.

The poems by Paul Verlaine quoted in **Portrait of Julia** were published in *Selected Poems Paul Verlaine, Translated by C.F. MacIntyre*, University of California Press, Berkeley, Los Angeles, London, Copyright 1948 by The Regents of the University of California, Copyright renewed 1976 by C.F. MacIntyre. ISBN 0-520-01298-4

Library and Archives Canada Cataloguing in Publication

MacNeil, Robert, 1931-, author
    Portrait of Julia / Robert MacNeil.

ISBN 978-1-4595-0279-6 (bound)

    I. Title.

PS3563.A3242P67 2013   813'.54   C2013-903881-7

Formac Publishing Company Limited
5502 Atlantic Street
Halifax, Nova Scotia, Canada
B3H 1G4
www.formac.ca

Printed and bound in Canada

"To My Fave."

1

When she entered the café, he had decided. His previous paintings of nudes had all been, in some way, reticent: half clothed, their bodies turned away or eyes averted. This would be different; the model, not in bed partially covered, not reclining, not seated, not turning away. She would stand, one knee bent with hip and shoulders classically tilted to sweeten the line, but she would face forward and her eyes would address you candidly.

In his first sight of her at the hotel, something had stirred—a flicker of optimism, a breath of fresh energy. He had been uneasy about her visit, reluctant to be found stalled and wrung out like this, so he had not gone to the Nice station. Then, catching her standing by the reception desk—tall and assured, the blonde chignon above the dark collar—her youth and her vitality had moved him. He was glad she had come.

Julia couldn't see it in his wan smile and was disappointed. Morrice appeared so much older, shrunken, physically depleted. And shorter. He'd always looked oldish, bald even in his thirties, but now his fine hooked nose seemed beakier, the blue eyes more protuberant and dimmer. Was that drink or just his mood? Clearly he wasn't overjoyed that she had invited herself. Though polite as always, the gentleman in his well-cut tweed suit, his neat beard.

"I'm glad to see you again, Julia." Wary of what she might impose on him, she sensed, ever jealous of his privacy.

Perhaps she'd been exaggerating how close they had been before the war, remembering a charming uncle-niece intimacy, curiously charged with undercurrents of other possibilities. Coming impulsively from Paris, sure she'd be welcome again, she felt deflated by his reticence.

"I hope you'll excuse my barging in on you. I really needed a change of scenery to help me think things through...and someone sensible to talk to."

A feeble laugh. "I don't know how sensible you'll find me these days, but I'll be happy to talk." He seemed depressed, withdrawn into himself.

"Is Léa here?"

"Yes, she's here."

"Will she mind?"

"Léa doesn't mind anything. She's in her little house in Cagnes. A few kilometres away. She's happy there. And I am happy here." He nodded around the lobby of the Hôtel La Méditerranée. He had always lived separately from his mistress, wanting to insulate his painting from all but the minimal domesticity. The intervening years had given Julia a lot of perspective. At her knowing smile, Morrice seemed to perk up a little.

"I like it. Matisse is staying here too."

"I'm dying to see your work—and his."

"Plenty of time for that. Why don't you get settled in your room and then, if you like, join me in the café next door? Just on the left."

Upstairs, as the chambermaid opened shutters, Julia

wondered about her let-down feeling. She'd been sick that morning and had eaten nothing. He'd always been shy and diffident with her. Even so, hearing his accent had given her a little rush of comfort, a voice from the same tribe, the Montreal English.

J. W. Morrice settled gratefully into the café like someone putting on a familiar and comfortable garment. In thirty years in France cafés had become his other home. He ordered a rum and lit his pipe to wait. Incredible to realize, he had known this girl since she was born, the year he came to France. On visits home he'd hardly noticed her; then, suddenly, twenty years had gone by and she'd arrived in Paris a striking woman, eager to study art. Her father, an old friend of his, had let her come on condition that Morrice keep an eye on her.

He was visualizing the planes of her face from cheekbone to jawline, changed since he'd painted her in 1913, when he was enjoying a small flurry of figure painting. The lovely grey eyes he remembered and the sculpted mouth, the little smile lines at the corners now more deeply etched. Her face had scarcely aged yet it was leaner, and in the tilt of her head, the more assured way she pointed that delicate jaw, there was also something defiant and brave. He knew her husband had been killed, his sister had written him. He began to be curious about what was bothering her; why had she wanted to run down to Nice to see him? Why was she even in France?

Outside the café, people scurried with wind-tormented umbrellas, clasping coats to their chins. The rainy wind tossed the fronds of the palms on the Promenade des Anglais and stirred the Mediterranean not to the usual azure or turquoise, but to molten steel.

Automatically he studied the composition, the restless sea framed in retreating layers of perspective, like a theatre set: the foreground a few occupied tables, then the café windows, street with people hurrying, promenade with palm trees, balustrade, and finally the sea. It was a mood and light he had not rendered. He absorbed it, feeling no stimulus to work on it, merely registering the tones and shapes. There had been periods like this in the past when work required too much concentration, too much energy. Curiously, though, her arrival had changed something.

From her room above the palm trees, Julia Robertson gazed down at the sea and wondered whether she should have come. How could she explain to this shy and withdrawn man how stupid she had been? Why had she believed she would draw comfort from him?

And she found herself in tears, actually sobbing. It's too much, she thought, too much! But by taking a few deep breaths she got the tears to stop and gradually felt calmer.

Well, at least Morrice would not burden her with bourgeois moralizing. He had defied the rigorous Presbyterianism of his parents while conforming superficially in reassuring ways that left them content to support him. In Paris he kept his mistress inconspicuous and he dressed like a gentleman. Julia's father, who had known Morrice at school, had had no qualms about letting her come to study with him—an unmarried artist. Morrice had behaved impeccably, like an affable uncle, but an uncle about whom she had been spinning private legends since her school days. Their twenty-four-year age difference was inhibiting, but perhaps also titillating. If the effervescence of being a young, adventurous artist in Paris occasionally let her imagination stray into other possibilities, Morrice had always appeared too preoccupied with his painting, or with Léa, or with drink, to take any notice.

Perhaps she had just wanted the relief of being able to speak in English, after weeks in Paris with Suzanne Perret. Most urgently, she needed relief from the prickling anxiety that now shadowed all her thoughts. But to suddenly dissolve into tears like this was new—and disturbing.

Well, she had to join him. She washed her eyes and powdered her face. When she entered the café, Morrice was not sketching or painting, just sitting, smoking, with two saucers on the table from drinks consumed. He looked up at her and he looked sick. She noticed the pouches under his eyes. He's destroying himself, she thought. His drinking no longer seemed like charming bohemian self-indulgence. But why would he throw away so much talent and such achievement?

She sat down and said, "Jim, I was sorry to hear of your parents dying suddenly—so close together—like that."

"Thank you. It did make me think. You know how strictly they lived, what a stern church man my father was. But he never questioned the life I chose and he supported me all the way. Even bought paintings. Put one of my Saint-Malo pieces into the holy of holies, the Mount Royal Club."

"Well I kept hearing how proud they were of your success."

Morrice sipped his drink and brooded over that a while

before saying, "Your dad and mother all right?"

"They're fine, I suppose. I've been travelling and my letters...haven't caught up with me."

He appeared to be struggling to overcome his shyness. "I should have told you how very sorry I was to learn about your husband. His name was—"

"Charles."

"I'm sorry I never met him."

"I was going to bring him to Paris after the war. He was eager to meet you."

"Did he like my painting of you?"

"He liked it"—suddenly, there was the enchanting smile he remembered—"privately. In Halifax I kept it in our bedroom cupboard. He didn't like the idea of other people looking at me."

He laughed and raised a finger to the waiter. "What would you like to drink?"

"May I have something to eat? I'm starved."

She ordered an omelette and he another rum and water. Compared with her father, Morrice didn't look so old. The hair framing his bald crown was still tawny coloured and, like his eyebrows and beard, just touched with grey. Not so much old as unhealthy. His cheeks looked puffy.

"When did you do the self-portrait—the one that hung in your studio on Quai des Grands-Augustins?"

"It's still there, or rather, in the new studio. You know I had to move? Quai de la Tournelle now, facing the Île St-Louis. I did the self-portrait nearly twenty years ago."

"I was thinking that only now you're beginning to look as you thought you looked then."

"When I was only thirty-five?" He laughed. "The artist ahead of his time? Ahead of his time, and behind his time, but always in his own time, or should I say"—he raised his glass—"in his own good time."

It wasn't going to be easy to plunge into her story; it would take time to become reacquainted, time she could not afford.

"I looked for your paintings at the Salon d'Automne but found only two."

"That's all I thought worth sending. Both painted on a trip a few years ago, one in Cuba and one in Jamaica."

"Well, I liked them both very much. So assured."

"I'm glad." He raised his rum glass and his hand shook. "The fact is—you'll know sooner or later—I haven't done anything in a long time."

"That's too bad. Have you been ill?"

"A little. Mostly I just haven't felt like it. The spark hasn't been there. Dried up or gone out, whatever sparks do." He laughed. "I've been waiting for it to come back."

"Perhaps you should take a trip."

"Yes, that usually stirs me up, but I haven't even felt like that."

She saw the trembling hand and wanted to ask, have they told you again to stop drinking? He'd had a big slump when doctors made him give up absinthe, but that was ten years ago at least. It would be easier to chat if he would ask some questions. But he seemed content to be silent, smiling at her, looking past her at the view outside. Finally it felt awkward and she got up.

"You know, I've been sitting in the train such a long time. I'd love some fresh air and a little walk."

"It's pretty miserable out."

"But it's so much warmer and fresher than Paris—and there's the sea and the light. And I haven't seen palm trees since Bermuda—before the war. I don't need to drag you out. Stay and be comfortable."

He did prefer to stay dry in the café, drinking and smoking, absorbing the scene. He would have liked to go on studying the clean lines of her face, but he cheerfully waved her out.

"The hotel will lend you an umbrella. If you'd like to have dinner with me, I'll ask for a table."

"Thank you. I'd love that."

When she went out, Morrice asked the waiter for paper and a pencil. His hand shook as it approached the paper. To steady it, he placed the tip of the pencil on the paper and rapidly drew a sinuous and fluent line.

She walked towards the casino, the wind whipping her clothes, plastering coat and skirt against her wet stockings. Morrice seemed so withdrawn, so absorbed in himself, that she might not be able to talk to him. Still, it cheered her to be here, even in this weather; to smell the sea, to feel the softer air on her skin, the fine rain on her face.

It made her think of the moist spring morning in Halifax when the letter had come.

2

Usually Julia loved such days, loved the fog drifting in smoky wraiths through the ranks of black spruce, the appetizing tang of brine in the air, the strangely intimate moan of the foghorn.

That May day, the weather made her indecisive and dithery: too cold for a cotton dress, too warm for wool. It distracted her as she worked at her painting. It darkened the room, but she wouldn't turn on the electric light because it would alter the colours. As she tried to concentrate she felt an emotional pull, like a child tugging her skirt, urging her to leave the work, wishing her out of the house, in the fog, at the seacoast.

Often, disconcertingly, the fog brought Charles into her thoughts, giving her that irrational feeling that he could reappear at will—had merely wandered off a few steps and might just step back into visibility, that he would undissolve into materiality. Sailing his boat, they said, he had always found his way in the fog.

And sometimes it gave her momentary, breathtaking intuitions that he was not dead, was really in the next room or just outside. In a landscape so often rendered indistinct or invisible, you had to remember what was really there, or you began to imagine it.

She was still living in his house, with his clothes untouched.

Then, in late morning, the letter had come, making

work impossible. An engraved crest and London address, both unfamiliar, yet from whom she instantly knew, and the recognition seemed to suffuse her entire body.

May 16, 1919

My dear Mrs. Robertson,

I hope you won't mind my writing to remind you of our brief acquaintance. We met in Halifax during the war when I was serving in HMS Changuinola. *Since the Armistice my life has changed rather dramatically. Through family connections, I find myself attached to the Royal Household as an equerry to HRH, the Prince of Wales. As you know, Prince Edward will visit Halifax on August 17–18 as he begins his tour of Canada and the United States. Since I will be coming along as a general factotum, I thought I'd be in touch with a few people who were kind to me in Halifax, yourself among them, to invite you to a small dinner, separate from the large receptions and other public events. It would give me, and I'm sure HRH, great pleasure to have you in the company. You'll find him a refreshing change from the stuffy or intimidating image you may have of royalty. I've known him since we were cadets together at Osborne. He's particularly keen to meet people of his own generation. In the routine way, the palace has been in touch with Ottawa for suggestions, but this dinner will be more relaxed, less "on duty", so to speak. So, could you possibly suggest one or two other young people the Prince would enjoy?*

May I say that I learned with enormous distress of your husband's tragic death in action in France. I am in awe of the gallantry that earned him the VC, although I imagine that was small consolation to you and his parents. I am also writing to them and your sister-in-law, Lucy Traverse.

Yours,
With pleasant anticipation,

Neville Boiscoyne

In an instant the letter had rekindled the feelings that she had suppressed in her mad escape to Montreal two years ago. Even her breathing had quickened.

"Ridiculous!" she said aloud.

Impatient, embarrassed at the memory, she put the letter aside, meaning to forget it, ignore it. Of course, she'd have to respond politely. In good time. No need to let it fluster her. But what a lot of bother this would cause, just when there was so much to do to be ready to leave for Europe.

Julia dipped her brush in the thin mixture of turpentine and colour she had learned from Morrice and turned to the canvas. Then, without intending to, she walked back to the table, the brush forgotten in her hand, and began to analyze the letter.

"With pleasant anticipation" seemed to echo his charmingly brazen manner in the moments which had aroused her so inappropriately in the summer of 1917. Months before Charles was killed. Although the grey, foggy day made the house chilly, she now felt too warm.

Was it as casual and offhand as it seemed? Did he merely wish to repay a slight social obligation? Hundreds of British naval officers had been entertained in Halifax, but even for the most punctilious a brief bread-and-butter note sufficed. Or, knowing he would be in Halifax, was he amusing himself—as many officers did—with a flirtation in the colonies? Or was she reading all that into it?

And just how would she tell Stewart? It was part of their arrangement that they told each other everything.

The telephone ringing made her put down the letter to go downstairs to answer. It was Lucy.

"Julia, aren't you thrilled to bits? Not only dinner with the Prince of Wales, but this must be the man at the Government House ball—wasn't that his name? Neville Boiscoyne? He danced with you all evening. Totally monopolized you. In your emerald dress. Devastatingly handsome man. Even Daddy liked him."

Since Charles's death, Lucy had become more a close sister than a sister-in-law.

Lucy asked, "But how did someone at Buckingham Palace know all our addresses?"

"Why Buckingham Palace?"

"Well, the letterhead. Where he wrote the letter."

"Not mine. Mine's from a private address in London. Wilton Crescent."

"Really?" Lucy, the excited schoolgirl. "That's very significant! What does yours say?"

Julia read her the letter.

"That's a lot more than mine or Mother's—much more personal. I think yours is definitely a billet-doux."

"Don't be silly."

"Well, come over and we'll compare them. And talk about whom to suggest. It's too delicious. We could make enemies for life! So we've got to talk but I can't leave the house because the girls are due back from the Waeg."

"They aren't swimming today?"

"I wouldn't, but they don't feel the cold."

"The morning was so chilly I felt like starting a fire."

"I know, I lit ours. Come over for a cozy cup of tea, and we'll examine the clues like Sherlock Holmes. Although, I think it's obvious. He fell madly in love with you two years ago, sailed away with a broken heart because you were married, has been pining ever since but now he knows you're free. Fate brings him to Halifax—it's his big chance. He's coming back to sweep you off your feet and carry you away to his...what does he have? A castle in England?"

Julia laughed. "I don't know what he has. I've had only two conversations with him in my life."

"I saw the conversation you were having waltzing around the ballroom at Government House. Every woman there saw it and was burning with jealousy. He's the handsomest man I ever saw. And he's got to be pretty blue-blooded to be part of the royal household. Honestly, my dear. I think your future's made."

"Lucy, I can't come now. I'm expecting Stewart."

"Oh, Julia! Now you listen to me. Friendly advice. I haven't said anything for a while, but just listen. He's a lovely man. He's been sweet to you and marvellous to Betty. But if you go on spending all your time with Stewart MacPherson, you'll never meet someone really suitable. Stewart is a good friend, I know. I like him enormously. But he's just too... unusual. You'll soon be thirty and—"

"I'm just twenty-eight, and you're beginning to sound like my mother. Goodbye."

"Well, think about whom to suggest."

"Of course I'll suggest Stewart."

"Oh no! I've just told you: all wrong! He'll stick out like a sore thumb. And he's not the least bit interested in social things. I doubt he's had evening dress on since his parents made him wear it years ago."

Julia felt a little temper rising. "Lucy, I know what you think, but if the damned Prince of Wales—excuse me—if the Prince of Wales wants to meet interesting people of his generation, who is more interesting than Stewart? Look at the fascinating work he's done."

"But if he comes, you'll queer the pitch with Neville Boiscoyne. He'll think you're tied up, spoken for, off the market."

"Well, I am tied up," Julia said proudly, "and I am not, as you put it so delicately, on 'the market.'"

"But you're not engaged to him."

"Because we've decided not to be. We wanted to give ourselves some time."

The guileless Lucy adopted her arch tone. "Well, if you suggest Stewart, I'll suggest Susan Gastonguy."

Julia laughed. "To try and pry him away from me?"

"She's a very nice girl."

"Yes, a very nice girl who's been after Stewart for years."

"Who knows, she might even turn the prince's head."

"Good luck to her."

"You think about what I said. You're so headstrong. Think how Stewart MacPherson will fit in, looking like a tousled teddy bear at the dinner table with those immaculate Englishmen. And, my God, what are we going to wear? Of course, you could just trot out the same green dress that dazzled him the last time—"

"Lucy, goodbye!"

After the call Julia thought, yes, she would ask them to invite Stewart. That would show Neville Boiscoyne—and everyone else—exactly where things stood.

The phone rang again and Lucy said, "Seriously, there is something I want to talk to you about—but not on the telephone. Could you come over later? Would you mind? Come and have supper with me." Something tremulous in Lucy's normally jaunty tone persuaded Julia.

"All right. What time would you like me?"

"About seven? It'll be just us two. Mother and Daddy are taking the girls for the weekend to open up the cottage."

The green evening gown was at the back of Julia's cupboard, untouched since that evening. With it was the black dress, which carried other associations. Fortunately, there were a few things Lucy didn't know.

Julia had repeatedly resolved to give the dresses away, get rid of them, but somehow kept forgetting. Doubtless unconscious motives at work, Stewart would say, and probably correctly. They had talked so much about Freud and Jung's theories of the unconscious that she had acquired Stewart's habit of analyzing things in that way herself. It was how they managed the relationship: they discussed and analyzed everything with a candour that exhilarated her at first because it seemed to fit the new spirit of the times. It felt as though they were sweeping away the suffocating and hypocritical restrictions of the past, facing life rationally, free of superstition and taboo.

Like being rational about Neville Boiscoyne, who, to be honest about it, had awakened fantasies of other men for the first time since her marriage to Charles. Even though she had resolutely avoided that temptation, clearly, when she looked back, meeting Neville had unlocked something in her, which had later put her in the frame of mind to encourage Peter Wentworth in those months of madness after Charles was killed.

And Stewart knew all this from the wretched diary and all their talks since.

She looked again at the salutation closing the letter. *Yours, with pleasant anticipation.* Certainly unusual. The ink looked different after the comma, as though he had paused, intending to write only a terse *Yours*, then reconsidered, wanting to say more. Which might argue some feeling or, cynically, a desire to sweeten the bait. How absurd. Probably had to stop to refill his pen. She was letting herself drift into silly reveries over tiny differences in the darkness of the ink? Madness.

Well then, why hadn't she given away the dresses as she'd so often intended? What unconscious motivation was at work? Aware that she would be discussing this with Stewart, she had a sudden resolve to test herself. She went upstairs, pushed other dresses aside, and pulled out the green gown and the black mourning dress with the lace at the throat. Both looked old fashioned, the line already out of date. But she was looking for something else, signs of those evenings that her subconscious must want her to cling to.

The fabric of the green dress was, as she had known without looking, stained under the arms. The excitement of dancing with Neville Boiscoyne that evening had made her perspire heavily. In fingering the material she could remember with perfect vividness the almost uncontrollable urge to kiss him, then coming home ashamed of her behaviour in front of Charles's sister and parents.

But that was nothing compared with the loss of control months later, in the compartment on the night train from Montreal to Halifax.

She examined the collar and found the stitches with which she had reattached the lace torn away in those feverish seconds. The memory provoked the nausea she still felt on seeing Peter Wentworth, as she could not help doing in a small city like Halifax, with the cathedral just across the park. Nausea but also...what? Titillation? Too namby-pamby a word. Sexual arousal, obviously: however overlaid with shame and disgust at her own weakness, the undeniable sensation was sexual excitement. She had felt echoes of it (or were they premonitions?) ever since opening Neville Boiscoyne's letter.

So, keeping the dresses against her conscious determination not to was simply a way of clinging to those feelings, as some women kept flowers pressed in books. Yet in her newly liberated way of thinking, there was nothing shameful in those feelings. They were normal and healthy. And discussable. Stewart and she were free to discuss such things, to understand them, and themselves, better.

I am going to live in the modern way, she said to herself, as she often did.

The problem—no, it wasn't a problem—the reality was that as deeply fond as she was of Stewart—no, as much as she loved him—as wonderful and as open as their relationship was, he did not kindle quite such feelings—or not feelings of this degree, the swooning desire to let everything go, abandon all caution. Of course she had never felt that swoony with Charles either.

She sighed. Well, understanding made one feel better. But at the very least these dresses were reminders of distress and they should go. Always happier with decisions that produced action, she bundled the dresses together and parked them on the kitchen table, where Mollie couldn't miss them.

Back upstairs cleaning her brushes, she noticed the room was lighter, the morning fog beginning to burn off. Even more strongly she wanted to be out of doors. She had to ring three times to find Stewart at home.

"Would you think I was crazy if I suggested a picnic, instead of having lunch here? It's brightening up and all morning I've been dying to get out of the house and smell the sea. Couldn't we put on some old clothes and go down to the shore somewhere?"

"Let's go to Herring Cove."

"You really don't mind?"

"The only thing I mind is not being alone enough with you."

"We'll be more alone this way than having lunch here."

Mollie found her making sandwiches.

"That's the chicken I roasted for your lunch. And they had some asparagus I thought would go nice with it."

"I'm sorry to change our plans. I just need to get some fresh air. So we're going to have a picnic."

"You're going to make that poor man sit on the ground and eat sandwiches when he could eat in your dining room nice and comfortable?"

Mollie, a fisherman's widow from Mahone Bay, did not see the romance of picnicking. She picked up the dresses. "What are you doing with them?"

"I want to get rid of them. You can find someone who'll use them, can't you?"

"I don't know any woman's got a waist small as yours to fit into them. Unless we was to make something out of the green one for Betty."

"No," Julia said firmly, "I'd like them out of the house."

Mollie looked at her shrewdly. "Well, all right. I'll get

them out of here. I remember the last time you wore that green dress..."

God. Did the entire city of Halifax know about that night?

Mollie put on an apron. "Now you let me fix them sandwiches. I'll make a neater job of it than what you can, worked up like you are."

"Worked up? What do you mean?"

"You've got that bright look in your eyes I haven't seen for a while."

Julia sat at the scrubbed kitchen table and dissembled a little. "Well, I am excited. We're going to take a trip to Europe, Stewart and I."

"Oh, my dear!"

"In September. I haven't told anyone else yet. But I'm sure you and Betty will be fine here for a while."

"Oh, we'd be fine. But would you want us staying here when you wasn't here yourself."

"Mollie, for heaven's sake, this is your home and Betty's. Of course I would. And in September she'll be back in school at the convent, so she'll need to be nearby."

"How long wills you be gone over there?"

"Probably about three months. Say till Christmastime."

"My dear!"

"We have a lot of things we want to do. I want to see Charles's grave in England."

"I thought Mr. Robertson wants to bring him back and bury him at home here."

"He does. But Mrs. Robertson doesn't, and I don't think it's a good idea. So I want to see where he's buried in England. And I want to go to France to see all the new painting. Stewart wants to see psychologists in England and Germany, and he also has an idea that doctors there might have some different ideas about Betty. So there are a lot of reasons to go"—she smiled candidly—"besides the fun of going."

Mollie said, "I imagine there's people might say something about you and him going off like this when you wasn't married."

"They might...and I don't care. These are modern times and I'm determined to live in a modern way. Does it bother you?"

Mollie cut a piece of waxed paper and wrapped the sandwiches. "What you do, dear, doesn't bother me. You're a good soul. And you've been some good to me. I'm just thinking of them people that does all the talking about how other people lives. You know what I mean. "

"Do you think I should marry him?"

"Does he want you to?"

"Yes, although we haven't talked about it for quite a while."

"Course he does. You can see it all over him. And, if you asked me, you could do a sight worse. But you always knowed your own mind, and I suppose you'll know in good time." She gave Julia one of her looks. "You aren't planning to get married whiles you're far away over there, are you? With no one to fuss about it? Like, on the sly?"

"You're a romantic old soul, aren't you? I never thought of it. We both think we need more time together before committing ourselves."

"Well, don't mind me talking plain, but you just be careful you don't find yourself in the family way, like my niece—"

"Mollie!" She blushed. Usually she enjoyed Mollie's frankness, but this was startling. How had she been careless? What had Mollie noticed?

"Times may be changing but you'd be in a pickle, and then you'd have to marry him whether yous wanted to or not."

Uncanny of Mollie to have suggested that.

To cover her embarrassment Julia said, "But the fellow didn't come back to marry your niece. What did you say? 'Some man come in a fog and left in the morning.'"

"Well, if he hadn't come by, I suppose, we'd have no little ones in the family besides Betty," Mollie said, "with Winnie and her baby and Tom lost in the explosion and our other boys lost at sea." She wiped her eyes with the back of her hand.

To lighten the tone, Julia said, "But Stewart didn't come in a fog, and he's not gone in the morning."

Mollie smiled, "My dear, the fog's in your head, like it's in the head of every woman now and then. I remember what happened with that Britisher. I seen them roses he sent you, and how you ran off home to Montreal quick as a flash. The fog on the shore is no worse than the fog in women's heads." She laughed. "The Lord knows I've had enough in mine."

Even with Mollie there were limits. Julia did not feel like discussing the Boiscoyne letter or birth control. So she changed the subject again.

"Sometimes I have the strangest sense that Charles is still alive. I know that's impossible...but I feel it, especially on foggy days like this."

"That's natural, dear. And when your man's lost at sea, like mine, you often feel he's just out there in the fog, waiting to come in..."

The sound of her voice made Julia's eyes fill with tears.

3

Back in La Méditerranée Julia was taking off her wet clothes and draping them on lukewarm radiators when a maid knocked with flowers and a note from Morrice: "I had clean forgotten (and I think you too) that it's New Year's Eve. So, I have booked us in the dining room. They're suggesting evening dress. Will you join me at 8:30? Jim."

By that hour Morrice had rediscovered the good spirits that made him such charming company when he was in the mood.

To cap the first full year of peace and launch them into the optimistic 1920s, Hotel La Méditerranée et Cote d'Azur had mounted a gala *repas du réveillon* of many courses and wines. The ornate ballroom was brilliant with electric chandeliers and wall sconces augmented by many candles. The music of a small orchestra and the excitement of some diners ensured that no pocket was empty of sound. A large table of young Americans in evening dress radiated enough festivity for the entire room, and there was no escaping the program of dishes timed so as to keep the exercise going till midnight. Certainly no atmosphere in which to broach what she had to discuss.

She had no appetite for the rich food. She had been sick that morning and expected it would happen the next. So she picked at each dish and sipped champagne, the waiter refilling her glass so smoothly that she had little sense of how much she had drunk. Morrice ate stolidly through everything placed in front of him, emptied each glass, and gradually grew more cheerful.

She watched people dancing between the courses, waltzes for the pleasure of older English and foreign couples and the latest jumpy dance numbers, plus tentative sallies into jazz, just finding its way into Europe. The jazz numbers animated the girls from the American table, some with bobbed hair, into exuberant efforts, their beads and fringes flying, while the older couples sat out or gamely adapted their own steps to the frenzied beat. Whatever their ages or nationalities, they all seemed to be having the time of their lives, a gaiety Julia and Morrice watched but did not share.

"We could have avoided this by looking for a restaurant on one of the side streets," he said. "But it's a nasty night out, and most restaurants are probably doing their own version of this. I don't think you can escape it tonight."

"When I think of New Year's, I think of really cold, crisp nights in Montreal, don't you? Huge snow banks six feet tall, black nights, twenty below zero, under sparkling stars, horse-drawn sleighs swishing through the cold, buried in furs that are cold to touch but warm underneath. I loved it."

"So did I, as a boy. I like it when I go back, for a little while. But I'm glad I live here. Canadian life is not congenial to me."

That seemed to raise the question of where Julia wanted to live and gave her an opening, but she let it slip by, watching the waiters, wondering what their families were up to that evening. She couldn't help observing small things in the people who served her. She had done it all her life, she supposed out of some embarrassment at being served by anyone who had a life of her own to get on with. She had felt it first at home as she became old enough to notice the cheapness of their maids' clothes and shoes compared to hers, and the pathetic knick-knacks decorating their rooms, where she snooped on their days off. A child growing up with servants, two in her parents' home, could develop insensitivity or sympathy—sometimes hypersensitive sympathy—to which she was more inclined, which is why Mollie in Halifax had become more friend or aunt to her than maid. But she had never lost her curiosity about the people serving her. Automatically she was looking at the wear on the heels of the waiters' shoes, for signs of frayed cuffs on their trousers; at shirt cuffs and collars for wear and freshness; at the elbows of their dinner jackets or tails, or the knees of their evening trousers, for the shine of much wear. She looked at how much they needed a haircut, how tired they appeared; and the same with waitresses—shoes, stockings, skirt hems, slips showing, hair, nails, makeup—curious whether they had had enough sleep and in what manner of bedrooms; what they had eaten before in the hotel kitchen; what went on behind their deferential but vacant eyes, like the haunting eyes of the girl in Manet's *A Bar at the Folies-Bergère*. And in Europe you could not help but wonder how recently they had taken baths. She had always had a rather earthy mind, curious about how people coped with the fundamentals of life, and her own bodily processes were much on her mind this evening.

A dark-haired young American left his table to come over to say charmingly to Morrice, "Sir, I hope you'll excuse me if I say it's a crying shame that a girl as beautiful as your daughter isn't asked to dance on a night like this."

Morrice laughed. "Well, it is a shame. Go right ahead."

The young man crooked his arm in a gesture already very old fashioned to Julia. "Won't you do me the honour?"

"You're very kind, thank you, but we're just enjoying a

quiet dinner and talking." She smiled at Morrice. "My father and I haven't seen each other for a long time."

"But it's New Year's Eve!"

"So we have noticed, young man," Morrice said, "and we are celebrating in our own way."

"I understand, sir, but we couldn't help looking over and noticing you."

"Thank you." She raised her champagne glass. "Enjoy yourself. Happy New Year."

"And the same to you, ma'am, sir." He bowed like a recent military-college graduate and went back to his jolly table.

"He's right, Julia," Morrice said. "You are an exceptionally beautiful woman, with your life still ahead of you. What are you going to do with it? Perhaps that's what the polite young man really wanted to know. He's been looking over this way all evening—highly irritating to one of the young women beside him."

She felt it one of those exquisitely delicate moments when in an instant you thought you apprehended wordlessly many layers of meaning. She felt a rush of poignant feelings for this man, assuming that he had been contemplating the worn-out husk of his own life, staring at his own mortality. He'd also drunk a lot of champagne, but so had she.

"You are much more beautiful now than when I painted you as a girl. You really were just a girl in Paris before the war. But riper now, like fruit at its perfection."

"Somewhat past that!" She laughed. "The bloom is definitely off this peach!"

"Metaphorically, you may think. Peaches may be painted at many stages. But fruit's an unfortunate metaphor. I have never had much taste for still life, probably because I'm not very good at it. A few years ago I painted some flowers to please Léa."

Julia had forgotten about Léa. "Isn't she going to be sad not being with you tonight?"

"Léa is with her own friends. She'll be quite all right."

"But I'm keeping you from joining them!"

"No, no. She's used to me not being there. But regarding still life, I've always been repelled by those *natures mortes* where the ripeness of the peach is calculated to the second before overripeness and decay set in." He must have been a little tipsy because he rarely talked about painting and hated any pretentious talk about art.

"With a bee or wasp attacking the glistening drop of juice just oozing through the skin?"

"Exactly, full of tactile imagery, but freighted with romantic melancholy. All is decline from this moment. We are supposed to brood on such profundities and be edified. I'm very glad that I have lived most of my life—at least my life as an artist—in a time when we can cast off the pathetic, the sentimental. In Cézanne's fruit, there is no sense of the pathetic. His apples are not burdened with naive sermons on the impermanence of life. They are apples, gorgeous in themselves as objects, not messengers from some banal religiosity. And the artists saw this long before the rest of society. Who needs sweating fruit to remind us now that men rot too? That we have left millions of young men rotting in France, like fruit tipped into the ditch because it had passed its ripeness and would not sell the next day."

He lifted his glass and his eyes filled with tears. "I'm sorry, my dear. That was tactless. I think tonight's festivities are making me morbid. Why don't you go and dance with your young admirer from Baltimore?"

"Why Baltimore?"

"I have no idea. I like the sound of the name."

"I don't feel like dancing."

In fact the notion of dancing, the constant awareness of dancers in the background, was unsettling her, reminding her of Neville and all that had happened. Now she had backed herself into quite a corner.

"You didn't answer when I asked what you are going to do now with your life."

It was easier to begin obliquely. "Well, for one thing I have stopped painting."

He smiled. "Again?"

"This time for good. Don't you think that's sensible? I have realized I can never be good enough to satisfy myself."

"Who is? Or what serious artist is ever? I think it is the untalented or the weakly talented who are satisfied with their own work."

"I mean good enough to call myself a serious artist."

"I understand." He didn't argue with her, didn't dispute her judgment, and she was probably hoping for some little demur like, *Oh, you're much better than you let yourself think.* But he didn't say anything like that. This artist she so greatly admired, and in a mild way, she supposed, loved, indulged in no diplomacy to spare her feelings, but simply agreed. "I understand."

She covered it with a little laugh. "Besides I've heard your opinion of women painters."

"From whom?"

"I ran into MacTavish in a gallery in Montreal. A few years ago. He'd had a letter from you about some show, and you talked about the inevitable lady painters."

"I certainly didn't mean you. I meant English lady water-colourists who flock like birds to Saint-Malo in the summer. I don't see why you have to give it up. I still play the flute for my own amusement, sometimes for friends. I knew from the beginning I would never be good enough to give concerts in public. Never cared about that. It gives me pleasure just to play for myself."

"Painting has meant more than that to me."

"You told me years ago, when you were married—you wrote me—that you were content to leave painting behind and find a rich life in your marriage."

"I did. I really did for a while. But when Charles was overseas for so long, I had a lot of time to think about my life, even before—"

"I know."

"I felt so useless and restless."

"Understandable with him away."

"Not just with him away. But with all that time to think and, frankly, all the loneliness, I gradually realized that I must do something with my life—something useful. Something meaningful."

She was embarrassed to hear herself sounding like a whining schoolgirl, but he gently encouraged her to talk.

"Knowing one's value is...I don't know...as rare perhaps as perfect pitch. Years ago, I went to Tangiers when Henri was painting there. For two winters. We spent a lot of time together. And I had no trouble assessing his work. It was obvious. Even at its most casual-seeming, his sketchiest, he never made a stroke that was banal, or tired, or lacking freshness, energy, any criterion you can think of. And the colour! His colour evolved so astonishingly that I was—I am—stunned by it, totally captivated by its daring, its confidence, its joie de vivre, its humour. All convincing even when most starkly new."

Julia said, "If they awarded stars for artists, as they do for hotels, how many stars would you give yourself and how many to Matisse?"

"Well, if you want to play a game like that...if five stars were the top, I would give six stars for Henri. No contest."

"But your own worth?"

"My own? How many stars to award myself? Certainly not six. Two, three, four maybe. Sometimes one painting of mine feels as good as anything he does, although we couldn't be more different. Others fall short."

"But there in Tangiers, when you were looking at his paintings, what did Matisse think of your work?"

"I didn't show it to him."

This stunned her. "You didn't? Why?"

"It didn't matter. Beside his, it wasn't important."

"But he knew your work before, when you showed together at the Salon?"

"That was different. That wasn't asking for his opinion."

"Well, what did you tell him about his painting that you admired so much?"

"Nothing."

She laughed, incredulous. "Really—nothing?"

"It wasn't important, what I felt."

"Didn't it hurt his feelings to have you look and say nothing?"

"He understands. We are friends. We were on the Salon d'Automne jury together." He laughed. "We voted to reject Braque. It was unanimous. *Non à le cubisme!*"

"But you have no doubts about your own standing. Look what the French critics say. You have an international reputation."

"I do. Some critics think so, some do not, as you know. Some buyers and collectors are enthusiasts; many are not, especially in Canada. But all this talk of stars is nonsense anyway. There is no Michelin for painters. There is no competition."

"There is market competition."

"But if I wanted to be in that competition in Canada I would be painting syrupy Dutch landscapes. The market is very slow to appreciate quality or originality."

"But what I'm trying to say—and I'm sure the champagne is making me terribly boring about it—is that however hard I worked, even with coaching from someone like you, my painting would never come near any serious ranking. So"— she raised her glass—"no stars for Julia!"

He laughed and clinked his glass with hers and she was filled with fondness for him.

"If it is stars you are reaching for, you need to find them in another sphere, that's all."

"It's a little late, at twenty-eight, to be setting out to learn some different skill. Besides, what would it be? I have no aptitude for anything else I can think of."

The small orchestra cranked out a fanfare of reeds and strings, lacking the brass to give it importance, but a fanfare and it was midnight. The American women squealed and jumped up to run around their table, kissing the men, throwing paper streamers, and blowing whistles and tin horns. The dining room was filled with cries of *"Bonne année"* and "Happy New Year," the streamers festooning tables, as though they were ships being launched onto the perilous waters of the 1920s.

Morrice stood up, only a little unsteady. They hugged and kissed like uncle and niece, all ancient possibilities long evaporated from her feelings; the orchestra was playing and people were singing "Auld Lang Syne." More champagne corks popped but there was a louder popping outside. The waiters threw back the drapes and opened the French windows and they went out. The sky was clear and the wind had died. Fireworks were exploding over the calm sea. Holding their champagne glasses, the diners crowded out onto the small balconies and cheered each screaming rocket until it burst into showers of light like the petals of a giant, shaggy chrysanthemum, reflected in the dark Mediterranean. By leaning out they could see other fireworks, tiny sprinkles of light from nearby towns along the Riviera.

Julia began to shiver, unsure whether it was her internal state or the actual temperature. She had known nights in winter when her blood seemed to flow so hot that she could have rushed outside and rolled naked in the snow without feeling chilled. In other moods even on a warm day in summer, she would begin to tremble and feel frail, and all from interior chemistry and the emotions that drove it. She knew then, as they came inside to see the hundreds of candle flames wavering in the breath from the sea outside, that a particular chemistry was commanding her.

"You've been so sweet to listen to all my nonsense. I think I'll go up, if you wouldn't mind."

"Not at all. Maybe I'll sit a moment and have a drop of cognac before I turn in."

"Thank you for such a nice evening."

"I enjoyed it. I think I'm the envy of all male eyes in the room. See you in the morning."

She kissed his cheek and squeezed his arm affectionately, and he said, "We'll go to see Henri's work soon—he's off in Paris for a few days—and that will cheer us both up."

"That's very generous of you."

"Just the truth...which isn't a bad way to start the new year, is it? Happy New Year."

They had parted and Julia was a few feet away when he called and came up to her, noticeably less wobbly from drink, in the instant seeming younger and more decisive. With sudden enthusiasm, he said, "What I was beginning to say, when we got a little sidetracked, is that I would love to paint you again—as you are now."

That produced a strange jumble of emotions, and to blow them away, she laughed. "You mean here?"

"While you're down here. With the light here, gorgeous on your skin, your colouring. And I haven't painted a figure in a long while."

"I don't know that I feel very paintable right now."

"Will you think it over?"

"I will."

"I began thinking about it the moment I saw you again."

That sent her to bed as though given a present. To please him by sitting for him, to gratify whatever whim abruptly made him want to work again; to gratify her own vanity by modelling for such an important painter; to be thought interesting enough to stimulate some curiosity in him; and the pleasure of seeing what he would make of her seven years since the last portrait.

Her room was chilly, her clothes from the afternoon walk still damp on the ineffectual radiators, and she got into bed quickly, thinking how uncomfortable it would be to pose in such a cold room. She hadn't asked what he intended—nude, like the earlier one, or clothed, full length or just head and shoulders. If nude, she could hear herself saying to him, "We'd better do it soon, unless you want a study of a pregnant woman." She laughed, but that flicker of amusement quickly dissolved into a shiver of fear.

4

Jim Morrice sat in the wreck of the dining room, an obstacle to waiters clearing tables of glasses, streamers, and paper horns, smoking a cigar and sipping his cognac. What was he up to? He wanted to be nice to her—she was clearly upset and it couldn't be just about painting. Her painting couldn't be taken that seriously, and she had the taste and eye to know it. She had a very good eye. She knew what was good. Something else had brought her to Nice believing he could help her. He couldn't imagine how. But a desire to help her was not what had given him the sudden notion of painting her. Not at all. It was quite involuntary, this spontaneous conviction that he had to pick up his work again, which came with a rush of full confidence that he could work well. Her arrival had provoked that. Looking at her in the café, and remembering exactly how he had rendered the flesh tones previously—he now wanted to do it differently—he recognized with delight that the urge for so long dormant had come back.

"*Garçon! S'il vous plaît, encore un cognac.*"

It was 1920. God, in August he would be fifty-five. And for months he'd felt about eighty. No energy. No ambition. In practical terms, ever since the war painting. The only commission he'd ever accepted and a bad decision. Max Aitken, ludicrous now that he was Lord Beaverbrook. Lord Beaverbrook! He'd come after Morrice as he had every Canadian artist he could rope in to go and paint the battlefields, document the heroic Canadian war effort. To make a permanent record. Because they didn't have enough photographers. Should have seen the message in that. But he was not suited to paint records or documents. His instincts were too lyrical, his taste too delicate. That sounded effete, like art for art's sake, and he'd long outgrown that. Most of the artists recruited were younger chaps, some who had visited him in Paris, paying homage. After Passchendaele, they gave him a captain's rank. Photographed him in Paris in the uniform that looked strange without insignia, like an officer disgraced and stripped of his rank. So he went off to Picardy in January, the front near Amiens, where curiously one of his paintings hung in the museum. Or had until they packed the collection away for safety from German shelling that was reducing centuries of civilization to rubble.

They were kind enough to the old codger, as he soon knew they considered him. The army provided a special liaison officer to work with the artists, a Captain Robertson, and he was entirely cheerful, did everything to make Captain Morrice comfortable. Interesting that Robertson was the name of Julia's dead husband. Morrice had had a miserable time, sketching in the cold, snow, mud, freezing rain, whatever. Some artists, like Varley, concentrated on the horror, piles of corpses. It had disturbed Morrice more than he'd expected. The filth, men crawling with lice, up to their thighs in liquid mud that stank of shit and piss; smoking, joking, singing, cursing whenever he saw them, except when they were marching to the front. Then they were silent. That was the subject he chose to work up for the final painting. The suppressed horror of it. That silent straggle of men, heavily burdened, trying to keep some marching order, sloshing up the muddy, half-frozen road in the snow, guns muttering ahead of them, light flashes on the horizon. Almost certainly by the numbers many of them were slogging to their deaths, and just as certainly they knew it. They knew it and they kept marching up there. The horror of it haunted him. His own young countrymen. Healthy lads half-a-foot taller than he, with all their lives ahead of them. He knew their willingness should have inspired him. He whose life had always been so protected, who had been free to go where he wished, as he liked. That they should have been compelled to go to their deaths did not inspire. It haunted him, as did the phrase of Wilfred Owen's...*these who die as cattle*. It haunted him and it made him sick.

They wanted a big painting and he wasn't comfortable with big. He had laboured to perfect small paintings, subjects perceived with great care, evaluated and internalized, then rendered with long thought. He disliked the big painting. The whole exercise depressed him. But he supposed he owed something to his country when young men were prepared to keep marching up that road and die like cattle for it. So he had to finish it. Almost seven feet by nine. Went down to Concarneau to work up the finished canvas in the studio, where he had the space for it. But even being in Brittany failed to cheer him up. A doctor suspected he'd picked up pneumonia at the front and told him to drink less and get outside in the spring sunshine. He did, but the work was slow and painful. Took until June to finish it, knowing it was a failure. And he couldn't paint at all after that. The whole experience had shut down the urge. Hadn't even bothered to go over to London when the prime minister opened the war paintings exhibition at the Royal Academy. And that was almost a year ago. A year of lying fallow. And now, remarkably, like the morning an invalid wakens after a long illness feeling miraculously restored, he really felt the joy of work again.

As she lay awake Julia could still hear faint cheers and shouts from revellers excited to be out in the first hours of the new year. Listening to them with a quickening of the heart, Julia felt her anxiety return. Time was passing, the growth happening within her was inexorable. She had to make decisions.

Suzanne Perret had been wonderfully sympathetic, extraordinarily generous for a new friend, offering to let her stay in her apartment indefinitely. She had lost her fiancé in the war and that created an instant bond.

In the few days past Julia's second missed period, hoping from hour to hour that it might yet arrive, that the previous month's miss had been a fluke, she had known quite well that the sensations that always preceded it were absent. The sickness the last two mornings before breakfast was undeniable. Through all that huge cloud of preoccupation, beginning at Suzanne's in Paris, then on the train journey and the change at Marseilles—visiting the smelly lavatory every few hours to check—then another train along the Riviera, she had been endlessly considering what to do, yet not wanting to decide.

She believed that years ago, Léa Cadoret, Morrice's amiable and loyal mistress, had had a baby. Morrice was secretive about Léa—many of his wide circle of artist and writer friends had not been invited to meet her; some did not know she existed. But Julia knew because she had come once unannounced to Quai des Grands-Augustins, up the curved staircase to the third-floor studio and surprised them. She knew Morrice did not want the liaison known in Montreal and she had told no one. But she knew, and she thought there had been a child, either before or just after Morrice began keeping her in 1898 or 1899. His child, or someone else's, Julia never asked. Léa treated her very courteously, convinced Julia was part of Morrice's extended Canadian family and knowing it was a wealthy and distinguished family. Julia was sure she could ask Léa for advice.

Stewart MacPherson would have helped. With his medical contacts he was one of the few men who would know how, but she shrank from asking him. He was off in Germany seeing the people he wanted to see and she had not written. Admitting that she was pregnant would have meant admitting a lot more and she had not been up to that.

The curious thing about deciding to be absolutely truthful to each other, as she had most willingly, seeing freedom in it, was that she had found it confining. When she was honest, sometimes against her better judgment, she could see it hurt him, which she never wanted to do. And she began finding it harder and harder to be candid.

That awkwardness went back to the spring in Halifax, the day of Neville's letter.

5

For their picnic Julia had said old clothes but found herself dressing to please Stewart, washing her hands carefully to erase the smell of turpentine, putting scent on her wrists and behind her ears, loosening her hair from its casual morning ribbon to do the chignon he liked. For a moment she let it hang to her shoulders. Should she cut it for the trip? Or for the dinner with Neville Boiscoyne and the prince? Long hair was already beginning to look dated on young women who were no longer girls. Or should she wait till London or Paris, see how the women looked and have it done there? It annoyed her to catch herself in such calculation, but when Stewart took the wicker picnic basket from her and said, "You are quite simply the most beautiful woman in the world," it pleased her, although she said, "Isn't that a bit sweeping and reckless for a scientist?"

"Even scientists need intuitive leaps, and you are mine."

Feeling watched in Halifax, she never kissed Stewart in public but sat companionably close to him in the front seat of his old black Paige. When they were out of her neighbourhood and crossing the Common, she kissed him warmly on the cheek and slipped her hand around his arm.

"Oh, I am so glad to get out of that house. I was feeling stifled all morning. Thank you for rescuing me."

If he never really aroused her physically, it was worth it to have the intimate companionship she had valued in him from the beginning.

"I picked up the tickets," Stewart said.

"Oh, that's thrilling. That makes it real."

"And I walked home daydreaming about all that delicious time alone with you, until I ran into the Very Reverend Peter Wentworth, and even that didn't spoil it."

"Oh, don't tell me! I can't wait to be away from here and not have to worry about bumping into him. It's another reason for moving from that house but I can't until Charles's estate is settled and it's taking forever. The Robertsons are very sweet about it, saying I must consider the house mine to dispose of as I wish, but I can't do that legally...until the probate, or whatever it is, is finished. It's a little spooky. It's as though he's not letting go of me. I got that weird feeling again the other day that if I just walked into the next room quickly enough—before he had time to flit away—he'd be there. Do you think that's normal?"

"Do you ever dream about him?"

"No. At least not for a very long time." She considered saying more, then changed the subject. "You must tell me exactly what my ticket comes to."

"I wish you'd let me pay for it."

"No. I want to pay my way for everything on this trip."

"Are we going to have ugly scenes in restaurants, each counting out our coins for the tip?"

"I just want to feel independent, in that way. Heaven knows I'm dependent enough on you emotionally. Oh, I told Mollie we were going."

"And how did she react?"

"'*Oh, moy deer!*' I love the way she talks. And then she said 'There's people might say something about you and him going off like this when you wasn't married.'" And she's right. I'm still a little shy about telling Lucy and the Robertsons."

"What did you tell her?"

"I told her these are modern times and I'm determined to live in a modern way."

"Wonderful!"

She was about to go on and say, "She told me to be careful not to get in the family way," but felt inhibited, did not say it, and wondered why. She had certainly been open with him about the need to be careful. In London she intended to find a doctor from whom she could discreetly obtain a diaphragm, because she could not in Halifax.

Stewart laughed. "I'll bet she told you to marry me and make an honest woman of yourself."

She squeezed his arm. "You don't think I'm an honest woman now?" and abruptly decided her shyness was silly. It was more open to tell him of Mollie's warning, but Stewart prevented her by saying, "Anyway, when I ran into the new dean he was hugging himself because he's received an invitation to a dinner with the Prince of Wales—"

"He hasn't!"

"Well, as I told him, he's become a civic landmark, the personification of our civilian courage"—he must have noticed that she was not laughing as he'd expected—"...and so on."

"Stewart, I've had a letter too."

"As the VC widow? Oh, that's unkind, I didn't mean—"

"No, I know what you meant and it's partly that, I suppose. At least it's mentioned. No, it's more personal..." Her hesitation was slight but must have been noticeable. "It's from Neville Boiscoyne."

"Lieutenant B?"

"You see! You instantly make the connection and so did Lucy and so did Mollie. It is so embarrassing!"

"Lucy and Mollie didn't read the diary."

"Oh, Stewart." She said it with affectionate annoyance. "They're women, for heaven's sake! They didn't need to read the diary to see what was going on."

"Obviously it's upset you. I can hear it in your voice."

"It has upset me. I brought it with me. You can read it when we stop. You'll see what I mean." Stewart said, "The fog's burning off a bit."

He turned off into the road that wound through Herring Cove village. Fish houses of weathered shingle perched on seaweedy legs by the rickety docks. The narrow slit in the granite coast sheltered a few fishing boats, with simple houses rising above the water, each with its tidy garden of potatoes, onions, beets, carrots, and cabbages, with beds of pansies, snapdragons, and sweet peas under the windows. They stopped to look at this picturesque serenity, the mouth of the tiny harbour just visible in the receding fog, hearing the boom of the tumultuous surf outside. Moored dories and sailing boats rode like ghosts on the glassy water. Huge gulls stood motionless and mute on roof ridges and on lobster pots stacked against the sheds.

"You should come and paint this," Stewart said.

"That's what everybody paints in Nova Scotia. It's so obvious it's banal," Julia said.

"Obvious but pretty. Nice to look at on your wall at home when you're not here."

"It's not what I'm trying to do," she said, turning away.

"I know," he said comfortingly, seeking no argument today.

"Yes, you do. You know better than anyone." She caught his mood and slipped her arm companionably through his. They walked back to the car and drove across the little strip of land that enclosed the harbour and parked overlooking the open Atlantic. They carried the picnic basket and rugs along the path that skirted the woods of balsam fir, fringed with bayberry bushes. She picked a bayberry leaf and crushed it, holding it under Stewart's nose.

"Smell."

"Nice."

"I love the smell. I never knew it before I came here. Oh, look, some wild strawberries!" She knelt down to pick a few tiny berries, smelling their perfume as she straightened up and held her cupped hand up to him.

"They're so ripe that it's hard to pick without squishing them. Have a taste."

He ate them out of her palm and his lips were red with them.

He leaned over. "A strawberry kiss." She kissed him and he licked his lips. "Mm-mm!"

But she did not feel like pursuing the kiss and walked on until they came to a small grassy clearing at the edge of the trees overlooking the sea, still grey under the receding fog, large waves hitting the rocks below them, the spray shooting upwards.

"Perfect!" She shook out one of the rugs to spread it. "And what a gorgeous day it's becoming! Aren't you glad we got out of town?"

Stewart took her in his arms. "I'm glad any time we're alone." He kissed her but she responded with a friendly peck and turned away.

"No one can see us here."

She smiled. "Do you know that from bringing other women here?"

"What is the gallant answer to that?" Of course he'd been here with other women.

"The gallant answer is, 'But never as gorgeous as you, my dear.'"

"That's also true," Stewart said, looking at her flushed face as she straightened up from spreading the other rug. She gave him another comradely, unprovocative touch of her lips and knelt on the tartan rug to take food out of the basket.

"Aren't you hungry? It's nearly two. I'm starved."

Stewart pulled out the tickets for the ocean crossing.

"Look. Two outside cabins, separate enough to be perfectly discreet—"

She laughed. "But close enough to be perfectly compromising. You are sweet, Professor MacPherson, and very thoughtful, but do you think that will fool anyone in Halifax?"

"I thought it observed the proprieties quite nicely."

"My dear, even if we bunked at opposite ends of the ship, on different decks, they'd assume we were travelling together."

"Does that bother you?"

"No. But I'm beginning to see it through their eyes."

"Through Mollie's eyes."

"Well, she's made me think about it, yes. Anyway, let's have lunch. Please!"

She knew that the moment she had suggested the picnic, he'd instantly thought of this spot and imagined they would eat and make love on the rugs. She could feel the little current of that expectation still running in him but the mood was wrong and, as they chatted through lunch, she knew the letter she intended to show him kept rising in his thoughts, because he brought up Peter Wentworth again.

"Peter's self-importance always makes me want to rib him. When he said he and Margery had been invited to the small dinner party for the prince, I couldn't resist saying, 'Not surprising, Peter. You've become one of the civic landmarks, a local attraction. They'll be trotting you out for official dinners until Judgment Day, or kingdom come—whichever is first.' And he said, 'Well, you may laugh, but I confess I'm quite thrilled to be asked to meet our future king—in such an intimate way.' The old Peter, still swimming in reverence for the mystical bonds of monarchy and the Church of England. He said the words 'our future king' with unction worthy of the Archbishop of Canterbury actually anointing the royal brow."

This brought a laugh from Julia, but anything to do with Peter still made her uneasy.

"As we parted, Peter said, 'Well, thank God everything is getting back to normal.' And I said, 'You mean, now that the god you're thanking has become bored with all the killing?' I wonder what he'll think up next to amuse himself. Honestly, Peter, there will never be 'normal,' as we knew it. Things will never be as they were. Just look at our own lives. Look at yours. The war has made you at thirty what you mightn't have been until fifty in peacetime."

Julia said, "I wonder how poor Margery is getting along?"

"I asked him and didn't get quite the defensive flare-up as in the past. He said, 'In some ways much better, she enjoys the bigger house. She and her mother are busy—you know...' I said, 'Erasing the Creightons' taste?' and Peter did smile: 'Well, you know Margery's mother.'"

"Lucy says they're spending a fortune on it, as though *he'd* become bishop, not Donald Creighton."

"Then Peter said rather oddly, 'And she goes out a lot more...' and looked embarrassed."

Julia knew that from Lucy too. People in the South End knew. The beautiful but hitherto listless Margery Wentworth had become socially aggressive and uninhibited—after an attempt at suicide. And the gossip pitied the new dean.

To get him out of her thoughts and clear the air with Stewart, she abruptly fished Neville's letter out of her bag. "Do you mind reading it so that we can discuss it?"

He did, and she imagined him feeling instantly jealous of the charisma rising from the page for her, the charged simplicity of the engraved aristocratic crest, the unassailable masculine self-confidence that flowed through the words. And Stewart knew the intensity of her reaction to Boiscoyne. She had been embarrassingly explicit about it in her diary, which had fallen into Peter's hands after the 1917 explosion, and Stewart had read it because Peter thought he might be able to identify the author.

"I suppose you can read it on two levels," he said evenly, handing the letter back. "You can read it as a perfectly straightforward, socially gracious gesture. Or you can read it more subjectively, as conveying more than an invitation to dinner."

"But is that really in it, or am I just imagining it?" She was ill at ease and saw that he noticed and leaned forward to kiss him. "You know, you're the only person with whom I could dream of being so honest about this."

"So you feel the second reading?"

"Well, yes and no." Even in the most candid conversations, in her desire to be totally honest with Stewart, some reticence restrained her. "I've wavered back and forth. Stupid, I know. But that's why I wanted you to see it."

"Difficult for me to be totally objective about it myself."

"I know."

"Knowing what I know."

"What do you think you know?"

"I suppose you still feel something about this fellow Boiscoyne?"

"I feel embarrassment. That's all. I'm embarrassed to be reminded of my wartime silliness. That's all it was."

"And if Lieutenant B wants to pursue something more when he comes?"

"As I said to Lucy, I am not on the market."

"You said that?"

"I did."

"I'm very glad to hear it."

"It can't come as a surprise, if you've just bought us cabins on the *Aquitania*."

"It's not a surprise but I'm very glad to hear you say it again."

She looked at Stewart, feeling a strong need to right things with him, and said, "Is there anyone at your house this afternoon?"

"No."

She kissed him again and said with a rush of held-up breath, "Could we go there now? It's nice here"—a kiss—"but not private enough."

In the car, sitting close to him, Julia said, "I didn't tell you something else Mollie said. I should be careful not to get in the family way." She kissed him lightly. "Now what do you suppose gave her that idea?"

"Probably sees the latent erotic content in your painting and puts two and two together."

"Oh, don't be mean!" She dug him in the ribs. "My painting is so awful! And so frustrating! Part of the reason I wanted to get out of the house was to not have to stare at it."

"You're too hard on yourself. If Henry Rosenberg's as keen on you as he says—"

"Oh, Rosenberg's just being nice. He has to be if he's giving me lessons. He has to encourage me."

"He wouldn't be giving you lessons if he didn't admire your work. You told me he stopped taking students years ago because he wants to do his own painting. And he's very good."

"He's a very good painter. I'm just running into the same thing as when I gave it up before I got married. Every day I see the limitations of my talent. The more I improve my technique, the better I see how modest my gift is. It's sad. But there it is. If I ever get uppity about it I just have to go downstairs and look at the little Matisse or my Morrice portrait, and then I know."

"But I see real development since you started again. You seem surer of yourself, and bolder, and your colour is a lot more sophisticated. Anyway, the object of art isn't to be as good as someone else or better than someone else."

"I know, you're right." She sighed. "You're right about everything. Anyway, it will be so refreshing to see all the new painting when we get to Paris. I can hardly wait."

Stewart told her about the clerk in the shipping line booking office, who had said almost exactly what Peter had: "Thank goodness everything's getting back to normal, sir."

"You know, I'm beginning to hear this everywhere. He said suddenly people want passages to Europe again. They're busier than they've been since the last summer before the war. Good I came early because the bookings are so heavy and shipping is so scarce."

"Because so many liners were sunk?"

"And because they still have thousands of soldiers to bring back. Oh, and there was something else. I still routinely ask everyone how they came through the explosion. And the elderly clerk said, 'Oh, I was all right, sir. But'—then he lowered his voice and leaned closer—'the young lady typist behind me lost her mother and sister.' As discreetly as I could

I glanced at the girl confidently typing—serene face, new short hairstyle, clothes suggesting a desire to look attractive. Fascinating that so many survivors give no outward sign of the tragedies that touched them. But the clerk whispered, 'Another of our girls had a terrible injury to her face. It's left her badly disfigured. But they gave her her job back, all right.' And I said, 'I should hope so,' and he said smugly, 'They just have her working upstairs now, where it won't distress people.' In other words, where people won't have to be reminded. Now how will such treatment affect the girl?"

Julia thought about that. "Well, isn't it a kindness to her?"

"I wonder. Perhaps I should go back and ask to see her, include her in my study."

For a man as sensitive as he was, sometimes Julia felt Stewart's zeal as a psychologist made him look too far beyond the obvious. She said, "If I were a girl with a disfigured face, I wouldn't want the public staring at me. I think everyone is putting all that behind them now."

"Well, you're right. It's amazing how resilient people are, behaving as if we'd just been through a great earthquake, a natural disaster, no fault of man. Bury the dead, repair the damage, and get on with life—survivors of the Halifax explosion, survivors of the carnage in France—putting it all behind them, getting back to normal."

"But, Stewart, you need to find people scarred psychologically to justify your thesis."

"Well, I have plenty of evidence" Stewart said evenly, not rising to her implied criticism. "I'm sure that shell shock doesn't happen just to soldiers."

In her mind was one of the private little strands of thought that accompanied even the most intimate and honest conversation. She kept going back to Lucy's reservations about

Stewart, whose house she was now approaching, in daylight, to make love, or have affectionate sex, which was and yet wasn't the same thing, because she wanted to reassure him or herself. But the momentary rush of that intention was evaporating in conflicting thoughts and the time it was taking to drive back into town.

They were coming down to the head of the Northwest Arm, seeing the pleasure boats moored in the cove at Armdale. She noticed a sloop that reminded her of Charles's boat, now four summers ashore in a cradle, its seams probably dried out. She looked at this seaworthy twin nodding jauntily on its mooring and then, it caught her again, that instant of conviction that Charles was not dead. He was about to come up from the cabin of that green boat, his sandy hair would appear as he slid back the companionway cover, a brown hand gripping the varnished rim.

Stewart heard her gasp for breath. "What's the matter?"

She let out the air she had suddenly drawn in. "I think I must be going mad. I saw that sailboat we were passing and I knew the next instant that Charles was going to stick his head up out of the cabin."

"Do you want to stop?"

She sighed. "No, let's keep going. But why do I feel that so strangely every now and then?"

"How often 'every now and then'?"

"More, recently. A few days ago, I told you. I was sure he was just in the next room. Then now. It's the first time with you, I mean when I'm with you. But it's uncanny, because when it happens, it feels so real."

"An hallucination."

"As real as real life. Not a dream. But just for a flash, and then it's gone and I'm quite normal again."

Stewart said, "It would be interesting to note each time, what you're doing or thinking, what you've just done, or about to do."

"You mean, like going to your house to..."

"Perhaps you'd prefer not to?"

"No," she said firmly, "I'd prefer to," but not feeling at all as firm.

The sexual promise in her emphasis excited him and he drove a little faster. To convince herself, she edged closer to hold his arm.

"What are you thinking?"

"I hate to say it but I'm wondering if you really do want to come to my house now."

"No I don't." He must have heard the relief in her voice. "Thank you for knowing that." She kissed his cheek. "You always know the right thing to say. I'm all at sixes and sevens today. Come home with me instead and Mollie will make tea for us."

"And chaperone us?"

She tried to say in her intimate tone, "You know what I mean."

Lying in bed in her hotel room in Nice eight months later, it was obvious that her fantasy that Charles was alive had provided a psychological mechanism for avoiding a real commitment to Stewart. Of course, as Mollie saw, he wanted to marry her: the question hovered unspoken but alive around every conversation. She was unquestionably very fond of Stewart (and always had been) and immeasurably grateful to him, not only for his kindness to Betty, but for helping her find a measure of sanity in her life. But she could not make herself be in love with him. It was awkward between them, each continually trying to pre-analyze the other's reaction to forestall misunderstandings and prevent hurt. Their attempts to make love reflected the ambivalence. Necessarily clandestine, on picnics, or in his car at remote places or, even more anxious about discovery, at his house on Victoria Road, these efforts were never satisfying. The physical reality of sex was so primitive and ridiculous that unless driven by strong desire, Julia was too aware of the mechanics and so became more observer than participant. Thus objectified, even with the kindliest, friendliest wish to please, the acts lost any personal excitement for her. And they were kind and friendly, but such sex left her empty, so she tried to put off these opportunities. Women had experienced this forever and had simulated excitement, or tolerated the lack of it, but she didn't. Yet she did not want a complete break with Stewart. She had no friend as valuable, as intelligent or understanding.

One thought came now and then, sometimes when they were actually trying to make the physical part right, that he knew from having read her diary how passionate she could be, how easily aroused with the right person. So she thought, *Well, he knows I'm not frigid, he must know it is not my fault.* And he had had past experiences that were satisfactory, so he must know they were sexually incompatible. It was one of the areas that defeated their efforts to be perfectly honest with each other.

Fear of pregnancy was another. One of Julia's motives in planning the European trip was to find effective birth control because her scandalized doctor in Halifax would not oblige, and a young war widow could hardly go around such a small city canvassing co-operative doctors. On the other hand, she had to be straight with herself and acknowledge that fear of pregnancy had not inhibited her when she was truly aroused. Stewart too, without being coarsely explicit, made it clear he believed that on their own, enjoying the anonymity and tolerance of sophisticated European hotels, and therefore more relaxed, her reluctance would dissolve and the awkwardness disappear. She did not think so. And it was when these considerations seemed to overwhelm her that she began to suspect Charles was not dead? My, my. She didn't need Stewart to analyze that!

Now it pleased her to think of him not dead. Little stories of how it might be possible had begun to unfold for her in moments like now, just as she was falling asleep...like the story of the switched uniforms...

6

Thursday, January 1, 1920

James Morrice awoke to see the sheer curtains stirring on the long French windows and felt the seductive, moist air of the Mediterranean, so entrancing to anyone from the north coming to the Côte d'Azur in winter. The hedonistic sunlight and the soft, luminous air always brought a lightness to his spirit—they promised relief from burdens and cares; they told of living as pleasure; they forced Calvinism back into the northern shadows; it was unnecessary and perverse to live where it was cold and gloomy. As potent a message to Morrice, a Canadian from Quebec, as to a northern Frenchman like Matisse from Picardy, men from darker winter latitudes, whose creative souls had unfolded like flowers under this beguiling light.

Morrice awoke remembering his desire to paint Julia and wondered soberly whether that had been mere drunken exuberance, of which he was frequently capable, or the birth of something, the rebirth he had been not too hopefully awaiting. In his stiff morning mind, he tried to re-grasp the elusive feather of thought that had brushed his imagination at midnight. No, the idea had come in the afternoon, in the café. He was not hungover; he drank too steadily to have hangovers. But he had a familiar pressure in his skull and dryness in the eye sockets. He wanted something to drink but did not yet feel like getting up to get it. He had eaten too much. He should have drunk whisky at the end of the evening. Something in cognac made his eyes hurt the next morning. He closed the lids and saw quite clearly, as though they were hanging in this hotel room, his early paintings of women. From the late 1890s, full-figure studies like *Young Woman in a Black Coat* or *Lady in Brown*, when his tonalities and colour harmonies were still inspired by Whistler, and two more intimate studies, *Femme au lit* and *Nude Reclining*, an homage to Manet. Then after the trips to Venice, and many paintings of its golden twilights, he'd begun to outgrow those influences and to be recognized by exhibitors, critics, and collectors for his own distinctive sensibility. For more than a decade he'd concentrated on landscape, travelling widely but painting mostly in France, in Quebec, then the two winters in Tangiers with Matisse, always looking to develop that personal style, to advance his technique, and to liberate his colour.

By 1910, he was well established as a landscapist. Louis Vauxcelles, the critic who had labeled Matisse and Derain *les fauves*, claimed that since Whistler's death Morrice was unquestionably the most noted American painter in Paris.

Then something had made him gravitate again to figure painting, not with calculation, not with any deliberate intention to freshen his eye for landscape, but he'd been stimulated by Bonnard and Matisse and wanted the different discipline, the different problems. *Nude with a Feather*, *Woman with a Fan*, *Nu de dos*, those paintings reappeared behind his eyes, familiar from almost daily viewing when they hung in the studio in Paris, now waiting at Léa's. The study of Julia in his wicker chair had been one of them, the least familiar because he had not seen it since 1913, when he had given it to her. He wished he could examine it carefully right now.

It was a fascinating challenge to return to the close-up, as they were saying in photography, after years of reducing the human figure to distant tiny flicks of the brush, mere ingredients in his landscapes of Paris, Venice, the coast of Normandy, the bars in Havana, the beaches of Trinidad. To come back from those half-inch twists and curls of the brush to a full canvas study had many implications. A huge journey mentally from the anonymous woman, minute at a distance, to the full-sized, real woman in the studio, her human presence, her body's presence, like the model's perfume, her personality filling the room, like her conversation—unless he asked her to be quiet. A very different proposition, in which he lost distance, and the sensual presence became a reality that was sometimes difficult to reduce to abstract questions of aesthetics or of technique.

It was in his nature to keep things at a remove until it suited him, or he needed to bring them close; like the way he had related to Léa all these years, with her amiable complicity. Partly his upbringing, he supposed, but he had never been comfortable living too cheek by jowl, being jostled physically by life. From his schooldays, when he was smaller physically than most of his schoolmates, and a good-natured whack from another boy could send him sprawling. He soon became more comfortable keeping life in spatial dimensions of his choosing. That is why he felt so comfortable sitting in a café with his specially made painting box, small enough to be unobtrusive, to slip into a jacket pocket, taking his time to observe penetratingly, from a sheltered sanctuary, the life swirling around him. He loved the French cafés for that, those in Venice too, and more recently the shady recesses of bars in Havana. From such a controlled perspective on life, such edited reality, to return to figure painting was a huge physical step closer to life. It was difficult to be in a small studio with a naked model without feeling her womanliness, without being aware, apart from everything else, that she was not simply a decorative object. She was tangible life brought very close, which might be why the world assumed that artists' models were inevitably mistresses too, because no layman could imagine being alone for hours with an attractive woman, of the sort of women they imagined being willing to take their clothes off and pose in the first place, without being dominated by sexual thoughts. When *La toilette* was exhibited in London, art critics considered it indecent, showing only they had dirty minds. But they had said that about Manet's *Olympia*, before which the younger Morrice had stood reverently for hours.

He had never really fully crossed the line, one of the most interesting lines in modern art, between figure painting that leaned towards portraiture, and that which was essentially decorative. It was a psychological as well as an aesthetic line and on which side of it any painting fell was only partly a matter of intention, more one of temperament and evolution, or feeling part of a movement, without being in the movement necessarily, or self-consciously part of a school, but of letting the work of others you admired lodge in your psyche, as part of the overall journey, the life's journey of finding yourself, your own individual identity as a painter. He had done that well enough. But the line was never a sharp one. It was as though that psychological-aesthetic line could stretch, so the line was actually a broad terrain across which individual artists went all, or only part of, the way, and not always consistently. Each of his figure paintings had strayed progressively further across that no man's land.

Lying there thinking, he could hold all the paintings in

mind. When he was working, he observed with such intensity of concentration that he carried hundreds of paintings around in his memory as composers did their music, as in fact he did the music by Chopin, or Schubert, or Mozart that he loved to play on the flute. The new painting, if Julia agreed, would carry him well beyond the last effort. In an odd way, each time he had devoted himself to figure painting, he had later noted a marked advance, a further maturing of his work in landscape. Could that possibly happen again?

His practical mind was occupied semi-consciously. Size of canvas: quite large for full-length figure. *Nude with a Feather* ended at her knees, so ninety centimetres by sixty would do. Where to pose her: somewhere you felt the luminosity of the south. Background: not the draped fabrics this time, focus more attention on the figure. To start with a ground colour wash on the raw canvas or not? He could feel a pale turquoise, the glaze in some Moorish tiles, a tone he had lightly brushed over the other colours in the Saint-Malo beach scene *Beneath the Ramparts*. Should he try some sketches first, or a small oil sketch, to play with the values before beginning in earnest? Now he felt like getting up. He needed a coffee with a little rum in it.

At least she was sick before breakfast and once the heaves had subsided, Julia was hungry and eager to be out in the glorious air she drank in from her window. Pale sunlight was turning the calm Mediterranean a cerulean blue where the water was deeper, shading to the palest opalescent turquoise where its waves lazily uncurled on the shingle beach. Drinking in the joy of those colours, she sighed. Whether she was going to continue painting or not, she could not help looking with the painter's eye. That was Morrice's great faculty, his delicate eye, an eye that could see with exquisite refinement and colour sense. Even Frenchmen, or the most discerning of them, were ravished by his paintings of Normandy and Brittany and especially Paris. The French government had bought three of them. Some critics had bought him for their private collections. Of the thousands of painters working in Paris, he was one of very few, particularly among foreign painters, to have earned real distinction. Measured by her small talent, Morrice was a giant, who should be stimulated by such admiration to fresh achievement. He should be at the height of his powers, not dissipating them as he was. The previous afternoon he had looked almost drained of energy—until, it was true, the evening had revived him. He had seemed quite vigorous when he suggested painting her.

If doing that would reawaken his ambition and get him back to work, it would be right to do it. But this morning she did not feel like it in the least. She turned away from the window to go on dressing, wondering at her reluctance. Anyone interested in art should be honoured to pose for an important artist. Quite selfishly, it conferred a little posterity. Whomever Morrice painted would be known and looked at in galleries for generations. Even in Canada, slow to appreciate him, Morrice was now hanging in the National Gallery and many others. She raised a leg to pull on a stocking and stopped. She had felt no shyness about posing for him before she was married. Why would it be different now? But it was, inexplicably. Before she decided, she wanted to take off her clothes alone and scrutinize her body carefully. To satisfy herself about what? Never mind. She could do it later. She needed to be out now in the charming streets she could see from the window, amid the cheerful noises and delicious smells. She pulled up the stocking and secured it.

Wanting some time to herself, she left the hotel so as not to pass the café where she guessed Morrice might be and walked up Rue Meyerbeer. It was absolutely true that changing the scenery helped change the spirits. The under-current of anxiety she'd been living with began to dissolve as she headed away from the sea towards the old city of Nice, absorbed in the busy life of the streets, the costumes, the shops, the architecture, the different odours of the region's cooking, the flowers strangely in season, the semi-tropical trees and foliage in the parks, all just exotic enough to be fascinating. By the time she had found a busy café on Place Masséna, with its shady arcades and terracotta- and pistachio-coloured buildings, she was cheerful. While she waited for her café au lait and croissants, she realized just what had been inhibiting her: Lucy.

7

"Oh, your cheeks are like ice!" Lucy said as they kissed. The coal fire made her living room cozy and inviting.

"The fog has come in again and it's really raw out."

"Come and sit near the fire and have something to warm you up." Lucy poured each a sherry. "Thanks to Daddy who keeps me supplied."

"Me too. And I never ask how he does it."

"My dear, the innocent Montrealer! Flouting the law is a Nova Scotia tradition. We've had pirates and privateers and smugglers forever. All our hundreds of little harbours, thousands of boats and ships. They used to go out and capture ships and steal their wines and brandies. Now they just sail over to St. Pierre and Miquelon and buy it from the French. So everyone knows a bootlegger."

"Mollie's people always seem to have some rum around."

"Of course. Prohibition isn't going to stop the schooners coming back with rum when they take fish and lumber down to the West Indies. Rum's in their blood. Anyway, it's just silly, outlawing drink, trying to bamboozle us with all that campaign to make Canada a better, cleaner, healthier place after the war."

Her jolliness didn't match Julia's mood. "Don't you think we're actually a sadder, more desperate place now? Such a heroic effort, and what are the men finding when they come? No jobs and the bosses richer than ever from the profits they made in the war."

"You could be talking of Daddy."

"Of course I'm not."

"Well, his shipyard did a roaring business. Of course it was essential and patriotic but he couldn't help making bushels of money. Now business is dead and he's laid off two-thirds of his workers. He's sitting pretty—we're sitting pretty—and what happens to them?"

"You make poor Archie sound like a hard-faced capitalist grinding the faces of the poor."

"No! But he can't pay them for not working. And the soldiers coming back all need jobs and that only makes it worse."

"I've never heard you sound so political."

"I'm not one bit political. You voted, I didn't."

Julia had voted for the first time. Since Borden's Unionist government had opportunistically given women the privilege, at least women with men overseas, she had to use it.

But Lucy's tone had changed and she said morosely, "I'm just feeling a little strange because Harry's coming back. And guilty." She looked meaningfully at Julia and squeezed her hand.

That evening more than usual she could see echoes of Charles in his sister's strong, freckled face. Her normal demeanour—the cheerful face of the hockey captain she had been at school—hid the resemblance. Now anxiety brought out the pensive, distracted, melancholy look so familiar in her dead brother.

"I didn't mean to get into this before I've even fed you."

"We can eat later. Let's keep talking. I'm not very hungry."

"At least let's have another sherry!"

"I'm not surprised you're feeling strange about Harry coming back. It's been so long. Longer than Charles—"

"He went before Charles."

"Charles went because of Harry."

"But when he could have come back after the Armistice, he agreed to stay on." She gave Julia a very direct look. "Didn't you think that was strange?"

"To be honest, Lucy, I did."

"Away for three years in the trenches, with a wife and two little girls desperately anxious for him hour by hour—especially after Charles was killed—and he chooses not to come home to us the first chance he gets?"

"I know what you mean."

"It's as though he's been avoiding us—avoiding me." Lucy's pale face was flushed and her voice was trembling.

"But it was an honour to be asked to help Borden with the peace conference, for a young officer straight out of the trenches."

"Oh, Daddy just fixed that up with Borden because Harry had worked for the same law firm after he graduated."

"Still, a great opportunity, to be present where history's being made."

"I know all that. Of course it is. And he's loved it, just as he loved the war. You remember his letters. Couldn't have been more different from the letters Charles sent you. Harry made the war sound like a great lark, like going off to rough it on a fishing trip. Without a scratch. It sounded as though he never even got his uniform dirty. Yet we know he was in some of the worst of it. Ypres. Men gassed, men killed all around him. And still a lark to him. The complete opposite of the poor fellows Stewart MacPherson's been dealing with, the shell-shocked men. As though some men like Harry get shocked the other way, shocked into joy. He loved it. And now he's loved the time in Paris. You can just imagine—after all, you've lived there, you can imagine what a good time they're having..."

"Do you mean—"

"Women? No I don't. Or of course I do, but I don't really. Because Harry's never been very interested in—all that. I think. No, what I mean—and it worries me—is that he feels for me about as much as he feels for the set of golf clubs in the cupboard out there. He'll come back, find them and say, 'Oh boy, I've missed these clubs! Can't wait to get out to Ashburn and get my swing back.' That's about how happy he'll be to see us."

"But not unhappy, Lucy. Isn't that just the way he is? His feelings don't engage the negatives. Like you, he's ninety percent positive about life."

"His feelings? I think his feelings are like those of a little boy who wakes up every morning excited about the fun he expects that day."

"But you don't mean that he doesn't care for you and the girls?"

"I mean—it's horrible to say it, but if I can't talk to you, I can't say it to anyone else. I feel he's as dead to me as though he'd been killed."

"Emotionally dead?"

"That's exactly it. Emotionally dead."

"You mean you feel that?"

"I do."

"So it's less his feelings that worry you when you see him on Sunday—"

"It may be Sunday, it may be late Saturday night."

"You're worried that you'll see him and you won't love him?"

"It's hard to know exactly what I feel. It's his indifference that I feel. That everything is more important to him than us: the war, Borden, even golf perhaps."

"Isn't that partly just men?"

"Men?"

"We get them in tender moments only when the world isn't using them for something else? And their mothers start pushing them towards that when they're still little boys. Pushing them away from the clingy, cuddly, affectionate behaviour into the practical ways of the world."

"What do I know about men?" Lucy looked reproachful.

"But you don't mean that Harry's turned against you? You don't feel hostility coming from him? He hasn't been saying unkind things to you?"

"No. Not a word. It's all the same cheery, optimistic way as usual."

"Perhaps you're just seeing more clearly the man you married because of all this distance from him. Because you've had to make your own life, make all your own decisions, you and the girls."

"You know—" Lucy giggled. "This is really wicked. I have actually thought that it's going to be very inconvenient having him around. He'll be in the way! And we'll have to ask him whether he wants this or that, what for dinner, what to do on Sunday. I've been making all those decisions without any fuss, to suit Lizzy and Sarah and me. Now I'm going to have someone around who'll be quite a stranger, like a lodger, and he'll upset our whole nice, cozy domestic arrangement." Lucy stifled another giggle. "Julia, you mustn't breathe a word of this to Mother."

"No. But I think she'd understand it all perfectly. She's a lot more understanding than my mother."

"Because she's not your mother!"

"When you say it's as though Harry died, I really don't

believe that. Yes, it is going to be very strange, having a man you haven't seen for four years come in here, eat meals with you and go upstairs and sleep in the same bed with you—"

"Julia!" Lucy was blushing into the hairline of her dark red hair.

"Well, be honest. You must be thinking of that too. I would be. I do anyway."

"You still do? About Charles?" Lucy asked shyly.

"No, not about Charles anymore. That did stop. I mean other men."

"You mean Stewart MacPherson?"

"Well—not only. But we're getting away from you. I'm sure it helps to talk about it. And talk as honestly as we can, because, when you put your feelings into words, it starts to relieve them. I think you're feeling better already just for this little talk. I can see it in your face. I knew when you giggled a minute ago."

"I think I'm feeling two glasses of sherry on an empty stomach! Come into the kitchen and we can talk while I put the food on the table. It's just a cold supper. I gave the maid the weekend off for the Queen's Birthday." Lucy must have realized what she'd just said because she added, "So she could go and see her family in Pictou."

Which transparent manoeuvre made Julia smile. "And it was thoughtful of your mother to take the girls for the weekend."

Lucy turned away. Julia could see the blush on her neck and jaw. "Daddy said, 'It'll be like a second honeymoon.'"

Julia said sympathetically, "Your mother wouldn't have said that."

Lucy was briskly cutting and arranging slices. "Cold tongue and pickles. I hope you don't mind."

"I love it. What have you made for Harry?"

"Oh, beefsteak and kidney pie. His favourite. It's baked. I can just stick it in the oven and warm it up. Anyway, they say the *Aquitania* will probably dock in the middle of the night."

"How romantic!"

"Don't make fun of me, Julia, please! It's so hard! He may not even like me anymore! Look at me! I'm not a beautiful woman like you. Men have never turned their heads to look at me twice. I'm just the plain old Lucy I was, only years older. I wish to God he weren't coming! I would gladly trade places with you."

"You won't think so when he's been back a few days and the awkwardness is over. And you're not plain old anything. You're a lovely woman, Lucy. You're young and vital and fresh—"

"I'm nearly thirty!"

"You're a wonderful mother. You're bringing up those girls beautifully. And you're the jolliest, most cheerful person I've ever met. You really kept me sane when Charles was killed. Any man in his right mind would be thrilled to be coming back to you."

Lucy smiled wanly. "In his right mind? He never says anything affectionate in a letter. Nothing like the lovely things that Charles wrote to you. Harry's so breezy and casual he could be writing to his brother."

"It'll be all right. You'll see. And if it isn't all right, I promise I'll help you out of it."

That startled Lucy. "Out of it? What do you mean?"

"Can I tell you something strange?" Julia had been determined not to tell Lucy, but it seemed the only way to divert her. "I keep having this feeling that Charles is still alive."

"No!" Lucy gasped and put down the plate she had just picked up. "What do you mean?"

"I mean every so often, it comes to me like a flash of

understanding. Like today." She described passing the sail-boat at Armdale and the seconds of certainty that Charles's head would emerge from the cabin.

"But we know he's dead. The Victoria Cross. The stained-glass window the family is putting in the cathedral."

"I know how absolutely silly I sound. It's just the strange tricks the mind plays. Like all your imaginings about Harry. It's just the inventions of the anxious mind."

In her diverted mood, Lucy was like a girl listening to a ghost story, round-eyed and credulous. "But you don't really think there's any chance?"

"No, and I've got to stop these silly imaginings. All his things are there and I haven't been able to touch them. His clothes could be really useful to someone. Would you come over tomorrow morning and help? Then I'll make myself do it. And perhaps that'll wash all this nonsense out of my head."

After all, Lucy had all day Saturday to get through.

"Of course I will. But I suppose we'd better eat something."

Halifax, May 26, 1919

Dear Mrs., Mr., or Miss Robertson,

I hope this intrusion does not cause you more suffering than the War may already have brought you, but a weird coincidence has just come to light that I must share with you.

Let me explain simply. My name is Julia Robertson. As you see, I live in Halifax, Nova Scotia. My husband, Charles Robertson, an acting Major in the 42nd Battalion, Royal Highlanders of Canada, was killed just after Passchendaele in December '17. Rather, he was wounded there, evacuated to England, and died in a military hospital two days later.

The-year-and-a half since then have passed somehow, I really don't know how. Some days were so long they felt like years, as though time were standing still—like a watch that has stopped—and would not move on, would not carry the pain away or let it be diminished by time, which is what everyone assures me will happen. Perhaps you are all too familiar with such emotions yourself. I have been unable to "get on with my life", as well-meaning family and friends advise, although I have done what I can to attempt that. I think I have been a little irrational in my sense of loss, and do not throw it off, as they say, as easily as others seem to do. A sense of inertia, like a paralysis, has seized me, as in those dreams in which you cannot flee some awful danger, because you cannot will yourself to move. And that brings me to the discovery that prompts this letter.

I could not face the task of disposing of Charles's things. I could not even open the cupboard to look at his clothes. There are many people who could use such clothing. There is great poverty here after the sudden end to the prosperity of war, and the city is still struggling to recover from the great explosion of which you may have heard. More than 1,600 known dead and many still missing!

Anyway, in the last few months I began to have the strangest feeling that Charles was not dead after all. I felt it particularly when there was fog—as there often is here. It makes me feel that he is just there, just out of sight, and might, at any moment, materialize out of the mist. I know how stupid this will sound to you, but please read on.

I had no rational reason to believe Charles alive. It was all officially recorded in forms and so on. In fact, he was awarded the Victoria Cross. His parents are arranging to have a memorial window installed in the cathedral here.

Yesterday, I got thoroughly annoyed at myself for being so foolish. Of course Charles was dead. I received his last letters,

*and some personal effects were eventually returned to me. There
is a grave in England where he is buried (in fact, I am going to
visit it on a trip this September).*

*To drive this mounting obsession away, with his sister, I
forced myself to take out his things. We examined a package
that had been sent to me a month or so after his death. I had
merely glanced at it and quickly put it away. Too painful to go
through it all and to what purpose? He was dead, and that was
it. But now I took everything out of the large official envelope:
a wrist watch, some French coins, a wallet and two official, not
personal, letters.*

*The watch did not look familiar but I had last seen my
husband in December 1915, when he went overseas, so he might
have replaced the watch I thought I remembered. (We were
married only a year before he left for the war.) The wallet was
familiar but also not familiar...but, to come to the point, the
wallet was not Charles's! The contents made that clear. They all
belonged to a Major James Robertson at the address to which I
am sending this letter, not knowing whether you are his mother,
his wife or sister, or father, and not knowing what happened
to him. But I assume that these effects were confused with my
husband's, in the chaos of those days. Someone has written in
ink on the OHMS envelope simply "Major Robertson". Now
Charles had just been made an acting Major, so the envelope was
probably handed over by someone who did not know there were
two Major Robertsons in the same place.*

*If you receive this and are kind enough to reply, I will
post James Robertson's belongings to you. As you will imagine,
however, this discovery has not banished my doubts, but fed them.
Did you, perhaps, receive the wrong package too? Do you have
things that belonged to my husband? I hate to cause you pain by
asking, but did Major James R. survive the war?*

I intend to pursue this also through "official channels" but I have no great confidence in their efficiency. I thought the first thing to do was to write you.

So, dear Miss or Mrs. or Mr. Robertson, with my deepest apologies for reopening what may be partly healed wounds, my most sincere good wishes.

Julia Robertson

"But this isn't Charles's wallet!"

She and Lucy had stared at each other as though they had passed into another realm of reality, the irrational world of dreams and ghosts, and Julia could feel the hair rising on her arms. A heart-stopping moment. It might have looked funny to anyone watching, two women frozen in fearful amazement, like actresses exaggerating in the pictures, their expressions frozen because for seconds they could not move.

And then Julia had said, "I've got to write to them immediately. I've got to know!"

"Ask my father. With his connections, he should be able to find out much faster whether...whatever there is to find out."

"Lucy, dear Lucy. Promise me you won't mention this to your parents. Not just yet. You and I are young. We can take shocks. But at their age, it would be awful to get their hopes up and then disappoint them again."

"What about *your* hopes?"

"I want to be absolutely sure that I'm not chasing some will o' the wisp."

Lucy said, "I won't say anything if you'll keep mum about what I said last night."

"Of course!"

"But you must promise to tell me the minute you know

anything more." Lucy, her freckled complexion pink from excitement, looked at Julia closely. "If he turned out to be alive now, would that...would you...I don't know how to put it delicately..."

"I'd be very confused."

"As I am."

"Although you're not getting a man back from the grave."

"It feels like it—as I told you last night."

Julia kissed Lucy and hugged her. "It'll be all right with Harry. As for Charles, if there's any chance he's alive, he could be...we have no idea what condition he could be in. He could have lost his mind or his memory—he mightn't know us. I've read stories like that. If it isn't something like that, why hasn't he been in touch, told us he's alive? I don't think we should allow ourselves to get very excited until we know more. I'd hate him to die twice."

8

Julia saw Jim Morrice cross the square, walking carefully. He came into the busy café and sat at a table without noticing her. She saw the waiter bring him a coffee and a bottle from which he poured liquor into the coffee. Seeing the artist's hand unsteady as he lifted the cup, she wanted to help him.

"Good morning. May I join you?"

He looked pleased to see her. "I looked for you in the hotel, then next door."

"It's such a gorgeous day, I had to get out. Thank you for being so kind to me last night."

"I should thank you for putting up with me."

"You were fun. Aren't you going to eat something?"

"You sound like Léa."

"Well, you should. I'll get you a croissant."

"I don't like 'em. Make my fingers all greasy. And I ate too much last night. Every damned thing in that colossal dinner."

"But you shouldn't drink on an empty stomach."

"I'm just having a coffee!"

"I saw what he put in it."

"Careful, my dear! Don't start sounding like the busybodies back in Canada, the land where everyone minds everyone else's business. Thank God I can live where church leaders and other self-appointed bigots can't force me onto their mean-spirited, narrow-minded path of virtue. It is a civilized country that permits me a *café arrosé* to start the day, in fact two. I had one at the café by the hotel—if you're keeping track."

"I'm sorry."

"Don't be. But do we understand each other?"

"Yes."

"Good. Now I've been thinking about the painting we discussed. No, I'm not pressing you for an answer. But several nude studies I did at the time I painted you are with paintings I'm keeping at Léa's house. I'd like a look at them again before we start yours. If you'd like we could go over to Cagnes and see her. She'd like to meet you again and she'd give us a good lunch. I can telegraph her."

"I'd like that. You're sure I won't be in the way?"

"You know me well enough to know I wouldn't ask you if I thought that. I arrange my life so that things don't get in my way. I have been blessed with the income to permit that and with a woman of infinite grace who understands it."

"What if she doesn't have time to go shopping to make lunch for three of us?"

"She will bless you for thinking of that. We'll eat in the little hotel on the square. She'd like that more than cooking anyway. I'll suggest it."

They made the trip in an open motor taxi with a fringed sunshade, the sea on the left, crossing the river Var and then an ancient stone bridge over the Cagnes. In both rivers women were washing, scrubbing clothes on the rocks and spreading them to dry. Julia thought of how hard it must be to wash in water coming icily from the Alps. They drove into Cros-de-Cagnes, a placid fishing village with boats drawn up on the stony beach and nets drying in the sun.

"It's all so beautiful and picturesque. I want to stop everywhere."

"The view is much better from Haut-de-Cagnes."

The motor laboured up a steep road through olive groves into the once-fortified hill town dominated by an ancient castle. The thick walls of the houses with roofs projecting like sunshades narrowed and darkened the cobbled street until they came out into a little square with a fountain at the centre, a large church, and the hotel garden shaded by tall palm trees.

"That's the hotel. Come along and we'll find Léa." Whether to see his mistress or his paintings, Morrice seemed quite eager now. They went down a narrow side street and he knocked at a small house. Julia watched Léa, clearly delighted, embrace him in the French manner with three kisses, murmuring "*Bonne année, chérie,*" and Morrice responding like a man impatient with any public demonstration. Léa was tiny and had to lean up to Morrice, but for a woman just over forty, she looked fresh and healthy, her chestnut hair giving off coppery lights and her brown eyes warm and amused.

"You remember Julia, Mademoiselle Montgomery? I mean Madame Robertson." Despite his thirty years in France, he still spoke French with a strong English, or English Canadian, accent.

Léa kissed her. "Certainly, my dear. I am happy to see you again. Come in, please." Julia followed her through cool rooms that smelled of lavender and coffee, passing Morrice paintings on the walls—including two Venetian scenes—and finally through French doors to a terrace with a breathtaking view over the hills back towards Nice and the sea.

Morrice pointed to a nearby hill. "There, the pink house, in the olive grove, that's Renoir's house. Poor old fellow died just before Christmas, but he worked to the end. His arthritis got so bad they had to tie the brush to his hand. When he couldn't paint, he made sculptures. I went to see him and he was sitting in a chair, with two assistants sculpting while he directed them with a long pointer. Well, if you both don't mind, I'd like to look at the paintings I came to see. Then we can have lunch." He went back into the house and Julia turned, but Léa touched her arm with a smile.

"He likes to do it alone. If you like, the weather is so nice, we could sit out here and have an aperitif and a little talk while he is looking." Her behaviour was gracious but deferential, as though Julia were a representative of a disapproving Montreal family.

In lieu of a garden on the gravel terrace were large terracotta pots with plantings of lavender and herbs. Lemon and orange trees were espaliered on the stone walls and geranium vines tumbled profusely over them.

"It is so beautiful it—" Julia couldn't immediately think of the French idiom and so fell into the literal—"it leaves me without breath. How do you say that?"

"*Ça me coupe le souffle?*"

Thank you. What a fabulous place to live!"

"I am very fortunate. I love living here. The air is soft. No snow and cold and the things grow all the year round. And Morrice likes it now. He spends more time here. Now that he doesn't travel so much, I see him more often. Still, you know, he likes to be alone. I never knew a man who liked to be alone so much. Or so silent! A very silent man, much of the time. Like when he is painting, he does not like to talk or for others to talk, and like just now, when he is looking. But a very kind man. Very kind to me." She chattered on, pleased to have a listener, and poured each a small glass of Lillet.

"Before, when he travelled more often, I never knew what he would do. He would disappear from Paris, sometimes send me a postcard as he left the Gare du Nord, or a card from New York, or Cuba, or Montreal, or London. Who knew where he was? Or how long he would be away. Two, three months would pass and then suddenly a card would arrive and he was back in Paris!" She was not complaining, just affectionately describing her lover's eccentricities.

The interval of seven years from last seeing Léa had changed Julia's vision. She could see the contented Frenchwoman as she might have been if she had stayed in her aunt's *pâtisserie* near the Boulevard Saint-Germaine, where she had come to work at sixteen, an orphan from a village in Côtes-du-Nord in Brittany, and had responded when Morrice advertised for a model. The aunt might well have passed on by now and Léa would be there, charming and affable with every customer, but a serious business-woman, on her feet from dawn to evening. In taking her away from that life, Morrice had given her a different status: a woman of leisure; a woman who could talk of the artists she knew and the gallery openings and concerts she went to; yet the ambiguous status of a woman who had surrendered another kind of dignity, of the respectable petite bourgeoi-sie. The difference would be very plain if she ever went back to her native village.

Distressingly, Julia also saw Léa through the eyes of her mother in Montreal, with her instinctive awareness of class, a sensibility Julia hated when she saw it surfacing in herself. Her mother would instantly mark Léa as of the serving classes, by her dress, her manners, her probable education. And the observation told Julia what she had missed years ago: why Morrice would be uncomfortable presenting Léa to his family. Listening to her bubbling on happily and unaffectedly, Julia also knew that it said something about

Morrice's need to conform, his own unwillingness—unusual for an artist—to flout convention too openly.

Léa was talking. "You know what he is doing? Before he can look, he has to unwrap all the paintings he sent down from Paris. *Beaucoup, beaucoup!* He is used to packaging and shipping to exhibitions and galleries all over the place, but in Paris he has someone who does the packaging. He worried when the war began. He thought the Boche might capture Paris, imagine! What would happen to all his work? So he sent it here where I have empty rooms. Hundreds of his oil sketches, his *pochades*, which he thinks are worth more than gold. Since I got him to move from Quai des Grands-Augustins—you remember it, so dirty and cramped?—he's never felt settled in Quai de la Tournelle and it made him worry if he's away a long time, someone might steal, you know? So, the result? I have a houseful of canvases. Only he does not want me to show them to anyone."

"Why not?"

She laughed good naturedly. "Who knows? He doesn't tell me. Ask him!"

Morrice had unpacked the three nudes. There was no easel—he never painted here—so he placed the canvases one at a time against a chair-back facing the light and studied them in the order in which he had painted them.

Nu de dos devant la cheminée, the Russian model with the reddish-blonde hair, her back turned. She was leaning on the mantel facing half a dozen framed oil sketches that provided tiny bright moments in a restrained palette. Interesting flesh tones and modelling, her buttocks prominent in the foreground. Too prominent? Too sensual for some. The whole effect harmonious but dated by more recent work.

He replaced it with *Nude with a Feather*; the colour advance was startling but, equally obvious, the awareness of Bonnard and Matisse. Good composition with the vertical lines of the patterned-fabric background emphasizing the soft curves of her neck and shoulders. Same girl had posed for all these paintings. Curious tones in the hand holding the feather on her breast, echoing the values in her hair and the chair-back, but unlike the rest of her skin. Creamy flesh on the breasts and then the startling white highlights, as though a gleam of light had splashed her chin and neck, or she'd just applied a lot of powder. Strongly drew the eye. Outlining a little severe under the right breast, making it seem to protrude unnaturally.

Woman with a Fan. The echo of Ingres's *La Grande Odalisque* immediately obvious on this fresh viewing. Radiant with colour, her skin tones creamy and ivory against the red chair and the bright-yellow flowered drape behind. Pale olive-violet shadow on her back was more intrusive than he remembered, and the line of her right thigh fell off lamely before the knee. Liked the touch of rose and pale cadmium on the cheek to reflect off the drape, and the violet shadow behind her elbow. But she looked inert, asleep, too languid. He wanted the new model—well, Julia—to be alive and in contact with the viewer, as in *Femme au lit*, which he still loved for its deep, affectionate gaze, but even that gaze was directed at someone just to one side, not bluntly at you like Manet's.

The question of reticence...the nature of his reticence. Of course it was aesthetic sense and restraint, a matter of taste, when holding back is refinement, when the extra step towards boldness will not only be out of character, not a creative step but a misstep, like a shocking mistake in grammar. He'd been praised for that restraint, which had always been as much unconscious as deliberate. Now, with his fresh urge to boldness, he wondered how much was personal. He had often felt something cautioning him, a resistance, curbing him. It wasn't a lack of daring, he felt daring; yet even when he had felt bold and freer than ever, he sensed this emotional curb, a self-governor. He had tried to suppress it with absinthe, briefly morphine, and all along with whisky or any other alcohol, striving to break this barrier of reticence, to reach beyond the normal state of consciousness. That was partly the state in which he'd painted many *pochades*, especially in the absinthe days, with a gradual loosening of inhibiting bonds. He would sit in a café for several hours, by preference as afternoon crept into twilight, letting unrestraint steal over him, as the water soaked through the sugar lump in the neck of the absinthe drip-glass, and he took occasional sips of the bitter, opalescent yellow-green liquid while his eyes and mind drank in the scene. When he saw precisely the touch of colour he wanted, he mixed it from the limited palette he carried, dipped a brush, and then bestowed a touch in just the right place. But in 1909 his doctor had forbidden absinthe, the year after the Swiss outlawed the liquor as dangerous to health, causing hallucinations and mental breakdown. The French government waited until 1915. Abstinence, and the lemonade cure the doctor required, had thrown him into a very low period, yet out of it had come the burst of figure painting—and these nudes. Now he needed to be governed less by good manners.

Léa was excited to be going out to lunch. If that meant Morrice did not take her very often, it made Julia a little sad for her, as did her clothes. Léa's satin dress with broad stripes and dramatic hat would have been a little flamboyant even in Paris. Could Léa have friends in this closed village? It felt like being inside the walls of a convent; the women she had glimpsed were all in workaday black. Léa was free to come and go as she wished, but would neighbours who had lived here for generations make her welcome?

This sympathy for Léa convinced Julia all at once not to bring up either her pregnancy or Léa's ancient one. After all, she had heard about it not from Léa or Morrice themselves, but in a group in a café years ago, all drinking and laughing. A young artist—she couldn't remember his name—was joking about Morrice. "The old codger keeps the gorgeous Léa out of sight. He tells young fellows like me, 'Don't chase the pretty young ones. You'll waste your time and neglect your work. Find some comfortable middle-aged woman who'll be nice to you and grateful for it.' Middle-aged! The joke is he always had Léa—and she was an eyeful at nineteen or twenty—he had her hidden, like the baby she had, tucked away somewhere inconspicuous in the country. He wouldn't let any other painter or sculptor use her as a model, wise old bird, so he'd have no worries." He went on to tell a story about a painter who spent a weekend with Morrice and Léa in the country and tried it on with Léa. Morrice never invited him again when he took Léa anywhere. Julia had taken the reference to the baby as fact, in the way you accept stories when you are young and want to feel part of a group. On reflection she didn't really know there had been a baby at all, and if so, whether Morrice was the father.

Among the guests in the dining room of the little hotel on the square was a young French army officer. His was the first military uniform Julia had seen since coming south and, unaccountably, tears filled her eyes. She had to wipe them to see the menu she was holding. Common still in northern France, a uniform looked out of place in this paradisiacal region where there wasn't the slightest evidence of the war that had just cost France a million-and-a-half lives. She felt Léa squeeze her hand and saw her smiling through the blur of her tears.

"Morrice told me about the tragedy of your husband." Léa squeezed again comfortingly. "I was so saddened to hear of it."

"Thank you." Julia wiped her eyes and smiled. "It was over two years ago. The feelings go away but, unexpectedly like that, they rush back."

Morrice said to Léa, "They awarded him the highest decoration the British can give for valour, the Victoria Cross."

"You know, that reminds me." Julia wondered whether she could tell it well enough in French. Well, she'd try. "My husband's parents want to make a memorial to him in the Anglican cathedral in Halifax where they live. They want to make a large window of—how do you say 'stained glass'?"

"*Un vitrail*," Morrice said.

"*Un vitrail* at the west end of the cathedral behind the altar."

"Very imposing," Léa said.

A waiter poured a Provencal wine and Morrice raised his glass. "Let us drink to him. To Charles Robertson."

With the first sip of the wine, Julia knew she could not eat. The menu offered dishes like knuckle of suckling pig, hot foie gras with truffled potatoes. She felt a reflexive spasm in her stomach. She put down her glass and rose. "I'm sorry but I don't feel well. I need to excuse myself."

By the time she reached the entrance she felt exhausted and had to sit in the nearest chair. Léa followed her out.

"Tell me, what is the matter?"

"Nothing. Really nothing serious. I'm just feeling a little ill and very tired. I'd really like to lie down."

"But of course, you come back to my house."

"Oh no, no. I don't want to spoil your nice lunch."

"Morrice will wait. I'll tell him and I'll go with you."

She was back in a moment. "He wanted to come too but I told him to stay and drink a glass of wine. Come now."

Surprisingly sturdy for her size, Léa took Julia's arm and they walked back to Léa's house. Everything in Julia's body felt heavy, hers legs, even her breasts. Léa made her lie down on a large soft bed; she took off Julia's shoes, covered her with a blanket, and brought her a glass of water.

"Perhaps it was the Lillet I gave you. A little too sweet, perhaps."

"No, all of a sudden I just felt exhausted. If I rest for a few minutes, I'll be fine. I'm so sorry to disturb you like this. Please. I beg you, I insist you go back and have your lunch. Please!"

Léa finally retreated and Julia gratefully let herself sink into the comfort of the bed and the silence of the house. Her clothing felt a little tight but she was too tired to sit up to loosen it.

She awoke twenty minutes later refreshed but still not hungry and too comfortable to move immediately, so she relaxed. It was good that Léa and Morrice could have lunch together. She could imagine Léa with a healthy French appetite working sturdily through four or five courses.

It would have been too big an effort to tell them the whole story about the stained glass in French. And there were parts too private to tell anyway. The cathedral window was the reason for the lunch at which she had lost her composure and spoken so angrily. The lunch at the Robertsons' in the summer...before the Prince of Wales came.

9

Julia didn't know how she had avoided the thought but, inevitably, as the new dean, Peter Wentworth had to be at the lunch. The Robertsons couldn't have known how she dreaded meeting him again, how strong a sense of shame she still bore after the night on the train with him. Now, after an even more bizarre experience, she could almost see the comic side of it: frustrated war widow throws herself at lusty clergyman, only to have the man of God shrink into an apologetic sponge and slink away to his own berth. Stewart had told her that Peter had confessed to him what had happened that night—and the equally remarkable sequel. After crawling abjectly out of the berth and scrambling in humiliation for his clerical clothes scattered around her compartment, the Reverend Mr. Wentworth had repaired to his bed and discovered— what? There was no God! Priceless! Well, bless the Church of England. Even in Canada, where there was a touch more Calvinism in all religions, the C. of E. had always been able to tolerate eccentricity and never demanded much in the way of belief. But the trials of his personal life had quickly eroded that fierce egotistical, dogmatic strain in Peter, that insinuating stare of his that had so unsettled her at first, and—on that one night—unleashed the most primitive responses, of desire, then anger, then shame that she could have been so abandoned—and with him! She had never been ashamed of having strong sexual feelings; if only they could always have been aroused in circumstances she did not have reason later to regret. What rankled additionally from that incident was the knowledge that Peter had read her diary when it fell into his hands in the chaos after the explosion; that knowledge still burned in her thoughts at the time of the luncheon at the Robertsons' big house on Young Avenue.

It was graciously done as was everything arranged by Elizabeth, who seemed to be surviving the death of her son with the same sweet intelligence she showed in all things. She and Archie had invited Margaret and Donald Creighton, the new bishop, who had chosen Peter to replace him as dean.

Julia's dread in facing Peter, fearing she might blush violently or break out in hives, proved groundless. They shook hands coolly and she saw on meeting his eyes a demeanour quite changed. The glittering, somewhat impertinent gaze that had so unsettled her before was gone, replaced by something more vulnerable, even anxious. The change in Margery was as startling. Even the persistent South End gossip about her had not prepared Julia for this stylish but ravenous-seeming woman. Margery greeted her with the vivacity of someone who had already had two sherries, the drink they were just being offered.

"I am so happy to see you again! It's been ages." Margery was wearing the style fashionable that summer of long knit skirt that fitted her more suggestively than you'd expect in a clergyman's wife. Her short hair and bare neck, bright red lips and mascara-ed eyes, the cigarette she articulated between long, polished nails, all made a flashy impression. But most of all what struck Julia was Margery's avidity. You could almost smell in her perfume eagerness for exciting experience and— the message was clear—men. She was hunting, and that might have explained the wary look in Peter's eyes.

"How smart you look, Margery," Julia said to be pleasant.

Margery gave her a quick, stabbing glance of doubt, arching her eyes away from the smoke she was exhaling, concluding swiftly that Julia was not being sarcastic, and dissolved with pleasure.

"Not easy in the pokey Halifax shops, as you know," she said in a way that made Julia wonder how much she knew about her. In fact Julia was wearing a summer dress bought in Montreal.

"Not just clothes. Fabrics. Mother and I had to go to New York to find the materials to do the house." She glanced around at the Creightons and leaned towards Julia. "You can't imagine how dowdy it looked the way they left it."

Julia smiled. "I hear you're doing a lot of work on it."

"We are. You must come and have dinner with us when we've finished. And bring Stewart MacPherson! I think it's so nice that you're seeing him."

Now Julia did blush, stupidly, but it was irritating to be in a place so small that everyone knew everything about her comings and goings, from Mollie to Margery Wentworth.

"Yes, he's become a good friend."

"Oh. I've known Stewart since we were children. We used to go to the same dances. He was rather awkward in those days. It's so nice that he's grown into his skin as a man. And very attractive!"

"He's been devoted to the little girl who lives with me. Perhaps you've heard? Betty Webber? The granddaughter of my maid. Her parents were killed in the explosion and Stewart found her wandering in the wreckage. She lost an eye. But she's fine now. She has a beautiful glass eye to match her own, and she goes to the convent."

"How sweet! So you and Stewart have become like a mother and father to her," she said archly.

"More like godparents, perhaps." Julia laughed, wanting to end this entirely too clever interrogation, hearing Elizabeth say, "Why don't we go into lunch?" when Margery added, mischievously but innocently, "Are you and Stewart going to adopt her?"

"Oh, I don't think that arises. She still has her grandmother, Mollie, and cousins in Mahone Bay, a lot of family of her own."

Margery was quicker than Julia remembered, but as they turned to go into lunch could not hide a hint of annoyance that she had not been able to make Julia define their relationship as a couple more precisely.

Harry had returned with Sir Robert Borden on the *Aquitania*, spent only three nights and had buzzed off to be with the prime minister in Ottawa, so Lucy and Julia were both alone.

"We do have an abundance of ladies," said Elizabeth, "so I'll just let Archie monopolize them." She put the bishop on her right and Peter on her left. At his end, Archie, a husky sixty-two with a red face dominated by shaggy eyebrows, had Margery and Margaret, with Lucy and Julia facing each other across the centre of the table. Peter was on Lucy's right so Julia faced him diagonally, Bishop Creighton on her left.

Julia heard Margery say to Archie in her newly aggressive social voice as she touched his arm, "Do you know, we've been invited to a small private dinner party with the Prince of Wales when he comes!" She said it loudly enough that Peter heard and Julia caught a shadow of embarrassment cross his face. "Isn't that exciting?"

"It is, my dear," Archie said, "and we've had a similar invitation."

"And so have Julia and I," Lucy said.

"Oh, really?" said Margery, a little let down.

"But we have not," Margaret Creighton said, as though comforting a child, "so it may indeed be quite exclusive."

The bishop cleared his throat importantly. "We are of course, my dear, invited to the formal events for His Royal Highness."

Elizabeth said, "Well, you never know, do you? Our letters all came from a young man we once entertained, with some other British officers, during the war. Neville Boiscoyne."

Not daring to catch Lucy's or Peter's eye, Julia looked only at Elizabeth.

Elizabeth continued, "I think it's lovely of him to remember all of us, when—" She looked at Julia, who sensed Elizabeth was about to smile and say, "Because as I recall, dear Julia, he only had eyes for you that night at Government House," but she hesitated, only a second, and said, "Well, it just goes to show, if you put yourself out for someone, you never know what good things will come of it."

Julia loved Elizabeth for her discretion. It was as though she had known just what Julia was feeling, a prickly heat inside her bodice, and was giving her time to calm down, take a sip of water, put her napkin to her lips, while she chattered on. How close Julia felt to her!

Elizabeth said, "Who would have guessed that inviting a few lonely officers to tea at the Saraguay would bring us an invitation to dine with the Prince of Wales! You girls seem so cool about it. I'm quite in a flutter myself."

"We're in an absolute panic, Mother," Lucy said. "I can't imagine what to wear."

"I can. I'm going to wear something absolutely delicious!" Margery said with pleasure.

"I'm sure you will, my dear," the bishop's wife said with an edge everyone but Margery must have felt. "I'm sure you will."

Julia thought they were safely out of Neville Boiscoyne territory when Archie said heartily, "I remember the fellow. He'd won the DSO and was damned modest about it." Julia let her eyes cross Peter's on the way to look at Archie and saw—what? Something? Nothing?

Archie continued, "Handsome devil. So now he's an equerry to the prince? Must be some blue-blood connection there. Borden will know. He's coming to Halifax and I'll ask him."

Lucy looked at Julia significantly and mouthed, "Borden." She was right. With the prime minister in town and Archie's friendship, it would be the fastest way to use official channels to solve the mystery of Charles. But it meant confiding her doubts to Archie and Elizabeth.

As though a little impatient at all this gossip about a party to which he was not invited, Donald Creighton cleared his throat again and repositioned the gold pince-nez he had been polishing in his table napkin. "Perhaps we should address the bittersweet business that has brought us together today."

Elizabeth said, "Excuse me, Donald. I was going to ask you to say grace."

"Yes, of course." Put out that he had needed reminding, the bishop launched into a long and rather tedious prayer that included a blessing for the food and begged divine guidance for the deliberations they were about to tackle "to acknowledge the glorious sacrifice in His name of our devoted Charles Robertson, the grief and generosity of Elizabeth and Archie, all to the glory of the Almighty Father..."

Julia had only slightly bowed her head and so caught a wink from Lucy and a glint from Peter Wentworth. But with the word "Amen," what came from Margery was an undisguised "Whew!"—like a child who can't believe some adult nonsense is taking so long.

"I could do with a drink after that," Margery whispered to Julia and then giggled.

They began eating cold cucumber soup and Donald Creighton resumed. "...the business both grievous and pleasant"—he turned and put his hand comfortingly on Julia's (it must have been Léa's gesture that had reminded her)—"...our painful duty to perform...the great embellishment of our cathedral church, which has been, I should add—Peter and Margery—been so spectacularly made whole by the generosity of your mother and father, George and Cynthia Tobin."

"Oh dear, Margery," said Elizabeth, "I should have invited your parents as well. It just didn't occur to me. How awful of me!"

Peter spoke for the first time. "Please don't apologize. The Tobins understand perfectly that this is a matter very personal to your family and to Mrs. Robertson. They are proud of what they were able to do in repairing the ravages of the explosion and delighted that the church they helped restore will soon be graced with the memorial to Charles, clearly one of Nova Scotia's greatest and most heroic sons."

"Hear, hear!" Archie grunted and the bishop echoed him.

Peter Wentworth had never needed lessons in unction from Donald Creighton.

"Well, I agree with you, Donald," Archie said. He finished his soup and put down the spoon noisily. "Let's get on with it."

"As the cathedral precincts are now the concern of my distinguished young successor," Creighton said, managing to invest even the compliment with heavy patronage, "I think we should ask Peter to guide us."

Now the Peter Julia recognized re-emerged as he confidently took charge. "As I promised some months ago, in our first meeting, I contacted the firm which makes most of the stained glass for churches in Canada. They're in Toronto—"

"Wouldn't you know!" said Lucy.

"—but they are closely in touch with the parent firm in London—"

"Sounds more like it," Archie said, winking at Lucy. Julia, from Montreal, was still tickled by the old virulence about Upper Canada in these Nova Scotians.-

"—and through them, I have received samples of two styles of windows,"—Peter produced a large envelope—"which can be the basis for our design. When we have considered which style is appropriate, when the Robertsons, all of you, are satisfied on the question of style, we'll tell them in detail what we want the memorial to convey, symbolically and literally, what actual words we wish to use. They will then work up a design and at that point they'll send a representative to Halifax with the design for our approval. We'll have an opportunity to make any comments we feel necessary, any changes we wish to suggest, and they'll go away and make the window."

"Sounds an eminently reasonable way of proceeding," said the bishop.

"How long will it take once we approve?" asked Archie.

"Unfortunately it won't be quick. They are under enormous pressure to meet the demand for memorial windows, for obvious reasons,"—a glance at Julia—"obvious and painful reasons, which is one justification for accepting one of their standard designs, with appropriate modification, of course. They call it customizing a standard design, because we'll be assured delivery and installation much sooner than if we want to have them design something from scratch. It means they can use glass in standard colours from stock, no special manufacture, and so on."

"Makes it sound like a factory," Archie said, "or a shipyard for that matter. We'd better look at the standard designs."

Before pulling them out of the envelope, Peter added, "There are basically two styles—in their own company terms, one ancient and one modern."

"Like the hymn tunes," the bishop said. "How appropriate."

"—and you see what that means, in the case of ancient, biblical figures in traditional costume or robes, and modern allegorical figures, not from scripture, in some form of modern dress, in uniform perhaps, or in armour like the knights of old, with flags, regimental crests, and badges as appropriate."

Peter then unveiled the samples, and the coloured plates went around the table to be inspected in silence or with quiet murmurs. Watching the Robertsons, Julia could feel this exercise was making the loss of Charles manifest in yet another dimension, their grief like her own unfolding in unexpected stages. Hers would recede into the background emotion of her daily mood, like the effect of the weather, then surge up suddenly at moments like this.

Margery said tartly, "They certainly look like church to me!" and handed them to Julia, who thought the designs were dreadful. Peter had described the styles well but they filled Julia with anger.

They were smug, safe, hackneyed groups of saints in garments conventionalized by centuries of religious painting, mournful eyes upturned to a sorrowing Jesus, who waited with outstretched arms to welcome the spirits of the fallen. In the modern, a knight in full armour but no helmet, with a Pre-Raphaelite face, was being wafted aloft by angels. To Julia's eye, this could keep Charles' memory alive for generations as a platitude. She bit her tongue and tried to breathe normally, passing the prints to the bishop, who'd obviously seen them in advance, because he quickly handed them to Elizabeth and said briskly, "Well, yes. That looks like the sort of thing one was expecting. I suppose, Peter, we could mix and match, so to speak, elements of one could be borrowed and fitted in if we—if the Robertsons—like something better, or would that greatly affect the cost and the delivery time?"

Peter said to Archie, "My understanding is that the more closely we adhere to one of their designs, the more reasonable the cost and the sooner the installation."

"Moderating the cost is not our chief concern," Archie said; as always when his feelings began to rise, so did tears in his blue eyes. "I mean, God damn it, sorry, Donald, but it's no secret to anyone in this room that we did bloody well out of the war financially. Just because things are tight now, we don't want to skimp on this, do we, my dear?"

"Of course not, Archie. I would far rather the shipyard had not made a penny from the war and have Sandy here with us." Elizabeth smiled at Julia. Sandy was their nickname for Charles.

"So, that's not the question," Archie said. "The question is, what do we think of the designs? Who likes the ancient and who likes the modern? I can see something in each of them myself. Lizzie?"

Elizabeth studied the prints. To Julia she seemed a model of something like perfection in the traditional roles for women of her class and time: wife, mother, household manager, hostess, and certainly mother-in-law. She seemed to do everything effortlessly, like this lunch, very simple but elegantly done, quite typical for the time of year—cucumber soup, a poached salmon from one of the Nova Scotia rivers, asparagus from her garden, strawberries from the market because hers were not quite ripe. The meal was the least let of her skills. What guided that household and kept the blustery, sentimental Archie in a husbandly paradise was the tact and intelligence that governed everything she did, applied so delicately it was scarcely felt.

She had told Julia, in one of their emotional moments together at the first news of Charles's death, that she felt closer to Julia than to her own daughter, Lucy. And one could see that Lucy owed more to her father's personality in her tomboyish temperament than to her entirely feminine mother. Elizabeth was the one in the family who kept urging Julia in quiet ways to make a new life for herself, to put this tragedy behind her, not to feel bound to them as a family, by which she meant finding a man, marrying, and having the children she had missed with Charles.

That had its ironic tinge now.

Elizabeth was one of the few human beings who really understood Julia—as she demonstrated at that luncheon—when Julia upset everyone else (except Margery, who enjoyed the fuss) by blurting out just what she felt about the proposed window.

"Why do we want—all of us who loved and admired Charles—to perpetuate his memory in a way that is so trite, devoid of any originality, as these designs are? He was unique to us, unique son, unique brother, unique husband to me, and everything that was unique about him will vanish in this safe, conventional treatment. They look smug to me. Smug and complacent. Cheaply sentimental and smug!" And with that, infuriating herself further, Julia began to cry.

Archie patted her arm. "There, there, old girl! We know you feel this strongly. We all feel it."

"Yes, I feel it strongly! I feel it as strongly as I did when I shocked you by trying to get his letters published."

"Well, my dear, no need to go into all that again. That's all behind us."

"But, don't you see? It's the same thing. It's smothering the truth about Charles. War hero, yes. VC winner, yes. But a man who passionately believed the war was madness. Once again, like the letters, we're smothering the real Charles under meaningless convention, so that people in future will go to your cathedral"—this to Peter hotly, as she realized at long last she could express her anger at him too—"people will go to pray and look up past your altar at a huge window and think, 'Well, it looks like every other window in every Anglican church in the world.' They'll probably have to go into a dark corner behind the altar and read a plaque to find it's about Charles."

Bishop Creighton cleared his throat ominously. "My dear Mrs. Robertson, and I say this in no censorious spirit but in a spirit of charity and compassion, admiring you as I do for the stalwart way in which you have borne your loss, I do not think it is out of the way, or the spirit of this discussion, to point out that you are not, in the daily run of things, a regular worshipper at the cathedral—"

Julia was knowingly rude. "Are you saying, Bishop, for that reason I should keep my mouth shut?"

Then, bluster, bluster, "Of course not my dear—"

"Well, Donald"—Elizabeth's voice was perfectly modulated to sound both sharply admonishing and affectionately humorous—"that's just the way I took it. Poor Julia should keep her opinions to herself, unless she's going to knuckle under and join the flock. Knowing her, I don't see her knuckling under to anything." And she laughed her observation away, which made everyone relax, especially Peter across the table, who had noted Julia's angry gaze and words with a look of some desperation, fear perhaps that she was so out of control that she would blurt out some awful words about their encounter on the train. Or perhaps he was hurt that she was accusing him of aesthetic naivety and ignorance.

Elizabeth stepped in as though the conversation had never been anything but polite. "Julia, of course we should have consulted you first. You are the artist among us. How stupid of us! With all your experience, you probably know just what we should do. So do tell us."

By now she had not only calmed Julia down, but left her considerably chastened. "Well, thank you. I do feel strongly. We have just been through a great catastrophe"—she could hear some words of Stewart's coming back to her—"in which human beings have shown themselves to be capable of evil—and capable of rationalizing it—on a scale greater than ever before in human history—"

Bishop Creighton snorted. "Well, I don't know about rationalizing on our side—"

"Let her finish, Donald."

"—so we have been through horrors unmatched in history and all of us have suffered"—a glare at the complacent bishop—"well, all of us related to Charles, so I feel it does not rise to the occasion to depict it with symbols used all the time to remember conventional happenings like the Boer War, things of the past, things of the nineteenth century."

"What would rise to the occasion?" Archie asked skeptically.

And so Julia plunged on, knowing as she began that she was entering a blind alley. "Even before the war, all sorts of fixed ideas were breaking up. There's been a revolution in political thought, in literature, in music, and in art. This time of horrendous destruction and human loss has also been a time of enormous creativity. Why don't we tap into those new currents and make something original, so original that people might come from all over the world to the cathedral, to see it and learn whose memory inspired it?"

When she had finished everyone looked to see everyone else's reaction and then Peter said in a reasonable voice, "Is that not secularizing the church by making its principal attraction a showplace for a work of art?"

"Does it secularize the Sistine Chapel?"

"Peter has a point," the bishop said. "A lot of those churches in Europe, in Venice or Florence, places like that, there's a constant swarm of people milling around to see the paintings and sculpture, constant clatter, not like a house of God, but as you say, Peter, like some art gallery."

Elizabeth: "But who would you suggest could make such a work that would draw the world to Halifax to see it?"

Julia knew she was wading in well over her head. "I know a remarkable Canadian painter, J.W. Morrice. He's very highly regarded in Europe and America."

"Where's he from?"

"He lives in Paris but he's from Montreal."

Archie exchanged a look with the others.

Lucy said, "Oh, he's the one you studied with, who did the nude portrait." Julia didn't think she meant to stir it up but Archie said, "A nude?"

"Oh, Archie! All great artists did studies of the nude form," Elizabeth, placatingly.

"Of course, of course, but aren't we getting away from the point?"

"Then there's Matisse," Julia said, "Henri Matisse, whom many consider one of the greatest artists of our time. I met him through Morrice."

Peter said, "Isn't there one of his pictures in your house?"

"I know it!" Archie said. "A mess of splotches and rough brushwork, looks only half painted to me, the colours are so garish it's a pain to look at—and you can't tell what it's supposed to be about."

"I quite like it, Archie," Elizabeth said. "Although it is very modern, it has something joyful about it."

"That's just what I think," Julia said. "Now if we were daring enough to ask Matisse—and I have no idea whether he'd be interested—we would have a monument to Charles and a landmark in the cathedral that would make it famous."

"Julia, my dear." Archie covered her hand with his. "You know I have the greatest affection for you, Lizzie and I both. But I'm not going to pay to bring some damned Frenchman across the Atlantic to make us a laughingstock among sensible people."

"Hear, hear, Archie!" Creighton said.

Archie said, "I suppose he's a Jew, as well as French, is he?"

"No, he's Catholic."

"A Catholic! Now why on earth would we want a Catholic decorating an Anglican cathedral?"

"I don't think his nationality or his religion matter."

"Well, I don't see, young lady, how that painting of yours makes life any better, or more joyful, and I'm as open-minded as any man—"

Elizabeth laughed. "Archie, you're nothing of the kind!"

"Well, I think I am. Anyway I want art in which I see the world I recognize, the world I see around me and love, that makes me feel grateful to my Maker, grateful to be alive, even if life has dealt us, and you, Julia, a cruel blow—"

"But what are we commemorating?" Julia asked.

"Charles's sacrifice and our belief that he has been resurrected and gone to heaven."

"But, if you believe that, it's not a literal thing, is it? The human body flying up into the clouds? It's an abstract thing, like an idea, like a dream. To portray it literally is childlike."

"I don't think these sample designs portray anything like that, Mrs. Robertson," the bishop said. "It is highly metaphorical and symbolical. But it is a symbolism with which our Anglican worshippers are well acquainted."

"I agree," Archie said, "and I think it's damned moving."

Pointless to argue further. As people were leaving, Elizabeth asked Julia upstairs to powder her nose and they had another of those candid talks they had shared before in her room, sitting together on the chaise longue.

"I know just what you mean, but it would be too controversial for us. You will go on with your life. You may well move away from Halifax. It can be very confining for someone of your spirit—and fire!" She laughed. "I love seeing Donald Creighton punctured now and then. But we must stay here and live with this. We and the community. I think Archie's instinct is right. We should have what we, we and the congregation, are comfortable with. Anything too novel will just distract and disturb. The vision of the world one artist sees may be exciting to some, but puzzling or upsetting to others. Do we want to be upset or puzzled where we go to be comforted?"

When Julia told all this to Stewart later, he said something very similar. "After all, the window's for them, for their comfort, for the rest of their lives, for their friends and the community. Reassurance that the things they believe and they trust haven't all fallen apart, that this is a world they still understand, this world and the next." This from the same Stewart who'd almost got himself sacked from Dalhousie University for lecturing on the abhorred Sigmund Freud. But he also said, "Did he really ask if Matisse was a Jew?"

"I think he was even more upset when he heard he was Catholic."

10

In Léa's house Julia got up from the bed and put on her shoes. The Morrice paintings in the living and dining rooms and hallway made her pause. First, two still lifes of flowers. Nothing out of the ordinary, not powerful like the late Manet. The Venetian scenes glowed with the nostalgic charm of which Morrice was such a master, a delicacy of colour that produced in the viewer an effect achingly mysterious and inexplicable. Several Quebec winter scenes, at which he excelled, not as literal as Gagnon, not as cloying as Suzor-Coté, affectionate and knowing, but not sentimental. The treatment of snow, the quality of light and sky colours so startling and yet so appropriate that each painting conveyed a total sense of the weather at that instant, that day or night, and precisely the mood such weather induced in someone who lived there. Familiar scenes of Paris, the subject to which he was most devoted and to which his spirit was so perfectly attuned that the French adored them. Here was one of his many treatments, in all weathers and seasons, of the Seine from his studio on Quai des Grands-Augustins.

She did not see the nudes he had come to look at. They must be in another room and she was shy about going to search. But the landscapes, both tiny oil sketches and fully painted canvases, brought back a sentiment that had startled her in Paris while she looked at his two paintings in the last Salon d'Automne. Even when the subject was nightlife in

Paris or Venice, often featuring women apparently on the prowl, his vision was innocent. Not naive, far from it, not cynical, far from that; but behind his obvious worldliness, his painterly sophistication, within this travel-worn and hard-used body resided a sensibility tinged with little or no irony: a tolerance not jaded but generous. In Paris it had leaped out of the contrast with other painters at the 1919 Salon d'Automne, but the feeling easily attached itself to these paintings in Léa's house. It gave Julia at twenty-eight the odd sensation, distasteful yet piquant, of feeling older than Morrice at fifty-four.

She hurried back to the hotel, where she found Morrice and Léa, their faces shining from food and drink, laughing together affectionately.

"Well, you look much better," Morrice said. "You had turned quite white."

"I'm fine now." She saw Léa's dessert arriving. "Oh, that looks delicious!"

"*Tarte chaude aux pommes caramelisées, madame*," the waiter said.

"May I have one like that?"

"Nothing else?"

"That's just what I'd like. And some coffee."

"And a cognac or something?"

"No, no thank you." She looked at them both, Lea in a faint perspiration, glowing like the Renoir women her full body resembled, Morrice with his cheeks flushed, sipping his cognac. How curious it was that he separated himself so wilfully from this accommodating and jolly woman, when he could have her comfort all the time. Clearly he was fond of her but sought her company infrequently, coming to Cagnes or asking her to Nice on his whim. It was the pattern he had chosen for twenty years in Paris, she in a flat he financed on Boulevard Saint-Germain, he isolated in his austere studio overlooking the Seine, with its monk-like iron bedstead, coming and going as he wished. To Julia it was a bizarre way to live, but then how conventional, or satisfying, had her own romantic life been? She who talked constantly about living in the modern way. What did she really mean by that? And how could she tell, for instance, her mother where it had led? And how—oh God!—her mother!

"I am very happy that you came to the south of France," Léa said. "Look at Morrice. You have woken him up. He is like a man who has awakened from a long sleep. He says he wants to begin working again, right away. He wants to make a painting of you."

No hint of any jealousy about that, obviously because he had painted many women and was still with her.

As they were being driven back to Nice in the dying winter light, Morrice debated silently whether to raise it. Léa thought Julia was pregnant: deduced that from her feeling ill, not wanting to eat, suddenly needing to lie down. So they had discussed it at lunch; she must want help. She had come because she was upset about something and needed to talk. If it were an unwanted pregnancy, what help did she want? Someone who would stop the pregnancy? Someone who would adopt the baby? I could talk to her myself, Léa said, but you have known her all her life; she knows you like her family, perhaps you should. Or should they be silent until she wanted to talk? She wasn't a child. She was old enough to know her own mind. Perhaps she had not made it up yet.

It should not be difficult for him to ask her, *What's on your mind? Can I help? Can Léa help?* She had talked freely enough about her painting at dinner the night before. He looked across where Julia was sitting only two feet away, looking out the other window, her fine profile silhouetted now by the grey and green foliage of winter, now by the Mediterranean, brilliant in the low-angled sunlight, ultramarine shading into Prussian blue and indigo on the horizon. But Julia seemed far away in spirit and he did not feel comfortable in raising the subject.

If she were pregnant, it must still be fairly early, because nothing showed. When she came back to the restaurant, he had glanced at her stomach below the waist, but her dress was closely fitted and there was no bulge. Would it show when she was nude? Would she not want to pose nude because of that? Was that why she had so far deflected his desire to paint her? She was a strong-minded young woman, more so now than before the war. And what would that do to the painting, the knowledge that she was expecting a baby? Because it would be in his mind and in hers and that would be bound to affect something. Intriguing thought. He was eager to begin. He'd been thinking about it all day. No sketches, at least no oil sketches. Just begin. Set the pose, study the lighting, and begin. He was impatient to do it. He could feel himself making the drawing and the painting. And the fact that he could feel it, and could see the values he wanted in the finished painting so clearly, excited him as he had not felt excited for many months. He wanted to begin the next morning. If it hadn't been for Léa's intuition about the pregnancy, he'd have asked Julia directly. He did not want this urge to go back to work to pass him by. It was a good urge, very positive, and he knew already that the desire to be less reticent meant that he was entering a new phase, a turning point artistically. A big or a little turning point, he didn't know.

Of course he would help her, if he could. She probably didn't need financial help; between her parents and her husband's family, he assumed she'd be secure for money. Would she want him to tell her father? Not her mother. Heather Montgomery was too dithery and petty. But Norman Montgomery was a reasonable fellow, for a pillar of the Montreal establishment. Odd that Norman and Heather, so conventional, should have a daughter like Julia, a strong and independent spirit, with some talent as a painter. Perhaps he had been too discouraging with her last evening.

"How are you feeling now?" That was a way to lead up to it.

Julia turned and smiled. "Oh, I'm fine." And as though to prevent him, quickly went on, "I've been looking at this glorious landscape...thinking about painting...thinking about our talk last night, about knowing your own value as an artist. When did you know you were really talented? Can you remember?"

Surprised, he needed a moment. Was painting the issue or was she avoiding the other?

"That is difficult. What does talent really mean—and all that. I suppose you feel it all along. At the beginning you tend to be in love with what you do, until you learn there are others who do it better. The sooner you know about those others, the better for you. Which is why, stuck in Canada in my early years, with taste as it was then, I didn't know. You fall into whatever tradition you are exposed to, for a while, to get some technique. I have never thought about it. I painted because when I was painting, I felt I was the person I wanted to be. But in soberer moments"—he laughed—"and I had a few, the exhibitions told me there were dozens of painters as talented or more, and that was healthy."

"But it didn't discourage you? Make you want to quit?"

"Some voice inside you inflates your confidence just enough to keep you afloat as the world keeps deflating it. That is the artist's life. Of course the minute I got to France, the dozens of talented painters became hundreds or thousands. But their genius did not inhibit me. It inspired me. It made me strive. Somerset Maugham isn't too intimidated to write because Henry James exists. So the answer is that you always know and you never know. You are always sure inside yourself and you are always unsure. Tonight, perhaps because we have had a charming day and because I am eager to start a picture, when all is infinite possibility, I am sure."

"You told me you knew Somerset Maugham when he lived in Paris?"

"Yes, we were part of a group in Montparnasse. Arnold Bennett, Clive Bell the critic. Gerald Kelly, an English painter I was giving lessons to, introduced us. We used to have dinner together quite often."

"Have you read *Of Human Bondage*?"

"Of course. He told me he'd used me in it."

"Oh, I didn't see that. Which character?"

"Cronshaw, the poet."

"But he didn't make me think of you. I'll have to look at it again."

"The resemblance is closer in his earlier novel, *The Magician*."

"In *Of Human Bondage* there's a character who really got under my skin: the pathetic girl who hangs herself because she's starving and trying to be a painter. She has absolutely no talent but won't believe it."

"There was a girl like that. I didn't know her but I heard about her."

"After she dies, his main character, Philip—"

"Who is very much Maugham himself."

"—he goes to ask advice from an old painting teacher, who tells him to quit, to take his courage in both hands and try his luck at something else. He'd give everything if someone had told him that when he was young, and he says, 'It is cruel to discover one's mediocrity only when it is too late.'"

"Well—" Morrice decided. "I'm going to take my courage in both hands and tell you something: Léa thinks you are pregnant."

Julia instantly blushed. "That's certainly changing the subject!"

"Is she right?"

"Oh, yes. I wondered if she'd guess, after the performance I put on at lunchtime."

"Want to tell me about it?"

"I suppose that's why I came down here. But it's such a mess, I'm not sure how to tell you. And some of it I don't think I should tell anyone. I'm embarrassed because I behaved so stupidly!" She pressed her fingertips together and raised them to her lips, a gesture he remembered, then let her hands fall helplessly. "I don't know how to begin."

"You could tell me while I'm painting. You'd have plenty of time."

"You do mean a nude painting?"

"Yes."

She laughed, protesting, "How can I talk about it like that?"

"It will put the nudity out of your mind."

"Some of it is very Halifax. It'd bore you to tears."

"You didn't think that when you decided suddenly to come all the way down here from Paris—telegraphing one day, arriving the next?"

"I came to give me time to think it through before I decide what to do next. I knew you'd be a sympathetic ear—and Léa. It's so entangled, like snarled-up string. I have to untangle it to know who I am."

"What is life but a search for who you are? Certainly the creative life. And what is the creative life but a search for your own identity?"

"Is that quoting someone?"

"I don't think so—or I've forgotten."

"Léa told me you didn't like talking when you paint."

"This is different."

The car was turning on Promenade des Anglais to the entrance of the Hôtel La Méditerranée.

"You didn't eat much at lunchtime. Will you feel like dinner?"

"I'm not sure yet."

"About the painting or dinner?"

"Both at the moment. But relieved that you know at least one of my secrets."

"Then come and sit with me on the café terrace and watch the twilight promenade. My favourite time of day."

"One odd thing you should know, although it has nothing to do with my...interesting condition. I had trouble convincing myself that Charles is really dead."

"My God, tell me why."

"I will later. I need to go upstairs. Enjoy your sunset. I saw two of your beautiful Venice twilights at Léa's. They are gorgeous."

"You can have one as a present if you'll pose for me."

"I'd adore one, but you don't need to bribe me. I think

I will be ready for some dinner. Is eight o'clock all right?"

"Meet me in the lobby at eight and we'll go somewhere nearby."

She was exhausted when she reached her room, too tired to throw more than a quick, appreciative glance at the spectacle of palms casting long shadows and the sea an ever-darkening blue, before collapsing gratefully on the bed. She desperately needed to sleep for a few minutes. Of course Léa would have guessed. It must have been written all over her. They must have been discussing it when she came back and found them finishing lunch, their faces like overripe fruit: Morrice, always elegant in his suit with waistcoat, neat collar, and tie, his hat on the empty chair; Léa happily perspiring in her loud satin dress. No wonder she was enjoying the outing: the selfish man had left her alone on New Year's Eve. They could have included Léa. But he wouldn't have. And she'd forgotten to tell them about the cathedral window. It was when she'd just begun to tell that she'd suddenly felt so tired.

Morrice took his accustomed seat in the café overlooking the seafront and ordered a whisky. Wherever he travelled, it comforted and stimulated him to be near water: to be able to contemplate the moods of the Seine or the Grand Canal, to lift his eyes to the ocean horizon in Tangiers or Havana, to ravish his vision with subtle reflections and the infinite play of light and colour. Water to stimulate the painter but water as the escape, the highway to variety, the allure of travel for its own sake. He'd always lived simply, his family thought meanly and frugally, so he could afford the pleasure of deciding impulsively to pick up and go. To wake up one morning and think, *I want to go to Cuba*, and immediately book a passage on the earliest ship, and then enjoy days of idle life at sea, the people met by chance, brief intense conviviality, holiday excitement in discardable acquaintance. Then, to arrive in the new place, unencumbered, the pleasure of a new hotel, new streets, new cafés, new light, new shapes, new smells, different coffee, different rolls, different life unfolding before him. All blissfully fresh, the sun rising on a new feast for the eye, a fresh beginning for the spirit. And when it began to be stale, moving on with no ties, moving back to Paris, where it was never stale. Perhaps the travel itch was coming back to him like the desire to work. They often came together. A burst of energy to paint so often meant the urge to jump on a train to Concarneau, Le Pouldu, Saint-Malo, or here, or the urge to cross the ocean. This was the longest he had gone without wanting to go anywhere. Fresh views demanded a fresh approach. They stimulated novelty. Was that restlessness an urge towards or an escape from? Both, perhaps. Well, it was just his nature. The pleasure was in the going and the coming and the not being static anywhere too long.

He drained his glass. Yes, he could feel that little tickle of anticipation. There must be a trip coming up. He caught the waiter's eye and with a tiny gesture of the forefinger ordered another whisky.

When Julia awoke it was dark. She had slept for forty-five minutes—deep, dreamless surrender to a drowsiness as heavy as those moments at thirteen when she couldn't stay awake another second, then awoke, like now, totally refreshed.

Of course, she had known the minute he asked her on New Year's Eve that she wanted him to paint her. In the days since the second missed period, she had not been totally in command of herself, her moods oscillating, but to be thought coy about anything always irritated her. To be certain, while the bath was running, she undressed and examined herself in the mirror. There was no sign. Or was there a little thickening just below the waistline? If so, imperceptible to anyone else. It couldn't be more than five weeks. If she looked in her pocket diary she could calculate to the day; if she tried she could do it in her head, but she did neither. If she had the baby, she would never again look like this. Satisfied there was no visible evidence, she got into the bath.

11

Friday, January 2, 1920

Morrice's room at the front of La Méditerranée had full-length French doors gracefully capped by an elliptical fanlight. Parting the floor-length curtains to open the doors and the louvred shutters, you found yourself on a small balcony over Promenade des Anglais and the sea. From inside the room the top of a palm tree was just apparent.

"It takes quite an effort to ignore the wallpaper," Morrice said, "but I've hidden some of it." He had hung several paintings over paper swimming with decoration.

"Like Oscar Wilde, either the wallpaper or I must go?"

"Not quite yet, I trust. Just look at how I see this." On a large new canvas pinned to the easel was a pencil sketch of a female form vaguely defined in the window, with one shutter and half the French door closed and one hand holding aside the diaphanous curtain.

"I like the drawing."

"Will you just stand there a moment in the window recess. I want to see how the light falls."

Julia did so, and he looked for a few seconds.

"Let's try it with the other shutter closed, this side open and you standing here. Yes, now that would put the lines of louvres behind you, unless I ignore them."

"It's going to be a little chilly with the door open. I mean it's nice but it's only the second of January."

"Don't worry, we can close the door for most of it and I'll open it only when I need to. Yes, I think that's good. The sun will come overhead and change the shadows, but we get a nice reflection off the wall. Good. Well, I think we can begin. I suggest we try an hour, then rest. And no more than two hours a day, because I want to keep the morning light. So, if you don't mind getting ready, you can use the bathroom to change."

He was brisk and businesslike in his incongruous three-piece suit and stiff collar and tie. With his bald head and Edward VII beard, he might have been banker going to work.

"What about my hair? Up or down?"

"I like it up, as you have it, leaving the neck free, although your chignon is a little severe. Could you do something still up but softer?"

In the bathroom, feeling disconnected from her body, Julia undressed and put on the robe she had brought. Then she loosened her hair and redid it in a knot on top of her head, letting it roll loosely to the sides.

"I like the hair that way," Morrice said when she emerged. "If you'll stand where you were...that's it. Now face me and put your weight on your right leg, and the left foot a few inches towards me. Good. Let your left arm just hang easily. Now raise your right hand just to brush the flimsy curtain back a few inches. Good. Finally, head up and look directly here." He pointed to the edge of the canvas stretcher, "No, a trifle higher. There. Good. I'll make a mark." With a stick of charcoal he marked it. "Now, how does that feel?"

"It feels all right. Except for this arm."

"Try letting it hang by your side. I like that better. Less coy."

"By all means, let's not be coy!"

He laughed. "Now relax a moment. He came forward and fastened the tie-backs to hold the curtains open, then went back and stood by the easel.

"Not sure about the curtains. But I can change that later. Now, if you don't mind, I'd like to see it without the robe."

Noticing that he was at pains to create the impersonal atmosphere of a studio, she tried to discard her robe as unselfconsciously as the models she'd drawn in life classes at the Julian.

He looked. "Yes, yes. Perhaps half a step back into the window opening. Yes, good. And relax the left leg again. Let the knee come in front, naturally. Fine. If you're ready, we'll start."

There was nothing coy about the pose now, considering that it meant a frank display of pubic hair. That didn't bother her aesthetically, but for the first few moments it made her feel more naked than the previous time she had posed for him, in his wicker chair in the studio on Quai des Grands-Augustins, her thighs demurely together and a wrist on the chair-arm obscuring the pubic area. The pose was ingeniously arranged to express, she supposed, a conception of ripeness and virginity, both then true, as she guessed he had chosen the new pose in part to express the more experienced woman she now was. Her condition might not show but knowing about it, wouldn't he perceive something that suggested it? Her breasts felt heavier. Would that be obvious? She glanced down and he said, "Eyes up here, please," causing her to blush.

Good painting was about essences, elusive, ineffable, often unconscious in the artist's mind. But a good artist sees what is not obvious, sees feelings, has feeling himself and applies it to the model, or mingles what he feels with what he senses in the model. It is subtle and it has to survive many hours, often days, sometimes weeks, in which the moods, feeling, digestion, emotions, reflections from the weather outside, preoccupation with a million concerns, continually flit across the thoughts of both model and painter and play over the model's face and body.

She stood, wondering how what she was thinking would show. And what was she thinking? Dismay? Anger? Fear? Disappointment? Anxiety? And even humour. All of these, but which would show in the finished painting? Some artists gabble away, saying *I see this as you, I see that, I want to capture this*. Morrice kept silent, so that her mind was free to roam.

She needed to do some fundamental planning. To arrange to have more money sent. Paris was one choice: Suzanne had offered to find a doctor, to arrange everything—assuming Julia would have the baby. She had not felt comfortable raising any alternative with Suzanne. But whom else to tell, she thought, that here I am at twenty-eight facing life as an unmarried mother in a society where I will be a constant embarrassment to everyone—to my parents first of all. And even if I can avoid Montreal, a deep embarrassment to the Robertsons, to Mollie and Betty—even to Stewart, who seems able to swallow everything I throw at him in good humour, but even for him there must be a limit. Of course if I told Lucy, she would tell Harry...

Harry had introduced Suzanne, whom he'd met through Borden. Improbably, in the midst of all that frenzy of meetings around the peace conference, while also running the Canadian government for months by telegraph from Paris, the prime minister actually stumped off every morning to have a French lesson with Mademoiselle Perret. And kept his diary in French! She was very funny about him. She told Julia he used to walk over from the Hotel Majestic on the Étoile, where the delegation stayed, to her flat on Rue Cortambert and bring his diary for her to correct. "Like a schoolboy. Very earnest," she said. "So proper, as though each day were a test. And so I would say to him, *'Bon garçon!'* and make the corrections. He was so earnest to do well, but he was too old and too busy to improve his French. He kept saying, 'The French language defeats me.'"

Suzanne was petite in the French way, beautiful and perfectly formed but tiny, as small at thirty as Julia had been as a girl of ten. She was all that Julia envied in Frenchwomen: innately chic, naturally elegant, frugal in her shopping and household management, yet a fine cook, a delightful companion.

What began out of politeness to Harry had become a close friendship. On the first visit to Paris, before the trip to the battlefields, Julia invited her to tea at the hotel. Suzanne told a charming story. According to Borden's diary, he got help in buying a coat for Laura in Paris. He enlisted none less than Nancy Astor, whom he had met in England when he had dedicated a new war cemetery for Canadians near the Astor estate.

"I think Sir Robert like very much to meet the grand personages of the time," Suzanne said, with a twinkle at her own English. Julia thought Borden must have had some sparkle himself to persuade one of the smartest and most aggressive women of the day to shop for his unsmart, passive wife, up to her melancholy ears in Ottawa snowdrifts! Bizarre. Lady Astor was notoriously straightlaced in the marital-fidelity department, but Borden might have enjoyed a platonic flirtation in a society infinitely more glittering than Ottawa's. His diary noted frequent letters from Laura saying how ill and lonely she felt.

Julia loved this glimpse into the stiff Sir Robert, whom she knew as a courtly, somewhat over-starched gentleman, with his bushy grey moustache and eyebrows and hair arranged in a rather dandified centre part. He had certainly given Mlle Perret an endless topic of conversation. Laced with her wry humour, the conversation long overran the time intended for tea at that first meeting.

"You must come to see me when you come to Paris again. Come and stay with me. I have room," she had said on parting.

If she told Lucy, she and Harry might feel they had to tell Julia's mother that her daughter was not making sensible judgments. But if she had to tell Mother herself? Disaster! And the baby's father? Unthinkable even to hint who it might be. And when the baby was delivered, what would she do with a tiny son or daughter? If it were delivered. A thread of fear shivered through her. If it were delivered and she kept it. In many places, otherwise quite-pleasant people could be deeply hostile to a woman with an illegitimate child. Others not so. Where she was going to live was not just a place to have the accouchement but where to live with the child.

"You're frowning," Morrice said.

"Sorry, I just thought of something I needed to resolve."

"Fine, just try to keep the facial expression neutral."

"Neutral never suits me."

"Wrong. From my point of view it suits you beautifully. You'll see. Your face is exquisite in repose."

"My thoughts are not in repose."

His drawing felt fluent and confident. He'd been a little startled, why he wasn't sure, to notice that her pubic hair was blonde. Perfectly reasonable that it should be but he hadn't remembered it from 1913. In Renoir's *Bather Arranging Her Hair*, there was a hint of blonde hair there and it added to the girl's charming innocence. Julia was a much leaner woman, smaller waist and hips—his pencil retraced that line—lean thighs, breasts high and firm, slim shoulders, and the amazing jaw line.

He was at ease and confident. The pale grey of the French doors would nicely set off the tones of her skin.

"Do you want to talk to pass the time? You told me about Charles last night. But not the other story."

"It won't disturb you?"

"If it does, I'll say."

"Well, there's more about Charles but I want to tell you in the right order."

"Any order you like."

"You'd think I was ridiculous if I told you how I allowed this to happen to me. The classic trap, like a Boccaccio story, a court commedia from the fourteenth century, but who'd believe it could happen to an intelligent woman of the twentieth century? Well, obviously not as intelligent as I thought in my desire to live in the modern way."

"What does that mean?"

"As a modern woman, who can make her own decisions, lead her own life, not be the prisoner of her biology. And I was encouraged by a really nice man. His name is Stewart MacPherson, he's a professor of psychology at Dalhousie University."

She told him how Stewart had appeared after the explosion, with Betty, and how comforting he was when the news came about Charles.

"So I began seeing him. We were planning a trip

to Europe when someone from the past turned up, an Englishman—Neville Boiscoyne."

She told Morrice a somewhat edited version of her instant attraction for Neville at a ball during the war, and how two years later he turned up with the Prince of Wales.

"He wrote asking me to dinner. So, to show everyone how indifferent I was to Neville, I asked Stewart to accompany me. But I wasn't indifferent at all. I was all atingle and Stewart knew that immediately."

Morrice grunted now and then to show he was listening, but he was so absorbed in his work she wondered if he really heard, like wondering whether a child being read to has gone to sleep, so she stopped.

And after a few seconds, he said, "Go on. I'm listening."

"The dinner was the first time I had been anywhere in public with Stewart as my companion, the first time I had seen Peter and Stewart together. And I went feeling protective of Stewart in the presence of Neville, because Stewart had, and knew it, every reason to be jealous."

"Wait, I'm lost." Morrice came out from behind the easel. "I'm lost. I've got Stewart and Neville but who is Peter?"

"Peter is an Anglican clergyman. He's very young but he's already the dean of the cathedral."

"And...?"

So she couldn't tell the story without Peter after all. "And he—it's a long story—but he and I had an embarrassing moment one night on the train from Montreal to Halifax. We both lost our heads. But that was well behind us. He was at the Prince of Wales's dinner too, with his wife, who is a handful."

"So there are three men you were concerned about at the dinner?" He was intrigued. Which of the three had fathered the child?

"Plus Charles's parents and his sister, Lucy, and her husband, Harry."

"Well, what happened?"

"Stewart and I both had a very detached view of royalty. Peter had a sort of mystical reverence for the monarchy, which Stewart and I found ridiculous and infantile. Going to dinner with our future king was to be a fascinating experience, not a surrender to the mystique of royalty. It makes me smile now to think how confident I was in the armour I wore as the emancipated, modern woman, intelligent and invulnerable, the sort of woman Shaw likes to celebrate. Well, Mr. Shaw would have thought me a weak member of my sex that evening!

"I had read every word the papers had to say about the prince beforehand. And we had laughed together at how abject and silly it seemed. The writers sounded like young girls with a crush, panting in admiration. Do you know Halifax?"

"Only to pass through to get a ship."

"It's sophisticated for its size. A long string of royal princes and dukes, including George V, have been stationed there and local society takes it in their stride, enjoying the vicarious prestige in a fairly grown-up way. So I thought this newspaper mooing about the Prince of Wales was embarrassing."

He saw her laugh, apparently oblivious of her nudity.

"But once I got into the presence, all my detachment evaporated in a puff of magic. First the trappings: out in the harbour to HMS *Renown*, the huge, sleek, menacing, grey battleship. Then we were greeted with all the pomp and glitter the navy always produces, but had ratcheted up considerably for royalty. But at the heart of it was this extraordinary young man, very boyish, with a sweet wistfulness about him that makes a woman want to cradle his head against her bosom—at the very least!"

She was ahead of herself. They had met the prince before the dinner. Neville sent a message asking if she and Lucy would go for an outing with them that afternoon.

"HRH—they all call him that—HRH wanted to escape from protocol for a while. The upshot was that we were picked up in a car on Sunday afternoon, driven to Point Pleasant Park, and deposited at the Young Avenue gate, just as another car dropped off the prince and Neville. And Lucy said, 'Oh my God! Do we curtsy?'"

They started to curtsy, very out of practice, but the prince stopped them by taking their hands and said, "It is so nice of you to give us a little of your time as we desperately needed to get our land legs, and yours were the first names Neville tossed out. You've both met Neville before, of course, and if I may say, even his rhapsodies do not do justice to the charms of you two ladies."

He was shorter than Julia had expected, shorter than her by an inch and several inches below Neville. And although he had a man's face, she felt the little boy lurking there, yearningly, she thought, and a little disconcertingly, the shadowlike boy in him—either yearning to be allowed to grow up, or the reverse, to go back to boyhood. Curiously, it brought back something she had felt about Charles. The pictures of him as a boy were so wistful they used to make her weep. However, there was nothing sad about the prince that day, as they set out briskly on the old path deeper into the park towards the Martello Tower, built by his great-great something-or-other.

The men were dressed for walking, in tweeds, with casual hats and walking sticks, less formal than the occasional people they passed, and none recognized the prince.

"Hold on," Morrice said, "you haven't described Neville and I gather he's to be the hero of the story."

"He's tall, dark brown hair, lean face and almost black eyes. A handsome man and totally self-assured."

"And is he still the hero?"

"Well, that's the point of the story," Julia said. "We walked four abreast when the road was wide enough, in twos when it narrowed, and the pairs evolved naturally into Lucy walking with Neville and I with HRH. I liked it, not only for the thrill of being with him, but because from furtive glances and a few words after the first handshake, I was trying to sort out my feelings about Neville."

Ever since his letter in May she had alternated between excited anticipation—he was going to reawaken all the repressed desire of their meetings eighteen months before—and indifference. But it took only a glimpse of the side of his dark head and his hand on the car door, as he held it for the prince, to tell her in an instant that she wanted him as she had then. Confirmed totally when he watched as they attempted to curtsy, his black eyes on hers, and the smile she recognized. And as she rose from the curtsy to take his hand, she understood perfectly that he had arranged all this specifically to see her and that she was very glad of it. So when she walked in a pair with the prince, she could feel a strong force close behind her.

Beyond the Martello Tower they needed to scramble over the old defensive fortifications, long overgrown with shrubs and trees, and the prince gave her his hand to help. She felt quite at ease with him and said, "You're holding my hand, sir, but I don't know what to call you."

"Call me David," he said, with one of those smiles that turned women's heads everywhere he went. "But if you do, I can't very well keep calling you Mrs. Robertson, can I? Let's be informal. I so much prefer it. Off duty. Your name is Julia."

"Yes, it is."

"I've known that for some time. Ever since Neville came back from Canada. And because he's moved around a bit since then, you can be sure that your fame has travelled far and wide."

He was flirting. It was unmistakable. They came down the far side of the embankment and turned to wait for Neville and Lucy. Her freckled face was glowing pink with the exercise and the excitement.

The prince leaned closer. "I don't want to raise a painful subject, but Neville told me about your late husband, his heroism, his tragic death. No wish to reopen old wounds but I would like you to know how personally I grieve for his loss—and yours."

"Thank you, sir." She was so moved at the simplicity and genuine feeling, she couldn't stop tears appearing.

"Not sir, David." He smiled. "It's simple. David in private, sir in public. Forget the Your Royal Highness nonsense, which I try to do as much as possible. That's what I tell people I like. The rest"—he laughed—"can Your Royal Highness me till they're blue in the face. And they do!" He kept laughing. It was impossible not to be enchanted with the performance, and she did think it was a performance. He was acting a role he'd made for himself: down to earth, unstuffy, let's shove the protocol aside, let's do as we wish, these are new times and deserve new behaviour from princes. And it was a brilliant success. As she knew now, millions of people all over Canada and the United States melted that summer at what they saw as this unaffected, regular fellow, democratic prince, apparently transforming relations between the Crown and people. But that captivating performance could be switched off in an instant, as she saw later.

He shouted, "Come on Neville! Miles to go and we'll be late for tea!"—sounding as he might have as a schoolboy of thirteen.

They came out at Point Pleasant, which divided the harbour from the Northwest Arm. Lucy showed them a patch of heather, supposed to have grown from seeds from the ticking of highland soldiers. The prince said, "We must have a piece for good luck." He waded in and picked a sprig for each of them. "Something for our memory books. Pity I haven't brought my bagpipes, isn't it, Neville? I could have given us a little concert."

"A great pity, sir." Neville smiled.

"Neville doesn't mean it. Always slopes off when I'm practising. No highland blood stirring in Boiscoyne veins. All Norman, isn't it? Back to the Conquest?"

"Well, at least not German, sir." Neville laughed.

The prince said, "I am very proud of my German connections, despite the recent unpleasantness due to my demented cousin, the Kaiser. But I liked my time there. Liked Germany a lot."

The cars met them at the Yacht Squadron and the prince said, "Never enough time for anything, is there, Neville? Why don't you come out to *Renown* with us and have tea, and we can continue this nice visit?"

"Be cutting it a bit fine for dinner, wouldn't it, sir," Neville said, clearly HRH's keeper. "I mean for the ladies."

"Quite right, Neville. I'm always trying to pack too much into a day."

Neville walked around to the car to hand Julia in and said, as he took her hand, "I really look forward to this evening— to dancing with you again."

"So do I." She got into the dark interior of the car and sank back beside Lucy.

"Well!" Lucy let out a huge breath and began to giggle. "What about that? Who's going to believe us?" She giggled like a schoolgirl. "Can you believe it? I want to see Margery Wentworth's face when I tell her."

"You wouldn't, Lucy! It's too mean."

"What did he say, the prince? I'm dying to hear every word. My God, he is so good looking! And as for your Neville Boiscoyne—"

"My Neville Boiscoyne?"

"My dear, the entire outing—the whole dinner invitation—is a put-up job. Believe me! I know it. It's all to get him together with you."

Julia said, "Lucy, he walked with *you* while the prince walked with me. What's put-up about that?"

"And what did he talk about while walking with me? You. Wanted to know everything. How you had been since Charles. Were there any children. Were you, very definitely put, seeing other people—"

"People, not men."

"Men, not people. Pumped me for every scrap of information he could get. Very offhandedly, of course. Nothing obvious but totally obvious to me. And, my dear! What an exquisite man. Handsome. Quite as charming as little Prince Charming himself."

"Which is saying a lot!"

"I'll say. If he'd even said a word to me, I'd have fainted dead away. But after saying how do you do, while I curtsied like an elephant—"

"You didn't. It was very nice."

"—he never addressed a word to me or even glanced at

me the entire time. But I'm used to that and I'm not looking for a husband—well, that's not very nice—but my hunch was right, you know, when those letters came in the spring. He is serious about you."

Julia happily listened to this girlish gush, which often irritated her, particularly when Lucy lectured her on Stewart MacPherson.

"Why, what was wrong with him?" Morrice asked.

"Oh, Lucy thinks he's too rumpled and professor-ish."

"And do you think so?"

"I am still very fond of him...but anyway, I found myself basking deliciously in Lucy's words, with images of Neville swimming in my head as she talked."

She had asked Lucy, "Tell me exactly what he said."

"Aha! So now you're intrigued?"

"You're making such a point of it, I'm just being polite to ask you to elaborate."

"Sure, sure. He said what a pleasure it was to be back in Halifax, where he'd so enjoyed his last visit. He said—oh, I asked him why the papers call him Lieutenant-Commander, the Honourable Neville Boiscoyne, and he said because his father's a viscount, so he and his sister are honourables. He doesn't use it but the Court puts it on lists. Didn't I tell you? He's a nobleman, an aristocrat, for heaven's sake!' Lucy fell back gasping. "I think this is the most exciting day of my life."

Julia saw Morrice come out from behind the easel and stretch.

"Am I boring you?"

"Not at all. I've never met anyone who's been so close to the Prince of Wales. I want to hear it all, but put on your robe and take a rest, I'm sure you need it."

She had half forgotten where she was and she wrapped herself gratefully in the robe and sat down. He stood back from the easel and looked. It was the first time since she'd come that she had seen him without a drink.

"All right?"

"Fine."

"Am I going to see it in stages?"

"If you like."

She got up, clasping her robe more self-consciously as she moved into his territory. The drawing was masterful, she thought, a minimum of lines, assured clear strokes, her body strange to her because, of course, she was seeing herself through other eyes. The French window and curtains were lightly suggested. The proud posture of the pencilled woman, her candid gaze, made Julia glad she had agreed.

"How did you get the mouth when I was gossiping all the time?"

"Very quickly—but this is just rough."

"You could sell it as finished."

He watched her body move beneath the robe as she went back and sat in the chair by the dressing table, the hips, breasts, thighs hidden yet revealed by the silk material. He would have liked to draw that too.

"Stay sitting for a few minutes, while I work in some of the background."

She watched as he squeezed colours on his palette and worked them together into a pale grey, then thinned it with turpentine. He was applying grey to the window frame around the outlines of the nude to kill a little time. Unexpectedly, an awareness of her body was distracting him. The knowledge that she had complications with several men at once had altered his focus. To clear his mind he worked on the rough background to her figure.

"I'm waiting to hear more about the prince and what he's like. The entire world seems to adore him."

12

Dinner on the battleship, Julia remembered, was not quite as informal as Neville's invitation had suggested. They had to sail for Prince Edward Island the next evening and this was the only dinner HRH could give, so he had to invite the prime minister, the premier of Nova Scotia, the lieutenant governor, and their wives.

For all his sometimes-rumpled professor look, Stewart's heavy figure in white tie was impressive. Not until she was sitting at her dressing table, in a new black evening dress, wondering what else she should do to herself, had the question of Stewart loomed up, as though he had appeared behind her in the mirror. She had insisted on his being invited, their first evening together in public. Yet it was Neville who filled her imagination, her senses tingling with anticipation of being with him. And Stewart would know, as Mollie had, the moment he saw the look in her eyes. And she'd been dreading this encounter. Well, it was too complicated to think through now. She touched her head to check the strands of hair at the back and stood up.

Curiously, just as she moved, she knew she was going to tell Neville Boiscoyne about the mystery of Charles. And she also knew that in part she was using it as a defence. Now she wanted to go to England more eagerly than ever, with no taste for more intimacy with Stewart, yet no wish to humiliate him. She looked into the mirror and said,

"We keep saying we should be honest. Then I'll just have to be honest."

Mollie was at the bottom of the stairs. "Oh, my dear, don't you look a picture! You don't mind if Betty comes out? She's dying to see to you all dressed up."

In fact, Betty's black curls were already halfway around the door frame from the kitchen. She always showed the half of her face with the good eye first and then revealed the other, with the glass eye.

Betty studied her thoughtfully.

"How do I look?"

"You look beautiful. But I wish your dress was a pretty colour. Instead of black."

"Why?"

"Because black's sad."

"But I'm not sad, sweetheart. I'm happy to be going to this party."

"I imagine!" Mollie said. "It's written all over you. And black looks real elegant on you. It shows off your blonde hair and your white skin."

Betty said, "I'm going to see the Prince of Wales tomorrow! All the school-children from the South End are going to the Grand Parade by St. Paul's Church."

In the shop in Montreal Julia had argued with her mother over the black dress.

"But dear, it's like going back into mourning, and you're long past the need to do that. And besides, black is so dramatic, isn't it? It makes such a bold statement. It's like that cruel painting by Sargent."

Morrice laughed. *"Madame X?"*

Julia had said, "Well, it doesn't leave my shoulders as bare as hers, Mother."

"I should think not. You don't want society in a small place like Halifax thinking there is something scandalous about you, do you dear?"

"The Merry Widow?"

"Well, Julia, laugh and make fun of me, but for the Prince of Wales"—said so the shop assistant couldn't miss it—"I would have thought something more demure..." She ruffled through several pastel colours Julia had rejected.

"But I like this dress!" Turning to the shop assistant. "Don't you think it suits me?"

"It suits you perfectly, madam."

"And it's not as though I'm a girl any longer. Those things all make me look like a debutante or a bridesmaid. I like this." And that's what she was wearing.

"That's exactly like your mother. She was fidgety and anxious when she was a girl," Morrice said.

They picked up Lucy and her husband, Harold Traverse, whom Julia had trouble reading: very contained emotionally, but with a perpetual good-humoured exterior. She felt rather cool towards him because she thought he treated Lucy abominably. In fact he was behaving just the way Borden, whom he worshipped, treated Laura, who was at the dinner that evening without him.

The prime minister had taken a spill at the start of the royal tour in St. John, New Brunswick. He'd hurt his leg and had been forced to stay in bed on the prince's ship ever since. The Prince of Wales loved it and made a point of slipping away at least three times that evening, each time announcing with a smile he was going to "comfort my distinguished patient."

Julia laughed. "Harry said later that Borden himself found it quite convenient. He didn't have to dance attendance on the impetuous prince minute by minute, a real chore because HRH was headstrong, continually changing his mind, chafing at protocol and upsetting long-made arrangements, to do things he found informal and fun. Borden had to play Dutch uncle, particularly over golf. HRH wanted to play as often as possible, including Sunday, when there was time free from the tour schedule, but hell to pay with the Lord's Day Alliance."

Morrice cheered. "The Lord's Day Alliance! I'd forgotten all about them! Another excellent reason to live in France!"

Julia said, "Borden actually had to speak sternly to the prince and remind him of constitutional custom: royals take advice from their ministers. And the prince backed off with great charm, saying, 'I hope, Sir Robert, I will never do anything to displease you.' That was the prince's pattern: push, test the limits of freedom as a child does, fret and sulk when he's crossed, dissolve the issue in a cloud of charming surrender. Borden considered him infantile and complained mightily to Harry. So the PM's enforced holiday from being governess to this royal boy was a relief. In any case, Borden was exhausted from the months at the Paris peace talks, plus all the political trials at home."

Morrice loved listening to her, her detachment and humour, but also her involvement with these people was titillating.

The dinner party guests all gathered at the appointed hour, having found the right jetty to meet the launch from HMS *Renown*.

Julia said, "Believe me, there is nothing more thrilling socially for Halifax women of any age than being invited to a party on board one of the visiting ships. The grander the ship, the greater the thrill, and this was the grandest of all: one of the great warships of the Royal Navy and the host no less than our future king. Who could be blasé about that? Even Stewart showed an amused sparkle when not—I felt it excruciatingly—trying to suppress his jealousy at the cause of my excitement. I have never met a man as unselfish as Stewart and as knowing. He's a man with feelings he isn't afraid to discuss, and he can be hurt."

Morrice noticed that she had slipped into the present tense.

"The prince came personally to the head of the gangway to welcome us aboard. He was in civilian evening dress. Junior officers and seamen yanked the ladies and older men out of the–bouncing launch and up the side of the battle-ship, looming above us as solid as a city. In the wardroom, he offered cocktails, still a pretty modern taste in Halifax. I noticed Margery Wentworth–accepted avidly. She looked glamorous that evening. And Peter, now in the actual pres-ence of royalty, had that look of ambitious intensity, that need to be noticed and marked for right conduct, which had always irritated me about him."

She had taken in all these details half consciously, only when politeness forced her to glance and smile at other guests and not stare too fixedly at Neville or HRH. Being in the same room with a famous politician paled beside the waves of magnetism that emanated from the prince. People knew where he was, even with their bodies turned. Some made a show of seeming not to notice, but no one quite turned away. Everyone was edging obliquely; all fourteen of them having drinks must have looked like a fleet of dinghies in a race, fluttering at different angles to the same royal breeze. And he was brilliant at this, exhibiting the greatest talent for meeting people and putting them at their ease, in fact charming them off their feet.

Neville presented the other guests to HRH, then came

over to Julia and said quietly, "I notice we're sitting together at dinner, so we'll have a chance to talk."

"I'm glad."

"May I say that you look absolutely stunning in that gown?"

"My mother said it made me look like the Merry Widow."

"Does she know something I don't?" He smiled.

"I know she'd give her eye teeth to be here tonight. In case you haven't noticed, we are all thrilled that you thought of us. It was very kind."

"We could have included your mother and father."

"Well—they're in Montreal."

"Ah, yes. Where you had to rush suddenly the last time I was here."

"At the time I thought it vital to go very quickly."

The prince joined them, cocktail glass in hand. "Neville, don't monopolize the pretty ladies. Mrs. Robertson, wasn't that jolly this afternoon? You were such good sports to come out with us."

"I enjoyed it very much, sir. I'm not sure our friends will believe it happened. Too much like a fairy story."

"Well, I didn't see any fairies in your woods, but I could show you some truly enchanted forest in England, if you came there."

Mostly for Neville's benefit, Julia said, "As it happens, I am going to England quite soon."

"I hope not too soon because we have to beetle all over Canada and the United States the next two months and we might miss you. Neville, find out when Mrs. Robertson plans to come. It would be delightful to entertain her there." She thought Neville frowned slightly as the prince said, "A good plan, indeed. Now I think I had better chivvy all these good people to the table. Lady Borden, with Sir Robert so fortuitously indisposed, I have the honour of taking you to dinner." He offered his arm to the shy Laura Borden.

"She's a melancholy lady by all accounts," Julia told Morrice, "a simple, unambitious but pretty, Halifax girl when she married Borden, a farm boy from Grand Pré, who rapidly became a prosperous lawyer. She never expected he would jump into politics, but he caught the bug and got elected to Parliament. Then, for seven years he left her behind in Halifax! People are amazing! I wouldn't put up with that for a minute. And when she did finally move to Ottawa and he succeeded Laurier as PM, Laura still moped, looked after her garden and did little else. He was away for seven months at the peace conference and she could easily have gone with him. One of his ministers took his wife and daughters to Paris and complained to Borden about their accommodation! I'd have jumped at the chance to be in Paris then. But Laura kept writing him plaintive letters about how lonely she was and how ill she felt. No gumption. She should have jumped on a ship and turned up in Paris to surprise him. Only, he was always such a dry stick of a man when I met him—very handsome but almost humourless—perhaps being with him wouldn't have been much fun."

Still, this evening Laura looked pleased with the attentions of HRH, who placed her on his right, with Mrs. Murray, wife of the Nova Scotia premier, on his left.

Julia found herself near the centre of the table, between Neville and Harry, facing Lucy, whose dinner partners were Peter and Stewart, so that if Neville had fixed the seating he had put Julia where her tiniest gesture could be scrutinized by those she was most sensitive about. Margery Wentworth was opposite Susan Gastonguy, an old friend of Julia's, with

Archie Robertson holding the end of the table, facing the prince at the other.

When they first sat down, everyone was a little shy and waited for HRH to speak, but as he began exercising his charm on the wives and officials close to him, the starchiness dissolved and the buzz of conversation grew louder.

Julia would have been content for a while just to look and listen, stealing glances up the table at the heart-wrenching face of the prince, as he bent his carefully combed fair head deferentially to Laura Borden or Premier Murray, no doubt convincing them, as he could Julia from a distance, that no companions, no topic, could have fascinated him more. And then, transferring his attention towards Elizabeth Robertson and the lieutenant governor, a momentary weariness clouded his eyes; he glanced absently down the table as though wondering where on earth he was, then refocused his attention and his rapt smile, which even on that young face caused lines to crinkle appealingly at his temples. In one of these moments Julia caught his eye, and for a second there was warm pulse in his glance while he continued to listen to his partner.

More important, just listening let her make a secret inspection of Neville. She noticed his lean hands holding knife and fork in the British manner, picking up his wineglass. The hands had comparatively little hair, which she liked.

Neville. So painful to recall all that now!

Julia gave an embarrassed laugh. "You're going to find all this stupid and girlish—"

"I'm enjoying the details," Morrice said.

She could see the condition of Neville's nails, recently trimmed with scissors, the little angled cuts still visible, not filed or buffed and, for some reason, she liked that. She liked that his dark chestnut hair was loosely combed and not stuck down with oil or brilliantine. In contrast she felt the prince a little too meticulously combed, not a blonde hair out of place. That was also true of his dress—she had noticed that afternoon. HRH wore clothes like a man who has just stepped away from his tailor or like an actor who has just left his dresser and hairdresser in the wings. That was as true of him in his walking tweeds as in white tie. He must be exquisitely particular about his clothes, while Neville, beautifully turned out, seemed more casual. And she very much liked that. Well, how surprising! She was falling in love with him, detail by detail, most willingly and frankly, observed at that glittering table by those who knew her best.

Her miasma could not have lasted more than a few seconds when Neville turned from polite chat with the lieutenant governor's wife to say, as though deliberately skipping time-wasting preliminaries, and by looking so directly into her eyes that she felt others must feel the intensity, "Well, where do we begin again? The last time, in your spectacular green dress, you told me you must not forget you were a married woman. The ball at Government House two years ago?"

"I remember you smirked and said, 'Are you likely to forget it?'"

"Surely I didn't smirk."

Neville's mouth curved in a way that made him seem to be smiling ironically even when he wasn't—the kind of look teachers hate because it carries the shadow of impertinence.

Julia said, "I thought you smirked."

"But it was impertinent of me to ask you that question—about forgetting you were married—and I have regretted it many times since."

"Have you?"

"Especially after I heard your sad news."

"Yes." She couldn't think of anything to add, and they were silent until Neville said, "The Prince of Wales calls you Julia and, I might add, refers to you frequently, especially since this afternoon. Is that merely royal prerogative, or might the privilege be shared with me?"

The silliness of words between new lovers! Silly if recalled when the heated moments had cooled, but how thrilling when the words were fashioning a fragile bridge over the rising torrent of emotion.

"You told HRH you were coming to England. When precisely might that be?"

She laughed. "Does he want to know or do you?"

"I do."

"We are sailing on September fifteenth."

"We?"

"Stewart MacPherson." She nodded towards him.

"You are travelling together?"

"We are travelling separately—as friends. Stewart has been a great friend to me since—since the war."

"Is it impertinent of me to ask—"

"You don't need to ask, I'll tell you. We are friends. We are not engaged to be married."

"Not yet?"

"Not going to be."

"Actually, I knew that."

"Because you asked Lucy?"

"I didn't have to, she volunteered it."

"Lucy is impossible!"

"The impertinence I was about to risk was to ask whether you would visit us in England?"

"Us?"

"Me, my family. My mother and my sister."

"That would be lovely. Where do you live?"

"In Wiltshire. West of London. Not too far. Lots of trains, or we could arrange a car."

"I have to go to Hampshire—"

"That's the county next to Wiltshire."

"—to find my husband's grave but also—I hesitate to tell you this—"

Just then the Prince of Wales asked for silence and he toasted the king, reminding them of the naval tradition to make that toast sitting down, because in Nelson's day they might have cracked their heads on the low deck beams. From that he rose to make a graceful toast to Halifax and the fond memories his father, George V, kept from his time there on the North Atlantic Station, and how delightful it was to able to meet a few people from Halifax away from the large receptions and crowds that would fill the next day. He concluded by asking them for one more toast, to dear Sir Robert Borden lying forsaken on his bed of pain. "I now intend to visit my patient and conduct his charming lady to his side." Everyone applauded as they left the wardroom.

Lucy glanced at Julia, then at Neville, and raised her eyes as if to say "Heavenly!" and to make a small mime of directing her applause to Julia, who heard Margery say petulantly, "Well, I hope we're going to dance. I chose this dress because it would be perfect for dancing."

"It is perfect, Margery," Stewart said comfortingly. "You look lovely in it."

"Thank you, sir!" Margery dropped an expert curtsy and sat down at the table. Archie gave Julia a benign smile and lifted his glass approvingly.

Susan Gastonguy said, "Did you hear the awful story

about the soldier killing his wife?" That silenced her end of the table. "We were just talking about it. It's in the paper. A sergeant who'd come back from the war beat his wife to death with a blacksmith's hammer. He'd been wounded in the head. His mother said they'd been quarrelling ever since he got back, that he was driven to a frenzy by gossip that while he was overseas his wife had gone out with American sailors. She'd been seen with them having suppers in cafés on Hollis Street. So he killed her with a hammer. Isn't that ghastly?"

Archie said, "Poor devil! I wonder how many chaps came back and found their wives had been straying a bit. I've heard a few stories."

Feeling her face get hot, Julia dared not look at anyone.

Neville said, "Probably the chap's head injury was the reason."

Margery was sulky. "I think that's a terrible story to tell at a party like this. It just spoils everything."

Peter, too far away to have heard the story, looked up at the words "spoils everything" and went around the table to lean over Margery. She wriggled her pretty shoulders crossly to shake him off, exclaiming, "I didn't mean anything!" and Peter retired uneasily to his place.

Stewart emphatically changed the subject. "Harry, it must have been fascinating to be in Paris for the peace conference."

"Oh, I was much too low on the totem pole to get near the actual conference," Harry said. He had a fair, Scottish colouring, and whenever he became the centre of attention, two little pink spots appeared on his cheekbones. "Most of my work was lugging stuff around for the PM. Running errands. Carrying papers about, going back and forth between Paris and the Canadian forces still serving on the

Armistice lines. But yes, it was great after all the horror to be doing something constructive."

"How constructive does Borden think the final result is?" Stewart asked.

"Best that could be achieved with the great powers acting like prima donnas, all grabbing for some territory or advantage. As far as I could tell, Canada was the only nation there not trying to snatch something for itself, in fact refusing a deal to give us the Alaskan panhandle. And the Americans, I suppose, came out with pretty clean hands."

"You mean the moral leadership of mankind isn't a trophy?" Stewart smiled and the others laughed.

Harry said, "President Wilson did put their backs up—especially the Brits and the French—with all his idealistic guff. For weeks our people thought Clemenceau was stalling and dragging things out in hopes that Wilson would pack up and go home, and leave the carving board to those who weren't afraid of blood."

"Which is about what happened, isn't it?" Stewart asked. "That's what I meant by constructive. Is it constructive to humiliate the Germans as thoroughly as we have?"

"Damned right!" Archie said. "Give them a taste of the misery they've inflicted on the world. Let them stew in their own sauerkraut."

Then Neville's voice came in, his accent to Julia sounding coolly musical among the harsher Canadian voices. "No I think Mr. MacPherson's point is a good one. Remember our history. Modern Germany was born when Bismarck humiliated the French and had the Kaiser crowned at Versailles. So the reciprocal gesture, forcing the Germans to come back to the Hall of Mirrors to sign their humiliation, was appropriate, and brilliant theatre for the French. I imagine right-thinking Germans saw the fitness of it. But symbolism aside, the Versailles Treaty is mean-spirited in the extreme and I fear we shall live to regret it."

"I agree," said Stewart. "It's interesting, if you can make an analogy between individuals and nations psychologically, how much humiliation the individual or the nation can stand. We usually know from childhood, from daily life as adults, where we deserve some reprimand, some punishment. But as nations we seem to abandon that sense of proportion, we lose the accurate barometer that tells us when the psychological pressure is unreasonable or dangerous. In Germany's case, we certainly read it incorrectly in 1914, and—"

Neville added, "And now the reparations we are imposing, the territorial annexations, the military restrictions of Versailles go beyond the reasonable to the point of being sadistic."

Stewart said, "When you create resentment, as in a child who feels unjustly or sadistically punished, that will simmer and come out in later behaviour."

Neville asked, "Have you heard about John Maynard Keynes, the economist who represented the Treasury at the peace talks?"

"Yes," said Harry. "He walked out of the British delegation."

"He resigned because he couldn't support the terms," Neville said. "He believes, and I think he makes a strong case—he's a brilliant fellow—simply on economic, not moral grounds, that the reparations will cause economic disaster, not only in Germany but in the world economy."

"Which would support my point," said Stewart.

"Indeed, and mine," said Neville.

To Julia it was sweet to hear Neville and Stewart agreeing in this manner, strengthening each other's arguments. It relieved some of her mounting apprehension that she had betrayed Stewart in her rush to deny they were engaged or would be. She felt that she had skipped a moral step in her haste, that she owed Stewart some easement of his own hopes. However tenuous her understanding with Neville might be, with no question it was what she wanted.

Harry was saying, "We had our own reservations, but Canada could not affect the final result. And you don't sell a difficult treaty to Parliament by dwelling on your reservations."

Neville said, "I saw a statement by a German nobleman the other day. Telling the Americans the reparations would be impossible to fulfill, flat out predicting that Germany would not pay them and would soon be a major power again."

"Well, if they raise their ugly heads again, we'll swat 'em down again!" Archie almost shouted.

Julia remembered sitting perfectly still, in a ladylike way, but feeling that her body was more alive than it had ever been, teeming with sensations, some undeniably sexual, others spiritual, all wrapped in a general mood of extraordinary happiness, a joy so palpable it rose like a lump in her throat and a sweet pain in her breast.

When the prince returned to the party, he said, "I am delighted to report that my patient is in high spirits, vital signs all good, took nourishment, and toasted us all with a little whisky. We are after all afloat on one of His Majesty's ships, Mr. Premier, so your prohibition laws do not touch us here. But Sir Robert sent me back to you with an absolute command—and you know, as a constitutional prince, I never disregard the sage counsel of my ministers! The prime minister urges us to dance, would join us if he were able, and commands us to enjoy ourselves without him. So, let us obey!"

As though he were in his own home, HRH went to the gramophone, apparently brought aboard for his amusement.

A steward had been posted beside it to keep it wound up. The prince selected a record, put it on, and without seeming to notice, unerringly chose the woman with whom protocol required he open the dancing: in Lady Borden's absence, the wife of the lieutenant governor, then Mrs. Murray. That brief duty done, he contented himself with the younger women for the rest of the night, as he'd clearly intended all along.

Julia told Morrice, "As this tour went on, the prince got more and more irked with the tedious and repetitive duties and occasionally neglected the deserving ladies for the more attractive. But this evening, he was still fresh and unjaded, cheerfully doing his duty. Yet you could see hints of a thoroughly self-absorbed and spoiled young man. But I'm probably reading back into that evening a lot of personal feelings, feelings that came later."

"Personal feelings for the prince?" Morrice asked.

"I'll get to that." Well, she thought, I can't tell him all of it. Aloud, she said, "The first time he danced with me, one of several, he said, 'Mrs. Robertson?'"

"Yes, sir?"

"You take this to be a public occasion?"

"I do, sir."

"I wish it were a private one. Perhaps, when you come to England, you will be my guest."

"That would be an honour."

"When is that precisely?"

"Mid-September."

"Oh yes. What a pity! We'll be rattling around Canada and the United States till the end of October, I fear."

"I'll be staying in England, or Europe, I think until Christmas at least."

"Splendid! Then we'll be back and I'll get Neville to fix something up. In the meantime, thousands of things like tomorrow ahead. Daunting prospect. Do you know, they gave a *thé dansant* for me the other day at Rothesay, in New Brunswick. Lieutenant-governor's house. Invited two thousand people! I think I shook the hand of every single one and danced with about five hundred. And that was just one event in the day!"

Morrice said, "All this makes him sound quite human."

"It's hard to separate the aura of his being the Prince of Wales from his charm as a man, which is real. He wasn't as conventionally masculine as Neville, more winsome than handsome. Winsome would sound too feminine for Neville. But being Englishmen of their class, they both have a softness of manner and speech that seem almost feminine and languid when compared to North American men. Don't you find that? Of course there are class differences among Canadian men too."

Morrice said, "I'm not big on Britain. Much happier in France."

Dancing and chatting with the prince, when Julia forgot for a few moments all the embellishments, she was drawn to him. It was nothing like the attraction to Neville, more something she and many people, she came to discover, were reading in David's eyes, in his wistful expression some generational message from the war. She later felt it most strongly in England, where people seemed far more disillusioned than Canadians. Many like Anne, Neville's sister, felt lost. They looked at their class and saw it decimated; they looked at the lower classes and saw unemployment and despair, and their leaders appeared exhausted or indifferent. The Prince of Wales was the only kind of leader they saw expressing the despair they felt, because he was their age and he had been at the war. The crowds saw their pain and their hopes embodied in him. He was the perfect medium, a happy coincidence in time, a king to be, perfectly in tune with his generation. And Julia felt some of that when she danced with him that evening, like dancing with history.

It held every excitement she could wish except that, when she was with David, she wasn't with Neville. In fact, she began to suspect that was somehow arranged and wondered: was Neville required to stand aside for any partner the prince wanted?

HRH did not monopolize her. He danced as often with Susan and Lucy and Margery and he danced tirelessly, almost never stopping. The minute a new record began he had another partner and was off again, leaving the men watching and trying gallantly to partner those the prince discarded. Julia saw Neville twice dancing with Elizabeth Robertson. In between such duties and when Julia was free he danced with her and she was in heaven. She wanted nothing more than to go off with him and be together—married, unmarried, it didn't matter—but alone, and she was almost certain he felt the same, although they had said very little and all obliquely. A lot had to be said because he would be on duty all the next day and sailing off that evening. The party was too small and the wardroom too open to allow them to sit unnoticed and talk alone. So they had to talk while seeming appropriately distant, the conversation direct and pointed.

"Why do you go to Hampshire?" he asked.

"I believe Charles's grave is there—if he is dead."

"If?"

She had changed her mind about raising the story—not wanting to alter the mood—but it gushed out.

He said, "Surely the facts can be tracked down pretty quickly."

"We've been trying. Archie Robertson, my father-in-law, is a friend of Borden's. The PM has ordered an investigation here and in England."

"What about the family you mention in Edinburgh?"

"Well, I've heard nothing and plan to go to Scotland myself."

"They may not be there."

"Surely the post office would have forwarded my letter."

"Apart from casualties in the war, so many people died in the 'flu last year."

"But I must go and find out what I can."

"How very upsetting for you"—they exchanged a long look—"...wanting to get on with your life."

"Especially that."

"I'd like to help you, if I may. Why don't I cable my mother? The war has made her a very effective organizer. She's directly involved with rehabilitation, helping demobbed and disabled soldiers pick up their lives. She'll certainly know how to track down the records of that hospital—where did you say in Hampshire?"

"It's near Andover."

"Just a few miles from us. Scarcely ten miles. You should stay with her and my sister."

They danced without talking for a few bars when he said, "It wouldn't surprise them."

"What do you mean?"

"Because I talked rather a lot about you at home after my last visit."

"And what did you say?"

"You would blush to hear."

"I blush quite easily."

"So I see."

There was excited laughter and applause behind them and they turned to see HRH and Margery Wentworth dancing a frenetic two-step to a very fast tune, Margery in ecstasy, flinging her bare arms in and out, her feet in delicate evening slippers mincing crisply through the steps. Everyone was stopping to watch, laughing, applauding but uneasily because, expert as she was and clearly practised in the steps, Margery looked on the edge of losing control. As Julia glanced over she saw that in Stewart's face, more anxiously in Peter's, in Susan's. The music got faster and Margery's feet and arms flew, the prince slowing down and applauding, as Margery cavorted alone. Then the music stopped, she opened her eyes and collapsed against the prince, exhausted and happy, as she might have leaned against a beau at a local dance. He had to embrace her to keep her from collapsing utterly, so there was Margery, radiant and panting for breath in a close embrace with the Prince of Wales, showing no sign of breaking it up.

HRH smiled indulgently, lifted one arm away, looked around for assistance, and Peter, thoroughly humiliated, came up and took Margery away.

"A marvellous dancer you are, Mrs. Wentworth, and all you charming ladies. You have given us an evening we will treasure—eh, Neville?"

"Indeed, sir."

"Now, I know many of us have a long day tomorrow. Lieutenant governor, Premier Murray, you have corner-stones to lay, speeches to make, and all that. Perhaps we should slip away now so we'll all be fresh for the morning." He went to each guest to thank them for coming and said to Julia very sincerely, "Do follow up with Neville, as I suggested. We'd be delighted to see you in England."

"Thank you, sir." She began to curtsy.

"No curtsies this time of night," and he moved on.

Neville said, "I'll see you into the launch." On the way—
she didn't need to tell Morrice all this—he turned back to
Julia. "Are you travelling with Mr. MacPherson, or not travelling with him, all your time abroad?"

"Some time together and some not. He wants to go to
Germany for a time."

"So, you might be unaccompanied in England some of
the time?"

"I can arrange it that way."

"I should like that very much."

"So would I. Very much."

"I'll be in touch when I have heard from my mother."

It sounded too sappy to tell Morrice that when they came
to a bend in the corridor leading to the deck, he had turned
again and said, "I would very much like to kiss you," and she
had whispered, "I would love you to," just when they heard
the others immediately behind them and moved on.

Aloud she said, "When Neville and the Prince of Wales
were together, someone knowing nothing might have
thought Neville the heir to the throne because of the set of
his head, the confident smile contrasted so vividly with the
shy, more diffident, apologetic look of the prince."

She had wanted to make love with Neville from her first
sight of him in a bathing costume in 1917 at the Saraguay.
The attraction was instant. It was fun to imagine some real-
ist, like a modern Bruegel, in meticulous detail rendering
that Sunday tea on the club lawn, blazers and flannels, chaste
dresses and parasols, the boats passing at the foot of the lawn,
a lady pouring tea from a large Spode pot, and in a corner

of the panorama a feverish couple, he dark, she blonde, her long skirts up, his flannels down, going at it; the rest as in Bruegel, paying no attention, passing teacups and dainty sandwiches, and the shadows of the setting Edwardian sun—setting later in Canada than in England—not quite touching the modern couple upsetting all the nice conventions as they edge into the twentieth century.

"And so what happened?" Morrice asked.

"I could not prevent myself from falling in love with him."

"So he remains the hero of the story?"

"I'm just exhausted from talking now." She put on her robe.

"And I want to stop." In fact he was already cleaning his brushes.

She paused at the easel on her way to change. The background had been washed in, using different pale colours. The figure remained bare canvas outlined in graphite.

"It looks intriguing like that."

"The serious work begins tomorrow morning," Morrice said.

When the bathroom door was closed he was more aware than he wanted to be of the sounds of her dressing. He had assumed his interest in her was purely as the subject for this painting, in fact its inspiration. The inspiration was still strong. He knew this painting would be bolder, simpler and more confident than any figure he had done. But between her divine body and her appetite for life, she was distracting him. That was it. Tomorrow he would ask her to be silent.

"I need a drink and some lunch," he said when she came out. "Will you join me? I'd like to hear more of your story."

"I keep meaning to summarize and then I start remembering details."

When they were outside the hotel, she said, "Would you mind if we had a short stroll first, by the sea? The air is so lovely, I'd like to drink it."

"You drink the air, I'll drink a whisky. When you feel like coming back, we'll have some lunch. How is that?"

"The walk would be better for you."

"Now!" He wagged his finger in front of his nose. "No Montreal moralizing, remember?"

13

This was the first morning Julia had not been sick. Perhaps the little anxiety about posing nude had distracted her. The actual posing disconcerted her for about two minutes, then it was devoid of emotion, like seeing a doctor—well, less: she still had that ahead of her. Morrice had made it entirely impersonal. And he seemed a new man, lively and excited by the work.

Even out here breathing the fresh sea air, the smell of oil, turpentine, and varnish lingered in her imagination. Yesterday he had told her, don't think, just paint, and the words had created an instant desire to do just that: push aside all her anxieties and hide here in Nice and paint, with Morrice available for expert advice. Perhaps he would paint with her, as he once had in the past. He was right. She should stop worrying whether she was good and just do it because she loved it, precisely because painting was so effective in taking her mind off other things.

She should go back to the café soon, before one drink turned into two or three.

But the story she'd been telling him was also nagging at her. The modern woman had mustered about as much resistance to Neville as a feather in the wind. And the way she had treated Stewart...

Even with the glow of that evening still warm in her heart, she'd had to confront what to tell Stewart and could not in good conscience postpone it. Even at this distance it made her heart ache again.

All was fine as the dinner guests came off together in the *Renown*'s launch, the excitement of the evening, the graciousness and warmth of the prince animating everyone. Now that they were out of his earshot, the men exclaimed how human and unaffected he was, what a good fellow, down to earth, breath of fresh air, damned good thing for the monarchy in these restive times, keep us from the revolutionary turmoil in other countries—phrases like that from the premier, the lieutenant governor, and Archie. And the women, young and old, sighed about his extraordinary good looks, his charm, his grace as a dancer, the fit of his evening clothes, what thoughtful things he had said to each, how sweet he had been to the PM and Laura Borden. Stewart was near Julia, she assumed smiling (the dark cabin was lit by occasional passing lights) but silent. Ashore at the dockyard they said good night to the others and got into Stewart's car with Harold and Lucy. Lucy bubbled all the way to their house, said she was too excited to go to bed, they must come in and have something to cap off the night. With the PM out of action for the official events, Harry said he wouldn't have to be on duty at the crack of dawn. It was also Lucy's way of acknowledging Stewart as Julia's escort, even though she must have sensed the electricity with Neville.

"What on earth do we drink to finish such a night as this? Harry, we must have a bottle of champagne downstairs. Daddy's always putting things in your wine cupboard when I'm not looking. There may even be some from before the war. I certainly haven't been drinking it, have I, Julia? She'll tell you. A sip of sherry on a cold night to keep the home fires burning. Harry please go and look!" She couldn't sit down in her excitement.

Julia said to Stewart, "You haven't said what you thought of our future king, when we were all chattering on the boat."

Stewart smiled through his spectacles and sat. "May I sit down? I'm exhausted from watching you all dance."

"Well, you took a few turns yourself," Lucy said. "It was like old times, at the dances when we were young." Not until then did it dawn on Julia that she had danced with Stewart only once the entire evening and had not noticed until this moment, with Lucy chattering on. "I like us both better now, Stewart. When we were children racing around, I think I was tougher than you were."

"You were—and faster and braver, a better tree climber—"

"All the demure, ladylike qualities mother despaired of my ever acquiring. Anyway, thank God, the grown-ups we've become are not the children we were! Or perhaps Julia is, gorgeous then, probably, and gorgeous now." Lucy, who had finally plopped down on a sofa, was a little tipsy. It made her even chattier than usual but it kept all eyes on her.

"—certainly the belle of the ball tonight, eh, Stewart? I lost count of how many times Prince Charming danced with Julia. Was it five—or six?"

"Now, Lucy, three or four, I think."

"Five or six, it seemed to me. He did his nice duty number once with me." She imitated HRH's accent. "'Are you originally from Halifax, Mrs. Traverse?' 'Oh yes, sir. A Haligonian, I am.' 'A Haligonian, you say? That's a new one to me.' 'That's what we call ourselves, sir.' 'Do you, indeed? I must remember that tomorrow when I'm greeting so many of your fellow Haligonians. Have you tried the Charleston, Mrs. Traverse?' 'No, sir. You can tell I'm not the world's niftiest dancer.'"

"You didn't say *niftiest* to him, Lucy!" Harold had returned with a bottle.

"I did. He liked it. He laughed and said, 'I must remember that. Niftiest. An American expression, is it?' 'No, sir,' I said, 'I think it's just the superlative of nifty. Nifty, niftier, niftiest!'" Lucy collapsed in giggles.

"I don't think you need another drop, my dear," Harry said. "Pity, because you were right. There's terrific stuff down there, hiding from the liquor police." He popped open the champagne and poured.

"Let's have a toast. What shall it be?"

"God bless the Prince of Wales!" said Lucy, jumping up. "And long may he reign over us, happy and glorious. He's the niftiest prince I've ever met—and of course the only one. But God bless him anyway, I say!"

She made them all laugh. And Stewart said, "You can't help liking the fellow. Think of keeping up that pleasant manner day after day, all the rest of his life. How awful! The energy it must take, just a small party like tonight's, being polite and interested in everyone."

"But he's born to it," Lucy said. "Ever since he was a little boy, they've been teaching him how to say"—and again she imitated him wonderfully—"'Are you originally from Halifax, Mrs. Traverse?'" and she dissolved into giggles again.

Julia said, "I think he was really enjoying himself this evening."

"Certainly with you!" Lucy said.

"Oh, come on, Lucy! He was with everybody. He was having fun. Wasn't that the point of the invitation? So that he could relax outside all the grinding stuff he has to do tomorrow?"

When they got into Stewart's car, she took a deep breath before saying, "Stewart. The only honest thing is to tell you right now. I know I'm in love with him."

He was silent for a moment, then gave a little grunting laugh.

"I don't suppose you mean Prince Charming?"

"I don't. I mean Neville."

"It's Neville, is it?"

"Yes. That's as direct as I can be."

"Of course, I expected it." And he started the engine. "And it was obvious enough tonight."

"Obvious? I hope not."

"Obvious to me because like any jealous fool I was looking for every hint of what I didn't want to see."

"My dear." She turned to him. "You are no fool."

"Jealous, though." He gave that little laugh again, half grunt, half chuckle. "Painfully, I must admit."

"I'm sorry to do this to you."

He turned to her and his spectacles reflected lights so that she couldn't see his eyes. "He's a deeper fellow than I imagined. Intelligent—as well as everything else."

When he stopped at her house and got out as usual to open the car door, she kissed him, which she had never wanted to do at her front door. She didn't care if Mollie was watching.

She had always acted impetuously and considered the consequences later. She went to bed that night, too keyed up to sleep for a long time, fluctuating between imagining being with Neville and fearing she had just dismissed the man whose loyalty and kindness had been assured for one who excited her but whose character she could only guess at.

She had reached the Nice casino and turned to go back. It wasn't fair to keep Morrice. She could walk after lunch.

She and Stewart had each thought about it for a few days and then met to decide about the travel arrangements. Oddly Julia felt no embarrassment at the prospect of being with him now, because she had nothing to hide.

"I suppose, skilled rationalizer that I am, it is better to have aspired and failed than to have achieved and be dismissed. I just hope this fellow is as fulfilling for you as you wish."

"But, Stewart, this frees you to look for someone else to make you happy."

"Right." He laughed. "In the meantime I will go as your undefined fellow traveller, at least as far as Southampton, and we'll improvise from there."

Too clever to play the hangdog disappointed lover, Stewart was as stimulating a companion as ever, and Julia did not have to feign a quality of affection or a physical ardour she did not share. They could avoid coy negotiations about visiting his cabin or hers. She could be with him exactly what she wanted to be, and he played his role delightfully. So she had a good time at sea, and so he appeared to: walking on deck, having meals with her, and returning to his—he had been quite right—distant cabin.

Once Stewart asked, "How did you explain me to Boiscoyne? I mean, you had me invited to the dinner."

"Yes, and he knows we're travelling together—as friends."

"And?"

"And not engaged to be married."

"A little ambiguous, surely?"

"Not in the way I said it to him."

In London, they had parted at Victoria Station, promising

to reconnect for their planned tour of the Western Front battlefields. After depositing her heavy luggage at her London hotel, Julia took the overnight train to Edinburgh.

14

Julia found Morrice in the café, to her surprise with only one drink saucer on his table, and he looked happy to see her back.

"I was getting hungry. Do you like bouillabaisse?"

"I love it and I'm starved."

"There's a small restaurant along here where they specialize—bouillabaisse, bourride, grilled fish, anything you like from the sea."

"Fine, but this must be my lunch. I haven't paid for anything."

"I didn't want to take advantage of a woman in your condition." He was jollier than she had seen him and she had not seen his hand shake today.

She wondered how they looked walking together, the bald, dapper little man and she much taller, trying to match his shorter stride. The *patron* of La Bouillabaisse greeted Morrice like a favoured regular and said, "The usual? A Pernod?"

"Thank you, I have just had a Pernod,"—he smiled at Julia—"one Pernod to tune my palate for your superb bouillabaise. It's fresh today?"

"It is fresh every day." The fat owner said to Julia, "He knows that but he asks each time. Bouillabaisse for mademoiselle, also?"

"And a bottle of your Côtes de Provence."

Above the dark wainscotting the upper walls sported

primitive paintings of men in fishing boats, hauling nets, and women in the fish market selling the catch from large wicker baskets.

"The modern movement has not overtaken all local art," Morrice said and then pointed to the shadowy rear wall, "except for that." Even in the dimmer light, she recognized the vibrant colours of an early Matisse.

"Fishing boats. One of dozens he did around the port at Collioure, with Derain. Before the Fauvist show in 1905. He gave them one."

"Why do they hide it back there?"

"Because the *patron* thinks it's garish, *trop voyant*, but he knows Matisse is becoming famous, so..."

"Why don't you give them a painting to hang if you come here a lot?"

"I don't do that much. My Scottish background maybe. I try to sell paintings and sell them well, for a good price. I don't even bargain. I set a price, say $700, and I stick to it. Drives the dealers mad when I won't be jewed down—"

Julia felt a reflexive wince at *jewed*. She had used it— it was common at home—but Stewart had protested. "There's enough anti-Semitism around without adding to it." Interesting that what Stewart said stuck like this.

"But you gave me one, my first portrait—"

"And I've promised you this one. I give to people I like and I give to other painters. And you are a painter."

"If you say so."

"But I hate to sell to people who I know have the money but, because it's just art, think it's a game to bid me down."

"Seven hundred dollars is a lot of money. You can buy a car for that."

"The car will wear out in a few years and my painting

won't. It will become more valuable as more people come to appreciate it. Matisse even more so."

"When is he coming back to Nice?"

"He said a few days. He's gone to see his wife and children in Paris."

"He lives apart from them now?"

"He feels he has to be free from distraction, at least that distraction."

The steaming bouillabaisse arrived bristling with pieces of lobster and other fish. They ate the fish first, drinking the crisp rosé, then spread the pungent *rouille* on toasted bread and stirred it in before eating the soup. At last Morrice removed the checked napkin from his collar and wiped his beard and moustache.

"While you were walking, I was thinking of what you said—yesterday was it?—about living in the modern way, being a modern woman."

"It must have sounded pretty lame, considering...what you know."

"No. It sounded fine. I approve. You should have the right to be as independent as I am. We're both fortunate to have families able, and willing, to support us. I assume you're all right financially, if that's not too personal?"

"Not at all. I'm fine financially. My father gave me some money, which produces an income. Charles's parents insist that I take his estate. And there's a house. No, financially I'm quite independent."

"So, like me, you can live as you choose. But you do have to choose. It's like modern painting. There is no right way anymore. There is no modern style. Modern means everyone searching for a style, each artist in his own career, continuing to search."

"Well, you're right," Julia said, "I am searching for a style of living, and not very successfully so far."

"This baby you are expecting will determine that to some extent. Excuse my bluntness, but do you intend to keep it?"

The direct question took her aback. "I am still considering what to do."

"If not having it is one of the possible options, of course, you cannot consider for too long."

"I understand."

"I am sure, perhaps you are hesitant to ask, but I am sure that option could be explored."

"Here, in Nice?"

"I don't know. I would have to ask."

"You'd ask Léa?"

He looked embarrassed. "She might have heard. You know, women talk. I can ask her, if you wish."

"No. Not yet. I want a few more days to think."

"And then, besides, if you give birth to the child, people can be found to adopt it."

Julia looked at him and wondered whether he might tell her about Léa's child, if there were such a child, if it were his, but there was no sign of it in his blue eyes.

She said, "I have some things to think through before making any decision. But it's kind of you to talk about it with me. You and Léa—and a friend in Paris—are the only people who know and I want to keep it that way for now."

"Is the friend in Paris—?"

She caught an implication in his tone and said, "A woman. I'll tell you about her."

"And the father?"

"He doesn't know." The way she said that discouraged Morrice from pursuing it. Instead, he said, "You didn't tell me what happened after the dinner with the prince."

"I had to tell Stewart I was in love with Neville."

"That was very direct and honest of you. How did he take that?"

"He took it very well. We still travelled together, that is on the same ship, to England."

Morrice said, "This Stewart must be a remarkably easy-going fellow—or else he suffers abominably."

She looked distressed. "I was concerned about him suffering. But he did take it very well."

"And when you arrived in England?"

"We separated and I went to Scotland."

She told him about the sad experience of finding the other Robertson family. Fresh off the train in Edinburgh, after putting her overnight bag in a hotel, she had set out by taxi to the address she had written to.

"And all the way I had this gnawing feeling in the pit of my stomach that I was going to find out something awful."

It was in a handsome but severe street of stone-terraced houses, respectable but shabby. A woman who answered the door said the Robertsons had moved but did not know a forwarding address. In the adjoining houses one family was newly arrived, the other door did not answer.

Julia asked for the nearest post office and found it after a long, chilly walk in the rain, her umbrella hard to control in the gusting, icy wind.

At the post office the man in charge listened to her story. Julia showed him some of the effects she was trying to deliver.

"It's a kind thing you're doing, to come such a long way." He found a file of mail-forwarding forms and went through it slowly as her umbrella dripped on the floor at his desk.

"I'm afraid they moved a long way for you, Mrs.

Robertson. Care of A. C. MacLeod, a street in Oban. Do you know where that is now?"

On a wall map he showed her the town on the west coast of Scotland and copied out the address.

"Of course, we could send the parcel, to save you the journey."

"I prefer to take it myself...to make sure."

For days she'd been rehearsing kind things to say to this widow—if that she was. Disappointed, she had to retreat to the gloomy hotel and have them book a ticket through Glasgow to Oban the next day. The weather was too wet for sightseeing so she had sat in the over-plush lounge, later in the dining room, seeing people coming and going, but off in a strange reverie unconnected to these surroundings.

On board *Aquitania* she had received a cable—in itself an excitement—from Neville's mother. "It would give us great pleasure to have you come and stay with us while you conduct your melancholy researches, in which my daughter and I would be eager to help." It was signed "Stephanie Boiscoyne," rather a girlish name for a woman Julia imagined to be a doughty and grand lady. But there was nothing else to judge by, no writing paper or hand-writing, merely the pasted words on the ship's cable form. Which left her to ruminate about her phrase "your melan-choly researches," which seemed endearing and full of personality.

There had been an earlier cable in Halifax, from Quebec City, in which Neville said he had contacted his mother and that Julia could expect to hear from her. His message concluded, "Greatly anticipate meeting in England late autumn. Neville." On these terse messages and a few hasty notes since, Julia had been constructing elaborate fantasies of a future life. Except in gothic novels, a man didn't invite a woman to stay with his mother and sister if he were up to no good. At least that was the gospel preached by the excitable Lucy. All Julia had known of Neville was from one tea and swimming party two summers before, and one ball at Government House where she had been so warmly attracted to him that she had taken the train to Montreal to remove herself from temptation. The whole matter had then lain dormant until his note inviting her to the prince's dinner, into which she had read volumes of secondary meaning while swearing she was not, but which seemed to be valid when she met him again and he appeared as smitten as she. On the strength of these brief encounters, she was now going to stay with his mother? Either quaintly Victorian behaviour—no, pre-Victorian, more Jane Austen—or something very modern and ruthless, perhaps, proposed in such an elegant manner.

Sitting in that dark-panelled Edinburgh dining room, with rain lashing the windows, her imagination stimulated by the eerie displacements of travel, she had to laugh because the image forming in her mind was of Jane Eyre setting out to be governess for the grim Mr. Rochester. She knew nothing about Neville's family, although everyone kept telling her it must be very grand. Stewart, always ironic but always practical, said, "An Englishwoman would rush for *Debrett's* and check the pedigree."

Julia had laughed. "You make it sound like horses."

"Well, the English take it almost as seriously. And if you're serious about him, you may end up bearing his children, so the breeding lines might be interesting. Not something we do in Canada, or we do it less overtly, I suppose. No *Debrett's* to make it easy for us."

Morrice noticed how often Stewart's name recurred. He also saw that the wine bottle was empty—and she had drunk only a glass.

"What would you like?"

"Oh, nothing, thanks. I'll get too sleepy."

"One Armagnac," he told the waiter.

Julia had felt her cheeks warming at the reference to having children. The assumption leaped over many others she was not prepared to acknowledge. She'd said a little testily to Stewart, "You're thinking a lot farther ahead than I am." And he had covered his own feelings with another laugh. "Well, someone has to do the thinking if you're lost in this fog of romance." Which wasn't far from the truth.

She asked Morrice, "Do you think I could have some coffee? Anyway, by late the next day I was in a very simple hotel in Oban. It's a small town built around a fishing port and a harbour for steamers. At breakfast, they fed me porridge!"

The weather was cheerful and warmer. She found the address, a small house of two floors in a meaner street than the Edinburgh address, and ran into the major's widow on the doorstep. She was coming from a shop with a full basket, wearing a pinny over a housedress and quite put out to see Julia, so prosperously dressed, at her door.

When Julia explained, she quickly whisked her inside and to a chair in the tiny front parlour. It was chilly even on this fine September day. She left to put away her shopping and came back without her pinafore, bringing tea and some biscuits. A child was crying in the back of the house, a nervous, unsettling cry. Julia noticed a cabbage-y cooking smell. The furnishings looked worn, the woman so careworn herself that Julia couldn't tell whether she was forty or sixty.

She wore no wedding ring. Her hands were red from house-work. Her name, oddly enough, was Elizabeth.

"That's the name of my husband's mother. Elizabeth Robertson. In Halifax. Nova Scotia."

"Where you wrote me from."

Julia noticed that her eyelids were red, which drew attention to quite red, carroty eyelashes.

"I'm sorry I didn't answer you. I put your letter in the kitchen and I've looked at it meaning to write but just haven't brought myself to it. There's always so much to do."

"Do you have children?"

"Aye. There's mine. They're at school. Then there's my sister's children. She went, poor thing, in the winter after the Armistice. In the 'flu that took so many."

"So you keep house for her husband?"

She met Julia's eyes at what the question suggested and then looked away. "I had nothing else to go on. Me and my children."

"Your husband—?"

"Took off with some woman from down south, in England. All I knew was when he was killed. A note in the papers. He must have given her as next of kin. I've never seen a penny of any pension money or allowances. So I can't be any help to you. I'm sorry about your husband. I suppose you loved him. You're still young enough." The way she said it suggested, *And silly enough!*

"We were married only a year when Charles went overseas."

"That's a shame. The war's taken a lot of good men and some...In your letter you asked if I'd received anything about your husband? Nothing. I'm sorry."

"I brought you the package I found of your late husband's things."

She stared at it. "Is there money in it?"

"Nothing to speak of. A few French coins."

"Then, as far as I'm concerned, you can take it and toss it into the sea out there. It'd do me as much good."

The voice of the crying child grew more frantic and she turned towards it.

"I'm keeping you from your work."

"Oh, he'll be all right for a little." She inspected Julia with a not unfriendly eye, her clothes, hat, and bag.

"It's cost you a pretty penny to come all the way here. Across the ocean and all. Most people around here think about going your way to make a new life in Canada. They say there's better chances there. Is that true?"

"I believe it is, generally. Though right now, with all the soldiers coming back, many people can't find work. If you like, I know where you could write to ask."

"I don't know. It's probably too late for him. Getting too old to make a move like that."

"I can write down the name and address of people who might know. Why don't I do that and mail it to you?" Julia got up to leave. The woman didn't reply but came to the door, shaking hands, her depressed eyes once again taking in everything in Julia's appearance. She didn't need to say anything. Clearly she was thinking, *She'll be all right. With her youth and her money, no need to feel sorry for her.*

Julia could imagine her when she had left, calculating the money she must have spent just to make the journey from London. She felt so uncomfortable about it that she posted her a note from the hotel giving Archie Robertson's address.

Morrice put down his Armagnac glass. "So, a dead end there regarding Charles."

"Yes but there's a lot more I learned after that. Believe it or not, with Neville's mother. She turned out to be—" She could not stop a huge yawn. "Oh, I'm sorry. All of a sudden I'm so sleepy I could curl up on this banquette."

"Go ahead. They won't mind."

"Oh, I couldn't!"

"The restaurant is empty."

She yawned again.

"Lie down. I'll have a word with the *patron*."

She couldn't resist. The lethargy was more powerful than any embarrassment and she stretched out. She heard Morrice murmuring. Was he saying that she was pregnant? She didn't care. It was so delicious to lie down for a moment.

Morrice tiptoed back with a fresh Armagnac and sat quietly at the table. He watched her sleeping, occasionally glancing up at the shadows of people passing the drawn curtains in the restaurant window, then looking down. Her face would be interesting to paint in this light, long eyelashes closed, the cheek facing him flushed with a pink like that he'd used often; it had become one of his trademarks. In the early nineties he'd found that pink in blanching down the palest rose madder while painting in the country on the banks of the Seine. *Sur les bords de la Seine*, olive-green grey in the old arched bridge, a tinge of pink in the sky and reflected in the river. Much heavier impasto than he used now. The American he'd met at the Julian, Maurice Prendergast, had said, "Now you're making your own style." They'd painted in Normandy that summer but Prendergast preferred Paris and Morrice had followed. Landscape painting did not have to mean bucolic. Apply the values of the landscape painter to the vibrant city life, with its reflections off the wet pavements and the rattling carriages, horse-drawn omnibuses, teeming cafés, and women in the soaring hats of the nineties, like ships in full sail on the boulevards.

Le bruit des cabarets, la fange des trottoirs...

How often his Verlaine, memorized from constant reading, expressed what he felt—

The noise of cabarets, the sidewalk's mire,
sycamores shedding leaves in the black air;
the omnibus, ill-hung on four wheels, rattles
and creaks, a storm of mud and old scrap metal,
rolling its red and green eyes as it goes...

One of his most successful early paintings was *The Omnibus*, expressing all the atmosphere of the poem on a cold, rainy night, the glowing café lights in the background, the rain-swept effect on the pavement under the horses' feet achieved by using both glaze and varnish...1896, when this girl must have been five or six.

How strange it was to be looking down at the daughter of his conventional friend Norman Montgomery, this quite unconventional daughter, whom he had seen that morning as a naked subject. And, unsettlingly, seen as a woman. As she lay fully clothed he remembered the flesh underneath. His eye was so experienced that he had already registered the delicately varied tones he would probably use here and there when he began to apply the paint tomorrow. If she left tonight and he had to paint without seeing her again, he could do it. But not as well. And this time he was going to do it very well. A turning point. He wished that the nerve transmitters in his fingertips were not telling his brain what those lean thighs would feel like. Or that his brain were not listening, but it was, or the part of the brain where sex arises

The drinking had taken a toll there as in everything else. His hand was shaking again as he lowered the Armagnac from his lips and silently signalled for another. After the operation for ulcers in the colon, the doctor had warned him. Later at Évian-les-Bains on Lac Léman, they had flushed out his kidneys and liver for weeks and new doctors had uttered new warnings. Unless you moderate your habits, take less distilled alcohol and drink wine instead, eat sensibly and take some exercise, your system will not last two or three years.

When they were younger and stayed out late in a café, Léa, the most good-natured of women, would sit with him as he got drunker, pleading nicely, jollying him along, never nagging, cajoling, "Just one, *chérie*, and we'll go home." Sometimes she would have said that six or seven times before she got him on his feet. Even then, at that age, when he fell into Léa's generous embrace, glory shone around. That glory was largely a spent force now, yet here were its faint signals coming back at the sight of Julia's breast under her white blouse, where the weight of her sleeping arm compressed it.

He put his fingers to his lips as the *patron* exchanged a full glass for the empty and leered as though he knew precisely where Morrice's thoughts had been.

And Morrice knew now what provoked the attraction, had known it in his bones but now it came floating up into his cloudy consciousness. She was one of his kind, the class, the attitudes, the collective taste he had grown up with and could not wait to leave behind. The girls, like Heather, Julia's mother, he'd known since childhood in Montreal were clean, rosy, blushing, straight-limbed; all wore pretty clothes, bathed frequently, had glossy hair and even teeth, and had aroused a strange ambivalence in him. He imagined intimacies with them, held them at Christmas dances, pushed them squealing into snowbanks during nighttime sleigh-ride parties, but had never become involved with any. Never got further than kisses glancing off averted Anglican lips and hands pushed away from Presbyterian legs, because the only way of going further was to marry one of them and the last thing he wanted was to be tied to someone like Heather Montgomery, practising law, which he'd have had to do to support her. It had taken Paris to give him guilt-less sexual release. The sleeping Julia reminded him of his unsatisfied yearnings at fifteen or sixteen for the girls he had affected to ignore. She was a woman like them, but frank and open, unashamed of her appetite for life. Had he possibly missed some signal from her when he painted her as a girl? A girl, because it was before she was married. Perhaps she had been telling him something in her eagerness to pose then. And perhaps not. He was slipping into the worst clichés about artists and their models.

He was gazing at her when Julia suddenly opened her eyes and sat up, her face now a darker rose from sleep, and shook her head.

"Oh, forgive me! How embarrassing. I am so sorry."

"No need. Do you feel better?"

"I feel—oh my God, you're not going to believe this, I'm hungry again! That huge lunch and I'm starved. You don't suppose they'd have something delicious for dessert?"

She ordered an ice flavoured with star anise, its odour

tantalizing him with echoes of absinthe. She was fully refreshed from her short sleep, still with a crease across one cheek from sleeping on it, her golden hair beginning to unpin itself, escaping from its topknot. Utterly charmed, Morrice watched her through eyes pleasantly beclouded from wine and Armagnac, thinking of Verlaine—

Et les soucis que vous pouvez avoir—

And the small cares you have are like the play
of swallows, my dear, in the lovely heaven
of afternoon, on a warm September day.

Doubtless not small cares to her, but to him they seemed innocent and manageable.

"Goodness, how late it must be! Shouldn't we be going?"

"No hurry. Your friend Stewart, what is he doing all this time in Europe?"

Why did he want to know about Stewart, she wondered. "He is a professor of psychology, I think I told you. He was working with soldiers suffering from shell shock. They got brutal treatment from the army. He was trying to help them with more enlightened methods. Then after the Halifax explosion, he wondered whether civilians suffered the same trauma if they're exposed to catastrophic events. He's calling it 'aftershock.' He's working on a paper. Is shell shock not just a military condition? What makes one person, one man in battle, susceptible and not another? So he's going around to see what they are doing in England, France, and Germany."

"Do you think that is important to do?"

She flared up a little. "It's very important! Do you remember my cousin, Jeffrey, the son of Daddy's younger brother,

Arthur? He and his wife were killed by an avalanche in Switzerland when Jeffrey was nine. In the war, Jeffrey joined up. He was an infantry officer in France and he was shell shocked. He couldn't function. He was court-martialled for cowardice. They were actually going to shoot him but sent him back to Canada to prison. I saw him there, an utterly broken man. Anyway, Stewart used his connections to get Jeffrey released and treated by a psychiatrist. He's much better and he's working in Daddy's company."

"Stewart sounds like a useful fellow to know. And kind."

"Very kind."

"Are you going to tell him about the baby?"

"I don't know...I suppose I'll have to, eventually."

"He might be helpful."

"It's a little awkward...under the circumstances."

"Of course. But he sounds very fond of you."

"There may be limits, even to that." Her little ironic laugh was pretty to see. She ran the spoon around the dish for a last drop of melted anise ice and licked it.

"I saw the war paintings when the exhibition was in Montreal. But I didn't see yours."

"I wasn't happy with it. But I felt I needed to do something. The whole experience depressed me."

"Did you see the exhibition when it was in London?"

"No, I didn't send my painting and I couldn't work up the interest to go over."

"Harry went with Borden when he opened the exhibition. The PM said some of the pictures were so modern and advanced that he couldn't understand them or appreciate them."

Morrice laughed. "I gave up a long time ago trying to improve Canadian taste."

"It was on in Montreal when I went up to say goodbye to Mother and Daddy. In fact Daddy came to the exhibition with me and we had quite different reactions. He thought it was brilliant. He was really moved. He thought they depicted a fierce truth. It made him very proud of what Canada had done."

"Exactly what Beaverbrook and the others wanted him to feel. But you?"

"It disturbed me. The paintings were fine—you know all of the artists, Cullen, Jefferys, Jackson, Varley—all highly competent, and they conveyed an experience most of us could not know. But did they convey it more tellingly than the photographs I had seen? No. The photographs appall me more because they are so matter of fact, laconic, in showing horrors we had never imagined our civilization capable of. I felt the paintings distanced me from the horror by making it beautiful, aesthetically pleasing, another human experience to be rendered by traditional respect for balance, form, colour—all the painterly values."

Morrice seemed to come freshly alive. "That is why so few European artists attempted to paint the war directly. Some of them were conscripted—Derain, Braque, and Léger. Matisse was too old but I think—you can ask him this—he felt instinctively what you're saying and so did I. It's a good observation. If we depict behaviour that breaks all moral conventions in a conventional way, are we not comforting ourselves by saying that what happened was comprehensible? That it occurred within a cultural frame we knew before and will still be the frame through which we see our culture in the future? But long before the war many artists in Europe had abandoned that cultural frame, cast it aside as irrelevant, as distorting to modern perceptions of reality, outdated, giving viewers a false sense of continuity with the past."

If she could keep him talking like this, perhaps he'd forget that his glass was empty.

She said, "Something else. The Canadian war paintings were full of mood, but they were so literal. There was something missing. And it struck me when I was looking at one by Stanley Turner. It shows civilians in Toronto staring at disabled soldiers as if they were beings from another planet. It was one of the few I can recall that expressed any irony about the war. Perhaps one or two by Varley. Everywhere at home I was hearing that oh yes, our losses were terrible but still the war was positive for Canada. Daddy feels it, Archie does, and Harry, and the smug writers of all the "glory" editorials. It cost us a lot but now we can hold our heads up among nations, especially to Britain. We showed them. Canada had only eight million people but we put more than half-a-million men in the field, one soldier for every sixteen Canadians.

"And I would say, 'But Harry—sixty thousand Canadians died!' And he said, 'We got a lot for it. We got a voice in the running of the Empire. Borden says it gave us a new stage in our nationhood. He fought Britain and the United States for a place at the peace conference table. He fought them for Canadian membership in the League of Nations.' What was missing in these paintings, I felt, was the other side that Charles expressed in the last letters to me: the gross immorality of the fighting, using men by the thousands to make points that could have been made in another manner. And refusing to negotiate in the last year. But, I suppose, that is how women have always looked at war."

"Tell me more about Charles, what you've found out?"

"I will, but do you mind if we move? I'm stiff from sitting on this banquette. I'd love to walk a little before it gets dark. But remember, this was my treat." She quickly called to the *patron*, "*Monsieur, s'il vous plaît, l'addition!*"

She paid, noting on the bill that he had drunk five Armagnacs and yet showed virtually no sign of it. He surprised her by suggesting the château gardens more than half a mile away as a destination.

"We can walk up there and look down into the port. If you get tired we can take a cab back."

"I'm not tired now."

The late afternoon sun was warm on the promenade as they passed other strollers, elegantly dressed, the women with parasols, the men swinging canes. Morrice lit one of the small cigars that he alternated with pipes of pungent French tobacco.

Julia strolled without talking for a time, basking in the warmth and beauty of the sea lapping gently on the pebbled beach. She debated how much to say about Stephanie Boiscoyne and decided there was really nothing to hold back now.

15

Whatever Julia had imagined Neville's mother to be, probably something approaching Queen Mary in dignity, Stephanie Boiscoyne contradicted. Julia couldn't quite believe her at first. She was standing at the barrier in the tiny train station, tall and odd looking, wearing a motoring duster coat and an absurd hat tied with a scarf under her chin. And she swept Julia up.

"Obviously you are Julia Robertson, so let me look at you! Well, I don't think that Neville exaggerated at all. You've probably noticed that he has a pretty way with words—so did his father—but about you, he outdid himself singing your praises."

She was tall, angular, and jolly, and when she laughed she showed long teeth with signs of elaborate bridge-work. She said she had arthritic knees and ankle joints, to explain why she walked so strangely: an unusual gliding way to ease the discomfort. Her knuckle joints were swollen and looked painful but she exuded absolute confidence in appearing to face the world entirely on her terms. Most surprising was the car she drove.

"I hope you don't mind an open car. It's my beautiful toy and I drive it every chance I get. I have a coat for you."

She was driving a sports car, a Hispano-Suiza, pale cream with brass fittings, very dashing, and quite astonishing for a woman of her age and position. She said, "This model was a favourite with the fighter pilots in the war. Have you noticed they're all photographed with their Hispanos?"

"I know very little about cars."

"It'll go seventy-five miles an hour!"

"And do you go that fast?"

"Whenever I get the chance, my dear!"

And she did. She forced her long legs into its cockpit, but once she was in, forgot any discomfort, zooming off as fast as she could go, the wind rushing past, as though they were flying. She shouted above the noise, "I am sorely tempted. Hispano have just shown a fabulous new model in Paris. They say it can go ninety and it has a beautiful wooden body. I am dying to see one. I hear you are going to Paris. Perhaps you'd let me come, and you could negotiate with the slippery Frenchmen. Anne, my daughter, thinks I am out of my mind. But I love it. And why shouldn't I do what I love if it doesn't hurt anyone? Besides, I do a few good things to balance it out. Pleasure and duty should be in balance— don't you think?"

"Did I understand you to say your husband is dead?"

"Oh no, but he's not been well for a long time. Didn't Neville tell you anything about us?"

"There wasn't much chance."

"Well, all in good time. The main thing is to make you comfortable and then plan how to solve your problem. May I express my deepest regrets about your husband. One has got so in the way of condolences these last few years that it has seemed more the rule than the exception. So don't think me unfeeling if I didn't say right away how sorry I am. Have you been out this way before?"

"Oh, years ago. I came to see Stonehenge and then we went on to Bath. It's lovely country."

"A little severe to my taste, so much denuded of forest centuries ago. My family are in Gloucestershire, where it feels much boskier and cozy to me, but now that I'm used to Wiltshire, I find it quite uplifting to see all this sky. I suppose that is why the ancient people chose it for their sacred places. Perhaps they felt nearer to heaven—if heaven was any part of their thinking. But I am chattering on. I haven't asked you anything about yourself. We'll just get you settled and then have a good talk. Anne's at home. She wanted to come but there isn't room in my little car. We'll send the large dull car over to the station for your trunks and boxes."

Julia told her she had brought only one case and left the rest in London.

"Oh, we thought you would stay with us for a while! But that's up to you. If you like us and wish to stay, we can easily send our man up to London for the rest."

Julia was not prepared for the house, which looked immense, or its beauty. After roaring through many roads so narrow that the car barely cleared the hedges on either side, they turned into a driveway flanked by symmetrically planted trees leading to a rise. Beyond it, settled into the landscape below, was a stone building, somewhat rambling from various additions, but drawn together by a neoclassical core.

"It's breathtaking!"

Stephanie laughed. "Yes, in some rooms it'll take your breath away on a winter morning when the wind sweeps over the downs and you're in a bedroom with no fire. To run it the way they used to took at least a dozen staff, but we can't do that nowadays. We lost two men to the war and the girls find more exciting things to do than be parlour maids. But from May to October it is a delight. The gardens are lovely. People come to see them, and some come to see the house and try to work out how old the old bits really are."

"How old are they?"

"No one seems really sure. Some thirteenth, fourteenth century perhaps. The family kept pulling pieces down and rebuilding."

"The same family?"

"Oh yes. If you're curious my husband knows a good deal about it, provided you can understand him. He's had two strokes and talks with great difficulty. Half the time I can't get a word he says and I have lived with the man for nearly half a century. Neville says you're interested in painting."

"Yes, I am. Very."

"You may find some things to interest you here. No one in the last two generations has paid much attention. Too busy being politicians or soldiers. Well, here were are!'

Her delight in her car, which had skidded to a stop in the gravel driveway, made Julia think of Kenneth Grahame's Mr. Toad, but there was nothing froglike about Stephanie when she threw off the hat and duster coat, revealing a willowy figure, her ash-silver hair still long in the pre-war manner done up on top of her head, exposing her fine forehead and blue eyes. The resemblance to Neville was much closer in Anne, who came to meet them. She had his dark eyes and hair and his high colour.

"Are you blown to bits from the drive? Mother is a menace in that car. We can't keep her out of it. She insists on driving to the station."

"Because it gives me a nice long motor," her mother said. "I love speed, I can't ride anymore and even walking's no fun for me, so I drive. An innocent pleasure."

"Not innocent when you barrel through the lanes"—they

were both addressing Julia, not each other—"frightening the horses, making the farmers jump into the hedges for their lives. She hasn't even got a licence to drive!"

"I do not have a licence to drive my horses and I don't see why I should have one to drive my motor car."

"If you persist, they'll come and drag you off to prison for contempt of court. They've had her up twice in Magistrate's Court."

"And the magistrate just laughed the charges away!"

"Because he's your pal, Mother. When they take you to the assizes, you won't have a friend to let you off."

"Very boring, dear! You are boring me and Julia. Why don't you show her upstairs and I'll see what's happening about lunch."

They went up a stone staircase that ascended in two wings from the main hall, the walls of stone until the first landing, where oak panelling began. Anne led her into one of the bedrooms.

"My grandmother called it the Prince of Wales room. Good Victorian lady that she was, she did not approve of the old Prince of Wales. He was a crony of my grandfather's and used to slip away here now and then for naughty weekends. My grandmother always managed to be away in London when he came. But it's the nicest guest room."

It was large with a canopied bed, armchairs facing a stone fireplace. A bay of mullioned windows overlooked gardens and lawns that stretched into the distance.

"What an exquisite view."

"More important, a real bathroom, with heated pipes. Quite an innovation when my grandfather fixed up this part of the house. And it has a matching twin." She opened a door in the panelled wall and they looked into an almost identical room. "So a lady he fancied could visit the prince—discreetly."

Back in Julia's room Anne stood in the bay, crossing her arms and leaning a shoulder against the window. "How well do you know my brother? I gather you first met two years ago?"

Julia said she knew him very little and explained how, and then told her why he'd suggested she visit his family.

Anne looked at her curiously. "You know, it's quite unusual. He's never done this before. Oh, I realize about your husband and I am terribly sorry about that. I lost someone I really liked—in fact I've lost several men in the war. All the girls I know have lost friends." She smiled. "We truly are the girls in sad shires, pulling down the blinds at tea time. The poem still makes me weep. I'm not used to it even now. It's no fun to be young and find all the men left are drips. When I came out, the season before the war, it seemed there were swarms of lovely young men. Very different now. Very lonely. But I'm being rude."

"No. I'd love to hear more."

"Really? The trouble is I have no one to talk to here—except Mother."

"Well, talk to me. I'd like it."

"I was going to say, it must be far worse to lose your husband. The boy I was keen on, I don't know whether it really would have led to anything—he hadn't said anything. But when you've committed and been married, it must be very hard." Her dark eyes were filling with tears, either for her own sadness or Julia's. When she blinked it made her long lashes shine wetly in the light from the window.

"It was very hard at first," Julia said.

"But now, is it true, you're not actually sure he did die?"

"It may all be foolishness on my part. I'll tell you everything about it."

"Mother is dying to help. And she can really make people snap to. You'll see. But you must have dust everywhere from her awful car. Take your time to tidy up, and you'll find us downstairs when you're ready for lunch."

She was about to leave but turned and smiled, her tears gone. "This is highly presumptuous but, you know—we'd love Neville to get married again."

Julia was stunned at what she said and how casually she said it.

"Again? I didn't know he had been married."

"Then we have a lot to talk about. After lunch."

That sent Julia into a fit of imaginings, and yet she felt immediately comfortable with these two women, quite unlike her advance notions of upper-class English women. She noted their total assurance that she was going to take to them and they to her instantly, but that life would go on if they didn't. Perhaps it was just this family. Neville radiated that assurance in a different, masculine way.

When she went downstairs for lunch, Stephanie glided into view. "After you've been with us a few days, I'll introduce my husband. I've told him you're here. He understands very well but has trouble expressing himself. Unbelievably frustrating for a politician used to speechifying. It's more comfortable for him, and us, if he keeps to his rooms. We have a nurse now, who's recently come out of the army. Quite a different thing looking after him than what she's been used to."

The sitting room was at the back of the house, with French doors open to a warm September day, bees busy in the late flowers, an air of quiet, almost drowsy, peace coming in from the garden. They ate lunch in a small room adjoining the sitting room.

"I think you should have today to take it easy, my dear. Tomorrow we can charge off on your errand. It's a hospital first, I think?"

Julia gave her the name of the military hospital.

"Oh, but of course, I know it. It's not half an hour from here. Why don't I ring up the man in charge and make an appointment for us? Just to be sure he'll be there. Wouldn't that be a good idea?"

"Wonderful, if it isn't too much trouble."

"Trouble? Nonsense! I deal with these places quite a lot in trying to help the men get back into civilian life. I hate to say it but many are still in hospital. Gradually some get well enough to come out. I'll just go and telephone."

Julia could hear her in the next room, asking the exchange for a trunk call and then, connected, raising her voice to say, "This is Lady Boiscoyne. I need a moment with the medical superintendent, if you please." And in a short while she had the gentleman, told the essentials with admirable crispness, and emerged with an appointment the next day.

"He operates first thing in the mornings. Horrible to imagine men still needing operations a year after the last fighting. But there it is. Now you two young people have a turn in the garden to settle your lunch. I have some things to see to and then we can have a good chat before tea."

"I'm sorry mother is so bossy," said Anne. "You don't have to walk in the garden at all if you don't want to. In fact, you don't have to put up with her crazed motoring, either. She loves having people to take places. It gives her a chance to roar around in that thing. If she were a man, I bet she'd be racing motor cars with the best of them. But if you put your foot down and said it made you sick or something, she'd dig up Mr. Watkins and make him take you in the Rolls."

"No, I think your mother's delightful. I have never met anyone like her."

"She was never like this, just the languid Edwardian lady. Then the war, and my father got ill. Something woke her up."

"Tell me about your brother's marriage."

"You really didn't know? While he was at Oxford—"

"I thought he was at the Naval College, with the Prince of Wales."

"Oh he was, but that was when they were very young. He got out at seventeen as a midshipman, clearly wasn't headed for the navy as a career, and went up to Oxford when the prince did. Anyway, in the London season, he met a woman who dazzled him into thinking it was him, not the title, she wanted and Neville fell for it. Much to everyone's disgust. We didn't like her at all. Not every English rose is as sweet as you might think, by any name. Her name was Constance, which turned out to be a joke, because my father showed no desire to shuffle off the mortal coil for her convenience. She found a young marquess who'd just inherited and ran off with him. Inconstancy, thy name is Constance!"

"And what happened?"

"Neville acted devastated, of course, but largely because it was expected of him. I think he'd had enough of her by then. So—divorce!"

"He was divorced?"

"Does that shock you? Shocked us. Never heard of such a thing in the family. But the best thing for him and good riddance to her."

"If life were a Jane Austen novel," Julia said, "she'd have got her comeuppance."

"Maybe she has. The marquess, I hear, is no paragon of constancy himself. So now you know the sordid history. But I'm dying to hear about you."

"There is just one thing I must ask, and please forgive my great ignorance. But what is the title you're referring to, that Constance wanted?"

Anne looked very surprised. "You really don't know?"

"I don't. Neville said his father—your father—is a viscount. Is that right?"

"Yes. And when he dies, Neville becomes Viscount Boiscoyne, the eighth. His wife becomes the viscountess."

Julia stopped and turned to Morrice. "I had to ask her to remind me where viscounts rank in the peerage."

Morrice said, "Only the bloody English understand all that stuff."

Anne recited as it must have been told her as a child: there were five degrees of the peerage. Dukes, marquesses, earls, viscounts, and barons. Viscounts were the fourth degree. They walked behind the earls at coronations and things. And if they could be bothered, they sat in the House of Lords, as her father had.

"He had a big political career and served in several governments. Like a good Tory, did his best to stop Lloyd George's reforms."

When Julia thanked her, Anne was smiling. "You really didn't know?"

"I really didn't," Julia said to Morrice. "How could I have been so...off in the clouds?"

"So suddenly you're imagining yourself a viscountess?"

Julia stopped and turned to him, reddening. "I'm chagrined to say I did. After that I couldn't help it."

❦

The sun was low in the sky behind Cap Ferrat.

The path led up from the sea through the dark greens of the gardens below the château, until they came out on a terrace above the tiny port sheltered between the château and Mont Boron.

"Why don't we sit and enjoy the view before turning back?"

Julia said, "So much happened so quickly, and so confusingly, last fall that it helps to go over it like this, to understand it."

The next day, she said, all the gaiety and excitement of Stephanie's driving did not dispel her mounting unease as they approached the hospital where Charles had been brought from France, where the records showed he had died and where, nearby, he was said to be buried. Until now her quest had been so abstract it was like reading someone else's story—the suspense thrilling but entirely vicarious. Now, inescapably, it was her story again and the emotional dread rose, so that she couldn't speak and was almost unaware of the daredevil driving that got them there.

Stephanie must have sensed this because she did not talk. She stopped the car in a skid of gravel in front of a large Georgian building with modern wings attached. She got out stiffly and walked around to Julia, removing her eccentric hat and coat, and took her arm.

"Whatever we find out, it's better to know, isn't it?"

"Yes. That's why I'm here."

But it was as though all the accumulated pain, anger, horror, from two years before had risen again, as though she were feeling it for the first time.

The medical superintendent, a tired but cheerful man, received them in his office, treating Stephanie with great respect, and got quickly to the point.

"We've already had inquiries about this matter from the Canadian people in London, acting on orders from their government in Canada, so we have looked through our records. The hospital has gradually been shrinking as the need declines, thank God. We have closed two of the five wards and we have sent the full dossiers on all those completed cases on to other authorities. But we have the basic ledger with a sheet on all cases we have handled since the hospital opened in 1915. I've had the ledger book for the period of Major Robertson's treatment brought in. You can see from the thickness it was a distressingly busy period, Passchendaele and its aftermath. We were at our most stretched..."

Julia knew from the way he prefaced all this that he would open the ledger (there was a slip marking a page) and, in a sense, she would be closer to Charles than at any time in the four years since he had sailed from Halifax. She did not want him to open the book. She listened to the drone of his voice, his quite reasonable, though bureaucratic, self-justifying tone.

"In the time of greatest stress we have made it the highest priority to keep impeccable records..." Finally he did open the ledger. "And so—I hope this will not distress you, Mrs. Robertson—here is the page devoted to your husband, all the notes by doctors and nurses who cared for him, including my own note as the surgeon who operated on him."

"You yourself?"

"I did, I see here with regret, with no hope of saving him."

"Do you remember him?"

"I'm afraid I do not. Too many cases, often four or five a morning, every morning for years. Let me bring it around so that you can see and we can go over it together. Some of it is technical and abbreviated, but here it is."

Suddenly it caught her like a painful stitch when running, an actual stab in her lungs, this was Charles alive, admitted on December 11, 1917, medical abstract of his condition plus additions in different pens and shades of ink...acute peritonitis...coma...temperature...blood pressure...surgery undertaken December 12 to cleanse wound area...morphine for pain.

"As you can see, he never regained consciousness."

"Then—why morphine for pain?"

"It is standard for a man so severely wounded, in case he becomes conscious. It is a kindness." He pointed to an entry. "You see, he died just after four a.m. The head nurse recorded that. A Canadian officer came from London to identify the body. That was unusual. He has signed here."

The signature was different from the English handwriting of the other entries. A Captain Richard Weeks had viewed the body in the morgue. Burial recorded at the military cemetery. Row number, plot number.

"I know the cemetery," Stephanie said. "We can go there."

"So, there seems to be no doubt about it, Mrs. Robertson. No ambiguity."

She was shivering, although the room was quite warm. The ledger was still open, its writing neat, remarkably careful and legible considering the conditions they must have worked under. But at the top of this page her husband had been alive, and by the bottom he was dead.

"One thing is quite clear from this. He did not suffer. From the time of his massive injury until his death he remained unconscious."

"Well, that's a blessing," said Stephanie.

"Mrs. Robertson, what has made you, and the Canadian government, doubt this record?"

"This." Julia produced the OHMS envelope. "This is what I received many months after his death was announced. You see, someone has written '*Major Robertson*' on the top. Last spring I discovered these are not my husband's things. They belong to a different Major Robertson." She handed him the package. "Look at the things inside and you'll see."

He looked carefully and whistled softly. "Well, I can understand your puzzlement. This is very strange. I see there is no date on the envelope. But it is the kind we use to send on small personal items when a patient dies."

"But where would my husband's envelope have gone—if he died here?"

"It is conceivable, we were as I say grossly overstretched for doctors, nurses, orderlies, at that period, it is conceivable despite all our care that there was a mix-up and the envelopes were switched. But two Major Robertsons at one time would have been rather unusual. Perhaps yours was sent to the other major's family."

"It wasn't. I went to Scotland to talk to his widow."

"Did you indeed?" He looked at her differently.

"I wrote to her when I discovered this. She has moved to Oban and I followed her there. She did not receive any envelope, and for her own personal reasons she did not wish to keep this. Her husband had left her. It was very sad to see her."

"Well, I admire your determination, Mrs. Robertson. I am disturbed by this...anomaly, if that is the word."

"Or mistake!" said Stephanie.

"Perhaps a mistake, Lady Boiscoyne. But it will take us some time to search the records again. This volume is just one of many. I suggest you let us do that, and if Mrs. Robertson will tell us where she can be reached, I will be in touch as soon as we get to the bottom of it—if we can."

"She is staying me with me and you'll find me on the telephone."

Julia hesitated to leave. However explicit and final the ledger page appeared, she felt more confident that something was wrong.

"If a man died here, what about all his other belongings, his clothing, uniforms, books, letters...?"

"Those would be the business of his regiment. I think you would have to contact them. I'm sure the Canadian authorities in London will assist you."

"Thank you. I will."

"I am really sorry about this. Whatever the explanation, it must be deeply distressing to you. However much we care, and we do, the individual can never touch us as he does those who loved him." He swallowed and reddened.

"If I may say, that is the most human thing I have ever heard a doctor say!" Stephanie exclaimed. "I commend you for that sentiment."

"It is sincere, Lady Boiscoyne. I lost...my wife and I...lost a son in the war so I have felt the other side of it. And I know that life is never the same after such a loss."

Stephanie stood up taller than the doctor or Julia. "I wonder, if there were the slightest chance of a wrong identification, if Mrs. Robertson and I shouldn't quickly walk through your wards to look at the faces." She turned to Julia. "One never knows. Would you like to? Just to see?"

Julian was floored by the suggestion that Charles might be alive in a bed in this hospital, and the shock indicated how convinced she must have been unconsciously that he was dead. Her emotions were too muddled to understand.

The doctor said, "Some of the sights are rather distressing to visitors."

"No," Julia said, "I'd like to see."

"Of course the chances of finding—" he looked at the two women and decided not to resist. "Come, I'll take you through."

They walked through the wards in turn and Julia looked at each face, or what part of a face she could see, of men in different positions of repose: sleeping, reading, chatting. The eyes of all the patients awake followed them, and Julia tried to smile encouragingly at each man. The kind autumn sunlight made the atmosphere quite cheerful, as were the ward nurses who greeted them.

Did she really want to find Charles there? Looking like any of these men, severely mutilated, burned, gassed—many with pathetically little of their bodies left? Condemned to a life, however much remained to them, of suffering, humiliation, pity; their vigor, their manhood, much of their humanity stripped from them; destined to remain out of sight for most of the countrymen they had fought for. And this was only one hospital of many here, in Canada, in all the countries that had fought in the war, those who had won, those who had lost. The war that had caused Peter Wentworth's dramatic promotion in the church, that had provided Harry's great opportunity with Borden, and that had brought Canada so much political recognition had also produced these living dead.

She wanted to be out quickly but Stephanie kept stopping and chatting with wonderful good humour, at one bed or another, as though the patients were her friends, with no sense of rank, no condescension. She was, Julia thought, like an unusually sympathetic school matron lifting homesick spirits in a dormitory.

Outside in the warm sunlight, their shoes crunching pleasantly on the gravel drive, they walked without talking. When they got to the car, Stephanie said, "Let's just pop over to the cemetery. We're close by. Then we'll have done it, don't you think?"

Julia shrank from the idea but Stephanie's forcefulness carried her along, and when they stopped a few minutes later she could see hundreds of white crosses in symmetrical rows.

"More than you need today, but let's just do it now and it will be behind us."

It took about fifteen minutes walking on the neatly mowed grass between the rows until they found it.

Major Charles A. Robertson
Royal Canadian Highland Regiment
1891–1917

They looked at it silently for a long time before Stephanie said, "Neville told us your husband was awarded the VC. I suppose that was after they put this up. I expect they'll add it when they put stone markers in place of the crosses."

Julia said, "His parents are giving a window in his memory for the cathedral in Halifax. The west window behind the altar. They're being awfully literal about everything, so I presume that will mention the VC. Charles's father will insist on it. He's very proud of it."

Stephanie walked on to let her be alone. Was Charles actually there under the earth?

That there's some corner of a foreign field
That is for ever England.

Canadians had learned it, everyone in the Empire had. Rupert Brooke making them all English. The grave looked so definite, official, case closed, ledger shut. If not Charles down there, somebody else. But probably Charles, after all. The record they had been shown left little doubt. Even if someone had mixed up the envelopes. Could it be the husband of the woman in Oban? Was a woman in England now grieving for him? But if Charles, what was left of him now? She shivered and turned to follow Stephanie, comforted by her strong presence. When they came out through the gate, she gave Julia an affectionate smile.

"Quite impertinent of me to ask this, but do you *want* him to be alive?"

"I did not want to find him in the hospital. I didn't want him to be one of those men. I don't know what I want. This stirs up so much."

"Of course it does. And you're a brave girl to do it. I admire you for it. Fancy running up to Edinburgh, and Oban, like that! You've got a good spirit in that pretty head of yours or a spirit in the heart. What is it? *'Tell me where is fancy bred, or in the heart or in the head?'*"

As they drove along, Julia could not shake off the feelings that conflicted: accept what the grave marker said and have done with it, but at the same time the ghoulish need still to prove it. The only way to be sure it was Charles in that grave would be to dig it up and have someone identify him. The idea made her shudder. It was what they did in murder cases, pathologists looking for traces of poison. But pathological examination would not identify Charles. Only one of them who knew his face could. And what would be left of his face now after nearly two years buried? The very idea was sickening. Who could stomach it? Archie? Lucy? But would the authorities agree to exhume him? Probably, if there were no other explanation, if Ottawa, if Borden insisted. Could she bear to look at him in that condition? She felt nausea at the ghastly images that flickered in her imagination.

"The doctor told us that a Canadian officer came from London to identify your husband."

"He did. His signature was there."

"My experience of the military mind—not always the brightest of creatures—is that it cannot issue lavatory paper without making a record of it. They must know who that officer is and where he is now. I think we should pursue it."

"I'm glad you think so. Thank you. I do too."

Nothing in her life had felt as detached from reality as that drive. As they bowled along the narrow lanes, a flushed pheasant whirred overhead, a farmer flattened himself to let this whirlwind pass. The car was driven by a woman whose son Julia felt so strongly about that her stomach contracted when she reminded myself. Yet she was doing everything to resurrect a husband whose existence would kill any future with Neville. Which is why, in her heart of hearts, she knew what she was doing.

She said to Morrice, "Obviously, I was going through these motions to ease my conscience. When I had done all I possibly could to resolve it, any feeling that I'd let Charles down with Neville, would be gone. Right? The moral ledger balanced? That was what I wanted."

Above the wind and the growl of her engine, Stephanie shouted, "You've seen Stonehenge, you say. Have you seen Old Sarum? Something to take your mind off things. It's only half an hour, and there's a village inn where we could have lunch. Would you like that?"

They drove south until Salisbury Cathedral came into view, then veered west to Old Sarum, an enormous moat circling a raised mound, with stone ruins blanketed with grass. They parked outside the ditch and Stephanie insisted on walking painfully up the hill. She described the Iron Age hill fort, eventually replaced by a Norman castle, then the first Salisbury cathedral and a military base. They sat on the remains of a wall.

"Eventually their water supply gave out and they had to move away to make the town." She pointed to Salisbury, whose cathedral now soared over the town, dominating the landscape to the south, its pale stone glowing in the autumn sunlight. "But think of the labour in digging these earthworks. Think of what one man can dig and how much earth he can move in a day, with no machines. They must have had a mighty fear for their safety to dig all this. And in all these years we've progressed to stinking trenches, barbed wire, and machine guns. Well, perhaps this war has put a stop to it."

"Neville believes the peace terms are just storing up trouble with Germany," Julia said. She had rapidly developed warm feelings for this woman but had felt shy of discussing Neville. She told Stephanie about the Prince of Wales's dinner and how funny he had been about visiting the invalid prime minister.

"David is full of charming gestures like that and he can be very amusing. He's been close to Neville ever since the king and queen let him out a little bit to breathe the same air as ordinary mortals. He and George, the Duke of York, had no friends until they went to Osborne. But we've watched David grow up. He comes to see us from time to time and now he's roped Neville in to do this Empire tour with him."

"Is that appointment permanent?"

"Oh no. I don't think Neville counted on more than a year or so. It's terribly confining and exhausting work. Thrilling in its way, of course. I had a go myself for a few years as a lady-in-waiting to the queen. Of course, we were both much younger. Can't imagine myself doing that now!" And she laughed her big-toothed laugh.

"What will Neville do afterwards?"

"He hasn't told you? What a strange young man he is at times."

"We've had very little chance to talk. When he was in Halifax he was always with the prince."

"That's precisely what I mean. You have no life of your own. No, Neville goes into the Foreign Office. He was appointed after Oxford but the war came, and like everyone, he had to go. Naturally with his naval training he went to sea. The palace couldn't risk that with David, despite his training. Even the biggest warships can be sunk. So he spent the war years as a staff officer, hating bitterly that he couldn't go into action, getting as close as he could to the front lines."

"Anne told me about Neville's marriage and divorce."

"Oh yes. I never liked the girl myself but from what I saw of her parents I wasn't surprised. Glad to see the back of her. I thought going to sea was a good way for Neville to forget her, as I'm sure the navy has been serving unhappy marriages since Nelson showed us the way."

"Or creating unhappy marriages?"

"Too true, my dear. Now what are you going to do, when all this is settled about Charles, assuming he is in fact dead. What will you do?"

"I'm trying to decide. I have taken up my painting again

but I don't think I'm good enough to devote my life to it. I'm going to spend some time in Paris, where I studied before the war. To look at everything new. Perhaps that will help me decide."

Stephanie looked at her with a casualness Julia was sure she feigned. "Will you have time to see Neville when he comes back?"

"Oh yes. I'm very much hoping to do that."

She smiled with her large teeth, the prominent bridge-work somehow a badge of her straightforwardness and lack of vanity. And her smile impelled Julia to say, aware that she was beginning to blush, "The truth is, Lady Boiscoyne, as I am sure you've probably guessed, I am in love with Neville."

"I had some suspicion of that sort. And please call me Stephanie."

"I felt it when I first met him two years ago but tried to put him out of my thoughts. When we met again last summer, I had no doubt."

"And he?"

"I think he feels the same."

"In my opinion, he'd be a fool not to. But who can speak for the hearts of others, especially one's own children? Such a mystery! Did you and your husband have children?"

"No."

"Well, you're still quite young enough."

That afternoon, Julia wrote to Lucy asking her to give Harry the name of Captain Weeks, and then there was nothing to do but wait. It became obvious that Stephanie did not like the idea of her straying too far on her own.

"Just think of this as your home. No need to stay in some expensive hotel in London when you can be comfortable here and give me and Anne such pleasure in your company. But if country life is too quiet for you, and you're dying for paintings, London is full of them. Take Anne to town for a few days and teach her about art. All she knows about is literature. She spends her life lost in a book. Do her good to get out. You can take the train or Watkins can run you up. We have a little flat in Belgravia from the days when my husband was active in politics. You can stay there and do the town. And Watkins can collect your things from the hotel where you left them and bring them back out here."

Anne jumped at the idea and so they went to town, driven by Watkins in a boxy Rolls Royce. Before they left, when Anne was out of the room, Stephanie said with the sharply focused air of indifference Julia was beginning to recognize, "Neville said you were travelling with another gentleman."

"Just as far as London. He is a friend from Halifax, a professor of psychology at the university there. His name is Stewart MacPherson."

"Psychology, indeed? And what has happened to him?"

"He has people to see in this country and on the Continent. People in his field."

"And will you undertake more of your travels together?"

"We have a plan to visit the battlefields in France and Belgium."

"Yes, I hear people are doing that."

"I want to see where Charles fought."

She looked at Julia with an amused appraisal. "Well, I'm sure it will be a comfort to have an old friend's company on such a melancholy journey. And a difficult one, I'm told, not easy to find cleared roads, or hotels or restaurants operating."

"He has made the arrangements."

"I believe Neville mentioned he was the partner you brought to the dinner David gave."

"He was."

Stephanie said, "Am I prying too much?"

Julia laughed. "I'm amazed how much Neville told you, considering how little he told me. I don't mind being direct with you. Stewart is not the person I am in England to see."

"Well, isn't it a good thing that young women like you can be so independent now? You'll need to be, with the times we're facing and the dreadful shortage of young men."

By sending Anne to London as well she could keep tabs on Julia. Had Neville suggested it? Not likely. Not in keeping with the devastating confidence he had shown. The more she absorbed the various hints and pressures, the more Julia began to feel mother and daughter exerting a careful plan, at Neville's wish perhaps, or for their own purposes, to examine, study, observe the specimen he had shipped back to them, like a botanist-explorer from his fieldwork overseas. And it gave her pleasure to be the object of so much distant thought. Was he communicating frequently with them, sending new questions to have answered? Or were they following their own curiosity? The scrutiny did not worry her. She had nothing to hide. She had probably been more direct than good manners suggested.

The little flat, in Wilton Crescent, turned out to be grander than advertised. With no one living there, the only staff was a woman who came twice a week to "do." So Julia and Anne did for themselves, went to museums and galleries until their legs gave out, ate in tea rooms and restaurants, and window-shopped. Then rather abruptly one morning Anne excused herself, saying she had to look up an old friend, reappearing late that afternoon bedraggled and depressed and then Julia found out what was governing her life. She wanted desperately to talk about a man she was involved with. She had told Julia the carnage in France had left only "drips." This involvement, secret from her parents, sounded more dangerous than a drip: an older man with an unsavoury reputation but fascinating to Anne in her loneliness. She was heavily involved emotionally and sexually, frightened that he would drop her, as he had other women. By listening sympathetically that evening Julia was clearly so useful to her that they became closer, although it made Julia uncomfortable that becoming Anne's ally put her in opposition to Stephanie. Very awkward. From Anne's distress it appeared that her affair was approaching a climax, which is why she had jumped at the excuse to come to London.

16

Julia turned to Morrice. "It's beginning to get chilly here."

"Right you are." He rose stiffly from the bench. "I was lost in your story. If we walk down here, there are usually some horse-drawn cabs at the bottom."

He helped her into a fiacre then climbed in awkwardly himself, pulling with both hands, one foot on the step but no spring in the leg pushing from the ground.

She preferred sleep to dinner and said good night in the hotel lobby.

"Nine o'clock in the morning?"

Morrice slipped into his favourite café overlooking the Mediterranean, ordered a whisky, and lit his pipe. He was tired but contented. She permeated his imagination. How sweet that she was willing to be so open with him. It had quite relaxed the tension between them. And her situation was becoming clearer. He could now form a picture of the haughty Englishman and his odd family. He could almost guess the rest. But, while diverting, that was in the background of his attention, in softer focus. What dominated his consciousness, and exhilarated him, was the painting upstairs in his room, merely begun, awaiting the next morning's work. He could feel it waiting, as though the canvas itself, like an ardent mistress, was impatient to resume. Even as he contemplated the scene in front of the café—passing strollers, carriages, and cars—in his mind he was beginning tomorrow's work: beginning, becoming distracted, then beginning again.

One distraction was a little embarrassment. He must clarify what he'd told her about prices. He loathed boastfulness. Probably too mellow from Armagnac, he'd told her $700. She'd picked up quickly: you could buy a car for that. It was a lot of money and he must have sounded casual about it. He did ask $700 in Canada, once even $800. Before the war he'd put $800 on *Venice, Night* at the Canadian National Exhibition in Toronto, but less—$500 and $600—at the spring exhibition of the Art Association of Montreal for *Une Parisienne* and *The Surf, Dieppe*, both a little smaller than *Venice*. But he didn't always get what he asked. Damned dealers were slippery, willing to bargain to make a sale even when he told them to stick to their price. Inevitably dealers played both sides, artist and customer. His London dealer, Goupil Gallery, always wanted him to keep the prices low, only £80 for *Red Houses, Venice*.

He must have this from his father, who had prospered without hypocrisy in that strange tension between model Christian gentleman and hard-headed businessman. By force of his own industry and character he had taken small elements of an infant textile industry in Canada, tiny by any rival British measure, and woven them into the Canadian Coloured Cotton Mills, a serious competitor on the imperial level.

Especially in the Canada of the 1880s and 1890s, such a successful man might have been a complacent philistine, but David Morrice was not. He gave generously to found the Art Association of Montreal and was astonishingly reasonable when his (third) son wanted to become a painter, not a lawyer as he'd hoped. If Morrice was serious, they would support him and not grudgingly. Once his talent began to be recognized his father had promoted his work, recommended it to galleries, to fellow businessmen, and to exhibitors. Totally unlike Matisse *père*, who had sourly given Henri a tiny allowance, then angrily cut him off when he too left the profession his father had chosen—also, coincidentally, the law. Matisse had struggled to survive and he considered Morrice a rich man. Morrice was very careful with his money. Apart from clothes, he lived frugally, not to embarrass fellow artists, but again a value instilled by his parents: no ostentation.Now that his parents—and sadly two of his brothers—were dead and the estate divided, Morrice was very comfortable. He could be more generous to Léa, and he had made a will in which she was well provided for.

As he was going to bed, he noticed that Julia had left her robe in his bathroom. Before turning out the light, he couldn't resist feeling the texture of the silk and putting his nose to it to catch her perfume.

17

Saturday, January 3, 1920

She awoke with Charles in her first thoughts. On her trip to London with Anne she'd gone to the Canadian government office by Trafalgar Square. The mystery had deepened, even as she convinced herself the more firmly that he was dead.

Solving it depended on finding the officer who had come to the hospital and identified his body. Julia was restless waiting for an answer from Lucy, which could take weeks. Besides, it was exciting to be in London in the hazy golden weather of October, with its cool nights and warm days, the flower stalls filled with huge dahlias and shaggy bronze chrysanthemums.

Early for her appointment, she got off the bus and walked through to Covent Garden to loiter in the riotous extravagance of colour. She mingled with people from flower shops, buyers for restaurants and hotels and large houses, doing business with the wholesalers in a chaotic noise of iron-shod barrow wheels rumbling on the cobbles; porters with stacks of baskets on their heads, shouting for a clear way to come through; sellers crying their wares at the tops of their voices; someone singing, an accordion or street organ playing in the background; the public houses nosily open here in the morning, stalls selling tea and buns, bacon and dripping sandwiches, another with cockles and jellied eels—so much life and energy all focused on the pleasant but doubtless hard business of buying and selling flowers.

Flowers were so much bigger a part of English life than Canadian. Everywhere she looked in the prosperous parts of London, lampposts sported hanging baskets of geraniums and lobelia. There were potted plants on windowsills inside and out, lining front steps by the black iron railings, in sunken areas outside kitchen windows.

Jostled by porters and buyers, she watched the market, thinking it showed no sign of there having been a great war only a year earlier. As she did everywhere she went, she looked carefully at employees in tea rooms, people waiting for buses, passersby on the pavements; she looked into the faces of women especially for signs of the great cataclysm but could seldom see any. If they had experienced personal tragedies, as statistically many of them must have, it did not show.

Under the smoky glass panes of the flower market roof, this cheerful, exuberant tumult of whistling, singing, shouting, shoving, hustling Londoners behaved as if nothing had ever dashed their joy in being alive or stopped them from going about their business. The scene so stimulated Julia that she bought a cup of tea from a cheerful woman in a stall, then sipped it leaning against the counter for protection from the racketing pushcarts and laden men shoving by. Like London taxi drivers, the tea lady was wearing several overcoats with a large apron over them all. On her head perched a perky felt hat with a feather. Her woollen gloves had the fingertips cut off. She saw Julia warming her hands on the mug.

"Nippy morning, isn't it? Always chillier in 'ere than what it is outside. It's the glass keeps the night cold in—and the flowers. Even summer mornings it's cool in here, except you don't mind it so much then. Tea all right, dear?"

"Very nice, thank you." It was strong and came ready

milked and sugared.

"Like a bun to go with it?"

"No thank you."

"Waiting for someone, are you?"

"No, I just came to look, on my way to somewhere else."

"Not from London, are you."

"No, I'm from Canada."

"Well, fancy that, then! My husband got mixed up with some Canadians in the war. Liked them well enough, he said. Of course, that was before he got killed." She said it philosophically, as she poured a mug of tea for a new customer.

"Tea, luv, that's three ha'pence."

"My husband was killed too," Julia said.

"Was he really? Awful, isn't it? I know ever so many lost their men. Terrible thing." But she went on, as she was talking, putting fresh water in a kettle to boil, scooping tea leaves out of a large pot, and chatting as though they had both said they'd had children with the 'flu. *Awful the way it's going round, isn't it?* As though this had been a small incident in her life and manageable.

"Do you notice a difference in the market since the war?"

"Here? Well, I see blokes missing as what I knew before. If you look at that stall over there, I knew a man ran that what didn't come back. There's lots of women working here that lost someone but what can they do? You can only go on working, can't you? Still got families to look after. I think it's busier now. It was slower for a few years but it's picked up again. Like it always was now. But then this isn't the busiest time. Most of the buyers have come and gone by now. This is just leftovers, late sleepers. If you want to see it really frantic, come at six in the morning. Only then I don't have time for a chat."

"Well, thank you for the tea."

"Ta ta, luv. Chin up!" She laughed.

Julia walked back through the entrance facing the Covent Garden church, thinking how impossible it would be for her to paint such a scene but also wondering how any painting could embrace what she had just been discussing with the tea woman, the marks of a great war. You couldn't, unless you made a pathetic show of widowhood in the foreground, or a disabled veteran on a crutch, trying to do his job. Even then, you'd have to label it, making it genre painting, sentimental and anecdotal. The flower market was a flower market. Gorgeous, rampant with colour and teeming with the human society that made commerce with flowers.

She walked the short distance down to the Strand and along to Trafalgar Square. Was she forcing herself to dwell too much on the war out of loyalty to Charles? No, she had resolved that a long time before. Out of guilt about Stewart? In any case the tea woman in Covent Garden had greatly improved her mood.

The military attaché knew about Charles from the inquiries from Ottawa. Julia told him about the hospital and asked if he could trace the Captain Weeks who had signed the book. Short of exhuming the body, that seemed to be the only practical step left. But why hadn't they thought of it? Probably because they thought the whole thing was her deranged invention.

"It shouldn't be difficult to trace him. Let me see what I can do while you're here." His show of eagerness betrayed the influence from higher up. He made two telephone calls to personnel records at the Canadian Military Headquarters in England about the current posting for Captain Richard Weeks.

"He could still be in England. We do have some units still

awaiting demobilization here."

"A year after the war ended?"

"Not desirable, I know. But scarcity of sea transport has slowed it down and the shortage of trains when they arrive in Canada."

"And the shortage of jobs when they do get back."

"All too true. Not good for morale. It isn't generally known but we had serious disturbances among our troops in England a few months ago."

"What happened?"

"Riots, fighting. Men fed up being kept in camps. Had to be put down by force."

"Was anyone hurt?"

He looked around but there was no one else in his office. "Twelve killed, twenty wounded."

"How terrible! I didn't know about that."

"British papers covered it but we kept it pretty quiet. Sir Robert Borden was here at the time and he gave the British papers hell for playing it up."

"But how can you keep something like that quiet? Surely the people at home have a right to know!"

"The army felt that publicity would only increase the frustration of the men and lead to more trouble."

"But what will you tell the families of men who were killed? After the war? How will you explain that?"

"Died on active service, I expect. Anyway, my point is, your captain could still be in England, or with our forces still in France, or he might have gone back to Canada and civilian life."

"Or he might have been killed too?"

"That is, unfortunately, a possibility. However, as they haven't called me back quickly, this may take some time and

I hate to keep you hanging about. If you'll tell me where I can reach you..."

A day later word came that Captain Weeks was in France on duty with Canadian forces there. He could remember going to the hospital and viewing the body. What questions did she wish him to be asked? She thought about it and sent a reply that she was going to France herself shortly, to visit the battlefields, and would like to talk to him in person. That seemed a good way to force her out of this drifting phase, in which fantasies anticipating Neville were constantly soured by her ambivalence.

She arrived at Morrice's room with a tray of coffee and crois-sants to smell the odour of fresh turpentine. He had just finished underpainting within the pencilled outline of her body. She had never seen him as casually dressed: pyjamas and dressing gown, his beard slightly dishevelled from sleep.

"Thank you. Time for a break. I wanted to apply this to give it some time to dry."

"You seem in good spirits. You must have slept well."

"I did, thank you."

He could tire and seem to age before her eyes, as on the previous evening, but this morning throw it off like a disguise.

"And I was eager to get back to work. That is a tonic."

While Julia poured coffee, he stood back to look. He had woken with a start before it was light, anxious about the drawing, with a fear in mind—some vague anxiety born in sleep—that he might have to paint it out and start again. When he left his bed and turned on a light, he was instantly reassured. The drawing was fine. Now in full daylight as he assessed the flat, painted, two-dimensional effect, his line showed its values even better. The composition pleased him, with her position slightly offset from the French window, one vertical line bisecting her right shoulder, bars from the closed shutter behind on the left providing dramatic horizontal stripes. But it was the way her figure planted itself in the picture that excited him. He had got that right. He had preserved his eye line relative to her height, so that Julia in the painting looked down slightly at the viewer, like Botticelli's Venus from her giant scallop shell. But the eyes of Venus had been dreamily averted, while Julia's looked challengingly at the spectator, with something like the amused frankness of Manet's model in *Le déjeuner sur l'herbe*. In his unconscious the Botticelli must have been lurking because Morrice had brought that delicious pose into the twentieth century, the weight on the rear foot, the rear shoulder lowered. Yet instead of Botticelli's maidenly Venus shielding her breasts and lap with her hands, Julia had both arms lowered undefensively. He had made her a modern woman, as she passionately wanted to be, her feet planted on the ground, in a pose that was in no way immodest, merely honest, hiding nothing. A woman for this century.

He was delighted not only by the composition but with the new freedom he had sensed while working, a new simplicity, and a looseness that nevertheless exerted perfect control from within. In this painting, only just begun, he knew he was moving into a new phase. He must work carefully to get the colour values and harmonies perfect, but he knew he could do it.

"We need to wait until that is dryer. It'll give me time to

dress properly. Excuse my appearance. I got out of bed and began working."

"Have your coffee before it gets cold."

"Very thoughtful of you to bring it."

Obviously, Julia had put Botticelli in his mind, perhaps years before, probably for the colour of her hair, so close to the honey blonde of the Venus in Florence. Not Julia's face, which was more angular, with a flatter plane to the cheek and a chiselled jawline, nor her body. Unlike the Botticelli ideal, Julia's body was lean, with square shoulders and legs and arms that clearly had usable muscles under the smooth skin. No superfluous flesh, no trace of those curious anklets like baby fat that slightly marred the Venus for Morrice, and not present in the perfect ankles of Botticelli's delicious women in *Primavera*. On his first visit to the Uffizi in Florence, Morrice had worshipped at both paintings for hours. No wonder they reigned so indelibly in his memory.

No, Julia's was a figure in no need of squeezing or corseting to achieve a fashionable shape. Hers was the new, desirable shape. Lean, unconstrained, and active.

"Are you very athletic?"

"Not much now. Why do you ask?"

"You have an active-looking body."

"Do I?" She laughed, a little self-conscious although still fully clothed. "Well, I used to ski in Switzerland and climb in the mountains while I was at school there. A lot of hiking. And tennis at home. So, yes, I was quite active as a girl."

"I'm interested in how much the female shape has actually changed over the centuries and how much it's just our idea of it. Haven't artists of the various periods exaggerated the features each period found attractive? In classical sculpture, Greek and Roman women, particularly in the Greek proportion, women look quite like women's figures today. Gothic women look emaciated, Rubens saw women like delectable dumplings, Renoir's tend to have huge hips and bottoms, Modigliani's are sweetly elongated—"

"And Picasso's look like pieces of shattered glass."

"Only some of them, depending on his mood." He got up. "If you don't mind, I'd like to get properly dressed."

"Then I'll leave you for half an hour."

18

How strange Morrice was, Julia thought, to need to get himself up in his customary three-piece suit, high collar and decorous tie, to paint a woman with no clothes on! Was that some Canadian sense of propriety that lingered in him, some mild redress for the way he flouted other conventions?

How much more casual she had found the British, at least those who had given her a taste of life in the upper classes. She had innocently supposed life in the mother country to be more hidebound, more deferential to established morality than in the supposedly freer society of the New World. Not a bit of it. Morality seemed to harden the more distantly it was planted from the fountainhead, more rigidly observed to keep society more like that in the old country than it actually was, to keep everything done in some fading colonial notion of the proper way, while at home British society itself went on changing its mores. It was Anne Boiscoyne who had made her feel at times the constricted colonial, and sometimes the freer spirit.

Anne and her friends wanted desperately to get back to a normal life, but were frustrated by the scarcity of young men they considered suitable. So she took an older man to bed. Conventions of all kinds had been overthrown by the war: by those who governed, those who ran the churches and supposedly set the morality. The Church of England (she had once taunted Peter Wentworth about it) had been as keen a cheerleader in the war effort as the generals and the newspapers. They gave their blessing, those keepers of the moral code, to some of the greatest bloodletting in human history. Not surprising that young people left behind, left over—and like all survivors in Stewart's view feeling guilty for remaining alive—should look on established social conventions as irrelevant.

When she and Julia really got talking about this, Anne had said slyly, "Of course, if Neville remarries, he couldn't do it in the church. The C. of E. won't remarry divorced people if the former husband or wife is still alive. So unless Lady Constance meets an untimely end, she's alive."

"What will he do?" Julia asked.

"I hope he'd tell the bloody Archbishop of Canterbury to stuff it and go to the registry office, like Bertrand Russell. Might be a little awkward if he wanted David as best man. You know, Defender of the Faith and all that? Divorce is the big bugaboo, even if the C. of E. was founded on Henry's divorce. It's all right to have mistresses, even to be quite openly adulterous, look at the late king—in our own house! Mrs. Keppel came to his deathbed with the queen's blessing. Everybody knows it. But divorce? How disgraceful! Children out of wedlock—how appalling! Yet half the great families in England, half of *Debrett's*, are probably descended from the wrong side of the blanket."

"Speaking of children out of wedlock, if you and Mr. X—"

Anne laughed. "Are sleeping together?"

"Are you—"

"Taking precautions? Of course! It's not the Middle Ages."

"It is in Canada."

"I can't believe it. I got fitted with a diaphragm. There's

a woman doctor who will do it. Just don't breathe a word to Mother. She'll have a fit."

So Anne had done what Julia had intended but not accomplished and had put off—until now it was too late.

From the way the conversation was going, now that they had fewer inhibitions, Julia could feel Anne wanting to know whether she and Neville had advanced that far, but Julia wouldn't discuss it.

With Anne becoming more candid, she leaped in maturity as Julia understood that the somewhat mopey, withdrawn girl she appeared at home was a persona adopted to keep her mother incurious. Anne was bright and far more widely read than Julia, certainly in the latest writers. She wanted to talk about D.H. Lawrence and Virginia Woolf. She had met Mr. X at a literary gathering. He was obviously well connected in the London world of book publishers and writers. She wanted to move to London to work and was calculating how to prepare the ground to persuade her mother.

Julia related her experience in Paris. Her parents would not have let her go if her father had not known Morrice and his family and decided he would be a stable influence.

Anne laughed. "If he's an artist, I'll bet he kept an eye on you."

"Well, he painted me."

"How, a portrait?"

"In the nude."

"Julia!" She was hysterical with pleasure. "When can I see it?"

"It's in my house in Halifax."

"Did Neville see it?"

"No. He was never at my house."

"And what else happened with the artist?" She added mockingly, "The trusted family friend!"

"Nothing. He helped me with my work."

"Nothing? You with no clothes on? I don't believe it."

"Seriously. Painting is serious business. Hard work. Great concentration."

"Oh, I know. I know. I'm not a fool. But artists' eyes have been known to stray, their attention to wander."

"Sometimes I wondered whether he thought about that."

"Did you?"

"He was much older."

"How much older?"

"Twenty-five years."

"Well, that's not so much. What happened to him?"

"He's still painting. I'm hoping to see him when I'm in France."

Anne looked as though Julia's little bohemian experience had sanctioned her current affair.

"But you take my point. Your family must have a lot of people in London whom they would feel—"

"Responsible."

"—comfortable with, as mine did with Morrice."

"It's the perfect idea. I don't know why I didn't think of it. Absolutely perfect."

"You'll just have to be careful that trusted family friend doesn't run into Mr. X."

"Oh, he could run into him, inevitably would, I suppose, but he wouldn't have to know about us."

"You don't believe it would show?" It was Julia's turn to smile.

When they returned to Wiltshire from London, now together a good deal, walking the surrounding countryside,

discussing books Anne gave Julia to read, they began bridg-
ing differences in their education. Anne had wanted to go to
Oxford after Neville. Her mother had been sympathetic but
overruled by her father. So Anne had been ready to do the
expected, the debutante season in London and marriage soon
after. The war had put a stop to that and derailed her whole
life. But Neville had spoken to his Oxford don, and Anne
had been reading with his advice, the don delighted to have
an unofficial student as bright and hungry to learn. Many of
the young men in his charge were floundering in the aftermath of the war, either frantically having a good time, or lost
in postwar confusion. It was another glimpse into Neville's
personality that he would take such trouble with his young
sister's intellectual development, more evidence of how close
they were. And, Julia assumed, that closeness explained the
role Anne was playing, with her mother, on Neville's behalf.

Julia grew more curious about this as the days passed,
very pleasant days, the more she felt embraced by the
family. Had it all been planned? Just what had Neville said
to them about her? Was their hospitality as casually offered
as it seemed? Or was it more directed, more constructed?
Of course she could not suppress her own speculations or
help pushing the story forward in her imagination. They
had dropped hints about marriage: had he told them it was
his intention to ask? He hadn't told her. And as she came
out of the intoxication of too many new impressions, like
looking at too many pictures in one visit to a gallery, she
realized that she was constantly pushing her imaginings
towards that, then putting herself on guard in case she
revealed such presumption.

The newspapers had frequent stories about the royal tour
of Canada, accounts of the rapturous reception the prince

was receiving as he travelled west, endless accolades for his skill in handling any crowd, always exceeding expectations. Even in Winnipeg, where labour riots had been put down by force, the prince's appeal had a magic effect.

Borden was worried that Bolshevism was as serious a threat in Canada as in Russia and Germany. When negotiations with Winnipeg strikers broke down and street riots followed, the government sent troops who opened fire, killing and wounding rioters. Now, just by travelling there, showing himself, attending receptions, shaking hands, opening this and that, really just being there, the Prince of Wales seemed to be healing the wounds.

Many of the strikers and rioters were returned soldiers. Some had seen him visiting the trenches on the Western Front. A mere glimpse of him was memorable. The British papers quoted an officer with the 85th Battalion, Nova Scotia Highlanders, saying that when the prince visited the battlefield, "he seemed to be the embodiment of modesty and virtue." The officer concluded, "Let us hope he will never forget what the manhood of the Empire are doing at this hour to secure international justice and secure for the future the safety of the throne he is destined to occupy."

Now he was a triumph in Canada, symbolically carrying the gratitude of the Empire to those who had fought to save it and, in their communities for a few hours, wiping away months of disillusion and anger. To read about the magic gift, even the fulsome rhetoric around it, made Julia weep, even if the sentiments were alien to her own view of the morality of the war. Canada had certainly fought to protect the British throne, and Borden believed Canadians were indirectly fighting for a measure of independence. When she read the jingoistic passage aloud Anne said, "I prefer my jingoism from Kipling. He warned us a long time ago against too much imperial hubris...you remember?

> *Far-called, our navies melt away;*
> *On dune and headland sinks the fire:*
> *Lo, all our pomp of yesterday*
> *Is one with Nineveh and Tyre!*

"Not fashionable to quote at the moment. My literary friend"—she looked around apprehensively—"my friend would think me very unprogressive."

Julia studied every photograph in the papers for possible glimpses of Neville somewhere behind the prince, but it wasn't until the *Illustrated London News* carried many pages on the tour that Anne pointed him out in a scene in the Rockies. Julia did not have a picture of Neville, so she kept slipping into the sitting room, where papers and periodicals were left on a table, to have another peek, until Anne, catching her, said, "We've all finished with it. Would you like to keep it as a souvenir? After all, it's your country." Julia took it to her room and gazed at it often, each time with a surge of strong feeling but eventually losing it as the picture, from too-close staring, resolved itself into the dots of the rotogravure process and meant nothing. Her own fantasies about Neville as she went to sleep were much more vivid.

Looking at one photo, Anne said, "Just look at David in that Indian headdress! He looks like a little boy."

"He looked that way to me in person," Julia said.

"But take care," Anne said. "This little boy likes married women."

Julia laughed but remembered all the attention he had paid to her and his repeated invitations to see him in England.

"He did say he would ask Neville to stay in touch when I was in England."

"Did he? So Neville has a rival?"

"Oh, that's nonsense."

"If he said that to you, I'll bet he invites you to something."

"Has he ever asked you?"

"No, for heaven's sake! I'm just Neville's little sister. Or too-big sister! I'm much too tall for him."

"I was taller when we danced."

"But I'm a lot taller—and I'm not married. Everybody notices. He only seems to get serious about women who are married."

"Why?"

"Who knows? I have one or two friends who do the lady-in-waiting business and they pick up a lot. One of them thinks he's looking for a mummy because his own is such an icicle to him. The king is very worried that he won't settle down. Of course, shooting him off all over the world like this doesn't help settling down, does it?"

"What do you think of him yourself?"

"I saw him so much when I was younger, just a little girl, I suppose I still think of him that way, as a child himself. He's very fussy about clothes. Loves all the dressing up he has to do. All the different uniforms, the Garter robes— adores all that!"

"Does Neville think of him as a friend?"

"I don't know these days. This tour will reveal a lot, I should think. Terribly wearing on everybody. Neville's a lot deeper than David. As far as I can tell, David never reads anything for pleasure. And he never concentrates on anything for very long. Keeps getting enthusiasms and dropping them."

"He'll have to concentrate as king."

"Oh, I think being king means skipping over the surface of many different things. What did you think of him? You danced with him, talked with him."

"And we had a long walk together."

"Alone?"

"No, no, Neville and Lucy Robertson too."

Anne said, "I'll bet you'll get an invitation, or he'll look you up here when he knows Neville's got you stashed away in the country."

"Is that what I am: stashed away? I don't really know anything Neville's told you about me."

"Really?"

"I don't. All he said to me was, 'Why don't you go and stay with my mother and sister? They'll help you find out what you need to.'"

"Which we are. Or Mother is. But, I told you, he's never done anything like this before."

"I know you said that. What does it mean?"

"It means he's mad about you! What else can it mean? Don't you think so?"

"I suppose I'll know when I see him again."

Later she asked Anne, "Tell me what happened to Neville in the war. He wouldn't say much about it."

"He was marvellous. We were terribly proud of him. Went to Buck House and got a gong pinned on him by the king. A DSO. Because he'd left the navy to go to Oxford, he was a reserve officer when the war came and just a lieutenant. Naturally the regular officers got all the plum jobs. They put Neville in a destroyer as a junior officer. Then the first lieutenant got a command of his own and the captain recommended Neville for his job. Their squadron got into a heavy battle with the German navy. Some of our ships sank, many were hit, hundreds of dead and wounded. His ship was hit several times, and the captain was killed on the bridge. The destroyer was in danger of sinking but Neville organized the damage control, kept her afloat, even kept her guns firing, and brought her back to port. They wrote later that he'd shown great courage, daring, and seamanship in the presence of the enemy. And because he's the heir to my father's title, of course the papers made a fuss over him. So, he had reason to expect promotion and his own ship, since they were desperate for good officers. But something happened and he got stuck in an armed merchant cruiser, the *Changuinola*, an old passenger liner converted into a warship."

"Was it the divorce?"

"How clever of you! Might well have been. We never knew. But it's as good a guess as any. Just redoubled his determination to get out of the navy as soon as the war was over."

"That's when I met him, when the *Changuinola* was in Halifax."

"And that's when he came back and told us about you."

"And said...?"

"My dear, it would give you a swelled head."

In fact, everything Anne and her mother said, or hinted at, suggested a man as infatuated as Julia was.

19

This awareness of being freer came back to Morrice as he painted. Julia had resumed the pose, and he had asked her not to talk as he worked on the face.

That must be what growth in an artist really meant, growing freer and freer, less constrained as one grew more confident and surer of oneself. It had felt like that at each new state in his development, a casting off of unneeded restraints, especially when he had found Manet. Manet had mesmerized Morrice at thirty, possessed him like a revelation, and left him freer in subject matter and style. Until then, except in life classes, he had never painted a nude, and *Nude Reclining* acknowledged his homage to Manet's *Olympia* in the Louvre. Then Whistler, then Matisse, then Bonnard, each one another influence. Influence. Such a trite and casual word, so easily tossed at artists. Artists absorb everything, but in particular they absorb from fellow artists; they possess other artists, as Beethoven possessed Mozart. They take other artists to reside in their psyches. Living with one's creative companions, one quotes, one borrows, one assimilates by merely breathing the air they breathed, and one's own work is subtly transformed, enlarged, enriched.

He stared hard at the side of her face more slightly in shadow, on the palette mixed a tone, looked again, and applied a few strokes, as freely as if he were sitting at a café table, his small painting box in his lap, working slowly on a *pochade* of life in the street.

And what had inspired this new freedom? Obviously the girl. Something in her energy was transmitted to him, as complex an amalgam of feeling as the colour he had just mixed was subtle, difficult to analyze.

His eyes left the face and transferred their attention to her body and legs, carefully studying the way light and shadow fell, then mixing a colour and applying it. Years before, he had sometimes applied a colour on top of another, then rubbed it in with a bit of cloth to blend the hues. It achieved some gratifying effects when used on wooden panels. Now he preferred using oils more like watercolours, a thinner medium, with washes that were more translucent for some effects.

Where the light fell most brightly on her near thigh, the relaxed one, it made the skin glow luminously. Not too many tones, he told himself, keep it simple, let it flow.

"If you want to talk again, please do."

"May I rest a little? My right leg is going to sleep."

"Of course. Let's stop for ten minutes."

Looking at the painting so as not to be seen watching, he could still see her peripherally as she put on her robe. And, perhaps because he had anticipated it would, it had the same effect on him as the day before. Nude, she was an object to be painted, presenting interesting challenges in light and form, but an object. With the clinging robe now covering her, she became a woman again and began to arouse his sensual awareness of that fact.

He found his box of small cigars and lit one, sitting in the armchair near her. He wanted her to talk, to dispel that atmosphere that had crept back in.

"You said you knew more about Charles but we were interrupted, or distracted by something else."

"Well...they found the officer who had viewed the body and I talked with him, when we went to France to visit the battlefields."

"Who is 'we'?"

"Stewart MacPherson, we had planned that all along, and Anne, Neville's sister."

"That's an interesting combination. How did it come about?"

"Her mother suggested it."

The Boiscoynes had made her entirely comfortable. The late viscount's efforts to modernize the house when Edward VII was king meant enough of the rooms had heating and hot water in the bathrooms that it could be run with a smaller staff. Comparable big houses needed maids to carry hot water and make fires in all the bedrooms.

"It's as though my grandfather knew that changes in society were coming," Anne said. "There used to be about twenty people on the staff, with a butler and housekeeper running it all, the way many houses still try to do. Now we manage with four—cook, upstairs maid, parlour maid who serves at table, and Watkins, who looks after the garden and who drives, when mother lets him. My father is a real skinflint, which is probably why he has hung onto to his money and some of the land."

When Julia announced that it was time to go on with the next stage of her plans, Stephanie said, "I know that what I am going to suggest may be quite inappropriate, but I was wondering if you'd let Anne go with you?"

And Anne immediately said, "Oh, I'd be fascinated to see it. Perhaps I could write an account of it that someone might publish."

Was this more evidence that she was being watched over? Julia wondered, then dismissed the idea as silly. She said she would be glad to have Anne's company and, she was sure, so would Stewart. "I'll just have to find him and see about the arrangements." Stewart would certainly not object to having an intelligent and attractive young woman accompany them, and if it smoothed the way between Julia and him, she would be pleased.

Nothing Julia had seen, or read, or heard, prepared her for the evidence they now saw of violence, of wanton destruction, of mindless rage, of human behaviour with all humanity subtracted. Towns that had taken ten centuries to build, the gorgeous tiered and gabled houses and shop fronts, medieval cathedrals, arcades, market squares, pounded into rubble as though some angry god had repeatedly lashed them with thunderbolts, his ravenous anger not satisfied until he had smashed all grace and charm.

In some towns, only a narrow path had been cleared through mountains of broken stone and brick, with an occasional arch or the cornice of a building rearing up, but life had resumed. She half expected to find survivors as dazed as she was, dumbfounded, stupefied, still raising a wild clamour about what had been visited upon them. But they were not. They had cleared paths and little roads. They had made channels of commerce for horse-drawn and people-drawn carts, and the occasional motor vehicle, to pass. The markets functioned; goods found their way out of the cellar workshops and supply rooms, where the residents had also hidden. Their famous textiles were on display, and pretty clothes, as well as fresh vegetables, meat, fish, wine, oil, nuts, bread.

Where mountains of rubble still existed, people were meticulously sorting and cleaning reuseable brick and stone to stack it in neat piles for others to cart away to building sites. Watching their hands sifting stones from a pile of rubble, she could see the human spirit patiently reasserting itself, gradually re-establishing its discipline over chaos. They might have been citizens in the Lorenzetti allegory in Siena trying to recreate the effects of good government after four years of government monstrously bad. Whatever they might have felt individually, they were reclaiming their tortured landscape for humanity, as their ancestors had done numerous times, because this terrain had been fought over repeatedly since the dawn of European history.

They were not merely stoic. The people did not look as crushed in spirit as Van Gogh's *The Potato Eaters*, which she had seen in Paris. These Belgians and French people seemed as cheerful, as full of life and zest, as any people who worked hard for a living might be—as cheerful as the workers at Covent Garden in London.

In the middle of an old Flemish market square, its rubble pushed aside like snow from a skating rink, was a small flower market, the autumn flowers vivid among the predominant greys of the stone and the black clothing of the market women. One flower seller sat smiling, her toothless gums munching something, her cheeks rosy and her blue eyes bright, humming to herself.

"Where are the shell-shocked civilians?" Julia asked Stewart. "Why hasn't so much violence driven them mad?

You have lots of cases in Halifax from just one explosion on one day."

"I don't know," Stewart said. "I want to see some hospitals, if we can find them."

"I would love to go with you and to see some of the people, if we could," Anne said. It pleased Julia to see that she and Stewart were enjoying each other's company.

After two days of travelling together, Anne had said, "He's a lovely man, your Professor MacPherson. Very interesting and droll."

"He's a very good friend," Julia had said.

"Of course he's dotty about you," Anne said. "He makes me think of Pierre in *War and Peace*."

Julia did not want to pursue that.

They were following the Western Front where it snaked into France, into Artois and Picardy, where trench warfare had stalled for nearly three years, subjecting troops and civilians to some of the most prolonged and destructive horror of the war. The Germans had briefly occupied the ancient city of Arras, famed for its architecture, had been driven out, and then subjected it to thirty-one months of siege and artillery bombardment.

Julia said to Morrice, "On our first morning in Arras, we met Captain Weeks, the officer said to have identified Charles's body. He looked very young and pleased to be excused from his routine. He had shown other visitors around, including Sir Robert Borden's party in March. So I asked, 'Did you meet a Major Traverse, Harold Traverse, who was with Borden?'"

"Oh yes, we were together for several days."

"He's my brother-in-law."

"A lawyer."

"Yes, but now he's heading into government, working for the prime minister's office."

"Well, that explains the urgency of the requests about your late husband."

While Stewart and Anne took the car and driver to visit hospitals, Julia sat down with Captain Weeks in the Hôtel de l'Univers. He told her about being sent down from London in December 1917, driving all night, reaching the hospital, and being shown to the morgue.

"I can't say categorically—you know I have been asked this a number of times—that I identified the body. When I got there, the chief medical officer was busy operating. He was free later and took me to the ward where Major Robertson had been treated. The head nurse told us he had died during the night. The CMO said, 'I suppose you want to see the body?' and I thought I should. At that point I had never seen a dead person." He laughed apologetically at such innocence. "I had not yet been at the front. We went to a separate building, used as a morgue, where the attendant showed us Major Robertson's body."

"They said it was Major Robertson."

"They said it was the body of the officer who had died during the night in the ward we had just visited asking for Major Robertson. I'm a lawyer in training myself or was, in civilian life. But at the time I was more concerned with not showing an emotion in the presence of death. Doubt about the identity of the dead man didn't arise. They assumed and I assumed it was Major Robertson."

"But you signed saying you identified him."

"Only in the sense that I did not challenge their identification. I had no reason to."

"What did he look like?"

"He was pale, with fair hair and freckles."

"You didn't see the colour of his eyes?"

"No. They were closed."

Julia produced her photograph. "Did he look like this?"

"Well, it's hard to say without the moustache."

"Charles did not have a moustache."

"The dead officer had one. Most of us have."

"Charles never wrote me that he had grown one."

"A lot of fellows have done it but keep it as a surprise for when they go home."

"What colour was the moustache?"

"Gosh, it's hard to remember after two years. The man was fair, I suppose the moustache was too."

"Not reddish hair? Charles had a red beard, although his hair was fair."

"I'm sorry. It didn't register with me, or else I don't remember. But I know there was a moustache."

"Did you see his injuries?"

"No, I saw only his shoulders and head. But may I ask why you are uncertain about the identification?"

She told him the story.

"That's very strange," he said. "She gave me the envelope, the nurse who told us he died, and I signed for it."

"And what did you do with it?"

"I turned it over to my CO in London, at Canadian HQ. It was all out of normal channels. They'd had a message from Ottawa saying the prime minister wanted to know."

"Do you know what happened to the envelope from there?"

"I don't."

"But you can't say for sure who the dead man you saw actually was?"

"Not in a court of law, I couldn't swear, now that a question has arisen. Does the description I gave you fit your husband?"

"Yes but many men fit that description."

"But does this help to resolve it for you?"

The question she was asking herself. Everything fit except the envelope...and the moustache. Everything else was consistent. It did sound like Charles—sandy hair, freckles. Normally he was tanned during the summer but this was December and he was dead; after being unconscious for days, loss of blood, he would have been pale. But only someone who actually had known him could have said for certain.

"The men who brought him in wounded, men from his own company, they must have known who they were taking to the field hospital?"

"They could have been stretcher bearers from another company or German prisoners bringing in wounded. It was often very confusing, with heavy casualties, and especially at night when we usually brought them in. I suppose the ward nurse could have given me the wrong envelope, if two Major Robertsons had died the same night. But that would have been so extraordinary she would have said, 'Which Major Robertson?' or something like that."

"You mean, the mix-up in the envelopes must have happened back in London?"

"I can't see any other probability. But even that doesn't sound very likely. You say the other officer was British army? Scottish? How would his effects come into Canadian hands? Unless your husband's envelope went somewhere else before it was sent to you."

Julia's head was dizzy with speculation. "Who would know that?"

"I don't know. We'd have to start with the duty officer that evening. A colonel I didn't know because I hadn't been posted in London very long, and I left for France right after that. But, you know, another thing occurs to me. Major Robertson was awarded the VC."

"Yes."

"They'd be pretty sure to know to whom they were giving the Victoria Cross. There was a detailed report of that action and his part in it. I remembered it coming through our office and going to Ottawa. Whichever senior officer signed that report would have known which major he was describing. It was very singular behaviour on your husband's part. Heroism of the highest... how does one say it now without sounding like a citation? I'm sure you know what I mean."

"I do, and thank you."

"I'm sorry I can't be more certain. If the inquiry goes further and it turns into a legal proceeding—like a coroner's inquest to settle the fact of death—of course I will gladly give evidence, but it'll be what I've told you. When the first request came several weeks ago, I went over it all carefully in my mind to give myself the clearest picture of what happened—or what I can remember. And that's what I've told you."

She told Morrice, "I thought then that Charles must be dead and it was foolish to pursue it further."

Foolish, when Neville would soon return from the trip—they were then in Washington seeing President Wilson—and at last she would really see him alone. It was good to have it resolved. It was time to put Charles finally to rest. Let them erect their banal window in the cathedral. The Robertsons deserved whatever comfort it could give them. Elizabeth in her sweet but firm way had repeatedly advised her to make a new life. Well, she was doing that—as usual flinging herself at the unknown—foolishly, as it turned out.

20

Morrice was painting again and Julia had slipped off her robe to resume the pose, always for the first few moments aware of her nudity, which talking made easier to forget.

"I think it really hit me later. A week before Neville was due to return, the Canadian forces office in London informed me that Charles's effects had been found. I went to the same attaché in Canada House. In an empty office he showed me a leather suitcase that I immediately recognized, and an army kitbag, and then discreetly left me alone with them."

They smelled musty, and when she opened the suitcase everything was mildewed. Both had been packed at his front-line quarters in France, two years before. There, ineffectually laundered or worn and not laundered, she found a civilian suit, tweed jacket and flannels, shoes, dress uniform, shirts, ties, underwear, pyjamas, socks, handkerchiefs, shaving kit, the twin military brushes she had given him as an advance Christmas present the year he left, a tin of Yardley's Brilliantine, and a bundle of her letters to him. A leather writing case with his initials embossed, a present from his mother, contained a tablet of writing paper, also mildewed, and his fountain pen.

"On the top sheet he had begun a letter. *'The Front, Somewhere in France, December 10, 1917.'* He had written, *'My darling—'* and nothing more. December tenth was the day he was wounded in the night action. He must have begun the letter, been interrupted, perhaps to plan the sortie that cost his life, and closed the tablet quickly, intending to continue when he came back."

"That must have been very distressing for you," Morrice said.

"No. I really felt he was dead. I picked up the clothing with distaste, as though it belonged to a stranger. I felt no intimacy with it."

Years before, in the first months when he had gone to the war, she would turn his jackets inside out to smell whether some scent of him lingered. That idea repelled her now.

"Even if he were alive, I would have wanted to discard these musty, sour-smelling clothes. They carried no emotion. I dropped them into the suitcase and wanted to wash my hands. I felt no tears. I took only his writing case and pen, and the bundle of my letters. I told the officer they could dispose of the rest as they wished. He asked me, 'Did the envelope turn up?'

"It took me a moment to realize what he was talking about. 'No, it has not turned up', I said. 'I don't think there is any more anyone can do.'

"As I stepped out into the street, busy with scarlet buses and shiny taxis, the window of Thomas Cook's across the street had a large poster advertising 'A New Life in Canada.' It felt like a message to me. There was a young family of eager British immigrants looking into a radiant future, gazing over fat wheat fields to the snow-capped Rockies. A part of Canada I've never been to and it looked foreign to me. I turned away feeling that a chapter in my life had closed for good."

Morrice, at work on the painting, took this in. "Does that mean you won't go back to Canada to live?"

"I don't know yet." She didn't want to talk about that. "Do you go back often now?"

"Not since my parents died in 1914. I used to go every year or so, to see them and to paint. I've always liked to do a few pictures in Quebec. I feel it's my scenery."

"Well, you paint it more subtly than anyone else."

"I feel it as a kind of reference point. As my style and colour have developed I like to go back there to measure it. I was painting with Maurice Cullen and he was using much brighter colours. He'd paid more attention to the Impressionists than I had. So I painted Sainte-Anne-de-Beaupré with the new colours and I later used the new palette back in France in painting the beach at Saint-Malo."

He looked at her shoulder where the light fell, mixed a tone, looked carefully again, and brushed it on.

"Today I have to prove to some critics that I am a Canadian painter. They think because I paint mostly in France I'm not Canadian."

"Do you think you are?"

"I never forget it. I'm happier living in France. They accept me, even with my tortured French, and they are kind about my painting. Some of them even forget now and then that I am not a French painter. A huge compliment, believe me. But I know my painting is not French. They love it when I paint snow in Paris, because they see I feel it. Someone wrote that I have a northern temperament. I don't know. I can't analyze it. I hate analyzing such things anyway. What I know is that when I look at the sky in Quebec, and the snow, they give me a feeling, and I can paint that feeling. And the more often I paint it, the better I do it. Just talking about it makes me want to go there and do another snow scene."

It was unlike Morrice to be so talkative. He leaned out from behind the easel to peer at her intensely, then disappeared, so that his voice came and went. If she dropped her eyes from the pose eye line, all she could see of him were his legs beneath the easel stand.

"They make me mad, some of them. What is a Canadian painter? Some of them today seem to think it is a painter who only goes out to paint the wilderness, the wild landscape of the north."

"Like Tom Thomson?" Julia said.

"Ah, Thomson was remarkable, the few things I have seen. A tragedy that he died. I'm not saying there aren't good men painting the wilderness...but almost never any people, no life. Why? Because they prefer looking at the wild terrain to looking at the cities. What gives me pleasure is the effect of man on nature, and I think it's foolish to say it's Canadian painting only if it's looking at empty woods and lakes."

"Perhaps they're reacting to all the horror in Europe. A lot of those painters were here, like you, at the front. Maybe they want to turn their backs on all that human ghastliness and look at nature unspoiled."

"Very true, I'm sure. But they may lose touch with where art is going. Where it is going is here, in Paris, here in Europe, however decadent and battered by disasters. This is where the imagination lives. This is where the new intellectual world rises from the ashes—not in Ontario. Anyway, it's foolish to make too much of nationality in art. Art is good or it is bad. It is important or it is unimportant."

"Where have you painted your best painting?"

"My best painting? I don't know. Here, right now. This one! But now the light is changing too much. We'll have to stop for today."

He could have worked longer, but his sensual imagination was interfering with the painterly discipline he needed, insinuating itself between his fingers and the brush they held. In applying a violet shadow under the breast, the brush stroking the canvas became his fingers touching her. And the fingers holding the brush were trembling again. She had not put any rum or eau-de-vie in the coffee, naturally. Léa would have thought of that.

A critic named Lyman had once said that Morrice's work did not appeal to the "fleshy" senses but seemed as pure painting poetry as Monet's. Huge exaggeration but he had been delighted by it. Yet that was just what he was risking now, slipping into the fleshy senses, becoming too aware of Julia's strong sexual appeal and having that leak into the painting. He wanted it to be subtler than that, to express her pride, her independence, as well as her sexuality and perhaps her imminent fecundity, yet also the mystery and the poetry of a beautiful woman. The warmer tones would express the sensuality, the cooler blues and greens her mystery and distance. He did not want the mystery to evaporate in sensuality rendered too literally. Lyman had also said that his painting was "unadulterated by verisimilitude." God, the highfalutin phrases the critics came up with! To mean he wasn't too literal? Well, that was right.

As he cleaned his palette and brushes he said, "I was thinking of going over to Cagnes to see Léa this afternoon. Will you be all right on your own?"

"Of course. Say hello to her from me and tell her she was quite right."

She studied the painting, the simplicity of form more obvious now with new colour applied. The work looked less fussed over, more sure of itself.

"It feels different from anything of yours I've seen."

"I think it is."

"How much more work does it need?"

"Tomorrow for sure. Perhaps the next day after that. If you can give me two more days?"

She was closing the bathroom door. "Yes, but I must get a grip on myself and make some decisions. I've been letting everything slide."

He called to her, "Don't forget your robe when you change. You left it behind yesterday."

Outside the hotel, intending to walk to clear her thoughts, she felt ravenous. She went back a few steps to the café she had just passed and found the table free where she had sat with Morrice. She ordered the first thing on the menu, fish soup and an omelette. She began gnawing at the bread the moment the waiter put it down.

This sudden imperative of food, like sleep, kept taking her unawares. It reinforced the message: she must think practically. The primitive force within her would not be ignored.

She had pushed out of her mind the letters that must be piling up at Thomas Cook's in Paris, the only address she had given anyone—inevitably letters, probably telegrams, from Neville. Perhaps from his mother and Anne, seeking explanation, although Anne might have guessed. I should have seen it coming. Anne kept warning me and I saw the way Neville kept retreating in the royal presence. It was bitterly satisfying to think of him discountenanced, his aplomb shaken. Too bad! There would be messages from Stewart, routine unless someone in Halifax had tracked him down in Germany. She had opened no letters for weeks— longer, since early December, ignoring Christmas, so her mother would be anxious too.

"Something to drink, *madame*?"

"A glass of rosé, if you please." Her stomach felt stronger today, just empty.

Leaving England in such haste, she had told everyone simply that she would be travelling in France, but inevitably they would find her, through Thomas Cook or through Suzanne.

Accepting Suzanne's help would be the easiest. They had become close. Suzanne's fiancé, André, had died late in the war, like Charles, so she too had lived through years of anxiety.

With the withering wartime losses of the French, nearly one-and-a-half million dead, her chances of finding a husband were slimmer than Anne's.

Suzanne did not need the money she earned from giving lessons to a few select pupils like Sir Robert but liked meeting them. She was exhilarated to be chatting with the man who rubbed shoulders with the likes of Clemenceau, Lloyd George, and President Wilson. Borden shared a lot with her, the diary recording his frustration in trying to get Canada representation at the peace conference commensurate with its war effort. By the time Borden and Harry left she had become quite a little Canadian nationalist, had Mlle Perret, burning with indignation over slights the prime minister had confided to her.

"Do you know"—she was a fierce little bird, corseted and erect in her indignation—"they wanted to give Canada the same number of *sièges* as countries like Portugal, which did not fight in the war! Canada, whose men came to France in the thousands to die for us, for our soil, who spilled their blood for us, and this old villain, Clemenceau, wants to treat you like that? When he told me, I said to him, 'Bravo, Monsieur Borden!' and I applaud him like this!" She clapped daintily and collapsed in her chair with merry laughter.

She made many little references to Borden's charm, his handsome face, his twinkle, his strong hands. She was fascinated by his capacity for work, his simple honesty with himself, his willingness to speak up to anyone. She drew all this from the diary he kept bringing her so touchingly and ingenuously. She thought him deliciously naive and honourable.

"How he agonized in the matter of buying some new shoes, because his boots were worn out, and he needed open shoes for the evening. Terribly put out because new laces for his old shoes were so expensive! Can you imagine? A great statesman, meeting with dukes and counts and presidents to make the peace of the world, and is writing in his diary how much shoelaces cost? *Mon Dieu*! It is ridiculous—and adorable!"

Borden was taken many times to the theatre, which he welcomed to improve his French, but he never had anything to say about the play. "Oh, he would say, 'Madame So-and-so played well,' but when I asked him he had no conversation to discuss the play. It was good, it was not good. He liked it, he did not like it. Or he would pass it off with a smile that it was very well done."

Borden had had little chance to acquire culture, in which most Canadians had no interest, Julia told her. Rupert Brooke had gone to Canada before the war and found it a country without a soul.

"And did the war give it a soul?" Suzanne asked. A good question, Julia thought.

"I would ask, who were his favourite authors, to make conversation for his French," Suzanne said. "but it seemed to me that he had none. Poor man, to have none of these joys."

He did take long walks for his health. Sometimes he would walk instead of going to a dinner, if he could get out of it. He liked to walk about the streets of Paris.

"I would ask him if he could not use some of this walking time to go to the Louvre to see paintings, but he said he found that very tiring and it was better recreation for him just to walk, so that he could think about problems he had to solve or speeches he had to make."

Of course Borden had made an impression on her. Her life was tiny, circumscribed, a doll in her parents' apartment, her needs all met within a few streets. And she had in a sense retired from all her other interests to live with her grief and her blighted prospects. Well, Julia thought, until I came along.

21

At the Nice station Morrice had to wait for the next trolley that ran the few kilometres to Cagnes-sur-Mer. In the station bar he ordered a rum and sipped it in the shade, watching the people and traffic in the bright square outside. He was thinking of the colour he had used in part of the shading on Julia's flesh tones, the merest suggestion of contour. Close to the grey-blue green of the water in his canvas of the Venice harbour many years ago, the green of a pale silk he had once seen in a Venetian shop, a jade so diluted in the misty sea luminescence of the lagoon it was almost colourless, like the Venetian ice dropped by a child on the paving stones of San Marco, its colour evaporating as it melted. Evaporated colour. He liked the idea.

The tones were similar to those in *The Port of Saint-Servan*, which the critic Henri Marcel had liked for its "indefinable shades of grey, mauve, pale green, before which one stands mesmerized." Liked so much he bought it at the 1902 Societé Nationale, where Morrice had also sent two Venice studies. Indefinable shades...that was a good phrase for a critic. Morrice drew the deepest pleasure from mixing shades that were almost impossible to describe in words. It was one of his singular talents, like the green today subtly defining Julia's thigh and torso. Let them leave words alone: let them be mesmerized.

Venice had perfectly suited his personality as a painter in those years striving for a subtle balance of harmonies, usually at twilight, in the mood of the Chopin nocturnes, as Whistler had called his evening studies of the Thames. Morrice himself had appropriated the title for the first painting he sent to the Societé Nationale des Beaux-Arts salon in 1896.

He'd been thinking about Venice. Interesting now how his colour sense had changed over the nine or ten years of those Venice sessions. Out of Whistler, through the Fauves, into his own personal palette and style. The illusive green he had used that morning might echo earlier work, but the style was quite new. Julia had noticed; her eyes really saw, those candid, often amused, grey eyes. How had Norman and Heather Montgomery bred this Venus, this Aphrodite? No wonder her romantic life was complicated. It made a man ache to look at her. How had this escaped him in 1913, when she posed nude in his wicker chair? He couldn't remember. Or had the knowledge that she was Norman's daughter made her taboo?

He saw the trolley arrive. When he put down his glass his trembling hand made it rattle on the zinc counter.

Julia paid one franc sixty for her café lunch, leaving the forty centimes change, an overgenerous tip but she felt generous. Living in France was reasonable. Not at resort hotels like La Méditerranée in season, but elsewhere you could have a simple meal, like her lunch for two francs, about a shilling and sixpence in British money, and dinner in a good restaurant for six francs. When she made up her mind, she could rent a flat or a small house in the country. When the Halifax house on South Park Street was sold, it might let her buy something in France without touching the capital invested in Montreal. If she stayed in France.

Today was another day worthy of the colourful posters sprouting again all over France advertising Nice as the "City of Winter." Julia walked on the promenade rejoicing in the warmth and soft brilliance of the sunlight, reflected off glossy palm fronds overhead, sparkling from a million facets of the sea, and causing the sails of distant boats to gleam like starched linen.

She came to where the Paillon River emptied into the Mediterranean, and saw scores of women kneeling on rocks in the riverbed doing laundry. Sheets were spread over rocks to dry or hung from trees or the stone walls of the river embankment. She leaned on the rail and watched the women, all swarthy from working in the sun, wearing coarse skirts with many petticoats, scrubbing clothes on the stones, wringing, spreading out, applying soap, scrubbing again, then rinsing in the cold, moving water. They were chattering cheerfully and loudly enough to match the clattering of horses' hooves and motors on the bridge.

How many of these young and middle-aged women might have lost someone in the war? Her thoughts went back to Anne Boiscoyne, whose social position gave her little to do but grieve for herself and a generation of her class.

After viewing the things in Charles's suitcase, she had told Anne about her coldness towards the musty, mildewed clothes: stronger than indifference, actual revulsion, as though they had just been taken off a dead body.

"You really must think him dead," Anne said. "If you didn't, wouldn't you have wept over them—to be reminded of him so tangibly?"

Perhaps she wanted Julia's experience for herself, to give her own grief more fuel, as though she regretted that her dead friend's clothing had not come to her.

At twenty-three, she was more world-weary, despairing of civilization, unhopeful about the future than Julia, five years older and widowed. In that sense Anne was more of the modern age, however advanced Julia's taste in music and painting. Perhaps prompted by her literary friends, Anne truly felt herself part of a generation that was damned, if not lost—that feeling, so common among young Europeans, comparatively rare in Canada. The intellectual avant-garde had foreshadowed it all, knowing that civilization had created machines, weapons, science, social pathologies, that dispossessed them of Edwardian assumptions of endless progress, the triumphal march of civilizing humanity. In a sense the intellectuals had already absorbed the lessons of the war as an abstraction before it happened. The war only fulfilled what had become expectations of dislocation, brutality, violence—humanity at its most savage. This was a watershed in human behaviour, a lurch in the orbit of the planet. Nothing would ever be the same.

Yet for these laundrywomen everything was the same, whether or not they had lost men in the war. They came here every day with loads of dirty laundry, knelt on wadded pieces of cloth among the rocks, washed in the cold waters of the river, spread their work to dry, folded it, and carried it back to the customer. Then, presumably, they walked to their own homes to cook and care for their families. There was no modern way for them. A way of life might be overthrown for some like Anne, for the Russians in their revolution, but in the mundane ways everyone felt, life was back to normal.

22

From the swaying trolley car Morrice caught flashes of cobalt blue where the Mediterranean scintillated through the gaps in passing trees and houses. On his right the foot-hills of the Alpes Maritimes wheeled by, covered with the greyish green of winter foliage.

Tomorrow she would come back and he would add detail—highlights, firmer outlines, more definition here and there. He could not keep her here but from the moment she had asked how much longer, he'd felt a certain sadness, an emptiness, at the prospect of her leaving. She was deciding what to do. She didn't want to tell him everything, naturally. Some of it must be too intimate to discuss. Obviously, she had given herself to the confident Englishman, and then something had happened. He had soured on her or she on him. And she was left with a baby.

He had said to her casually, *Oh, Léa might know, women talk*. In the old house at 45 Quai des Grands-Augustins a midwife lived on the second floor. One passed her sign, *Sage-femme*, coming up the curved stairs to his small apart-ment. That midwives also discreetly helped women out of difficulties in certain cases was of course assumed by many. Léa would know. If the *sage-femme* in his building, or another, could help a woman desperate for an accidental miscarriage and not a child, Léa would know.

Was Julia the kind of woman to take such a course? Illegal as it was, but often winked at when the practitioners were discreet? Better for society to have wanted babies or no babies was his own view, but that was a sentiment easier to defend in Paris than in Montreal. But if she were going to go back there to live, Julia would have to conform or be unhappy. He guessed that a woman with an illegitimate child would be treated cruelly. Better for her to begin life afresh, without such an encumbrance. But that was a decision she would have to come to herself.

He did not see her making a life as a painter. Her talent was real but unremarkable. The daring she showed in her spirit, intellectually, in her nonconformity, did not appear on canvas.

She had such a good eye and knowledge of painting that she would make a better critic than a painter. If the art world would ever listen to a woman critic. But to be a critic she would need to see new painting constantly, so she would have to stay in France, at least in Europe. Or, if she had a little money, she could open a small gallery and sell young painters she liked. She could attract the Americans and Canadians now beginning to travel to Europe again. He could put his own paintings in her gallery. They could remain friends. If he were a younger man he would probably be falling in love with her, doing just what he had always warned young painters to avoid: emotional entanglements that would spoil their work.

Overcome with sleepiness again, Julia lay down in her room, the French windows open, the faintest breeze from the sea licking the gauze curtains in the sunlight. It would be delicious to stay here forever, in this Mediterranean air that bathed every common thing in such healing light that it filled the spirit with hope.

In the lobby she had seen Henri Matisse collecting his key. She must remember to tell Morrice. That would be something to tell Anne, that she had seen Matisse.

Only—it came back—she would not be seeing Anne again. Or Stephanie...*How could I have let this happen?* But of course, to her dismay, she knew.

She had never been as keyed up for anything as in the few days before Neville's return: electric with anticipation, every part of her alert for the moment. Never in her life had any meeting been so long anticipated—more than two years, if she included both conscious and unconscious yearnings. To be truthful about it now, all the time she had been trying to make a relationship with Stewart, Neville was in the back of her mind, personifying the passion she missed. Unfair to Stewart, but in the end fair because she was square with him as soon as she'd recognized what was what. But she had been brought to that pitch in the middle of August, only to have him snatched away by the Prince of Wales.

All through those weeks in Wiltshire, in London, over to France and back, she was being treated virtually as though she and Neville were actually betrothed, that everything had been settled and announced, all arrangements made. He had only to come back and carry her off, not only willingly, mind you, but as eagerly as she had ever wanted anything. Yet, of course, nothing was settled except in the few words they had spoken in Halifax, more in the looks they had exchanged. She behaving like a lovesick girl, she *was* a lovesick girl, mooning over his photograph from the *Illustrated London News*.

Now that she was certain about Charles, she thought of asking Stephanie to drive her back to the cemetery, where she could put flowers on his grave. Soon it would be November eleventh, the first anniversary of the Armistice. It would be nice to ask Anne, too, but that would mean taking the big car...In her preoccupation with Neville's return, the idea slipped away.

Nothing was simple with royalty involved, even with the Prince of Wales trying famously to abbreviate or bypass protocol. So at the end of the tour as an equerry, Neville had to endure all the formalities of princely homecoming receptions, public and private, with the king and queen before he could come to Wiltshire. The day they knew he was coming, or thought he was, Julia was as nervous as if it had been her wedding day. She had washed her hair the day before and fussed over how to put it up, not liking the result and doing it again, as usual becoming impatient with herself for thinking it mattered so much. If he loves you it doesn't matter which way you put up your hair, stupid! But it mattered, as did the dresses she put on and took off, not certain whether he would appear at lunch, or tea, or dinner. So much repressed longing, so many doubts that sprang up from the shadows in the middle of the night to be squelched with firm talking to herself. So much excitement building and swelling that at times during the day she had to force herself to take long, slow breaths to calm down.

Her imagination would leap from the most explicitly erotic with Neville to frightening indifference, when she feared she would instantly see in his face that she had imagined the whole thing. His letters did not hint at any such change of heart but they had been hastily scribbled, on the run. In a few seconds' daydreaming, she could have them decorously shaking hands in public, indecorously embracing in private, kissing passionately and in bed together blissfully coupled. All this could be imagined in the space of stopping on the main staircase to look out the mullioned windows at the autumn flower beds or in the second it took to turn to a looking glass and catch her complexion flushed from such reveries. Nothing shy or inhibited about her daydreaming! She had even calculated, while making polite conversation at lunch, the number of days until her next period, as though they were long married and he were her husband returning from a trip. Eager? She was emotionally and physically at concert pitch. She was the violin string anticipating the bow.

23

"Léa wanted to come to Nice today to shop. I suggested we have lunch together."

"That would be nice."

"Then you and she could have some time. She wanted to talk to you."

So the shy Montrealer and his mistress had been discussing Julia like anxious parents.

"If you'll get ready, I just need an hour or so to finish this."

She went to change, and Morrice tried to concentrate on the painting. He had not intended to arrange the meeting with Léa so unsubtly, but Julia's presence this morning overwhelmed him, the small breeze of perfumed soap or scent arriving with her had acted on his senses as though on a boy of sixteen who had never been alone in a bedroom with a woman.

The evening before he'd spent with Léa but had come back to Nice at midnight. At four-thirty when it was still dark he had snapped awake, alert as if he had been drinking coffee for hours. He awoke with an image filling his mind, as though he had been rehearsing it in his sleep, of Julia, arriving to pose again and removing her clothes. He had never witnessed that, since she had always retired to the bathroom, but in this vision she disrobed unaffectedly in front of him.

And when she was naked, she came and sat on his bed, leaned over, and embraced his burning face with her cool, firm breasts. So vivid was the experience that, with his nose pressed into the sweet softness of her flesh, he could smell the scent that always came into the room with her.

Sur votre jeune sein laissez rouler ma tête...

Let my head, still ringing with your last
kisses, settle on your soft young breast;
and when the splendid hurricane has passed,
perhaps I'll sleep a little while you rest.

Perhaps because he had discovered Verlaine so young, or for some other reason, in the image of Julia's breast, mingled with its accompanying sensual knowledge, there was something connected with the linen cupboard in his home in Montreal. He remembered as a small boy the scent of clean linen. When he thought of his home in those days, the linen cupboard was a recurrent image, like the vision of winter light filling the house: the dazzling brilliance of snow-reflected light shining upward into all the rooms, then reflected down from the white plaster of the ceilings, exposing heavy, dark furniture, tasselled velvets in dark vermillions and purples. And with those colours went the sound of bells jingling on the harnesses of passing sleigh-horses, long before the motor cars with clanking chains replaced the sleighs. And the sound evoked the smells of porridge and toast and the poached kippered herrings his father ate on Sunday mornings before church.

Julia would have known all those smells and sounds. She would have been precisely the kind of girl, outwardly at least, whom his mother had wished he would find and marry, as his brothers had; a girl of their kind, a girl he associated with, or thought his mother did, with the word *clean*; clean like the fresh laundry in the linen closet upstairs with its smell of ironing but also of some dried lavender that sweetened the odour. But that was just the kind of girl he had considered a trap in those years when his private desires, sexual and life-directional, were clearly at odds with the route planned for him. The girls from the "nice" families his parents knew, with their pretty hair and trim ankles and good teeth, who smelled sweet and flowery when he held them at dances, were baiting the trap set for his life. But here was Julia, one of them, not a generation later but as though back with him a generation younger: he was her age and suddenly she was what he wanted. Now she was standing in the position where she normally posed, the light bathing her, haloing the contours of her body, and he was on his knees at her feet, his arms around her thighs, burying his face in the blonde curls there.

He had risen hastily, bathed, dressed, and gone outside to watch the dawn and drink several cups of coffee. Then he returned to study the problems left in the painting but still could not entirely banish the sensations lingering from his fantasies. To have her arrive in a subtle cloud of the very scent he had imagined, after such explicit reveries, was disconcerting. Without thinking he mentioned Léa's desire to have a private word, and he noticed the knowing look Julia returned.

Undressing, putting on and tying the robe, and coming back into his bedroom studio, she felt more than the usual momentary self-consciousness. It made her tone more challenging than she intended. "Does Léa have advice for my...predicament?"

"It might be easier if you talked with her. I think of your mother and father—"

"Please don't." Just to think of them in this context horrified her and she hastily added, "No need to disturb them now."

"No, no, I won't." But invoking them did channel his thoughts in a more responsible direction. Useful, because it was shaming to consider what Norman Montgomery would think if he knew what Jim Morrice had been fantasizing about.

Actually, when she slipped off her robe and resumed the pose, the sight of her nudity erased the prurient thoughts. Now again she was a painting exercise. He studied her carefully. What had he not quite got? Nothing obvious. The face was really fine, he thought, her regard a nicely mysterious mix of the defiant and the demure, a reticence that suggested a profound spiritual life animating and making more complex the radiant sensuality of her flesh. Though not too radiant; restrained by the cool tones in the shadows, stimulating, if an observer looked long enough, a tension. Odd that the word *reticence* should occur to him; this was in no way a reticent painting. It was as bold as anything he had ever done. It expressed powerfully the tensions he felt in her presence, yet it was in no way anecdotal. This was not an explicit situation. This woman had not just said or done something, nor was something about to be said or done to her. Yet anything could have happened or be about to happen—or nothing. He stared, as Julia stared back, at the charcoal mark on the edge of the stretcher. The only question in his mind was whether her face was too literally her face. Was it too specifically a portrait because of those grey eyes—which, incidentally, he had caught well—that nose, that mouth?

Leave that thought for a moment and come back to the overall style of the painting. It was a departure, or rather a marked step in the direction in which he had been tending for several years, towards simpler forms, elimination of unneeded detail. The surrounding wallpaper, curtains, window frame, louvred shutters, carpet were as much part of the design and composition as the woman. This was a painting, not a window on the world, but a decoration intended to give you more profound and complex feelings the longer you contemplated it. A painting to be lived with and experienced over many years.

The colour values? For thirty years he had been pursuing colour, searching for colour, looking with infinite care to see the fine tones that would, in balance or in tension with each other, induce feeling in the observer. The colours in this painting were the product of thirty years of applying himself to that challenge. He could not have painted this picture at any time in those thirty years until now.

Painting brought to light so many tensions: the tension between his own natural diffidence and the struggle to be more assertive; between his appetites and the training to repress them; between recklessness and discipline; between the resistance he felt when moving further from the traditional, in life as much as in painting; between being himself or what others expected him to be; between the man luxuriating in the light and restorative warmth of the south, and the soul that felt it morally belonged to snow and the north. He could see all this in the painting, but he doubted anyone else ever would.

Finally, it brought out what every painting had, from his earliest watercolours: the tension between his talent, to the degree he had trained it, and whatever it was, innate or acquired, that limited his talent.

"Well," he said at last, "it's finished."

"But I haven't seen you add anything to it."

"I didn't need to. It's finished."

"May I look?"

"Of course."

She turned away from him as she slipped into the robe. "Now I can do my hair the usual way. This always feels about to fall down."

She tied the robe and came behind the easel to stand beside him, and again he became strongly aware of her body's close presence and the scent it carried.

"I think it's wonderful. It makes me see all over again what a really fine painter you are."

"I'm happy with it. If you don't mind, I'd like to send it to the Salon this autumn."

Julia hesitated, trying to disentangle the emotion of seeing herself depicted thus, so recognizable and so frankly naked, from her aesthetic sense. Impossible, since the two currents were constantly intermingling. Who in Paris would see it? Suzanne Perret? But she did not go to see modern art. Someone from Canada on a visit?

"If you don't put my name on it—all right? For the time being?"

"I wasn't going to, since I consider it much more than a portrait." He laughed. "And I won't show it in Canada."

"Oh dear!"

"Or London."

He could almost feel her stiffen, and when he looked she was blushing vividly down to her neck.

"But I promised it to you and I'll send it after the Salon."

Julia said, "I was imagining my maid—she's a wonderful, salty old thing—I was thinking of her looking at it. And what she'd say."

"And...?"

"She knows nothing about painting but she's very shrewd. She actually warned me about getting in the family way."

"So you are thinking about moving back to Halifax?"

She looked at Morrice questioningly. "No, I was just thinking of Mollie."

"And I'd like to show it to Henri, when he's back."

"Oh, he's back! I meant to tell to you. I saw him in the lobby last night."

"Wonderful! Then, let's ask him to lunch with us. It's Sunday. On Sunday in France one goes out for lunch. Besides, I think we should celebrate. Before you came, I hadn't worked for months. And now look! A totally fresh start. The beauty has awakened the sleeping prince."

She saw him excited, moving as though he wanted to kiss her but, as their eyes met, hesitating—and retreating.

"...and I am very grateful to you."

24

"*Cher ami!*" As they gathered in the lobby, Matisse greeted Morrice with a handshake and an affectionate pat on the shoulder. Bowing first over Léa's hand, then Julia's, the Frenchman looked younger at fifty by ten or fifteen years than Morrice's fifty-four, his complexion healthy, his eyes luminous behind his glasses. Matisse was slightly less bald; otherwise, it was remarkable how similar the two painters were—both short, bearded, neatly suited, like two insurance salesmen off to work.

Matisse said to Léa, "Charming to see you again," and to Julia when Morrice introduced her, "Certainly, I remember you, *madame*. You came to my studio with Morrice and you bought my small painting—from Morocco." He turned to Morrice. "The little sketch in red and green that Shchukin did not want."

Now she had to try to think in French again. "I love that painting. I wanted it more than anything before I left Paris. It has kept me happy through many sad times."

"It gives me a lot of pleasure to hear you say that."

She would have liked to go on and say that the startling conjunction of colours had come to represent for her both the sadness and sweetness of life, that at times the painting seemed mysteriously to hold the secret to her own happiness.

Matisse said, "You know Shchukin lives on the Côte d'Azur now? A few kilometres. But a changed man. He has lost interest in modern art since the Bolsheviks took everything from him. I suppose somewhere they have all those paintings of mine."

They were setting off for the restaurant, Léa on Morrice's arm, proud in a Sunday dress of green linen with black appliqué.

Matisse walked beside Julia. "It is a comfort for me to have a friend like Morrice here. The Côte d'Azur is a delight but a little isolated culturally. It is good to have someone to talk to. He likes music as I do...his flute, my violin...everything."

"I have known him since I was a child in Montreal. He was a legend in our family, the independent way he lived."

"Ah, well he is rich. He can afford independence. He is like a bird—always on the move, here, there, always restless. But when he alights in one place, he is a delightful companion, in every sense a gentleman."

"He has just finished a painting of me."

"So he told me this morning. He said you have inspired him to paint again, which is very good. It made me sad to see him vegetating...and drinking."

"Well, he hasn't stopped that."

"Oh, I assume he never will. This passion for whisky is part of him. I have spent many delightful evenings with him, in Tangiers, here, Paris. Wonderful companion, only I drink as many mineral waters as he does whiskies. But the important thing is his eye—the most delicate painter's eye. It is a miracle that you have made him open it again. But a miracle that is understandable. You possess a beauty any artist would like to paint."

As they entered La Bouillabaisse Julia whispered to Léa, "We had lunch here the other day. I got so sleepy I fell asleep on the banquette. But there was no one here."

Léa's warm brown eyes smiled complicitly. "I thought, after lunch, we could chat a little...if you would like?"

"I would. We can be alone if you come up to my room."

In the languor induced by the slow serving of the Sunday meal in the crowded restaurant, Matisse and Morrice talked diagonally across the table, making direct conversation difficult for the women, but Léa was happily occupied in listening and giving serious attention to the food.

Matisse was telling Morrice about the art scene in Paris, about Marquet and Camoin and other painters they both knew, and Miró and Juan Gris, with whom he'd become friends.

"Are you arranging an exhibition?"

"No, just trying to sell some paintings. You know as well as I do, they do not sell themselves. You have to pay attention to it."

"I know."

"And to the men who write about it in the newspapers and art journals. I resolved a long time ago, never refuse to see journalists, however stupid they may be. It is essential to be mentioned, to be talked about. No, I have not had an exhibition for two years—since the show with Picasso at Paul Guillaume's."

"I always heard you were bitter rivals," Julia said.

"Oh, that was people creating stupid competition. Long before the war. Gertrude Stein and her friends liked to divide people into Picassoites or Matissites. Just for something to talk about. The war did away with those cliques." He smiled. "But you know, I learned this after the Armistice, the French army had two camouflage battalions. They named one of them Picasso and one Matisse. That's amusing, isn't it?"

"And which was the better at fooling the Germans?" Morrice asked.

"In nature the best camouflage is colour, so I leave it to you. Who is the better colourist?"

"But Picasso can make a woman look like a machine," said Léa. "Perhaps he could make a war machine look like a woman!" And everyone laughed.

It intrigued Julia to observe them together. Both men had emerged late as artists; each had toed the parental line, each submitting reluctantly but dutifully to years of training in the law before breaking free. And the affinities did not stop there. Both were men with sensibilities shaped in the narrower light and mores of the north, but whose souls craved the luxury of southern light and spirit.

"In the autumn," Julia said to Matisse, "I made a tour of the battlefields in your part of France, in Artois and Picardy. The destruction was almost beyond my comprehension. I wonder how your town, your family, came through it."

"Ah, *madame*." Matisse wiped his lips and lifted his glasses to wipe his eyes with the napkin. "It was occupied by the Germans. My mother and my brother's family were virtual prisoners there. My brother was taken to Germany as a prisoner of war. We had to send him food parcels. I made engravings to pay for them. When I went immediately after the Armistice, the road from Arras to Bohain was strewn with dead horses. My mother was near death but she had vowed to wait for me."

"Then I must have been very close because we visited Arras, and Vimy, where so many Canadians were killed."

"They were glorious, those Canadians. Everyone in the region talks about that."

"My husband was killed after Passchendaele and I wanted to see the battlefields for myself."

Morrice said, "Julia's husband was a hero. They awarded him the Victoria Cross. It is the highest award the British make."

Matisse raised his wineglass solemnly. "Then I drink to his memory, *madame*, and to his courage—and yours."

"Thank you," Julia said, wondering how often in her life this little ceremony would happen, and then she remembered the cathedral window.

"In memory of Charles—my husband's name was Charles—his parents are putting a large stained-glass window in the cathedral in Halifax."

She described the argument about style, what the Robertsons had preferred, and her own suggestion that they should commission a leading modern artist, like Matisse or Morrice.

Morrice snorted, Matisse listened with full attention, asking Julia to describe the church, where the window would be, and how large. She told them her idea had been brushed aside but, if they had been willing, would either artist have considered such a commission?

"Not me, thank you!" Morrice said. "I had enough of churches when I was young and I don't like commissions."

But Matisse was nodding, thinking about it. He asked where Halifax was and Morrice reminded him of the explosion of the French munitions ship in 1917. Of course, Matisse said, that would be a very long way to go, many weeks away from all other work, and the conversation moved on.

That was a difference in the two men: Morrice dismissive but Matisse's curiosity instantly engaged. But then, he had endured years of poverty, scraping for every franc to support his wife and three children, while Morrice, with his private income and no responsibilities, had lived for himself and his art, unburdened by financial anxiety. Was that why Morrice's paintings preserved behind all their worldliness some hint of innocence?

As usual, he was emptying his glass more rapidly than the others, ordering another bottle.

Julia said, "Jim and I were talking about painters in the war. Did you do any pictures of the war itself?"

"No," Matisse said. "There would have been no point. I am not a journalist. I do not make records."

"That's about what I told her." Morrice was proud to be exposing Julia to Matisse, who loved talking theory as much as Morrice disliked it. And proud of Julia who talked well in French, whose colour rose as she talked, making her more beautiful.

Matisse said, "But the war is in every painting I did during the war. Every painting. In the colour first, of course, but in the faces and the eyes of people I painted. In the gravity of the faces, you see the war. Come and see. I have some of those pictures here in Nice. Come and look."

"Thank you, I'd love to."

Julia mentioned the Canadian war paintings and her feeling that, while intending to portray the horror, the conventions of painting made that horror somehow morally acceptable.

"Painters have usually depicted war as heroism or national glory, and so they romanticized it or sentimentalized it, because we considered war cruel but necessary. To the French this last war was necessary. Our homeland was invaded. We had to defend it. It has made us serious and it leaves us with no illusions about war in the future."

Morrice said, "Goya had no illusions about war. His painting in the Prado of French soldiers executing Spanish hostages at point-blank range is full of disgust."

"It is a great painting, but Goya was Spanish," Matisse said. "In this war, French soldiers executed fellow Frenchmen who refused to fight—hundreds of them—to hold the front lines. What French painter would have the heart to paint such scenes? Think of the mothers of those Frenchmen!"

What French commanders had the lack of heart to order such executions? Julia felt herself flaring for an argument but let the spurt of anger subside because Matisse was saying, "During the war, I painted Greta Prozor, a woman in touch with modern schools of poetry. She told me about Rilke, watching the war from his country, Germany. He was in despair because he owed too much to France, to Russia, to others to reject or hate any of them. She said his whole occupation was to refuse to understand."

"If enough of us refused to understand..." Julia could not immediately finish the thought. "But I know people in Canada who have illusions, who kept their innocence and feel quite cheerful about it."

"But this is a conversation so serious and sad!" cried Léa. "The war is finished. Can't we make ourselves happy again?"

"You are right, my dear!" Matisse beamed. "We should make ourselves happy with a miraculous dessert!"

25

In her room at the hotel, Julia said, "Do you mind if I lie down while we talk?" She stretched out on the bed, while Léa settled into the small armchair with a grateful sigh.

"I always eat too much when we go out. And Morrice drinks too much. But I have never been able to change that. Nor have his doctors."

"Has he been seriously ill?"

"Absolutely. He had ulcers in the colon. That is serious. They had to do an operation to remove part of it. I was very worried about him. It was a long recovery. That's why he began spending more time in Nice. But he was soon back to his old ways again."

"How well is he now, do you think?"

"Who can tell? He won't discuss it. He won't tell me what the doctors say. But anyone can look at him and see he is not the picture of health. How do you think he looks?"

"I haven't seen him for seven years, so he looks different to me. No, to be honest, he doesn't look well."

"But, my dear, how it has lifted his spirits to see you! And he is working! He showed me the painting. It is very beautiful and"—she laughed—"looking at it, who would know your condition?"

"You knew four days ago when you saw me at Cagnes."

"Sometimes I think I can tell—when a woman's eyes look

big like a cat's. And then you felt ill and you had to sleep. So, I made a guess."

"What has Morrice told you?"

"Almost nothing. Well, that you need to make some decisions."

"I must. I think I'm somewhere in the fifth or sixth week."

"And the father does not know?"

"No."

"And you do not wish him to know?"

"No."

"Well." With a sigh Léa got up and went to the window to look at the view. Then she let the flimsy curtain drop and came to sit on the dressing-table chair, close to Julia, speaking more quietly.

"Twice in my life I have been in the same situation. Both times I thought I could not live with a baby. There was no prospect of marriage or a regulated life. You know what I mean."

"Of course."

"Did Morrice ever tell you about this?"

"No, nothing."

Léa pulled a dainty handkerchief from her sleeve because her dark eyes were beginning to moisten.

"He knew, but really he didn't want to know. Everything must be clear for his work. Like Matisse, like other artists they know. They may be great painters, but as men they are very selfish. As husbands? Disasters, most of them. They are like children. They can think only of themselves. Morrice was always very honest about it. Matisse has that wife and three children and he just leaves them! When they were little, he went off for months at a time to Tangiers. Like Morrice. Going off whenever he liked. I could not raise children like that. It is too cruel."

She mopped her eyes.

"The first time I was caught, I was only nineteen, I knew nothing. I was afraid to tell my aunt, anyone, until it was too late to do anything but to have the baby. So I had it, it was a boy, and he was immediately adopted. And I went back to my life in Paris. The life I enjoyed. In those days I liked all the excitement of the city. Morrice would take me to the concerts, the openings of all the painting exhibitions; we would sit in the cafés on the boulevards; we would go to dinners with his friends at the Closerie des Lilas. He let me buy beautiful clothes. I loved it. Then I got pregnant again, and this time I thought I was much wiser. I knew a certain woman who helped me, and I had a miscarriage. You follow me?"

"Of course."

"And I continued with my life. Free of that burden. I believe that woman is still there, in Paris. A year ago I know she was, if you follow me."

"I do."

"But, strange as it may seem, the way I did it the second time—a sin, of course, not strictly legal, of course—that disturbed me less than the first. Oh, after the miscarriage I felt out of sorts for a while, but the pain of giving away the first child, the little boy, has stayed with me every day.

"And since I guessed your situation and began thinking what you would do, that pain has come back to me with great force. And I will tell you this—between us—because I have not told Morrice and I don't know what he will say: I want to go back and find my child. Does that seem terrible to you? To come into his life now? He will be twenty-two next month. I want him to know I am his mother."

She began to cry and Julia got up and hugged her until the heaving of her chest subsided.

"Léa, I understand what you're telling me. And you are wonderful to share it with me."

"You won't tell Morrice?"

"Of course not."

"He may be upset, but I am determined to do it."

"I think it is very brave of you."

Lea smiled happily. "You think so?"

"I think Morrice is lucky to have someone as devoted as you. He must be a difficult man to love—no, not difficult to love, difficult to put up with."

"I have not given you much help."

"No, no, no. You have."

"If you tell me, I will send that woman a note, immediately."

"I'll tell you."

"You should decide quickly."

"That I know."

Léa looked at her for a moment, shaking her head. Finally she patted Julia affectionately on the arm. "I have wept so much my face is a mess. If you don't mind, I'll use your bathroom to put myself to rights before we join them to see Matisse's new pictures."

"Of course."

Julia lay quite relaxed and she heard herself say to Neville, "My face is a mess."

26

It had happened almost as Julia had imagined. Neville arrived at tea time, and the first sight of him emerging from the Prince of Wales's car sent an electric thrill through her that she could feel in every sensitive part of her body. Neville looked leaner for his travels and exhausted. There were dark circles under his eyes, but the eyes instantly fastened on hers in a way that was unmistakably reassuring. And in front of his mother and sister he kissed her —actually for the first time, but as though they had often kissed before, an affectionate, homecoming kiss.

She sat with him on the small sofa in the sitting room while tea was served, the few inches separating his thigh and hers charged, for her, with currents of warmth and pent-up desire.

Putting down her cup, Stephanie said in a friendly but commanding tone, "Well, you two will have a lot to talk over, so we'll leave you to it." Anne's dark eyes, so like her brother's, swept Julia's with a long, soulful look as she shut the door to the sitting room.

And they were actually alone for the first time.

He stood up and held out his hand, which she took, letting herself be pulled up to him.

"I have been thinking of this moment ever since we parted on *Renown* the night of the dinner party."

"So have I."

"We talked that night about whether it would be presumptuous of me to say this or that. Would it be presumptuous now to do this?"

He kissed her, his lips pressing hers in a light, questioning way, and she pressed her lips back. He pulled away to whisper, "And presumptuous of me to do this?" And he kissed her again, with his lips parted, his tongue moving through her lips in a way that sent a hot wave through her. She put her arms around his neck and responded to the kiss, and he pulled her body to his so that she could feel his arousal. When she drew away slightly to catch her breath, she felt the slight rasp of his shaven cheek against hers, and she glued her mouth again to his, wanting to disappear into him, yet wanting to consume him so that their bodies were transformed into one body.

She gently pulled away.

"Your mother said we must have a lot to talk about. I can't think of anything to say except I love you. I have longed for you, not just since this summer, but for two years. I have been counting the minutes until this moment."

"I love you, Julia, and I was stupid not to say it the first time we met, because I knew it then."

"But I was married then."

"Yes. What have you found out about Charles?"

"He is dead. I know that now. I want to tell you about it. And now I know that you were married."

"You know that?"

"Your mother and Anne told me. I think they told me everything. Did you tell them to do that?"

"I told them you were very special to me and asked them to look after you."

"They have done that beautifully and I like them very much, but you had said so little to me I didn't know what you really thought."

"I wanted to be with you to say it, to be absolutely sure you felt as I do."

"Once bitten, twice shy?"

"Perhaps. But my experience with—"

"Constance? The inconstant Constance?"

"Believe me, she never awakened in me one one-thousandth of what I feel for you. It was a silly, adolescent thing. But you fill me with the most wonderful feeling of completeness, of being united with my soul's partner, my other half."

"Oh Neville!" She pulled him to her and they kissed again.

He whispered, "We can be together later...if you'd like."

"Like? I'm dying to be with you."

"After dinner, when they all go to bed, I can come to your room. Is that all right?"

She breathed into his neck, "I can't wait till then."

She turned and saw herself in a gilt mirror over the mantel. "Oh God, look at my face. And I left my bag upstairs."

"You can slip upstairs. I'm sure they've withdrawn a discreet distance, the kitchen or somewhere. You're free to run up."

"I love your house. No, I like your house. I love you. But I like your house a lot."

"Would you like to live in it?"

"I have been living in it, virtually, for months."

He came to where she was standing with one hand on the doorknob and put his hand over hers. "Would you like to live in it permanently?"

"You mean..."

"I mean if we were married, we could live here."

Their conversation had fallen naturally into the same bantering, pleasantly edgy tone of all their talks until then.

"Does that mean you are asking if I will marry you?"

"Clever girl. It means just that."

"Are you asking because it's the done thing, if you're going to come to my room tonight, or are you asking because you'd really like me to say yes."

"I would like you to say yes, quickly, with no more beating about the bush."

"Then I say yes, Neville. I will marry you and love you with all my heart."

"I think it's good form to seal that little arrangement with a kiss, if it's not too much trouble, if you haven't used them all up."

"I have a lifetime of kisses to give you, so I think I can spare a tiny one now."

"I'm glad. Then I suppose, Julia Robertson, we are engaged."

"We are." She kissed him, on one ear, then the other, then his neck on both sides, then lightly on the lips.

"When do you think we should tell them?"

"When would you like?"

"When I buy you a ring."

"That doesn't matter to me."

"But it does to me. In my first marriage I used an old family ring. She did give it back, but I think that would be bad luck. I want you to have something absolutely yours, just for you. So we'll go to London together, if you like, and choose one."

"I'd love that."

"We could go tomorrow. No, damn, David's coming. HRH. He was going to come tonight, but he had to stop at Windsor and he sent his car on with me. So he's joining us tomorrow. As soon as we're clear of him, I'll take you to London."

"I really need to run upstairs. My face is a mess."

"I hate to be separated from you now."

"Me too."

"But I'd better go along and tell my father I'm home."

"Neville?" She loved saying his name aloud. "I feel I'm home."

Léa came out of the bathroom. "There we are! Shall we join the painters before they forget us?"

27

In his hotel room Matisse said, "*Madame,* we have been to see your painting. May I say that my friend Morrice is fortunate in his model!"

"Do you like the painting?"

"I like it enormously. But the intelligence of the model adds to it. The beauty of course, but the interior light, the animation and spirit, that is what we all try to capture, and he has done that. As I say, I like it tremendously. It is both an advance for him and, perhaps, a renaissance?"

Through all this Morrice was smiling, his after-lunch face a shiny pink, enjoying the praise, while he looked through canvases stacked against the wall of Matisse's hotel room.

Matisse had only to put one canvas on the easel—depicting an open door with blackness outside—for Julia to feel she was witnessing a huge aesthetic leap.

"At lunch, you were talking of the war. This is the door at Collioure in 1914. The war had just begun."

A large empty rectangle of black dominated the picture, framed by slabs of pale blue, grey, and green.

"This is Greta Pozor, the woman who knows the poets." The woman was seated, in a blue dress and black hat, against a background of greys and an unpleasant yellow green, her form drawn through the dress in thick black lines, her neck encased in a rigid black collar, her eyes full of deep sadness.

"And then in 1916," Matisse said. "My model Laurette

in a green dress." Laurette floated on a pink chair in a black limbo. And the same painting reappeared in the next picture, on his easel, showing him painting her in his studio in Paris, the black relieved by a white wall and a severe city view through the window.

In each work he showed, his point was obvious: the mood was grim, solemn, reserved. The war existed in the eyes of the sitters or in the limited palette or severe design of other subjects, still lives, light in a forest, whereas none of the work Morrice had done in the war period, except for the one painting near the front, gave any hint of the war. That was it: the war resided in individual hearts and minds, whatever the external return to normality.

Perhaps Morrice in his subtle way had seen the war in Julia's eyes, not as starkly as Matisse in his sitters, but Matisse was conceptually, psychologically, in a different world: existed on a different plane of daring, of imagination, of innovation, of confidence, of risk-taking. She glanced at Morrice to see how he reacted. Did it hurt him, did he feel crushed by this force? No sign of it. He was smiling, drinking in each picture with delighted concentration. She had to remember, he had seen Matisse's work many times, had painted with him, knew and understood it intimately.

She was tempted to go back to his room to be sure, to look again at the portrait of herself, which only a few hours ago she had thought stunning, a daring step into new territory for Morrice. And that was true. It was bold for him and it was a fine painting. All his paintings were fine paintings.

It was not a competition, but in this room, almost identical to Morrice's, only the wallpaper a different pattern, they had moved into a different dimension. It was stunning that such a difference could exist a few rooms apart in the same hotel in the same city in the same country at the same moment, be part of the same general tendency in modern art. It was breathtaking to feel so much power coming from one rather ordinary-looking man, not very tall, balding, bearded, a little paunchy, with stubby, square-shaped workman's hands. To understand that so much creativity resided in one man and that he knew it filled her with awe, but also astonishment that he needed praise, as he revealed by recalling the same thing Morrice had told her.

Matisse said, "I never knew whether Morrice even liked my painting, because he would never say. He would come and look and make no comment. When we were in Tangiers I worried about it. I wrote to my family, 'I don't know whether Morrice likes my work.' Finally, after the second winter there, Morrice stayed longer and I got a letter from Charles Camoin. He said, 'Contrary to what you think, he very much likes what you do.' I was very relieved."

Morrice said, "Henri, you have better things to do than remember what I said. What I think about your work doesn't matter. Your painting is too important. My view of it is not important."

"You are too modest. It is important to me."

Now Matisse put up a series of utterly beautiful pencil sketches of a model with fascinating eyes and a sensuous mouth, wearing fantastic hats.

"I see that the war has ended," Julia said with a smile.

"It has, but not the pain. I am escaping from it by finding new pleasure in classical line and form."

"The model is very pretty."

"No more so than the model Morrice has been painting. And, may I say, you are fortunate to be painted in your youth by such a fine artist."

"I know that."

28

As they left the hotel to stroll on the promenade, Léa took Julia's hand, interlaced their fingers, and brought Julia's arm up to clasp it tightly to her side.

"My dear, what you have told me makes me feel so much emotion for you. I feel like you are my sister and I want to help you. I know I felt a little cold to you when we met many years ago, because...you know...to come, so to speak, from his family, and I know he does not speak of me to them, so I assumed..."

"You didn't have to assume anything. I liked you then. I have always thought how lucky Jim is to have you. His life might be completely off the rails if you had not steadied him and provided some stability and affection."

Léa was thinking. "You call him 'Jim.' You see, that is an intimacy I do not have with him."

Julia laughed. "Oh, I called him that as a child, when he was Uncle Jim to me. It does not mean any intimacy."

"No, but it means something. I have known him very well for more than twenty years now, and I call him only by his family name, Morrice. He has never said to me, 'Please call me Jim.'"

"You could just say it!"

"Oh, I wouldn't dare!" And Léa giggled. "Jim?" And she giggled afresh.

The two men, looking from behind almost like twins,

were walking ahead when Julia stopped Léa, who saw the serious expression on her face.

"I would like you to send a note to the woman in Paris. Tell her I will be in touch. Will you do that?"

Léa touched her arm. "Of course I will, dear."

"And give me the name and address?"

Léa opened the drawstring of her reticule and pulled out a piece of paper. "I wrote it down already—in case you needed it."

"I think it's time for me to go to Paris."

"I understand. It is better not to wait."

"Tomorrow. I think I should go tomorrow morning. If I take the early train I can be in Paris by evening."

"Will you write to me and tell me how it goes for you?"

"I will. I don't know what I'd have done without you."

"I will be so interested to hear what you do...after this."

Julia laughed. "I haven't got that far yet in my thinking."

"But it is good you can laugh. It means your thinking is positive, no?"

"If I'm going to go tomorrow, I'll have to arrange a ticket and do some packing."

Morrice and Matisse had stopped near the casino and were each gesticulating as though drawing large pictures in the air.

"I'm sorry to do this so suddenly, but I think I really need to go back to Paris tomorrow." She looked at Morrice. "I know you'll understand...in the circumstances. And the painting is finished."

"But so suddenly?"

Léa touched Morrice's arm and said, "Don't interfere, chérie. It's time for her to go."

"And I will need to go now and do some packing." To Matisse, "If you'll excuse me. Continue your walk. I am thrilled to have seen your paintings. More than I can say."

"And I yours, *madame*." Matisse lifted his hat. "I wish you bon voyage. It was good you came when you did. Your visit was a happy occurrence."

"Well, if this is to be the last night," Morrice said, "we should have a farewell dinner. Léa, Julia, Henri, you will join us?"

"I think I will not tonight, if you will excuse me. Two big meals in a day and I will become Bibendum, the Michelin Man." Matisse patted his prominent belly. "I am going to take up rowing. I have talked to the man at the *club nautique*, and he will give me lessons. If I go out for a little row each day it will empty my mind and reduce my front." Again he patted.

"Sounds terrible to me!" Morrice said. "Like voluntarily turning yourself into a galley slave."

Matisse raised his hat. "*Au revoir, madame.* Come to see me again when you are here or in Paris. I would be happy to see you." He bowed over Julia's hand and added, "I find the idea of the window for your cathedral has not left my mind since you mentioned it. If it were closer, it would interest me very much."

"Then I dearly wish it were closer," Julia said.

"Indeed."

"I will make an arrangement for dinner," Morrice called after her.

The hotel concierge booked her on the morning train and asked whether she needed a hotel in Paris. Julia hesitated. The rest of her luggage was at Suzanne Perret's apartment. But would Suzanne approve of what she was about to do? She would have hours to think on the train. "Yes, I would like a hotel."

She had opened her suitcase to begin packing when Léa knocked and came in.

"I wondered if you needed any help?"

"Oh, you're sweet. I brought only a few things, so it won't take me very long."

Léa sat in the armchair. "I really came to say something else. If you would like, I could come to Paris with you tomorrow. I have a small flat there and I could see you through the next few days. You know...since I have been there myself. If you wanted someone to be with you."

"Oh, Léa, you are so kind! I think I'll be fine, and I have a friend in Paris. A woman I was staying with before I came to Nice. My things are with her. So, thank you, but I think Morrice needs you more than I do."

"No question. I had better go and make sure he doesn't become too sodden before dinner. He is very happy today. Matisse likes your portrait. And when Morrice is very happy he wants to celebrate."

"And when he is sad?"

"He wants to drown his sorrows. Nothing will change him at this time of his life. But when I am sitting with him, he at least drinks more slowly, and I think just now he wants to paint. So—see you later!"

"Thank you." They kissed and Julia resumed her packing, impatient now to be on her way. If she had rushed she might have taken a night train, but then she would have arrived in Paris bedraggled and exhausted. Better to sleep in a good bed here, then travel by day.

Remembering Neville's homecoming had brought about this decision, because inevitably it made her relive what came afterwards.

The hotel had returned a bundle of clean laundry and as she undid it, she found the nightdress she had worn.

29

There were no guests at the Boiscoynes' for dinner that evening. Stephanie and Anne must have known perfectly well what Neville and Julia were feeling, but a stranger watching would have witnessed nothing but a polite and relaxed dinner for four, with the women asking about the royal trip.

Neville said, "The vaunted royal charm was wearing a little thin and brittle by the last few weeks. But what they put him through! There can't be a debutante in Canada he hasn't chatted with, danced with, drunk tea with, and her mother and aunts, and the mothers' and aunts' mothers and aunts. They said Canada has only eight million people, but there seem to be twenty million women panting to see the fellow. I couldn't do it. All I had to do was tag along and watch from the proverbial three steps behind. I didn't have to dance with them all or make charming small talk with them. And he doesn't even drink! He holds a champagne or wineglass, whatever they put in his hand, could have been maple syrup for all I know, and he holds it and holds it, looks as though he's drinking it but the glass is always almost full. All he really likes drinking is tea, and that got to him because they make rotten tea in Canada. So we were brewing up for him on the train. Most of us were hitting the whisky or gin to keep our spirits up, but David runs on tea."

"He doesn't drink tea at dinners, does he?" Anne asked.

"He would, if they put it there."

Julia loved listening to him talk, watching him across the table, his high colour rising from his cheekbones into his dark hair, watching the curve of his upper lip, which at first she had thought arrogant, but now thought mischievous. She watched his hands as he manipulated his knife and fork, and when she thought of them soon to be touching her body, a little shudder of desire would go through her.

"Your brother-in-law, Harry Traverse, is a good fellow. He was along a lot of the trip, keeping an eye on HRH for Borden, who came in again at the end."

Julia said to Stephanie and Anne, "Harry is married to Charles's sister, Lucy, who has become a good friend to me."

"Oh, Lucy was fun," Neville said. "The night of the dinner on board, I danced with her. Big, strapping girl with red hair and freckles. David found her very amusing."

"Harry is one of those men, people are now saying, who had a good war," Julia said. "He was in the thick of it, mentioned in dispatches, decorated several times but came through it as though it hadn't even mussed up his hair. Lucy thought he never got his uniform dirty. He was a lawyer in Borden's firm before the war, and now he's been an aide to the prime minister since the peace conference."

Neville said, "Isn't he a bit stiff to be married to such a jolly woman?"

"'Stiff.'" Julia laughed and said to the women, "Actually, he's one of those men, you'd recognize it instantly, who rub women the wrong way. Whether it's his training as a lawyer, or his time with Borden, he loves to lay down the law as he talks. *'My dear Julia...my dear Lucy...you must understand...it is perfectly clear to everyone...'*"

Stephanie looked at Anne. "Well, we know a man like that who is not a thousand miles from this table."

Julia said, "No wonder women bridle, because it suggests that if only we women wouldn't interfere with our inconvenient opinions, the affairs of the world would be run quite satisfactorily by men, thank you."

"I wish your father could hear this," Stephanie said to Neville.

"I'm not sure she doesn't mean it for me," Neville said.

"Well…" Julia was about to say, *I think I was born to be a thorn in the flesh of such men*, but thought better of it and said instead, "I can set Harry off, put him out of countenance, by just the slightest smile when he's talking, while I'm paying avid attention. If he notices the smile, his chin goes up another inch, and little red spots glow on his cheekbones."

Anne said, "Neville, I'd listen to all this very carefully if I were you."

"I'm listening and I'm terrified."

"But you're not pompous." Julia gave him a warm smile.

"Isn't he just! You'll see. Pompous and supremely arrogant, if you cross him," said Anne.

"But I don't want to cross him," Julia said sweetly, and the look she received set off a new flutter of anticipation.

Stephanie asked how Neville planned to entertain HRH, and Julia began to wish she had stayed in London in a hotel, where she and Neville could be together in private.

"I suppose David wants a few days of quiet, *en famille*," Stephanie said.

"His idea of relaxing may be rather exhausting," Anne said. "Not likely to curl up by the fire with a good book. Not sure he's ever read a good book!"

Her mother said, "Be nice to him, darling. No need to put his nose out of joint."

"Since we don't have horses now, he'll probably want to drag us out for hare and hounds or something equally ghastly. He'll have you running over the hills in the freezing rain for hours. And then want to dance all night afterwards. You'll see."

Stephanie said, "Well, dancing might be rather fun, dear."

"Mother, we have no dance music. He can't do the foxtrot to your Galli-Curci records!"

"The foxtrot? That sounds rather sweet." Stephanie said.

Anne said to Neville, "I'll bet you didn't know what you were in for when you agreed to this equerry business. Anyway, I want to go to London."

"You can't go off with David coming."

"David is the last person in the world I want to see. But if we have to entertain him, why don't we take him to London?"

In perpetual crisis with her older literary figure, Anne was always dying for an excuse to go to town.

"I think the point, dear, is a quiet few days in the country. David can go to nightclubs in London any time he likes, and he's welcome to them."

It seemed to Julia like an hour, not just after they had all said their good nights and gone upstairs, but an hour even after she had gone to bed, turned out her light and lay expectantly, listening to every sound in the old house, as full of creaking noises as if half a dozen guests were tiptoe-ing to assignations. She began imagining reasons why he might not come after all: that he was so tired he had fallen asleep, that he worried that his mother or sister might hear him moving about, that he regretted having so impetu-ously asked her to marry him. To marry him. That was where her fantasies had been leading but she had not really allowed herself to imagine it. If they married, no, now *when* they married, she would come to live here. Would that be a good idea with his parents still alive? Or had he meant when his father died and the house would be his? And the title. She had forgotten about that. He would be Viscount Boiscoyne someday and she would be the viscountess! She smiled in the dark and found herself laughing. She knew exactly who would be thrilled to bits: her mother. Julia could imagine shopping with her in Montreal, or perhaps London, and her mother making sure, in quite a well-bred way of course, that the saleswomen knew that her daughter, Lady Boiscoyne, had this or that engagement to go to and needed a certain kind of dress. Eventually David would become king, and probably they would go to his coronation. Her mother would die to be there. And what would Elizabeth and Archie say? Archie had liked Neville. Well, Julia was doing just what Elizabeth had been urging her to do, making her own life, although Elizabeth might be a little shocked if she knew that on the day they had become engaged, a few hours later, Julia was waiting, her body aching with expectation, for Neville to come into her room. Or she might not. Why was he taking so long?

"Julia!" His whisper was so close to her ear that she started, then sighed with delight and reached for him.

"My darling."

"It's a little chilly out here."

"Then come," she whispered.

She raised the bedclothes and he slipped in and they were in a close embrace, kissing, caressing, in a fever of impatience.

"I love you."

"Oh darling, I love you."

No erotic daydream she had concocted in the preceding weeks came close to the sweetness and fulfillment of these minutes. Nor had any past sexual experience been as rich and satisfying.

It was the best night of her life. If she were honest now, here in France two months later—and she didn't want to be honest, she wanted to despise him—that night she was in heaven. Everything about him was delicious to her, the feel of his body, the taste of his mouth, his breath, his weight on her, his caresses, the music of his voice.

A long time later, she asked, "How did you get in? I was straining every nerve to hear. I began to worry because you were so long."

"I'm sure they know just what's going on, but I didn't want to give them the satisfaction of actually hearing me. Our bedrooms are in the other wing. I went down the back stairs through the pantry and up the front stairs to the room next door."

She laughed. "You must have done this before, if you know the way so well."

"I swear I haven't."

"I'm glad."

"You are delectable. Your skin feels like the skin of a tomato that's been warming in the sun."

"Not very poetic, a tomato."

"Well, I'm not a poet."

"Think of a romantic vegetable, with a skin you'd love to touch."

"A potato?"

"No! I think you'd better feel my skin more carefully until you find just the right image."

"Like this?"

"Yes—and more."

"Like this?"

"Oh!" She sighed and moved with his hands, then rolled over to him and crushed her mouth on his.

"How long can you stay?"

"How long would you like?"

"Years. Years and years. I want to go to sleep with you and wake up with you every night and every morning for the rest of my life."

"I think we can arrange that."

Luxuriously she stretched beside him, feeling his legs with hers, while their hands continued to explore.

"I know almost nothing about you. I know about the navy, and your marriage, and that you're going into the Foreign Office—-does that mean we'll be living in different countries?"

"Unless we start running embassies here in the United Kingdom. Would you like that?"

"I'd love it. I love travelling."

"Can't guarantee they'll all be exotic places. But some would be."

"But I don't know anything really about you. What you read, what music you like, what painters; what you like to eat, what you drink, which side of the bed you like to sleep on."

"Is this side all right?"

"It's fine with me."

"And it's fine with me."

"Thank God, we've settled that."

"Do you believe in God, Neville?"

"Well, I suppose so. Don't you?"

"No, I don't"

"Does he know?"

"He can't know if he doesn't exist."

"He can if he exists for me and if I tell him."

"You wouldn't tell him and make him angry at me?"

"You shouldn't care about him being angry since you don't believe in him."

"Do you go to church?"

"When I have to."

"Do you like going?"

"I suppose I do sometimes. You know the English and the church. You go to be christened, and married and buried, and Christmas and Easter."

"Anne says the church won't marry you because of the divorce."

"Depends on the vicar. The village church used to be part of this place, and the lord of the manor had the living and appointed the vicar. Now some bishop up the road does it and I don't think he does any better job of it than my father and grandfather did. But he seems a reasonable fellow. I'll have a chat with him. But, look here, isn't this a bit deep for...where we are, and what you're doing to me right now?"

"Don't you like it?"

"Making it very difficult to think about God—or anything else."

"Good."

"Anything else."

"Then don't."

They lay embracing, then talking, the minutes slipping imperceptibly away as they grew serious, and then silly, then passionate; whispering, murmuring, forgetting and letting their voices rise, then fall nervously to whispers again.

"I love you."

"I love you."

"I couldn't wait a day longer for you to come. I was going mad with waiting."

"I worried that my family would drive you away. I know how overbearing they can be."

"They've been sweet to me. They acted as though we were already engaged."

Neville said, "They knew that's what I wanted."

"Did you tell them that?"

"In a way."

"And you didn't tell me? Even in your little notes. I've been living with your family, talking about you all the time, and thinking, what if he comes and has changed his mind?"

When, finally, after many lingering kisses, whispered words, and caresses, he left silently, Julia turned on the light to see that it was nearly four o'clock. He had been there for almost five hours!

She turned on her side to settle for sleep, her body and spirit glowing with the matchless pleasure of finding that the one she loved loved her.

How much richer love was, she felt as sleep began to enfold her, how much richer when you were mature, with some experience, after suffering, and then you willingly let down your guard and accepted another fully, knowingly.

At the Hotel Méditerranée she closed the suitcase. The last things could be packed in the morning. To go to dinner she put on the dress she planned to travel in the next day. When she fastened it, the waistband was, for the first time, a little tight.

30

When Morrice awoke it was already light. As he got out of bed, Léa stirred and he said, "Go back to sleep. I want to do some work." She murmured and pulled the covers over her bare shoulder. He quickly dressed with his usual care, then opened the small painting box he had not touched in months. He squeezed touches of his usual seven colours onto the palette, slid it carefully into its grooves and next to it a fresh wood panel. He closed the box and slipped it into his jacket pocket.

On the few steps from the hotel to the café he gratefully breathed in the delicious morning air. The sun had not yet risen above the hills behind the town, so the light on the sea was innocent and shadowless. A waiter was opening the café, repositioning the bentwood chairs that had been stacked on the tables. Morrice sat in his favourite place, ordered a black coffee with rum, opened the painting case, and sat back to gaze for several minutes at the pattern he had been seeing in his mind since the evening before. His coffee arrived and the waiter poured in a splash of dark rum. Morrice took a sip. He felt perfect contentment.

The visit to Matisse's room had been deeply comforting. After his wild adventures, his flirtations with abstraction and Cubism, the stark brooding of his wartime work, he felt

Matisse was coming back towards him. The grey nude by the window, Madame Matisse with her parasol, the girl reading by the window, the harem girl by the black table, felt to Morrice like vindication. It was a gradual return to a spirit they shared: the effort to extract joy and light from the pain and darkness of life and to give that pleasure to others.

He looked hard at the tone of a sky still untainted by the brassiness of a rising sun. He mixed a blue he could never describe in words, diluted it with turpentine, drew a horizon line with his brush, and washed in the colour above it.

The Julia nude was still on the easel in his room. Looking at it, Léa had said, "This girl has truly stirred up something in you, hasn't she? I can see it. There is more feeling in this than in your painting for a long time."

He could not put into words, least of all to Léa, what feelings Julia had aroused. They went too deeply into the past, to his childhood, and to his chosen exile from that life. It was a feeling as much of regret as arousal. What had been aroused was nostalgia for what might have been, some connection he had missed by the choice he had made to escape a life he did not want and perhaps now missed? Not artistic, but personal. He couldn't explain it. He couldn't explain feelings except in colour and form and, for once, as Morrice reached for words to express a feeling, his beloved Verlaine could not help.

When he rejoined Léa to take Julia to the station, he said, "I'm beginning to feel like taking a trip again. A change of scenery. Would you like to come with me this time?"

"I would be very happy to come. Where are you thinking of?"

"Perhaps North Africa—Morocco, Algeria, Tunisia. The light is pure there, like the early morning here."

For Julia, as they waited at the Nice station, the loveliness of the morning was an enticement to stay. Even with the smells of horse-drawn carriages and motor cars delivering passengers, the air had the moist freshness and the special light of the Côte d'Azur. In her mind it bathed the semi-tropical foliage, the extravagant architecture, even the hurrying people, in an atmosphere of languor and indulgence.

Julia stood with her hand baggage looking at Morrice and Léa, feeling something fateful in the moment. On top of the usual dislocation of starting a long journey—waking too early, her stomach unsettled, anxieties about luggage, tipping, tickets—she had the sense not of beginning a journey, but of abandoning part of her life.

"I wish I weren't going," she said. "I hate to leave this."

"Then come right back!" Léa said. She took Julia's arm and held it tightly to her side to lead her a few steps away.

"You come back here when it's over. Don't worry. The discomfort is small. But come back and I will look after you."

"You are too kind to me."

"No, no! It is you who are kind. You have saved my life, because you have saved his—for the moment." She glanced back at Morrice, in a hat, leaning on a cane. "He was slowly dying here. Remember that. You have given him the desire to live and work."

"Well, I am very glad about that."

Léa pulled a small envelope from her bag. "I was thinking last night. It is quicker if I write the woman a note and you take it to her immediately. Quicker than the post, more discreet than a telegram, if you follow me?"

"I do. You are right."

"So, I have written her to be kind to you. You arrive in Paris tonight? You take it to her tomorrow morning and everything will be all right."

The small train from Monte Carlo that would take her to Aix-en-Provence to change for Paris was snorting into the station.

She hugged Léa and kissed her. "I came because I was sure it would be a help to talk to you. But you have given me much more than I expected. Goodbye, Léa, and thank you."

"*Au revoir. À bientôt, chérie.*"

"*À bientôt.*"

She moved over to hug Morrice, noticing again how small he was. "Thank you for letting me dump my messed-up life on you like this."

"Your life is not at all messed up. You'll move beyond this little problem and then—you're not even thirty?—a whole life opens up for you. With your gifts, my dear Julia, I know it will be a very rich life. And you have brought me an enormous gift."

"I will stay in touch. I'll want to know about the painting at the Salon, if I'm not in Paris."

"And when you tell me where, I will send it to you—after I've shown it in Montreal, of course!"

"You wouldn't!" But she saw his smile. "Oh, you're joking!"

"It would be fun to see their faces, though, wouldn't it? That reminds me. Please send my good wishes to your mother and father."

There were shouts from the train guard.

"I must get on. Goodbye. Love to you both. Take care. *Au revoir*, Léa."

She settled into her seat, feeling her emotions unable to catch up with her decisions and movements, as though they had spilled out of a suitcase and were littering the tracks behind her. As the train began moving, her thoughts went back to the previous evening.

Surprisingly, Morrice had drunk little at dinner and excused himself before dessert to go to bed.

"I want to get up and work in the morning. But I'll come to the station."

Léa had stayed on with Julia, in her usual buoyant spirits. They ordered dessert, Léa enthusiastically, Julia to keep her company.

After a while Léa said, "You may not wish to tell me about it, but he"—she indicated Morrice with a nod upwards—"said you were trying to find out about your husband? He didn't say what you found out in the end."

"In the end? I didn't tell him."

She had rapidly become fond of Léa and annoyed with Morrice for being ashamed of her while depending on her emotionally. Léa was direct and positive about life, eating her *meringue glacée* with unselfconscious pleasure, as she would drink the Grand Marnier she had ordered with her coffee.

"Do you know what happened?"

"Yes."

"Is it a very sad story?" Léa was like a child, her warm eyes filling even in anticipation.

"I'll tell you. You know the big battle of Passchendaele? Well, shortly after that, in December 1917, Charles crawled out one night towards the German lines to reconnoitre for infiltrators. He went with two NCOs. As acting major, Charles was second in command of a company, so he had information valuable to the Germans if he were caught and forced to talk. One of the NCOs exchanged jackets with him, so the Germans wouldn't know which was the officer—the NCO couldn't divulge secrets he didn't know. They came upon an unexpectedly large German force getting ready to launch a surprise attack. The NCO wearing my husband's jacket was badly wounded. In the dark and confusion he was brought back by volunteers. The official report said one NCO was killed. That was Charles, but he was really only unconscious from a wound in the head. The Germans overran the spot and he was picked up. They saw he was alive and took him to a hospital. When he'd recovered enough, he was interned as a prisoner of war. But his head wound had affected his memory. In the prison camp he did not know his name, so they gave him a name. When the war ended and he was released, he thought that was his name. They took him to a hospital in England for men who had lost their minds in the war. He felt perfectly well physically but he still couldn't remember who he was. He stayed there until the spring came and the nurses began to let him go out for walks, longer and longer walks as he got stronger. One day he just kept on walking. He didn't want to go back to the hospital with all those poor, half-mad men screaming in the night. He wanted to be away from there and to find out who he was. So he kept on walking.

"English farmers saw a soldier walking alone and were kind to him. Their wives gave him food and places to sleep, sometimes in their houses, sometimes on the hay in their barns. They asked him to stay and work for them because they were so short of men. But he kept on walking in the warm spring sunshine, admiring the flowers and the blossoming trees until he came to the sea. There is a small seaside village, a little port. He saw they were building sailboats there. And he knew that he could to do that. Before the war Charles was a sailor and he studied marine engineering in college, because he was going to join his father's shipyard after the war. So in this little English shipyard he went to work building sailing yachts. He was very happy. He loved the work. Gradually he got used to the name he had been given and became less anxious about finding his old identity. He was very handsome, with sandy-coloured hair and bright blue eyes and a lot of freckles from being out in the sun. The young women in the village were lonely because so many young men had not come back from the war, so they were very friendly to Charles. He began seeing one of them regularly. She was a young war widow and he began living at her house. When the Armistice came and the war was over, he joined in all the festivities in the village. He has become one of them. And that is the story."

"And he is there now?"

"Yes, he is living happily in that village."

Léa's excitement was rising. "Do you know which village? Can you go there?"

"No, I don't know which village."

"But you can find out!"

"No. It is impossible."

"Do you not want to know because of—" Léa looked at Julia's stomach.

"Not because of that."

"But of course, that is it!" Léa was eager with certainty. "But, my dear. Don't let such a matter keep you apart."

"It is not that, Léa."

"I am sure it is. You are ashamed to tell him you have a baby by another man. But I beg you not to be so noble."

"I am not being noble."

"Then why?"

"Because it is just a story."

"What do you mean?"

"It did not really happen like that."

"Oh no!" There were tears in Léa's eyes.

"I made it up."

"But you made it so real and so sweet."

"It is sweeter to me than the truth," Julia said.

*Sweeter than the truth...sweeter than the truth...*the train wheels seemed to be saying.

"And you do not want to tell me who is the father of the baby?" Léa had been eager for more stories.

"Do you want the truth or do you want a story?"

"For the baby, surely the truth is better."

"The truth is I don't know."

"*O, mon Dieu!* Julia!" Léa began to smile, then laugh. "Oh, my dear!"

"I can't tell you. It is too bizarre. You'd think I was making it up."

31

The morning after Julia's first night with Neville, they had waited almost till noon for the Prince of Wales.

"Typical of David!" Anne said, looking out at the rain-sodden garden. "Keeping everybody hanging about, waiting on his bloody royal pleasure."

"I know we are very modern, Annie dear," her mother said, "but do you think 'bloody' is suitable for a young lady of your refinement?"

"It's good enough for Bernard Shaw."

"For a Cockney flower girl."

"And I don't like to be called Annie!"

"Yes, dear."

Stephanie smiled at Julia. Neville was reading articles they had saved about the royal tour, glancing over the paper to exchange warm glances with Julia. In a few moments alone in the breakfast room they had touched and kissed, she still feeling detached from reality, tired but suffused with the wonder of those recent hours.

Finally Neville put down his paper and said, "How about going for a walk?"

"It's pouring, Neville," Anne said.

"Never mind. We have lots of mackintoshes and wellies. Come along, Julia. If you're going to be English, you'll have to love the rain."

"Is she going to be English?" Anne asked.

"I love the rain anyway," Julia said.

"But you'll get that nice dress all muddy, dear," Stephanie said.

"You're right. I'll just take a moment to put on something that doesn't matter."

She had chosen the dress to please Neville, but also of course because the Prince of Wales was coming. And whenever she caught herself primping, it annoyed her to notice, even as she carried on with it.

In coats, boots, and hats, they escaped through the garden and over the nearest rise into a small woods, and under a large tree fell into each other's arms. They kissed hungrily, ignoring the rain running down their faces into their necks.

"Oh, I'm so glad you got us out of there. I've been dying to hold you."

"Only the English can arrange things so they have to make love in the rain."

"In Canada some people make love in the snow," Julia said. She kissed the side of his mouth where a raindrop had stopped.

"Pretty desperate people, I expect."

"People in love, like me."

"Odd that I didn't notice anybody doing that on the royal tour."

"You were too early. Snow lovemaking begins in January."

"One day you must show me just how you do that."

"With pleasure, Lieutenant-Commander Boiscoyne."

"Commander, if you please. My running around with HRH must have impressed the Admiralty because they gave me a brass hat."

"I knew there was a reason to kiss you." She did so. "Congratulations. And congratulations. And congratulations!"

"Jolly good thing they didn't make me an admiral. You'd never stop."

"I don't ever want to."

"I love you."

"I love you and I loved the night with you."

"So did I."

"I still feel unreal, in a dream, in a wonderland."

"Through the looking glass?"

"In another part of the forest."

"Once upon a time, long ago."

"And they lived happily ever after," Julia said. "That's how it ends."

"I never got to the end before."

"You will now. We will now."

When they got back to the house, Stephanie said, "Neville, David called. He's changed his mind. He's asking you and Julia and Anne to go over to Windsor and spend the day. He'll send his car."

Neville looked at Julia questioningly. "I'll ring him up and have a word."

Stephanie said to Julia, "It might be fun for you. The castle is fascinating—you could spend days just looking at the pictures. It's not much of a day for anything else...I'd love to see Anne get out and stop being so irritable."

With each reason piled on, Julia felt Neville's mother making excuses. When royalty wanted something, you found reasons to fall in, as Neville did when he came back from the phone.

"It could be amusing. The king and queen have gone to Sandringham, so it won't be formal, and David's asking us to spend the night."

"Oh Julia, that will be a treat! You should do it at least once."

Julia said, "I suppose you can't say no?"

Stephanie said, "One just doesn't." And if she was thinking about food or other preparations to entertain the prince now being made so casually redundant, she did not show it.

"What on earth do I wear?" Julia asked Anne as they went upstairs to pack a bag.

"Since it's just David, any old thing. With his mama and papa, it'd be ghastly court dresses and tiaras for dinner." At the top of the stairs she whispered, "Since we'll be in Windsor, it's almost to London. Perhaps we can slip into town tomorrow."

The large black car took them to Windsor Castle in time for lunch. Whatever resistance Julia had felt about being thus hijacked by royal command evaporated as the car swept through a narrow, arched entrance to the castle and the prince came to the door to meet them. There again was the strangely heart-tugging, boyish face, the fair hair immaculately combed, the slight figure in what on any other man might have been a casual country suit but on him was severely tailored and close fitting.

"So good of you to come, Mrs. Robertson. How delightful. I've been so looking forward to seeing you again. It's really good of Neville to have kept in touch with you."

Julia caught Neville's eye and raised her eyebrows.

"And Anne, how lovely. It's been a long time."

Julia was surprised to hear Anne say, "How are you, sir?" and begin a small curtsy, which the prince prevented.-

"No sirs, no curtsies while you are my guests. Come in out of the rain. I thought you'd all be going mad staring at the gloomy Wiltshire countryside. Why not come over here? You've never been to the castle, Julia?"

"No." And curiously his aura was such that Julia almost said "sir" herself. It was uncanny that in these surroundings the man's presence subtly conveyed such a different tone: a gentle imperative, an expectation, clothed in the most unassuming manner, but an expectation that whatever he wished would happen.

"Well, after lunch, if you like, I can give you a little tour. I didn't know my parents and my brothers would all be away, and it's rare to have the place to myself, so we can relax and enjoy ourselves. Now, they'll take you to your rooms for a wash and brush-up, if you like, then we'll have lunch. And Julia, I'm dying to hear everything you've been up to since we saw you last."

"I know what you've been up to," Julia said. "We've been following you in the papers."

"The most ghastly reading, I expect. Pictures of yours truly in dreadful warrior headdresses and the like. But—I have some news for you about Canada. When we meet for lunch."

The prince might be relaxed and informal but the staff were not. A footman in livery carried her overnight case up to a room in the private apartments, where a ladies' maid took it and curtsied.

"I'll unpack, madam, when you've gone down to lunch," she said and discreetly withdrew.

In the bathroom, Julia examined old-fashioned but gleaming fittings, towels, soap, brushes, combs, nail file, all meticulously laid out. She wanted to remember every detail to be able to tell...whom? She looked at everything, the quality of the towelling and that of the linen on the huge bed, where the sheets were turned down, she supposed in case she wanted to nap. On the desk she found writing paper engraved simply "Windsor Castle" and wondered if they would notice if she took a sheet to write to someone. Then, again, to whom? The only person she wanted to think about, to be with, to communicate with, and that devouringly, was Neville. And how could he possibly find his way to her room in this vast place?

Before lunch, in a small drawing room furnished in the French style, they were served sherry, which she noticed David held but scarcely sipped. It was apparent that Neville behaved differently in David's presence, still bantering and easygoing, but his personality turned one notch more reserved, and to the smallest degree possible, deferential. Again she felt, as she had in Halifax, that Neville would have made the more princely figure, taller, with a more commanding bearing. In other centuries he would have sworn allegiance to this prince, perhaps in this very castle, and followed him to the death. But his family might well have fought David's ancestors for the crown. Now in David's presence he was, so faintly as to be almost unobservable, diminished, and it saddened her to notice it.

"What I wanted to tell you, Julia, is that I have acquired a piece of your beautiful country. Neville knows because he came to see it with me. In Alberta, I've bought a ranch. Most spectacular place. Thousands of acres. Wonderful for horses, that country. Good for cattle too, and in the distance you can see the beginnings of the Rocky Mountains. You must come and see it sometime, when you're in the west."

"I've never been to western Canada at all."

"Have you not? Now isn't that extraordinary. I'd have thought that Canadians who are full of pride in their country would be jumping on the trains just to see those vast spaces."

"They don't all have private trains provided by the Canadian Pacific Railway," Neville said dryly. "Quite a train, like a hotel on wheels."

"Well, come along and let's eat. Aren't you hungry, Anne? You always were."

"Well, I am, in fact."

"When we were young and I stayed with the Boiscoynes, it was hard getting one's share at tea time. Anne has a very long reach, and if you were the tiniest bit late, she'd have snaffled all the cakes. Well, lots to eat here. I've asked them to do a little buffet so we can serve ourselves and not have the footmen standing around. Nice and cozy, don't you think?"

When they entered a small dining room, with a fire burning, Julia gasped. "Goodness, look at the Canalettos!" On symmetrical sections of wall, between the windows and doors, hung matched scenes of Venice.

"You know the painter, do you? What's the name?"

Anne said with an edge, "Oh David! Everyone knows Canaletto. But not everyone has a set in his dining room."

"Never paid much attention to them. The castle is crammed with stuff my ancestors have bought or plundered here and there."

"Do you think the room was designed around the paintings, or were they bought for the room?" Anne asked.

"I don't know. Probably someone called up the artist and ordered them, you know. When was he painting, this fellow?"

"Middle 1700s, I think."

"Then George II, perhaps George III. When he wasn't busy losing America and suppressing the Scots, he liked to collect things. I dare say he got someone in London to go and see this fellow and tell him the size and colour he needed."

It was almost as though he were sending them up with this display of happy philistinism, but Anne wouldn't let him get away with it. "David, Canaletto was a great Italian master. He lived in Venice."

"He did paint in London too," Julia said.

"Well, there you are! I have heard the name, now that you mention it. But if you spend all the time gawking at the pictures, we'll all starve!" and again Julia could see the thirteen-year-old boy.

From a sideboard under the Canalettos they served themselves from silver chafing dishes.

"You know, we got rather fond of old Borden, your prime minister, didn't we, Neville?"

"You saw rather more of him than I did."

"And your brother-in-law, Harry Traverse, a capital fellow. Told me I'd visited his battalion at the front and shook hands with him. All across the country demobbed soldiers came down to the train, cheering away, and I met many who said I'd visited them. Canada should be very proud of its effort. Borden told me that Canada not only gained recognition, but the war actually changed the way the Empire is run. From now on much more autonomy for the dominions. We can't sit in London, my father's ministers in Whitehall, and just tell Ottawa what to do. And a very good thing, too."

Neville said, "There was a move a few months ago to give Canada its own embassy in Washington but the Colonial Office quashed it. Too much like a step towards independence."

"Independence?" the prince said incredulously. "You mean like the Americans? What would happen to the Empire we've all been fighting for, if our dominions started becoming independent? But I do think a bigger say in their own affairs is well deserved, don't you?" He looked at Julia.

"Yes. I just hope that what we've gained that way is worth the loss of sixty thousand lives."

"I know. Frightful. Heard it over and over. Sixty thousand out of eight million people, and that includes all the women and children."

"Julia's late husband among them," Neville said, as though used to prompting David. "Charles Robertson, the VC."

"Of course I remember, with deep sadness."

"And Anne lost very close friends."

"Yes, Anne, I know. So sad."

Watching Neville slip effortlessly into this role, Julia felt a faint bristling in herself, a resistance to this assumption that all his life, however successful he became as a diplomat, whatever glories he earned, Neville would always have to be a little obsequious with David, even more so when David became king. She felt it a little in herself, this being in thrall. She wondered if it was ever galling to Neville or whether it came so naturally he didn't notice. She wanted to ask him, if they could ever be alone again.

For the rest of the afternoon and evening, whenever for a moment she found herself beside him, close enough unobtrusively to touch his fingers or to let their hips touch familiarly, HRH chose that moment to turn, to follow them around that corner.

He led them on a tour of the castle, surprising footmen, maids, or other members of the staff whose duty seemed to be to stand and wait, like guards in a museum, but who quickly bowed or curtsied when they saw the prince.

The Canalettos were soon overshadowed by a bewildering array of works by legendary painters —Van Dyck, Holbein, Rembrandt, Dürer, Rubens, Andrea del Sarto, Hogarth, Memling, and others Julia did not know. If they were portraits of his ancestors, as many were, the prince identified them—Charles I, Elizabeth I as a princess, and in St. George's Hall, many kings from James I to George IV. Other subjects, like a Rubens of the Holy Family in the King's Drawing Room, he passed without comment. He did not linger, he almost sprinted from one apartment to the next, like an impatient real estate agent showing a house he knew the people wouldn't buy. On top of the rapid pace, Julia was tired from too little sleep and distracted by being so close to Neville but able to touch him only furtively.

The prince much preferred showing the fortifications, whose history he knew from before William the Conqueror. From the Norman Round Tower they looked down on the town of Windsor and Eton College, with the Thames meandering through its meadows. Even in the rain two rowing crews were on the river.

They finished in St. George's Chapel, with stalls for Knights of the Garter, the tombs of Henry VIII and other kings. As he described these monuments to a thousand years of British history, Julia watched him curiously, trying to connect this charming but sometimes callow young man with the extraordinary deeds that people of his blood had performed. It was true that he had already moved the hearts of millions of his future subjects. He'd been installed as a Knight of the Garter. One day he would sit there in the royal pew that Henry VIII, he said, had built for Catherine of Aragon. Eventually he would be buried here, with the remains of Charles I and all the others. He was royal enough, even imperious in quick flashes, but somehow incongruous in this context, lighting a cigarette the moment they left the chapel.

"Marvellous, it's stopped raining. We can go for a walk in the Home Park. Come along and I'll find us coats and things."

Anne, who had been tagging along like a sulky child, said to Julia, "What did I tell you? "

"What was that?" The prince turned.

"I told them your idea of a quiet country weekend was like a continual steeplechase, David. Don't you ever sit down? Don't you ever feel like curling up in front of the fire with a good book?"

"Of course."

"What are you reading right now?"

"Let me see. No. Gone clean out of my mind."

Anne rolled her eyes.

"We'd better hurry if we want to stretch our legs before the rain starts again."

So the race continued, with the prince leading them at a forced-march pace around the private gardens, then out into the Windsor Home Park and a loop around the Frogmore Mausoleum, containing the remains of Queen Victoria and Prince Albert.

Anne fell back to walk with Julia. "I've discovered what he's doing. He thinks the faster he gets through his boyhood, the sooner he'll be a grown-up." She smiled wickedly. "But he's only up to thirteen, so he has to hurry."

Indeed, impatience with the slow passage of time seemed to govern HRH, because every activity appeared to be undertaken to make the time go more rapidly and to make him physically tired. Perhaps that was it: he had insomnia and was desperate to exhaust himself to sleep at night.

"Half an hour to tidy up before cocktails," he announced like the leader of a guided tour. "But no dressing for dinner, right, ladies? Neville? Absolute informality this evening."

"Where's your room?" Julia whispered to Neville as they mounted the stairs. "Mine's there."

"Down that corridor."

She was about to say, "Too far away," when Anne came upstairs behind them.

"God, I'm exhausted. I may fall asleep in the bath. If I'm not down in an hour, send someone."

When she had passed them, Neville said, "Show me your door, so I'll know."

Julia opened her door and blew him a kiss before closing it.

The maid was waiting. "I've laid out the frock I think you'll want this evening, madam, and I've drawn your bath."

"Thank you very much."

"No trouble, madam. If there's anything else, just ring."

Julia tested the water, wondering what signal had told the maid when to have the tub ready and hot, with some scented bath crystals already dissolved, towels warming on the heated rack, her clothes laid out on the bed as if for an inspection.

She slid gratefully into the hot water; the tub was so long she found she could float in it. If the palace servants kept such an intimate eye on the guests, would they be watching in the corridor at night? Exhausting or not, the day had been fascinating. How often did one get to sleep under a royal roof? Well, perhaps that was not so far-fetched, given the prince's evident fondness for Neville. Was it a real friendship? Could it be a real friendship? How close did anyone get to a man like David, whose hyperactivity seemed almost a defence against letting anyone know him, a defence against intimacy. Neville had known him since they were boys, so perhaps that made them real friends. Yet several times she had seen Neville rein in, or hold back, knowing which fence to jump and which to shy away from. And could it be real friendship when their interests seemed so different, and Neville appeared so much deeper and more thoughtful? Well, she didn't really know how deep. She really knew very little about him, except that she loved him, and the knowledge that he would come to her again tonight filled her with a delicious languor. She stretched out her legs in the scented hot water.

When offered a champagne cocktail, Anne said, "Thank God!" and Julia followed her lead. When their glasses were empty, Anne accepted refills for them both, murmuring, "You'll need this. It's going to be one of those exhausting nights!" So by the time they sat for dinner, Julia felt a pleasant buzz.

At dinner the prince was as voluble and energetic as he had been all day.

"My father wants me to make another tour, as soon as possible. But longer, Australia and New Zealand, then on right away to India. He thinks it's important to show the flag, so to speak, while the Empire is still feeling the glow from the effort in the war and the victory."

"Won't he give you a little time at home, David?" Anne said.

"My argument, exactly. I said to the king, 'Surely I have earned a little time off—what do they say of prisoners?— time off for good behaviour.' But he wants to strike while the iron is hot. I must say, the prospect of another one right away is pretty daunting, don't you think, Neville?"

"Judging by the pace of what we've just been through, yes. Several times he shook so many hands, his right hand swelled up and he had to use his left. No, in your shoes, I'd try to insist on some time off."

"'Insist' is not a word you would use with my father. 'Insist' would get very short shrift. 'Duty,' now there's a word he likes. How do I make it my duty to stay at home? That's the question."

Julia felt a shadow on her happiness at the hint that Neville might be expected on another royal tour. She wished he would speak up.

Anne said, "David, you could tell him you feel it's your duty to get to know your own people a bit. After all, the British deserve to be thanked for our war effort just as much as the colonies."

"Too true, Anne. I'll try that approach and I thank you for it. But the king thinks if I'm within reach of London, I'll just hang around nightclubs having a good time."

"Is he wrong?" Anne laughed. She seemed less deferential than Neville. "A few nights in the West End might be great for your spirits."

"I think my father loathes nightclubs as he does Bolsheviks, not surprising seeing what Lenin and Co. did to our cousins. No, he seems to be adamant about another trip. I'm just trying to stall him as long as possible. I mean, a chap of my age deserves a bit of fun, doesn't he? Before the weight of the world falls on his shoulders?"

Neville said, "I told the Foreign Office I'd take up my appointment when we came back from North America, so they're expecting me at the first of the year."

"Oh, the Foreign Office, Neville! I'm sure the king could talk the Foreign Secretary into sparing you to come with me. You wouldn't refuse to come? Now that Neville knows the ropes so well, he's invaluable to me."

Neville exchanged an anxious glance with Julia, but why didn't he speak up? His deference seemed slightly unmanning. Apart from her own desires, it seemed intolerable that he might have to postpone an important career for the whims of this young man simply because one was the future king and the other his subject.

"In any case, that's in the future. Right now, the king's away and we can play. Our duty is to have a good time tonight. What would you like, a spot of billiards, cards? I wouldn't mind a little dancing, myself."

So of course they danced, with the prince putting on the records and winding up the gramophone. Julia remembered the tunes from the night on *Renown*.

The prince was not subtle about wanting to dance with Julia; he appeared to share her a little grudgingly with Neville, which made Julia long for the evening to end. She was exhausted, and when Anne accepted a cognac, she did too.

To be so close to him, to be touching Neville when they did dance, made her want only the more strongly to be alone with him. She wanted to say to him, "Stand up for your rights, or tell him we are engaged," but she didn't want to put him in an awkward position. And she had to admit to herself that, while she longed to be in Neville's arms, it was exhilarating to be dancing and chatting with the Prince of Wales.

"I'm giving a little party for some friends at St. James's Palace next Friday. If you'd come it would give me great pleasure, and I'm sure you'd like them."

"That would be delightful. And Neville?"

"Well, Neville, of course, although I don't know how much he enjoys that sort of party."

"What sort of party do you mean?"

"Oh, a little dinner and then finish the evening at one of the clubs." And before she could say anything, he was rattling on, "It is lovely to see you again. You've often been in my thoughts since we met in Halifax."

"I'm flattered, sir." Where had the *sir* come from? Not from coquetry, which she did not feel. Perhaps from an effort to put a little distance between them.

"Ah, ah! No 'sir.' 'David,' remember?" He was looking at her warmly, his blue eyes crinkling charmingly at the corners. "Yes, very often, and as Neville and I encountered most of the female population of Canada between twelve and eighty, I can say without qualification that we needn't have gone any farther than Halifax to find their most delightful representative."

"Well, that is very charming, sir."

"I mean it, Julia," he said, his right hand in the small of her back slightly increasing its pressure, obliging her to move closer to him. "We talked about you a lot, Neville and I."

"Oh, what did he say?"

"Well, he's seems quite smitten."

"I'm glad."

"You're glad?"

"Because I'm quite smitten with him."

"Well, he's a capital fellow and I'm very fond of him," David said, as though that dispensed with Neville.

When that number ended, she saw Anne go out and excused herself to follow. In the ladies' lavatory, Anne said, "This is no fun. It's clear he wants to dance with you and suffers me only to be polite—and not very polite at that."

"Then let's stop it," Julia said. Whether from frustration or drink, she felt bolder.

"How?"

"I'll say I'm dying to play billiards."

"Oh good. Let's do that. He'll love showing us how good he is, and you're someone new to show off to. Little boys... you know?"

"I think he looks sad, trying so hard to have a good time."

"Just don't let him get us into charades. He'll be at it all night."

"Neville seems a different person when he's around David. Do you see that?"

"Of course. But almost everybody is with David or any royals."

"You're not," Julia said. "I hear your little digs."

"Well, you seem to be quite yourself."

"I haven't had much training in being deferential. Neville's so much more forceful and commanding by himself."

Anne said, "Do Neville good to get away from him after all these months."

"You don't think HRH would insist that Neville go to Australia and India with him? You heard about getting the king to talk to the Foreign Office."

"It's up to Neville. He just has to put his foot down. But, you know, this atmosphere—" They were walking through a reception room filled with gilt furniture and paintings. "All this turns some people to mush. It's like an invisible gas. They breathe it and go all monarchical."

Julia said, "Not Neville?"

"Oh no, he's known David too long. He'll just have to be firm. David's not used to people crossing him, except his mother and father who can be beastly to him—real martinets—and that may be the trouble. They're so censorious that he has to get his way with other people."

The prince jumped at Julia's suggestion and led the way to the billiard room.

"My uncle created the room. He loved the game but Queen Victoria did not approve. Worse than Mr. Borden about my golfing on Sundays!" And he winked at Julia.

Neville and she sat and watched as David played with Anne, who was good, neatly sinking a series of balls with crisp, decisive shots.

"Not fair! You've been practising while I've been away. Not fair, Neville! Your sister's taking unfair advantage!"

"Try her at golf, David," Neville said. "She's getting pretty good at that, too."

"Is this a conspiracy to humiliate me in front of our guest from Canada?"

"Julia suggested the billiards."

"I'll bet you put her up to it."

Neville whispered to Julia, "He hates to be beaten at anything. You should see him at polo. He'll kill himself trying to win. They put him on a bucking bronco in Saskatoon and he amazed them by staying on!"

Julia moved her head close to his and whispered, "I'm so tired. I'm dying for the evening to end."

"Too tired?" She smiled and shook her head.

The prince said, "Bad form for spectators to whisper while a chap is making a shot!" His cue ball snicked its target and the other ball wobbled away.

"You see!"

"No, keep whispering!" Anne laughed.

Julia watched the prince, totally absorbed in his game, and her annoyance softened a little. How complicated her reactions to him were! Intellectually, her Modern Woman despised the notion of hereditary rulers, divine right. It was absurd—she turned to glance at Neville's fine profile and met his almost black eyes—absurd in the twentieth century to give one man mystical sway because of his lineage. She looked back at the boyish figure excitedly watching Anne make a shot. On one level he was a sweet-looking young man, who did stir something like maternal feelings in her. But on another level she couldn't help it. It was thrilling to be in the room with him, in this room in this castle, and to have him glance up at her with his crinkly smile. It was disarming, even though she was sitting beside the man she was crazy about—and was going to marry. And, curiously, the more Neville deferred—*deferred* was too strong—exhibiting in his own confident way that he knew his place in the chain of being, and the more he showed it was habitual to him, the more it transformed the prince into something more powerful.

It was creeping into her feelings: she itched even more for Neville to challenge him. She wanted to hear him say, *"David, I can't go to India with you, because I'm going into the Foreign Office, and Julia and I are going to be married."* She felt the emotion of those unsaid words. It was as though the very presence of the heir to the throne cast an inhibiting spell over them all, but particularly Neville. What must it have been like five or six hundred years ago, when his ancestors kept this as a real castle? A king annoyed at a courtier like Neville could simply have him done away with, his head cut off, imprisoned in the tower, murdered in the night. And that was the truth of this feeling. While he was serving as an equerry, Neville was a courtier and had to behave like one. The three English people present—two members of the hereditary aristocracy and one hereditary king-in-waiting—were so used to it they gave no sign of even being aware of any tension. Her passport said, "A Canadian citizen is a British subject." Perhaps, she thought, I do not like the idea of being a subject: a citizen, yes, a person, but not a subject, not subject to any arbitrary power or royal whims. And yet, I feel the magic. Something he gives off that conveys that he knows his power, he knows that everyone will in some way abase themselves in his presence—and love doing it.

A train official opened the door of the compartment: *"Messieurs, dames, Aix-en-Provence, cinq minutes!"* She had to gather her things to change platforms and trains, and hoped her luggage would be transferred too.

32

Julia had an hour to wait before the Paris train arrived from Marseilles. Having had no breakfast in Nice, she now found a table in the station café to order coffee and a brioche.

On the wall was a poster advertising Nice as "The Capital of Winter." The style was contemporary poster art, banal, of interest for a second's attention. The French railway would be better to commission Matisse to do its poster for Nice, now that he had come out of his stark war period and was again lyrical and hedonistic. Or Morrice, if Morrice wouldn't balk at the mere idea of a commission, as he had over the cathedral window. Always adamant about his prerogatives of freedom as an artist. Daring to live in a manner that would be considered quite radical in Montreal, yet in his work, compared to Matisse, not as daring. Morrice had always been innovative in careful increments: original in small steps, never bold leaps.

What could explain such a difference in two men similar in so many ways? Temperament, but what made temperament? A matter of nationality? The French were revolutionaries, like Americans. Canadians certainly were not. Borden, according to Harry, was proud of winning tiny gains in autonomy from Britain—for sixty thousand lives. But there were plenty of daring Canadians. They had just shown it in the war. Was there a psychic reticence in Morrice, as with Canada, an inability to break radically with the past?

She remembered Matisse talking about Apollinaire, who had been wounded in the war but had died of 'flu just at the Armistice. At a dinner in Paris, the poet had said to Matisse, "Have pity on us who must live out the long quarrel between order and adventure."

That quarrel took place inside everyone, not just artists. Some took very small steps, some leaped. The quarrel is in me, she told herself, and I am too inclined to leap.

Neville had been a foolish leap.

When the evening at Windsor Castle had finally ended, the prince said eagerly, "We can go riding in the morning if anyone would like to." Anne murmured, "God, he's got tomorrow's marathon planned already," and aloud, "Since it's Sunday, Your Royal Highness, couldn't we have a nice little lie in—please!"

"Can't have the future Defender of the Faith shirking his duty. We can go out for a canter and be back in time for the service in St. George's Chapel. You'll love it. Excellent music from the choir school." Almost in the same breath he asked who wanted a drink to take to bed. "Cup of tea anyone? Cocoa?"

This active day after a night of little sleep, the cocktails and wine she'd drunk, had left Julia drooping.

It was delicious to lie in the dark, waiting for Neville, more exciting even than the night before in Wiltshire because of the certainty and the knowledge from those hours. She could remember and anticipate, her excitement mounting as she relived explicitly each caress, and imagined feeling them afresh. Yet she had to struggle to stay awake.

Of course Neville knew what he was doing with the prince. Silly of her to have felt disappointed that he had not spoken up when HRH had mentioned new tours. Neville knew how to handle him, had been doing it for years. He knew not to embarrass a member of the royal family by challenging him in front of others. Of course it wasn't done. As his mother had said, "One just doesn't." Neville was perfectly capable of standing up for what he wanted when the right moment came. God! A trip to Australia, New Zealand, and India would be unbearably long. Unbearable to part with him just when they had come together with such joy and understanding.

She was aching for him, knowing how difficult it might be for him to come unseen. She was so sleepy she felt herself drifting off. She threw back the blankets and slipped off her nightdress and lay back naked, her anticipation the more heightened knowing she would surprise him by being totally ready for him. The night before he had arrived without her hearing anything; that was in his own house. Should she turn on the light to stay awake? No, it was more thrilling to wait for him in the dark, like this, in this strange, high bed, wondering what famous or royal people might have slept in it. Whoever it was no one could have been as eagerly awaited in it as Neville was now: her lover, her husband-to-be, a man so gorgeous to look at that every woman's eye turned to watch him pass. But the minutes passed and she could not stay awake. It was blissful to let herself go, to surrender...and she couldn't resist.

She was deeply asleep when his hand on her shoulder awoke her. She whispered, "Oh darling, I've been dying for you to come. Come quickly, quickly." She opened the bedclothes for him and gathered him to her with her arms and legs. "My love, my love!"

But it felt different. She was embracing him with her entire body—strangely, he felt lighter. "Please, please!"—opening herself to him—"Oh yes"—taking him into her—"Ah!"

But the weight, the feel, the scent! It was not Neville!

In an instant, now fully awake, she knew. The man now panting in her ear was not Neville. The back her arms had automatically clasped to her was slighter, the feel of the rapid lovemaking different. It was not Neville! It was the prince! Who now gave a long groan of pleasure as she felt the pulsing of his ejaculation. All in a few seconds.

She was bewildered. Confused. Frightened. Horrified. Angry. She didn't know which. It had happened so quickly, but the seconds it had taken to realize who it was had numbed all her own physical sensations.

The prince, still lying on her, took several deep breaths and expelled them in long sighs. "Marvellous, Julia! Absolutely marvellous. I've been thinking about it all day, actually began thinking about it months ago. But today, watching you, and seeing you watching me, I got the message."

"No."

"No, what?"

What could she say? She had been looking at him all day, it was true, but out of the curiosity his presence inspired. And he took it as an invitation?

"You're very quiet."

She said evenly, "I'm thinking."

When she called him "darling" two minutes ago, he thought she had meant him?

"And...?"

"I want you to leave. Please."

"Oh!" He sounded genuinely surprised. "Rather awkward for a chap to be told that in this position." He moved himself off her.

Why couldn't she find more words? Rage was rising in her throat, but awareness of who he was left her almost speechless.

"I mean it. I wish you to go."

"You were glad enough to see me a few moments ago. You were lying here just waiting for me."

She felt like shouting at him, *I was waiting for Neville!* But the words froze before they reached her tongue. Neville! Had Neville known? Was it a plan? Did Neville help? No, it was too awful to think.

David was sitting on the bedside now, she could just make him out in the shadows, looking down at her.

"Well, sorry if you have regrets now. Perhaps the next time it'll be all right for you. As I said, it was marvellous for me. You are an unbelievably lovely and passionate woman." He sounded as casual as he would in a receiving line, shaking hands. Then he put his hand on her breast to caress it, and her anger escaped from its timidity. She swept his hand away and said, "I wish you to leave—now!" with as much contempt as she could muster.

"All right. I can take a hint. What do they say? Woman's prerogative to change her mind. Just need to find my things." The prince was quite pleased with himself, not at all put out by her anger.

"Sleep on it, my dear. See if we can be friends again in the morning. Good night!" The last said almost gaily as he left.

But when the door closed, she was no longer in a rage. She was frightened. Her future with Neville was evaporating second by second, like soap bubbles popping in the sunlight. If Neville had connived...if Neville had passively acqui-esced...if Neville had ensnared her for just this purpose? It was too cynical a thought to bear. It was like something out of the Middle Ages—for God's sake, tricked into sleeping with the future king?

And if Neville knew nothing? But how could he not know? She had been sure he was coming. She knew he was coming. But if he had come and seen the prince entering, what would he have thought?

Her anger had become more like grief. She was sobbing. No, she was furious again. She would march down to Neville's room and tell him! Tell him what? And discover that he already knew? The sheepish look on his face would break her heart. What could she do?

How could Neville have played with her like this? If he had, how foolish had she been! How gullible! Utterly naive! She searched her memory for clues to Neville's astonishing behaviour. How could any honourable man allow himself to be used this way? Prince or no prince? To be, in effect, a pimp, a procurer? She was outraged that she could have been so neatly tricked.

She did not want to it to be fully light, so at just after six a.m. she opened her door stealthily, carrying her bag, and crept along the corridor and downstairs to the entrance. A footman, half asleep, was startled awake.

"Can I help you, madam?"

"Thank you. Would you order me a taxi? I find I have a train to catch earlier than I had expected."

"Certainly, madam. I'll just call the porter's lodge. They'll have a car take you to the station in a few minutes."

"That would be very kind."

"Do you wish to inform His Royal Highness?"

"I do not, thank you. No need to disturb him."

So, before anyone was stirring, she was driven out of the tower gate in the drizzling, grey November dawn to the Windsor station. She had to wait less than twenty minutes for a London train. At Paddington she took a taxi to Victoria Station and bought a ticket to Paris.

❧

Now, in Aix-en-Provence, the Marseilles-Paris train was announced and she gathered her things. She found that her reserved seat faced forward, which pleased her. She had done enough looking back; she needed to face the future.

As the train raced up the fertile valley of the Rhône, stopping at Avignon, Orange, Valence, Lyon, she tried to imagine a future beyond the next few days.

She would go to the hotel, so as not to surprise Suzanne Perret, then call. Then tomorrow she should go to Quai des Grands-Augustins to see Léa's woman, up the stairs where she had gone as a young woman to be painted by Morrice in the dusty third-floor studio overlooking the Seine.

Could she tell Suzanne? She had discovered quite soon that Suzanne's stiff notions of what was proper did not preclude a woman having a baby outside marriage. During the war it had become common, and since the war the shortage of marriageable men probably made women less insistent about marriage as the precondition. Julia wondered whether Suzanne and her fiancé had crossed that threshold. Had Suzanne been pregnant herself? Would that explain her equanimity? But it was too intimate a question to ask when Julia was being so guarded about her own secrets.

"In any case," Suzanne had said, "many women are left with babies to bring up without husbands. It is a condition of the times and France needs children."

But how would Suzanne react to a miscarriage that was not spontaneous? How would anyone? Why should anyone know? Only Suzanne, Lea, and Morrice knew of her pregnancy.

As the day advanced and the reality of the northern winter season slowly closed in, the light gradually lost the heartening irradiance of the south and, as if in sympathy, her spirits fell.

Have I really been fooling myself all along? she thought. Believing I could live my life as I chose, that being the silly Modern Woman I thought I was actually made me different? That I wouldn't be governed, constrained, by the same realities as any other woman? Priding myself on my courage, my daring, my impulsiveness, not ashamed of my strong physical desires. Well, where did all that get me? Tricked by a man I thought I loved, possibly pregnant by him, or—would anyone believe it?—possibly by the future king. Imagine sitting down and telling Mother I might be pregnant by the Price of Wales! So bizarre that it's ludicrous to imagine.

Why have I not seen this before? It must have been Léa handing me the note to the woman in Paris. Suddenly it became real. That I was on my way to Paris to end this pregnancy! What would Stewart say? Have you really thought it through? Have you thought of this, thought of that? But whatever he said, he would add, "Whatever you decide, I'll support you." Unless I've pushed him too far.

I need to talk to him, talk reality, because I must have been living in a dream, or a fog, as Mollie said, the fog in women's heads.

The fog about Neville. Even so I saw him shrinking back in the royal presence. The Royal Presence! If I hadn't been asleep. But I was dead tired, as I am now. And obviously a little tipsy...more than a little? Well, it's hours until Paris... So sleepy! All right to nod off now.

She lay back against the headrest and fell asleep.

33

Julia was still half asleep when she left the train at the Gare de Lyon, her legs stiff from sitting all day, and looked for a porter to collect her bag and find a taxi.

And there waiting—was Neville!

"Julia, I have been searching for you for weeks!"

He did look strained and tired, deeply anxious, but with the dark good looks that had turned her to jelly in the past. Now she was determined to give him no comfort and said nothing.

"I must talk to you."

"I have nothing to say to you."

"But we must talk. You ran away that morning. Everyone has been desperately worried about you."

"No one needs to worry. As you can see I am fine."

She turned to flag a porter. Neville noticed and grabbed the porter's arm. "Where is your luggage?"

"On the train." She gave the porter the ticket with the seat number.

"How did you know I was coming here?"

"I have tried everybody. I got in touch with Harry Traverse in Halifax. He told me about Mlle Perret, who told me about Morrice. I was desperate to find you."

Her eyes looked at him coldly, but stirring within her disgust was the old feeling for him.

"Please sit down and talk to me for half an hour. I've been going mad with not knowing."

She looked at him unbelievingly and saw that his eyes did look wounded.

"How can you not know? I don't believe you."

He took her arm. "Can't we go somewhere to talk?"

She shook his hand off. "I don't want to talk."

"Could we have dinner?"

"I've had dinner."

"Find a café nearby and talk for a few minutes. Julia, please. I must talk."

She examined his face. He looked sincere, but she was dubious, and yet she wanted to abandon her doubts, to believe him, and to embrace him. She weakened a little.

"I'm very tired from travelling all day. I want to go to my hotel. But if you come with me, we can talk for a few minutes."

He smiled with relief. "Good."

The porter came out of the train with her bag; they followed him out to a taxi and she gave the address of her hotel. Her emotions grew more confused as they entered the taxi together. Even moving to the far corner she was instantly aware of being in a confined space with him. And she had to admit to herself that she was becoming curious about what he thought.

"How are your mother and Anne?"

"Desperately concerned about you."

"What did you tell them?"

"I knew nothing to tell them except that you'd run off from Windsor Castle before dawn."

"Anne probably guessed why."

Neville said nothing but turned and looked at her. In the passing lights from the boulevard, for the first time since she had known him, she saw real anguish in his face and it moved her. If he felt it so strongly...

At the hotel she registered, giving her passport, but when Neville moved to follow her into the small elevator, she said, "Please wait for me here. I'll be down in a moment."

She removed her coat, used the toilet, and washed her face and hands. While drying her face she looked at herself in the mirror. How could she hate him and feel for him at the same time? What do I tell him? What do I want him to tell me?

He was still standing in the lobby and she took him into the small lounge where she had entertained Suzanne Perret at tea; it seemed a long time ago.

"You've been in Nice."

"I went to see an old friend."

"James Morrice, I know."

"If you've been in touch with Harry in Halifax, they must be worried about me."

"It was the only way I could find you."

An elderly waiter appeared to ask whether they wanted anything.

Julia hesitated. Neville said, "I need a brandy—and soda."

It was becoming too social, she felt, too reasonable for the huge pressure of her conflicting emotions.

"A coffee, please."

She looked at him carefully. It was difficult to believe that a few words from him could dispel the weeks of rage and revulsion that had been stewing in her since the night at Windsor. She said, "You'll have to speak first. I can't bring myself to talk about it until I know what you know."

"I know that when we got up that Sunday morning, you were gone. A footman said you had slipped out before dawn."

"And why did you think I had done that?"

The waiter arrived and slowly put the drinks on the table. Neville added soda to his brandy and drank a large gulp.

"Why, Neville? I know why. I want to know what you know. What I assume I know has filled me with horror. But I want to hear you tell me."

Neville looked haggard now. He drained the brandy and put down the glass.

"I saw David go into your room."

Just to hear him say it made her feel a clutch of fear, a spasm in her abdomen.

"Then what else is there to say? You knew."

"I had come to the end of that corridor. He was just opening and closing the door."

"Well? What did you think?"

"I thought David was being David. It was not the first time I'd seen him go into a bedroom not his own."

"Perhaps the first time that it was the bedroom of your fiancée."

"Yes." Neville gulped.

"So you went back to your room? What did you feel? Anger? Jealousy? Rage? Disappointment?"

"I felt all those things."

"What did you think happened between him and me?"

"I tried not to imagine."

"Well, I will tell you." Her anger was rising now above sympathy for him. "He forced himself on me. For a tiny moment in the dark I thought it was you. I'd been waiting for you. It took me a second to know who it was and by that time he was finished. I asked him to leave. He left but he was quite pleased with himself."

"I'm sorry."

"Is that all you are? Sorry?"

"I am deeply unhappy about it," Neville said.

"Well, I'll tell you what has given me more anguish than

what happened. Far more anguish. Did you know he was going to come to my room?"

"Certainly not!"

"You didn't plan it with him?

"For God's sake, no!"

"My turn tonight, your turn tomorrow?"

"How can you possibly think such a thing of me?"

"Well, I can. And I have—for six weeks."

"It is too dishonourable to think of."

"That's why it has given me such pain. To think that you would lend yourself to that."

"I would not. I did not."

"But you said it was not the first time."

"Quite different. The others were his affair. He's the Prince of Wales. Women throw themselves at him."

"What did you do about it?"

"What do you mean?"

"What did you say to him, when you found I had left?"

"I took him aside and told him what I had seen."

"And?"

"He laughed. He said it had been good fun. And then I told him that you and I were engaged to be married."

"And what did he say to that?'"

"He was most apologetic. Said, if only he'd known... he should have guessed...he would never have violated our friendship...and so on."

"Did you believe he didn't know?"

Neville said, "I did. I had to. And you were right. Anne got it immediately. Knew right away. Said she'd seen it all coming."

"And you didn't?"

"No, I did not!"

Julia asked, "And what did you really think? Did you think I had asked him? Made an assignation with him?"

"Not for a moment. I love you too much to think that."

"That gave me as much pain as thinking you knew in advance, that you might suspect I had asked him."

"My darling, I did not." He reached and took her hand."I knew we would have to say all this. I've been going over it all in my head for weeks. I knew almost every word we would each say to the other. But there is one thing I could not know."

Julia was inclined to remove her hand from his but did not. "And what's that?"

"I have said I love you. I mean now. I love you no matter what happened that night. But I don't know what you still feel about me."

Julia looked at him. She took her hand away from his and moved herself farther from him on the settee.

"I don't know what I feel right now. My feelings cannot run so quickly and keep up. When I left that morning, I hated you because I thought...well, I've told you what I thought."

"And now?"

"I've told you I don't know. Are you going to go to Australia and India with him?"

"No. I told him I wanted to get on with life in the F.O."

"I'm glad. I was afraid that day that you were going to cave in, when he said he'd get the king to call the Foreign Office."

"He did, and I told the Foreign Secretary that my career was more important to me than escorting HRH on another royal tour."

"Did you? I'm glad you did that—for your own sake."

"I did it for ours, Julia. Of course mine, but yours too. I could not bear the thought of being away from you for many months, perhaps a year."

She was finding it hard to breathe. He was saying precisely what she had longed for him to say that evening... but he was saying it now.

"What did the prince say?"

"He was disappointed but, in view of what...we've been talking about, he didn't press me. In fact he apologized again."

"How did he apologize?"

"He asked me to give you something. He ordered it from Asprey's."

"Jewellery?"

"It's how he's thanked people in the past."

"People? You mean women?"

"The sort of jewellery he sends would look a bit odd on a man." He smiled for the first time.

"Well, I would like you to send it back to him."

"You don't want to look at it first?"

"I don't."

"I'm glad to hear you say that."

"Well, of course I say it! Am I going to wear his jewel like a scarlet letter?"

"Or you could sell it and buy some marvellous painting you've longed for. It's probably worth thousands. He's incredibly generous."

"Is he? Well, I suppose he can afford to be."

"Julia, if we had gone to Asprey's, you and I, before Windsor Castle, all this would not have happened."

"Is he a respecter of engagement rings? Anne said he has a penchant for married women. Why not engaged ones?"

"No. It was my fault. We should have told everyone right away, the moment we became engaged. It was silly to wait for the ring. We should have announced it."

"Well...it's too late to think of that now."

"But that's what I'm saying, Julia. It isn't too late. Put what's happened behind you, behind us. I want to marry you. But I realize I have to ask again. So, I am asking. Will you marry me? This time, so there's no mistake, I have this!"

Neville pulled out a ring set with two large diamonds. "Will you accept it?"

She felt two people struggling within her, one feeling a rush of affection and relief, the other saying *be careful, you have suffered too much to fall at his feet like a leaf.*

"It's a lovely ring. But it is too sudden for me. I need to sleep on it."

He reached out. "Take it and sleep on it."

"No. Let me consider a day or so. I'm really bewildered. My feelings are all confused."

"Have lunch with me tomorrow. I'll come and pick you up here. With a good night's sleep, perhaps things will be clearer."

"Tomorrow, oh no, I can't." She had Léa's note in her bag. She had to take it to the woman on Quai des Grands-Augustins. "I have an appointment."

"Come to dinner then. That will give you enough time."

"Perhaps, dinner, yes." By then she should know. "Is there somewhere I can telephone you?"

"No. I'll come at seven to get you for dinner."

"And if I don't feel like dinner?"

"We'll make another plan."

Interestingly, the forceful, confident Neville she had first fallen in love with had returned. There was no sign of the man who had been so deferential with David. Should she confide in him? No. Her instinct was not to. At least until she had delivered Léa's note and knew more. She got up.

"I am really tired, Neville. I need to go up."

"Believe me, there is nothing I want more than to make my life with you. Is there any hope that you might feel the same?"

"Thank you for taking all this trouble to find me. And the ring."

She found herself leaning up to kiss his cheek—

The door to the first-class compartment slid open and a train man said, *"Auxerre! Cinq minutes. Auxerre!"*

Startled awake, Julia saw an elderly couple lifting their small luggage and packages from the rack over their seats. They put on their coats.

"Auxerre?" she asked. "How long is it still to Paris?"

"About two hours. Have a pleasant trip." They went out into the corridor.

Through the window Julia saw cathedral spires coming into view, the stone glowing in the late afternoon light. They were crossing a river.

She got up to stretch her legs. Auxerre was too small for the train to stop more than a minute or two. She had the compartment to herself. She sat down again, wanting to recapture her daydream. She had imagined in him everything she would have wished but had not trusted him enough to tell him about the baby. What would he have said, this improbable Neville she had been conjuring up for herself? What could he say?

"Darling, it doesn't make any difference! We can be married right away, and who'll know the difference? I love you. It's our baby. I'm thrilled to know."

Yes, he could say that. A little gushy, but in keeping with the Neville she had created for herself. Or he could say, "But whose baby is it?'"

"I can't be sure."

"Really? It could be mine or it could be—"

"David's."

And he would struggle with that. She could see it in his face, his fine brow furrowing, and then he would take her shoulders and kiss her, hold her close to him and say, "Darling, it doesn't matter whose it is. It is ours. And we'll love it."

"What if it looks like David?" she'd have to ask.

"No matter. Anyway, babies don't look exactly like their fathers anyway."

"It really won't matter to you? If people say, *Neville's son looks awfully like*...assuming it's a boy."

"If it's a girl it wouldn't matter."

"What does that mean?"

"I mean...well..." He was embarrassed, but he said, "I meant any family resemblance in a girl mightn't be quite so obvious. But in either case we'd have a child with royal blood."

Julia said, "I didn't think of that. A pretender to the throne?"

"I wonder what David would think, if he knew?"

"Neville, you must promise me one thing. He is not going to know."

"Of course I promise. You didn't need ask," this totally obliging Neville said.

The train began moving again and the town of Auxerre was slipping away.

Or Neville could say, "What are you going to do about it?"

"What do you mean?"

"Are you going to have the baby?"

"What do you think?"

"Can you get rid of it?"

"You mean…"

"There are ways, aren't there?"

"You mean you don't want me to have the child?"

"I'm just thinking it might be a little awkward."

"How?"

"To have a baby so soon after we're married. When would it be?"

"About mid-July. Seven-and-a half months. Not too premature."

"What if it looks so much like David that it's obvious to everyone?"

"Would that embarrass you?"

"Would it embarrass you?"

"I could have it and then have someone adopt it. I know a woman who did that."

"Then we'd have to hide you somewhere till mid-July. So people wouldn't know you were pregnant."

"We could go abroad, travel. We are abroad now. We could stay in France."

"Would you risk having a baby in France?"

"Why not? Frenchwomen do it every day."

"But you're not French! You're British."

"I'm Canadian."

"That's British."

"Only in part. But that doesn't matter. Having babies works the same whatever you are."

"Well," this Neville said, "I think you should get rid of it. Less embarrassing all round. And we'll have our own children later."

"What if getting rid of it makes it impossible to have our children?"

"Does it?"

"It can. But I can go to a good person. I've been given an introduction."

"Someone you can trust?"

"I believe so."

"Then I think you should do that. Get rid of it."

And, to her amazement, Julia, looking out the train window, heard herself saying aloud, "No."

The imaginary Neville had no reply to that.

I don't want to get rid of it. I don't want to see the woman tomorrow morning.

She let that realization sink in. That meant having the baby. That meant...many other decisions. Time enough for them. Right now she was stunned by the way something in her had suddenly rebelled. She put her hand on her lower abdomen. There was nothing to feel, but through her dress she sensed a great warmth there.

The corridor door slid open and a waiter said, "Dinner is being served now in the restaurant car. Two hours to Paris."

"Thank you very much."

She'd eaten nothing since her brioche at Aix. In the restaurant car she felt strangely like celebrating. She remembered Léa saying at one of their meals, "Red wine is good for expectant mothers. French doctors recommend it." They were just leaving northern Burgundy, and to celebrate that she drank a glass of Chambertin, amused to think of trying that on a Canadian train. By the time she had eaten and nearly finished the wine, her spirits were higher than they had been in many weeks.

That did not change when the train entered the Gare de Lyon and she saw standing there not Neville, but Stewart MacPherson.

"Oh Stewart! Thank God it's you!" She hugged him and sobbed, "I've been such a fool!"

Embracing her tightly, Stewart asked, "Perfidious Albion?"

"And gullible me," she murmured.

The End

ACKNOWLEDGEMENTS

This is a work of fiction but a number of real people figure in the action, especially the Canadian painter, J.W. Morrice (1865 – 1924), much of whose work can be seen at the National Gallery of Canada in Ottawa, the Montreal Museum of Fine Arts, and the Art Gallery of Ontario in Toronto. For insight into his life and work and for her critical advice, I am particularly indebted to Lucie Dorais, who has made a life-long study of the artist. Her monograph, *J.W. Morrice*, was published by the National Gallery in 1985.

Other actual people who appear in this story are: Léa Cadoret, the long-term mistress of J.W. Morrice; his friend Henri Matisse; Sir Robert Borden, Canada's prime minister at the 1919 Paris Peace Conference, and Edward, Prince of Wales, the future King Edward VIII. Everything they do, or say, or think in this novel is imagined, as are all the other characters.

For their assistance in my research I am grateful to the National Archives of Canada, the Nova Scotia Archives and the New York Public Library.

In some publishing today editing may be a dying or neglected art, but this book benefits substantially from the penetrating editing of Marie-Lynn Hammond.